Sixteen Diamonds

English Edition

By Harita Willebrands

PROLOGUE

Six years ago…

Vivian Foster walked across a dazzling white marble corridor
following a secretary. Every two meters on either side, elegant
potted white orchids sat on steel grey concrete pillars. Even
though she'd already set foot on the premises, it was still hard
to believe she'd been invited for a job interview in this
magnificent building: Frenay & Iams, a well-known company
that only hired the best architects and interior designers for its
international projects.
This job vacancy had of course caught half the town's
attention, and she felt fortunate to be one of the candidates
invited for an interview. After the secretary had stopped in front
of a tall, impressive doorway, she knocked slowly. She paused
for a moment, then opened the doors and peeped her head
between the gap.
    'Mr. Maldini, the candidate for the eleven o'clock interview is
here,' she announced, before turning around with a friendly
smile and motioning for Vivian to enter. With a hammering
heart, Vivian entered the room.
Mr. Maldini's office was as splendid as the corridor she'd
passed through; in the middle of the room, there was a creamy
colored oval meeting table flanked by twelve high-backed
chairs in a majestic striped pattern.

Above the table hung a large, luxurious chandelier in matching cream.

George Maldini rose from his chair and greeted Vivian with a firm but gentle handshake.

'Vivian Foster, welcome to Frenay & Iams. Please take a seat. Can I offer you something to drink?'

'Thank you. If it's not too much trouble, I'd like a glass of water.' Vivian sat down in the chair Mr. Maldini offered her, then buzzed his secretary on the intercom to bring a glass of water and a cappuccino.

Mr. Maldini sat across from Vivian and studied her resume. While waiting, Vivian subtly observed the man whom she estimated was in his late fifties. He was handsome, with a well-maintained physique, caramel skin and shaved head. His big hazel eyes were adorned with fine wrinkles, which were more defined when he smiled. She didn't know why, but she felt safe in his presence, as though she had known him for a long time.

'Vivian. I've studied your resume, and I'm impressed by your Bachelor's degree with summa cum laude.'

'Thank you, Mr. Maldini. I'm grateful to have finished my Master's degree as well. Even though it was challenging, the sacrifices I made paid off.'

For a second time, Mr. Maldini studied her resume, while Vivian sipped her water.

'Hmm, so, let's start with a little test. It's very easy. I'll say a word, and you tell me the first thing that comes to mind.'

3

'You mean, technically?'

'Yes, exactly. In theme or style. I'll start with the word… casino.'

'Cheap kitsch.'

Mr. Maldini raised his eyebrows and roared with laughter, deepening the wrinkles around his eyes.

'Very entertaining.' Vivian's face flushed red.

'Well, sorry, that's really the first thing that came to my mind.'

'No, no. You don't have to apologize. I think what you thought is original, although honestly, I haven't the faintest idea what cheap kitsch looks like. Very well, next words... wellness and spa.'

'Hearing those words, what appeared in my mind was Bali and jasmine.'

'Hmm, interesting... you have a fresh perspective on specific things. Now tell me, why do you want this job?'

Vivian shifted in her seat, straightened her back and stared straight at Mr. Maldini.

'As a teenager, my mother dragged me with her to her office, where I'd read magazines containing pictures of all Frenay & Iams' projects. I dreamed that one day, my works would be commissioned. Since gazing at design photos in those magazines, I became addicted. I redecorated my bedroom at least a hundred times and my friends' bedrooms too. Until their mothers were annoyed because of it.'

Mr. Maldini listened carefully.

Vivian took a deep breath and continued.

'Mr. Maldini, I know I don't have experience and maybe there are a hundred resumes from far more competent applicants. However, I truly want this position. With all my capabilities, and having completed my studies, I believe I can do this job. Maybe you assume I am too young and have no experience, but I hope you will give me a chance, so I can prove it to you and to myself that I can. I won't disappoint you, sir.'

Mr. Maldini rose from his seat and walked to the curved floor-to-ceiling window looking out over the Hudson River. For a while, he stood with his back to her. She suddenly grew worried that her answer would crush her chance to work there. Mr. Maldini turned toward her, and looked at her calmly, his hands in his pockets.

'Vivian... besides experience, there are a lot of other aspects that are very important for this position, such as one's family situation, passion for one's career, high interest within your field of work, and many other aspects.' He returned to his chair, put his elbows on the table, and folded his hands as though in prayer.

'Before I end this interview, I have one more question... have you planned your summer vacation?'

Vivian shrugged her shoulders and confidently shook her head.

'No, right after I graduated, I went on vacation to Bali.'

'Ah, so that's why you answered Bali earlier,' he said with a small smile.

'Do you have any questions for me, Vivian?'

She thought for a while and considered what would make a wise question.

Despite the risks she asked, 'If I may know, how many applicants were invited for an interview so I can predict my chances of getting this position, and when will the successful applicant be announced?'

Mr. Maldini leaned back in his chair and folded his arms across his chest.

'We did receive hundreds of resumes for this position, and we only selected five applicants to be interviewed. You are the fourth. We will make a decision by Friday at the latest.'

Vivian heaved a sigh of relief. Twenty percent chance out of hundreds of applicants. Her face brightened, and a smile spread across her face. Her change in facial expression caught Mr. Maldini's attention.

'You have to be more like this, Vivian.'

Vivian stared questioningly at Mr. Maldini.

'You should smile more often. It suits you.'

She blushed. With her youth and lack of experience, she didn't know how to respond.

'Come on,' said Mr. Maldini. 'I'll walk you to the elevator.'

In silence, they walked down the lavish corridor toward the lift. Mr. Maldini pushed the button, and the lift opened immediately.

Vivian turned her head to Mr. Maldini and held out her hand.

'Mr. Maldini, thank you so much for your time,' she said with a genuine smile. He accepted her hand softly. Before stepping into the lift she said, 'I hope we'll meet again.'

Mr. Maldini laughed. He realized Vivian was already practicing his advice to smile more often.

'Don't you worry, Vivian. You'll get there.' Mr. Maldini winked at her and the lift's doors closed.

Now Vivian had to wait for three days.

On the following Friday afternoon, her waiting paid off. She was hired.

CHAPTER 1

Now…

A crash of noise carried across from the crowd and the deafening music. Despite the cacophony, Vivian savored the night she spent with her two best friends. After they graduated, these moments were so rare as it was difficult for them to find time to get together.

The booming music forced them to shout into each other's ears and use hand gestures. Vivian and Salfina slipped from the dancefloor and returned to the table where Genieva was waiting for them.

'Oh my god!' Salfina cried out. 'Look at my feet, they are completely swollen and hurt like hell!'

Vivian and Genieva giggled, while looking at Salfina's feet.

'Well, who told you to go out with shoes like that. Better to be like me, just wear flat shoes. Much comfier,' said Genieva smugly.

'Pffft, of course that's easy for you to say Genieva. You can't even walk in high heels'

'Well, that's true!' Genieva admitted. 'However, even if I could walk in high heels, I wouldn't hang out or dance in The Club with shoes like that.'

Vivian watched her best friends quarrel, then looked at each of them. She pointed at her shoes and said with a laugh,

'Or buy shoes like these. They're pricey, but you get real shoes.' They all laughed.

'Duh, not everyone can afford Manolo Blahniks, Viv.'

'Should we have one last drink, before going for a nightcap at my place?' Vivian asked.

'I agree with one last drink. I'll pass on the nightcap. I have to get up early to catch a flight to Vancouver,' Genieva said.

Vivian looked toward Salfina who suddenly focused on her phone then glanced around The Club as if she was looking for someone.

'Sal!' exclaimed Vivian.

'Yeah?'

'What's wrong? Who are you looking for?'

Salfina glanced at her phone and shrugged her shoulders. 'I'm not sure. Just wanted to check my phone to see what time it is, and then I saw a message from an unknown number. It says: "How is the lady you're dancing with? Ethan Stein must meet her".'

Vivian raised her eyebrows.

'You really don't know this number? How do they know your number? Also, who is Ethan Stein?'

'No, Viv, I don't know this number. However, I think it's best if we leave now.' Genieva stood up.

'Come on, Viv. Sal is right. It's better if we leave now. That Ethan guy is bad news, trust me, you don't want to meet him.'

'That's right,' added Salfina sternly.

Vivian rolled her eyes and helped Salfina to get up on her swollen and painful feet.

'You know what, let's share a cab. We can drop Genieva off and then go to your place, what do you say?' suggested Salfina.

'Yeah, whatever,' Vivian muttered.

When they were out of The Club they had trouble finding a taxi. After some time and effort they finally managed to stop one. They hurried in, and Vivian told the driver their destination.

'Okay, which one of you is going to explain to me why we left The Club in such a hurry after those stupid messages?'

Salfina was busy taking off her shoes. Her tight jeans made it difficult to move around in the cramped taxi.

'Just forget it Viv,' said Genieva, while searching for her key in her bag.

Vivian let out an irritated sigh, because she was sure both of them were deliberately hiding something from her.

Salfina's phone vibrated.

'It's the same number again.'

Genieva leaned over Vivian who was seated in the middle to look at Salfina with a frown.

'Don't reply and block the number.'

Vivian snapped and lost her patience.

'Wait a second! What is going on here? You both look like you're hiding something from me. The only thing I'm getting is "He's bad news" or "Just forget it Viv".

I want a clear answer, and I am mature enough and wise enough to decide for myself whether I want to meet this person or not. I don't need your help!'

'Sorry, Viv, you're right,' Genieva finally conceded.

'Of course I'm right,' Vivian snapped.

The driver pretended to cough, to signal they'd arrived in front of Genieva's apartment.

'Sorry, Viv, it's late. I'm tired, and in a few hours I need to be ready at the airport. If you want answers about Ethan, Sal will fill you in.'

Genieva opened the taxi door, climbed out, then closed it. Without looking back, she entered her apartment.

Vivian stared at Salfina full of questions. Salfina just shrugged.

'As soon as we get home, you are going to tell me everything there is to know about that Ethan Stein. Right?'

'Yes, I'll tell you everything,' Salfina said with a sigh. They continued their drive to the Upper West Side to Vivian's apartment.

Once they'd arrived Vivian asked, 'Would you care for some pizza while you fill me in?'

Salfina snorted and rolled her eyes, like she was already losing her patience.

'There's not much to tell actually. Ethan is just a dangerous playboy. Why do you even want to know about him anyway? Trust me, you better put some distance between you and him and try to stay as far away as possible.'

Vivian took off her shoes, poured a drink, and stood in the kitchen.

'Why is it hard for you both to give me information about this Ethan? By the way, are you still getting messages?'

'No, uhh, I don't know. I blocked the number and switched off my phone. Anyway, lend me a pair of your pajamas. These tight jeans and shirt are really uncomfortable. After pizza, I'll tell you about Ethan, okay?' Giggling she added, 'I communicate so much better with a full stomach.'

Vivian laughed out loud. She knew her friend weakened when hunger struck.

'Fine, but first you must tell me how you can eat so much but never gain weight. What's your secret?'

'Oh, that's easy, Viv! I have a deal with God. I forgave him for my small boobs in exchange for His forgiveness for my weakness for food.'

They cackled with laughter.

Twenty minutes later, they were stretched out on the couch with full stomachs.

Salfina sat up, took her tea from the table, and gripped the cup tightly. Vivian looked at her, concerned.

'Are you cold?'

'No, no, not that. I start shivering every time I think about Ethan. The appearance of that man is downright horrible news.' Salfina combed her long blond hair with her fingers, tied it messily and took a deep breath.

'Ethan Stein is a very dashing man. His father owns a diamond mine in South Africa and that's the source of their abundant wealth. Since childhood he's been pampered, he can get whatever he wants. Even now, when he wants something, he won't stop until he gets it.'

'What's so bad about that? I mean, there are far more evil things than pampered young men. Didn't you two overreact over a stupid text message?'

Salfina jumped off the couch and started pacing back and forth.

'No Vivian, you don'' understand. It's not just because he's rich and pampered.'

Vivian sat up on the couch.

'Why then?' Salfina sat down beside her.

'Eight years ago, two accidents happened. Two women who'd had a brief relationship with him were found dead. They both committed suicide. The rumor is that Ethan was behind all of this.'

Vivian's face filled with fear. Now it was her turn to pace back and forth.

'Didn't the authorities investigate the death of these two women? Was there any proof that Ethan was involved?'

'No, there was no proper investigation. Because they weren't crimes the cases were closed because they involved suicide. Shortly after that Ethan took off to Europe, and apparently, he's back.'

'Wait, all of this happened eight years ago, right?'

'Yes.'

'We were sixteen back then, what was Ethan's age at the time? How come you and Genieva know all of this? And again, how do they know your number?'

Panic engulfed Salfina. She grew pale and swallowed nervously.

'I have no idea how they got my number. Maybe someone from The Club. Since he's been back in town people have started gossiping again because no one has forgotten about these two girls. People believe he must have something to do with their deaths. Why else flee to Europe? Genieva and I always hang out when you're away on a business trip, and Ethan is the talk of the town right now.'

Salfina took a deep breath, loosened her shoulders, and continued.

'Vivian, you know what upset me the most? The fact that he has my number. If he sets his mind to it, it's only a matter of time before he gets yours. Be wise Viv, if you have any common sense, stay the hell away from him.'

Vivian looked at her best friend pitifully and noticed her exhausted face.

'How are you gonna handle this? You can't keep switching off your phone. Even if you've already blocked his number, they'll try to reach you with different numbers.'

'I know. Tomorrow I'll buy a new SIM card, and I'll only give

14

you, Genieva, my mom, and my colleagues the number. However, Genieva is right. I shouldn't respond to their messages.'

'Yeah, that might be for the best.'

They sat on the couch in silence for a moment, each caught up in their own thoughts. Vivian broke the silence.

'I'm sure everything is going to be alright. What if I fill up the tub so you can have a long warm bath? In the meantime I'll set up the guest room so you can sleep here. And to top it all off, I'll buy you breakfast at Sarabeth first thing tomorrow. How does that sound?'

'I'll take you up on the breakfast, but I'll pass on the tub. I think I'd better take a shower. What if I fell asleep in the tub and drowned then I might be Ethan's third victim.' She laughed at her own joke.

'It's not funny, Sal,' Vivian uttered sharply, yet she couldn't help but giggle.

Vivian stood in the bathroom and gazed at herself in the mirror. She had long brown wavy hair reaching down to her waist. Her slightly honeyed skin was supple and smooth. Big blue eyes were enlarged by long lashes. But fatigue emanated from her face. She tried to cover the dark shadows beneath her eyes with makeup. It was no use. She still looked tired.

The aroma of freshly brewed coffee penetrated her nostrils when she stepped into the living room with her shoes in her hand.

'Hmm, delicious, coffee.'

'Good morning to you too.' Salfina poured a cup of coffee for Vivian.

'Sleep well?' Vivian asked Salfina.

'Like a baby. It seems like you didn't get enough sleep. If only Ethan saw you in this state yesterday maybe then he wouldn't want to meet you.'

'I don't get why he wants to meet me at all.' Then she said quickly, 'Not that I want to meet him. Now I know about what's going on.'

Salfina sipped her steaming coffee while marveling at her friend through narrowed eyes.

'For God's sake, Viv. Every woman in NYC, including Nieva and me, would give anything to have your looks. The fact you don't see that yourself makes you even more beautiful.'

Vivian turned crimson, and didn't know how to respond.

'There's nothing fake about you. Your hair, your breasts, your nails, even your long eyelashes it's all real. You're really…'

She thought for a few seconds and made a dramatic gesture by putting her hand on her forehead.

'You're an exotic beauty. Really! Think about how many women wear fake nails, or hair extensions, or get boob jobs!'

Salfina was the funniest among her friends. She never took anything seriously and always looked on the bright side.

'Cut it out, Sal. You also know that most men prefer blonds. Look at you, you're always the center of attention.

They're lining up to get you.' Upon hearing this, Salfina almost choked.

'That's bullshit.'

'No it's not. When I call you, nine out of ten times you're on a date. So don't tell me it's bullshit.'

'Viv, going out for a drink with someone doesn't always mean it's dating, capisce?'

'I don't know, maybe you're right. It's just… I'm away from home most of the time, and I barely see you and Nieva. Sometimes I feel lonely, you know what I'm saying? I'm jealous of you guys.'

'Listen, you might think men line up for me. Did you ever consider that all these men think blonds are stupid and easy to get? You know the saying, "Blondes have more fun." Educated men are often surprised once they start talking to me because they don't expect I can keep up with them in a good conversation. So no, Viv, you don't have to envy me.'
She got up from her chair, brushed her hair to her back, and stared at Vivian mischievously.

'How about that breakfast at Sarabeth's you promised? Can we go now?'
As usual, Sarabeth was crowded, but luckily they didn't have to wait long for a table, and the waiter took their orders quickly. They both ordered omelets with a cafe latte and fresh orange juice. While waiting for their breakfast, they joked about the people passing by in front of the window.

17

A young couple walked by by holding hands, looking as though they were afraid of losing each other. Vivian gazed at the couple, then glanced at Salfina.

'I'm longing for a man in my life, you know. When I'm on location for work, I feel very lonely at night. At times like that, it would be nice if I could call someone I love.'

'I can imagine.'

'Sometimes I think of quitting my job at Frenay & Iams and working for my mother. She wants to expand her architect's firm and has asked me to be her partner over and over again.'

'Why don't you make that change? Don't get me wrong, because I do believe you have a great job over there at Frenay and Iams. However, if you can be part of your mom's firm, it means you become a co-owner. Right?'

The waiter served the lattes, and Vivian immediately took a sip.

'True, but you know my mom. We don't see eye to eye about a lot of things, and we are two opposites. Also, I enjoy the freedom I have at Frenay & Iams, and to be honest, I really would miss George if I left. He's like a father to me.'

'Isn't George gay?'

'Yes, he is. He's got a lovely partner. I've met him a few times.' The omelets and orange juice arrived, and without waiting for Sal, Vivian began eating.

'By the way, Viv, what about that guy? George's right hand man. You still work with him?' Vivian looked surprised and choked on her omelet. She coughed and turned bright red, quickly gulped her orange juice and breathed in.

'You mean Ferris?'

'Yes, him.'

Vivian tried to appear relaxed because she didn't want Salfina to find out she still had a thing for him.

'Umm, nope. We still keep in touch by phone, because George hasn't been at the office much recently.'

Salfina finished her breakfast and settled back in her chair with a satisfied grin.

'You still like him, don't you? I can see it.' She laughed and added, 'You can't hide anything from me, Viv. I know you too well.'

The last thing Vivian wanted was for her friends to mock her. Especially about men. Why was it so hard for her to lie? She knew Salfina wouldn't give it a rest before she got the truth.

'Alright, I still love him, but he's too old for me. He's nine years older than me.' She told Sal the truth, and crossed her fingers that her friend would leave it alone.

'Have you tried to seduce him or asked him out on a date?'

Vivian looked at her friend with surprise.

'Of course not.'

'Never seduced him or never asked him on a date?'

'Niether.'

'Well, you'll never know if you never try!' Vivian tried to change the subject.

'I asked George what's the deal with Ferris.'

'What do you mean?'

'No one at the office has ever seen him with a woman. He doesn't even look at women. So I asked George if Ferris was also gay.'

'What did George say?'

'He convinced me that Ferris is straight. The only thing he was willing to tell me is that he suffers from trauma from his previous relationship.'

'And then what?' Salfina asked eagerly.

'I don't know. George won't say anything more, so that's it.'

'But he knows something, right?'

'I guess so.'

'You really can't get any other information out of him? After all, he's like your father. If I were you, I'd do anything to get to the bottom of it.'

'Well, that's the difference between you and me. I respect someone's privacy while you keep digging and digging.'

'Oh, please don't make me laugh. You're dying to know what happened to him, but you are too chicken to ask him. Do you know what you need?'

'What?'

'You need to get laid. When was the last time you did it? Wasn't it almost two years ago with your ex, Nick? Gradually you'll become a nun, you know.'

Salfina cracked up. Vivian got annoyed and looked for a reason to escape. She knew for a fact Salfina wouldn't stop mocking her. Vivian despised herself for allowing Salfina to trick her into discussing these things.

'Sal, we need to go! I still need to go to my mom's house, and pack for tomorrow's trip.' Salfina looked surprised and called the waiter for the bill.

'Wow, time flies when you're having fun. I also have to hurry. I've got an appointment at two with a colleague to discuss new clients.' After they paid the bill, they walked outside and waited for a taxi.

'What's the destination this time?'

'Las Vegas. I have a project to design a newly-built hotel.'

'Wow, Las Vegas! How long will you stay? Maybe Nieva and I will come visit you!' Vivian's face brightened. She never got angry with her friends for long.

'I'll only be there for three weeks, but I'd be glad if you come visit me. Just let me know when, so I can arrange a room for you.' Finally a taxi stopped in front of them, and Salfina insisted Vivian take it. They hugged before parting. Vivian got in the cab, closed the door, then wound down the window and stuck her head out.

'Don't forget to give me your new number when you've got it.'

'Sure thing. You'll be the first to get it.' Then the taxi drove away.

CHAPTER 2

Vivian waited for her flight in the business lounge one of the many benefits of flying business class. She looked up at the big clock hanging on the wall, and found she still had thirty minutes before the gate opened. She reached into her bag and took out her phone, and searched for a contact under 'G'. Her thumb stopped on 'George'. After selecting his name, she listened to the dial tone until she heard, "Your call is being forwarded."

Vivian almost cut off the call before she heard a heavy voice.

'With Ferris Austin.' Her heart thumped wildly. His seductive voice made her instantly weak. What should she do? Cut off the call or respond? Ferris's voice always made her daydream about a man indulging a woman in a bedroom by whispering sweet things into her ear. How could someone's voice make her fantasize like this?

She had to be brave. Since Vivian had met Ferris, she hadn't seen any other men. It was unhealthy and would lead to obsession though Vivian vehemently denied this. In the end, she needed to be aware that this man was definitely not interested in her. Her bubble burst when she heard, 'Hello?'

'Hello Ferris, this is Vivian Foster,' she answered quickly.

'Hello Vivian, is there anything I can help you with?' Despite his formal tone, he was always kind to Vivian.

'I actually wanted to speak with George.'

'George has taken a leave of absence, so any call for him will be forwarded to me.'

Vivian thought for a second. Strangely, George hadn't told her he was taking leave.

'Oh, right... no wonder.'

'Is there anything else I could help you with?'

Forbidden thoughts entered her mind when Ferris asked that question. For Vivian, he could always help her with everything as long as it wasn't work-related.

'No, thank you. I just wanted to ask whether George will be coming to Las Vegas for my project.'

'Oh... That's right. You're in Vegas for the next few weeks. George asked if I could join you.' Vivian's face beamed imagining Ferris there with her. At the same time, she felt nervous. Her happiness didn't last long as Ferris continued, 'I couldn't find time for that as the workload in the office has become quite hectic. Vivian, I know the project in Vegas is massive, but George believes in you, and so do I. If you have a problem and need help or advice, you can always call me. I'll try to help from here.'

Vivian hid her disappointment and answered in a formal tone, 'Thank you, Ferris. It's good to know that you and George believe in my capabilities.'

'You're welcome.'

'I have to go now. My flight will take off soon.'

For a moment, there came no reply.

And then, 'Vivian?'

The way Ferris said her name was so enticing it made her whole body and intimate area tingle.

'Yes?' Her 'yes' was filled with longing.

'You have my number. Just call me until George comes back, okay?'

'All right. I must go. Goodbye, Ferris.' She hung up the phone feeling a mixture of anger, excitement, disappointment, and in particular sadness.

With a cold glass of champagne, Vivian leaned back in her plush leather seat with a blanket covering her feet. Fortunately, this flight would only take a few hours. A slim, blond female attendant appeared in the cabin and asked whether she'd like another glass of champagne. Vivian declined she wasn't a heavy drinker. She pulled the blanket up over her body and gazed out the window. All she could see were thick white clouds.

Suddenly she felt exhausted. She tried to keep her eyes open, but finally surrendered. With the push of a button her seat reclined, and she drifted off to sleep.

Light classical music awoke Vivian. When she opened her eyes, panic struck. She couldn't see anything, and couldn't move her hands and feet. She was tied up and blindfolded, lying on a soft bed. She tried to calm down and use her hearing and sense of smell. She could only hear the classical music, and in the air was the fragrance of fresh flowers. Where am I? Why am I here? Who blindfolded and tied me up? She panicked more when she realized not a single thread covered her body. She struggled to move but to no avail. Her arms were stretched up, and with her feet bound to each end of the bed her thighs were wide open. She could feel the soft fabric restraining her hands and feet. Vivian could only rely on her hearing. She concentrated on the voices around her, but she could only hear the faint music.

Trapped in confusion, she realized her mouth wasn't covered.

'Hello?'

Her voice was so soft it almost didn't make a sound. She tried again with a louder voice. 'Hello!?'

No one answered.

Vivian waited with a head spinning with questions when she heard the door open. She heard the footsteps of someone entering the room. Her heart shuddered wildly and her breath became labored. Her adrenaline pumped through the roof.

'Seems like my beauty just woke up.' Vivian focused hard on the voice. It was deep, husky, and very enticing. She knew this voice. It only took a moment to realize the voice belonged to Ferris.

'Ferris!?' Vivian could feel that Ferries was sitting at the foot of the bed where her feet were bound.

'You seem surprised, beautiful.' Vivian licked her lips

nervously. Before she could say anything Ferris continued,

'Vivian, do you realize how tantalizing it is when you wet your lips like that?'

Vivian tried to be rational, but couldn't. On one hand she was afraid, but on the other, she was thrilled because she desperately desired this man. But she wasn't sure she wanted him this way.

'Ferris, why are you doing this? Why am I here? You can't just strip someone without consent. Binding me and blindfolding me as well. You can't tie me up here against my will. You're scaring me!'

There was a lengthy pause until Ferris answered with a low and gravelly voice.

'Vivian, my beauty, the last thing I want is to make you feel afraid. I won't do anything that you don't want me to do.'

'Then release me this instant!' she snapped, tugging at her bound wrists. 'I don't like this game!'

'Are you sure, Vivian? Because if I remember correctly, since the very first time we met, you've been stripping me naked with your provocative big blue eyes.' Vivian's mind whirred. What should she do? What should she say? What Ferris said was true, but it never occurred to her that this man was aware of her deep admiration and burning desire for him.

'Beauty, let me spoil you. Let me make love to you. I have been waiting for this moment since the first time I saw you. You are so beautiful. I know you want all of this.'

26

His voice made her tremble. His lustful baritone and teasing words tickled all of her senses and sparked her recklessness. She had yearned for a man who would say that to her for a very long time. And there he was, right in front of her.

In the most confusing moment of her life, she chose an act of courage. She lifted her chin and caressed her lips with her tongue. 'Then touch me,' she said. Let me feel what it's like to be your woman. Please release me so I can see you.'

In a flash, Ferris sat astride Vivian and put his finger under her chin. With his thumb he traced Vivian's thin, plump lips.

'Everything has its time, beautiful. Just try to relax and enjoy it. Let me take you to the next level. You'll love it, believe me.'

Ferris brought his face closer to Vivian's lips and kissed her delicately. The kiss quickly became rough and vigorous. With his lips Ferris swept Vivian's neck down to her breast. He saw her chest tighten, and her nipples stiffen.

He nibbled her nipple and bit it carefully, while skillfully massaging her other breast. Vivian felt like she was going to explode, and thrust her chest toward Ferris, making him more aroused. He carefully nibbled her other nipple and sucked it. Vivian moaned. Her breath became heavy.

'Ferris,' she groaned, hoping he would let her go. Ferris's mouth descended to her stomach. He stuck the tip of his tongue on Vivian's belly button, and traced her torso down to the apex of her legs.

'Hmm, I can see you are ready for me, beautiful.

You're wet down there. But you need to be patient.'

Ferris's breath was heavy too. Greedily he licked her moistened folds and then explored deeper inside. Feeling completely helpless she cried, 'Ferris, I can't take it anymore!'

'Patient... wait for it, beautiful.' He started to lick again and then slowly inserted a finger, deftly pulling it in and out, over and over again until Vivian's whole body was shaking as she was on the verge of orgasm.

Suddenly Ferris stopped when Vivian said, 'Please release me, Ferris. I also want to touch you.'

Ferris untied her legs, but Vivian didn't move. Finally, he grabbed her hand and helped her to rest on her knees. Ferris sat in front of her a short distance away. With Vivian's hands still in his grip he placed them around his shoulders. Now Vivian could feel his body. His skin was smooth and warm. Slowly she moved her hands to his arms. She could feel his taught muscles. Her hands moved down to his flat, muscular stomach. Even though she was blindfold, Vivian's eyes followed her hands as she touched him. Her hands continued down until she reached the waist of his briefs. She gasped when she felt his hard male heat.

'Hmm... Vivian,' he moaned in her ear. 'I want you, and I want to be inside you.' His words gave her the courage to reach into his tight briefs. Vivian's hands wrapped around his throbbing erection, and as she gripped it tightly she gulped loudly. It was huge!

Before Vivian realized, Ferris sat on top of her and pushed his pulsating cock inside her. Vivian's pussy was tight, so Ferris paused for a few moments, allowing Vivian's depths to moisten and adjust. He ripped off the blindfold and stared at her. 'Are you okay? Am I hurting you?'

Her eyes widened. Pain and pleasure blended into one.

'Yes and no. It hurts, but it feels good.'

After he made sure he could go all the way, Ferris repositioned his hips. Vivian wrapped her legs around his butt so he could enter more deeply. Her fingers clung to his sturdy and muscular back.

Vivian groaned as Ferris thrust his driving flesh in and out, fast and rough. They panted together heavily. Vivian's slickened depths tightened around his cock. She was almost there. Ferris quickened his tempo to bring Vivian to a heaving orgasm. She gasped, groaned, and with her body shaking uncontrollably, Vivian came. She felt his cum spill out in a cool trickle.

'Ma'am, is everything all right?' Vivian was startled by the flight attendant's hand touching her shoulder and her friendly voice. She looked confused with her surroundings. The other passengers glanced toward her while giggling and raising their eyebrows. For heaven's sake! While she was asleep and dreaming, everyone seated in the surrounding rows could hear the erotic noises escaping her mouth.

'Yes, I'm fine. Thank you.'

Red-faced and ashamed, Vivian reclined in her seat. Damn it! It's Salfina's fault for saying she needed to get laid. There she sat, stuck in a plane full of shame with nowhere to hide. Fortunately, they were landing soon, as the fasten seatbelt sign had been switched on. In a short while she could escape from the passengers that kept throwing her bemused glances. Vivian collected her baggage and strode to a car rental counter. It took her a long time to complete all the forms. Helping with her luggage, an employee took her to the car and explained how its navigation system worked. After entering her destination, Vivian drove away.

The hotel's reception desk was crowded with people. Vivian walked toward them and eavesdropped on the conversation between a hotel employee and a guest. 'We're sorry, sir. We're fully booked but will do our best to settle the problem. Please take a seat first. If there is any progress, we will inform you as soon as possible.' With a sour face the man strode toward the lobby, almost crashing into Vivian. Not a single word of apology came from his mouth. It was now Vivian's turn, and what she worried about was true there was no room left for her too. 'How is this possible? The booking was made weeks ago. I don't understand,' said Vivian, staring in shock at the employee at the reception desk.

'Ma'am, don't worry, we will find a way out of this as soon as possible.' Vivian calmed herself and had to rethink to find the right polite words to say to the employee.

'What do you mean by "a way out"?'

The employee was startled by Vivian's question, and she blushed.

'Uhh, we will transfer our guests to another hotel, ma'am.'

Vivian glanced at her name tag.

'Listen, Sandra, I understand you can't do anything about it, but I don't want to transfer.' Her face began to redden.

'This booking was made a few weeks ago. I'm here to work, not for vacation. I chose this hotel because its name and service are well-known. So, I don't care how you will settle this problem, but transferring me to another hotel is not an option.'

The receptionist looked very confused.

'Uh, all right, Miss Foster, I understand. Bu... but would you mind taking a seat first? I will call the manager to meet you.'

'Thank you,' Vivian said firmly and then walked to a large seat in the lobby which was as far away from the sour-looking man as possible.

In a panic she fretted about what to do. Even though she often went away on business, she'd never had this problem before. Her stomach tightened when she considered calling Ferris for advice. Did she even have the courage to do so?

To hell with it, Ferris wouldn't be able to see her on the phone, and he didn't know that Vivian had just had an erotic dream about him. Vivian grabbed her Chloé bag from the floor and took out her phone. Hesitantly, she pushed the call button.

'Good afternoon, this is Ferris Austin from Frenay & Iams.'
Like usual, his voice was low and alluring. In a split second
scenes from her dream raced through her mind. She could feel
the dampness spread between her thighs. She pressed her legs
together tightly, as though the people around her might notice
what was happening to her.

'Hello, Ferris. It's Viv.'

'Hello, Vivian, what can I do for you? You're in Vegas
already?' Despite his rigid voice, Vivian couldn't stop her heart
from beating madly.

'Yes I've just arrived, but I already have a problem.'

'What's the problem, Vivian?'

She took a deep breath. 'The hotel is overbooked, and I…'
Ferris cut in, 'Which hotel?'

'The Bellagio. Someone at reception arranged for me to speak
with the manager.'

'You don't have to speak with the manager. I'll call you back
in a minute.' Ferris ended the call abruptly. After a few minutes
Vivian's phone rang. When she saw the screen the name made
her heart thump. 'Vivian here.'

'It's all clear, and you can check in during the next half hour.'
Vivian was shocked. 'How... How did you do that?'
Ferris laughed. For the first time, Vivian listened to this man
laugh. It completely charmed her.

'Connections. Let me know when you've successfully
checked in.'

'Thank you, Ferris. Of course, I'll call you once I'm in my room.' Vivian glanced around. Her eyes stopped on an attractive man behind the check-in counter. He looked like he was talking with Sandra, the young employee who had spoken with Vivian earlier. The man reminded her of Michael Buffer, the man behind the legendary phrase, "Let's get ready to rumble." Only this man seemed younger. It seemed like Sandra was receiving a briefing from the man. Observing from a distance, Vivian was surprised when Sandra pointed at her. The man said something to Sandra, then walked toward Vivian and held out his hand. 'Miss Foster?' Vivian stood up and shook his hand. 'Yes, that's right.'

'I'm Thomas Scott. I apologize for the inconvenience. Your room is ready. Please follow me. I will take you to your room.' Vivian turned red with discomfort as the man who almost collided with her glared at her.

'You can leave your luggage here. I will make sure it is sent to your room.'

'Thank you, Mr. Scott.' Thomas Scott signaled to a bell boy who immediately picked up her luggage. Vivian followed Thomas toward the lift, and then he pushed the thirty-sixth floor button.

'Mr. Austin told me that you're in Vegas to design a newly-built hotel?'

'Yes, that's right. Vivian couldn't contain her curiosity.

'Do you know Mr. Austin personally?'

33

'Of course. We're family.'

'Family?' Vivian had the urge to ask this man everything about Ferris, but she composed herself because she knew it would be highly inappropriate.

'Yes, Ferris is my nephew.' The lift opened. Thomas stepped out first and unlocked her room. She was overwhelmed by the view. It wasn't a standard room it was a suite.

'Welcome to The Bellagio's penthouse. We hope you will feel comfortable here during your stay.' Vivian was speechless. Thomas chuckled softly. Luckily, his phone rang because Vivian couldn't find a single word.

'If I weren't required downstairs I'd give you a tour, but duty calls. If there's anything you need, please contact me. I will gladly help,' Thomas said while giving her his name card.

'Thank you, Mr. Scott.'

'Please, call me Thomas.' Without a sound, a bellboy had brought her luggage inside. 'Only if you call me Vivian.'

'Agreed.' Thomas shook her hand and left her alone in the palatial room. She walked to the window, which looked out onto Las Vegas' famous dancing fountain. She could also see a replica of the Eiffel Tower. It was mesmerizing. She decided she would not be leaving her room today. She opened her suitcase and hung her clothes neatly in the spacious walk-in wardrobe, and arranged her toiletries in the bathroom, which was vast and extravagant. She should call Ferris but decided she would first take a bath.

CHAPTER 3

After thoroughly soaking in the hot water in the bath, Vivian relaxed on a large armchair while admiring her suite. She could easily spend three weeks in this lavish room, she thought. Smiling, she imagined what would her friends would say when they saw it. They must come to visit.

Vivian gazed around the room. Her eyes stopped on a big fruit basket and a vase of flowers on top of the dining table. They weren't there when she'd arrived. They must have been placed there while she was in the bath.

She got up from the armchair and walked over to the dining table. Pale pink peonies and white roses were beautifully arranged in the vase. The basket bulged with a colorful variety fruit, including strawberries and mangoes. In the middle of it there was a card. With her long and slender fingers, Vivian plucked out the note and read it:

"Vivian Foster, welcome to The Bellagio Penthouse Suite. We wish you a pleasant stay."

Between the fruit basket and the bouquet lay an ice bucket containing a bottle of expensive champagne. She felt like a movie star with this level of luxury! For as long as she worked at Frenay & Iams, she would have gotten used to staying in extravagant hotel rooms, but this time it felt special because she knew that Ferris was the one who arranged all of this for her.

She should call Ferris like she'd told him she would, but somehow, she was trying to ignore him. Vivian longed to call the man and hear his seductive voice, but she also wanted to avoid him, because she was afraid her feelings for him were already too deep. Her erotic dream on the flight had ignited her feelings and her desire for him was getting out of control. Although he sounded rigid with her on the phone, Vivian felt that him solving her problem was very noble.

How stupid she was. This man didn't have any feelings for her at all. She must stop these crazy and embarrassing thoughts about this man. If she didn't, she wouldn't open her heart to other men.

Vivian made a plan. First, she would drink a glass of champagne until she had the courage to call Ferris. Then she would call Salfina or Genieva. Vivian downed the cold champagne. It tasted incredible, so she spoiled herself with another. After she finished her second glass, she felt the bubbles go straight to her head. Her alcohol tolerance was very low, especially as she hadn't eaten yet. She ate some fruit from the basket to fill her stomach a little. She giggled while she knelt on the floor, picturing the scene from *Pretty Woman* when Julia Roberts sat on the floor in the hotel room, drinking champagne then eating the strawberry. When she remembered that Julia's character's name was Vivian, she laughed some more. Yes, she really should call Ferris now. She couldn't delay any longer.

With the third glass in her hand, she walked back to the seat, took out her phone and searched for Ferris's number.

'Hello, this is Ferris Austin.' Oh God, why did his voice always sound so formal and authoritarian? Did he know that it was she who was calling him?

'Hello Ferris.' She needed to concentrate hard so she wouldn't talk too much. Three glasses of champagne were too much for her.

'Are you settled in? Does the room fulfill your expectations?'

'Ferris, this isn't a standerd room; this is the Penthouse Suite! Also, your uncle, Thomas, he was very nice to me.'

'I'm glad you like it. Thomas is always very attentive.'

'While I was taking a bath they delievered flowers, fruit and champagne. It's wonderful! Once again, thank you so much.' She let out a small laugh, and Ferris laughed in return. It was the second time that day she heard him laugh. The sound of it made her whole body glow and tingle.

'You should laugh more often, Ferris,' the words tumbled from her mouth. There was an awkward pause.

'Do you think I laugh too little, Vivian?'

The alcohol made her brave enough to bare her heart. 'Yes, you rarely laugh. You're always so formal and serious.'

'Is that so?'

Vivian continued the conversation calmly. She knew her bravery was from the alcohol, but in that moment, she didn't care.

'Yes, it's true. I have been working at Frenay & Iams for a long time, but I have never heard or seen you laugh. It's too bad, as your laugh is amazing.'

Ferris roared with laughter, and Vivian tingled between her legs. 'I also rarely see you laughing, Vivian!'

'That's not true. I laugh a lot, especially when I'm with friends,' she defended herself.

'So do I, Vivian, so don't judge people so quickly.'

Vivian immediately sagged upon hearing Ferris's words get straight to the point. 'I'm sorry, you're right. I didn't mean to judge you.'

'Apology accepted. Is the project under control? If needed, I could send Trisha to be your assistant.' Vivian was disappointed because once again Ferris had deflected the conversation back to work matters.

'No, thank you. I can handle it. But thanks for the offer and for arranging this room.'

'You're welcome. It was nothing. If you need help, just let me know.'

'Yes, I will... Ferris?' Without Vivian realizing, the yearning in her voice was clear.

'Vivian?' For a moment she could swear she could hear longing in his voice too.

'Sorry, it's nothing.'

'What did you want to say, Vivian?' His voice was deep and husky, as though it was caressing Vivian's ears.

It was impossible to tell him the truth: that she wanted him body and soul. That she wanted to caress him and taste his lips and body. She couldn't be honest with him, so she lied. 'I actually want to ask if George is okay? He always tells me when he's going to take leave.'

Ferris took a deep breath. He needed a moment before he answered. 'Vivian, everything is fine with George. Don't worry. Is there anything else?'

'No, that's all. I will call you when there's some progress with the project.'

'Okay, fine.'

'Bye, Ferris.'

'Vivian?' Once again his voice seemed full of desire. Vivian gripped her phone tightly, hoping she would hear something that she'd waited for for so long: that he wanted her, the same way she wanted him.

'Sleep well.'

'Thank you. Talk to you later, Ferris.'

The disappointment struck her hard, but what more could she hope for? Did Vivian honestly think that Ferris's voice contained a secret desire for her, or was she hallucinating? She padded over to the big window with the view of the dancing fountain. Hundreds of people, including many couples, gathered around it. Some were embracing while watching the divine and romantic display. Vivian stood in front of the window alone, and lonely. Tears streamed down her cheeks.

She leaned her back on the wall then collapsed on the floor and sobbed. Why?

Why couldn't she erase this man from her mind? How long must she torture herself? Why couldn't she just hate him? Vivian almost went numb with self-pity. With great difficulty, she attempted to stand up but stumbled and fell toward the dining table where she'd placed the champagne. With shaking hands and blurred eyes, she poured the champagne to the rim. One more drink, then one more and one more... until the bottle was empty. Vivian felt totally intoxicated, but the sadness and heartbreak remained.

She needed more alcohol to feel completely numb. She walked to the minibar and took out a small bottle of Johnnie Walker Blue Label. She'd never tried whiskey before and took a big sip, which instantly made her cough as her throat burned from the liquid... She needed this to forget all her sorrow for a while.

The next day, Vivian woke early. She panicked for a second when she didn't realize where she was. She'd fallen asleep in the armchair. Her head felt like it was being hit with a hammer. She cautiously sat up, and eyed all the emptied whiskey bottles scattered on the floor. What had she done? This couldn't be happening. It was the stupidest thing she had done drinking to get rid of the sadness. She was not a drinker, and she didn't want to be so pathetic. Her eyes overflowed with tears again. Why did the rejection from this man hurt so much?

She picked up her phone, searched for Salfina's number,

and pushed the call button. She heard the dial tone.

'Hi, Viv, what's up?' After hearing her friend's bright voice, she began to cry again.

'Vivian, what's wrong? What happened?' Sal's cheery voice became panicked.

'Sal, I... I can't take it anymore!'

'What can't you take anymore? What exactly is going on, Vivian?'

Through her sobs, Vivian told her best friend what had happened, about her dream, the conversation with Ferris and that she'd gotten wasted the night before. Her best friend listened intently.

'What am I supposed to do, Sal? It will destroy me if this keeps going on.' Vivian cried.

'Listen, Viv, you must wake up. He doesn't deserve your tears! Maybe you're crazy about him because he is hard to get.'

Vivian snorted and wiped her nose with the back of her hand.

'Yeah... maybe you're right.'

'Duh, of course I'm right, I'm always right.' She listened to Salfina's laugh, and knew her friend was trying to cheer her up.

'Anyway, Viv, why do you want to sleep with an old man like him? Isn't he like ten years older than you?'

'Nine years older. Ferris is thirty-three.'

'Almost ancient then! Duh, Viv. Do you know what you need? A healthy young Adonis look-alike. A man who can satisfy you in bed!'

41

Through her tears Vivian couldn't help but chuckle, though her head still pounded from the drinking.

'See, you can still laugh! Oh, by the way, Viv. I will call Genieva today, and we'll see when we'll be able to visit you in Vegas. Probably this weekend. I want to see that luxurious penthouse.' Vivian felt a flood of relief. She could always count on their support.

'I'll be very glad if you can come!'

'Chill, Viv. I won't let you be there alone, and if Nieva can't come, I'll go alone. We''l have fun, okay?'

'Okay. Deal. Oh, Sal, I still have a question left.'

'Shoot.'

'How can you get rid of a hangover real quick?' Salfina snickered.

'Take a cold bath, then drink lots of water and take an aspirin.'

'Okay, thank you, Sal. I'll do that now. We'll talk later.'

'All right. See you later, Viv.'

Vivian sat for a while staring vacantly, before following her friend's advice.

With her iPad in hand and big black sunglasses masking her hangover, Vivian stepped into the hotel lobby that would over the next three weeks come to life under her care. She summoned a lot of effort and energy to choose furniture and décor that would bring the space to life.

The regal white sandstone mantels she would use for the fireplaces in the suite rooms were imported from France. This stone was from an eighteenth century castle. Luckily she had an unlimited budget for this project money was not an issue and everything must be built from the best materials.

From the lobby, she entered the conference room. This room was chaotic. Everyone was talking loudly, and Vivian couldn't stand it because she was still suffering from her hangover. She stopped at the door, looked around and thought how she would quell this riot that looked like a chicken coop.

A few employees noticed her standing there and elbowed each other. A few moments later, she had everyone's attention. She walked to the middle of the room with all eyes on her. The men ogled her, while the women focused on her classy shoes and clothes. Vivian introduced herself to the group of people that would be working with her for the next three weeks. Based on her previous experiences, she knew she must divide the people gathered into smaller groups as soon as possible. After she divided them, she gave them lists so they could catalog which items had already arrived and ensure they'd been placed on the right floor. When Vivian was confident with her crews and each of them had their list of tasks, she sought a quiet place to work. She had dozens of phone calls to make and emails to answer.

Firstly, she called the auction house in France to determine whether the fireplaces she ordered had been sent or not.

The employee assured her that her items had been sent with specialized transportation and would arrive in the next few weeks. Via email she was informed that the mirror she'd ordered from Venice would be delayed by a few days due to a worker's strike. Vivian glanced at her watch and realized it was lunchtime. She was so caught up in her calls and emails that she'd lost track of time. Work was a welcoming distraction for her, and not once did she think about Ferris.

She leaned back in her chair and sighed.

Her hangover had almost gone but the sadness remained. Out of the corner of her eye, she saw someone enter the room. It was a handsome young man, with an athletic and sun tanned body. His stylishly unkempt salt and pepper hair hung slightly over his eyes. He wore ripped jeans and a tight shirt which emphasized the contours of his muscles. He stopped in front of Vivian.

'I'm sorry to disturb you, but I've been watching you for a while, and I noticed you haven't had anything to eat or drink yet. Can I get you a coffee or something else?' Vivian stared at him thoroughly. He was a handsome man. Not as good-looking as Ferris, but still, not bad.

'I forgot about the time. I can get my own coffee, thank you, if you can tell me where I can get it.'

A teasing smile spread on his lips.

'If you want, I can accompany you to drink coffee. I also haven't taken a break for lunch.' Vivian thought for a second.

It was against her principle to socialize with her employees. She considered how to decline his offer politely.

'Hmm, how about this, if you're kindly offering to bring me a coffee, I'd happily accept, so I can continue my work here.' The man knew he'd been turned down, but he didn't show it.

'What kind of coffee would make you happy?'

'I'd like a café latte.'

'Okay, coming right up.' He turned and left. Even from afar, Vivian was still impressed by his butt.

When he brought the coffee, Vivian was pacing back and forth while talking on her phone. The man placed the coffee on the table next to her iPad. Vivian, still on the call, shrugged her shoulders apologetically and nodded her head in thanks. The man winked, combed his messy hair with his fingers, and vanished.

It was Friday morning. She'd already been in Vegas a week. Vivian's days were long and she always returned late at night to her room. When she arrived, she'd be exhausted and fall asleep immediately. Fortunately, everything went smoothly and according to plan. The building started to look like a real hotel. The gambling tables and machines would be installed that day. Vivian padded to the conference room which was serving as her temporary office. In the corridor, she heard two women discussing their weekend plans. They reminded Vivian of her best friends who until this day still hadn't called to say whether they would visit or not. She planned to call them soon.

Every lunchtime, the man with messy hair, Terry, would bring Vivian a café latte. He would open up a short, innocent conversation and then vanish for the rest of the day. While sipping her coffee, she called her friend, Salfina.

'Hi, Viv, I was just going to call you.'

'Telepathy.' Vivian smiled.

'Oh, Viv, I'm sorry, we can't come! Genieva broke her leg, and no one else can take care of her until she gets a cast.' Vivian tried very hard to mask her disappointment.

'It's okay, no problem. Of course, you need to take care of Nieva. I'm swamped anyway, and I don't even have time to eat a proper dinner. I even need to work on the weekends,' she lied.

'So, you don't mind?'

'No, Sal. It's okay. It's actually a good thing we can work on the weekends so it'll be ready on time.'

'Okay then, but when you're back home we need to hang out like usual, okay.'

'Noted. Take care of Nieva. Love and hugs from me.'

'I'll tell her. Bye-bye, Viv.' Her friend hung up the phone.

Vivian had just returned to her room when someone knocked on the door. With her Louboutin shoes still in her hand, she opened the door carefully. Surprised, she saw Thomas Scott in the doorway.

'Am I interrupting you, Vivian?'

'No, of course not. Please come in.'

She gestured with her other hand to welcome him inside. Together they crossed the room.

'I want to make sure that everything is satisfying.'

'Yes, everything is fine. Thank you.'

'I did"t want to meddle, but it seems like you never eat in our restaurant.' Vivian sat on the couch and looked at Thomas with a smile.

'I'm sorry. It's true. I work until late at night, and when I come back, I'm too tired to eat.' Of course, she wouldn't tell Thomas that she'd lost her appetite because of his nephew, Ferris.

'Then, I would be honored if you want to eat together with me right now. I insist, because I've already made a reservation for us downstairs.' He smiled at Vivian. It was impossible to refuse his offer. She knew that this was the right moment, because it was an opportunity to learn more about Ferris.

'The honor would be all mine.' She stood up and put her feet into her Louboutin stilettos. Thomas offered his arm, and they left the suite toward the restaurant.

When a piece of tender meat touched her tongue, she realized she was starving. Vivian listened to Thomas share the story of his work at Bellagio. The man described his work at the hotel as very dynamic. It seemed like he enjoyed his job, just like Vivian, who was always completely involved in her projects. Vivian had to refuse dessert because she was full and couldn't eat more.

She relaxed her position, and felt comfortable near Thomas.

'Thomas, can I ask you something?' she tried to find a way to open up a conversation about Ferris.

'Of course,' he said, while leaning back in his seat.

'Do you always do this? I mean, eating together with a guest.'

'No, I've violated a rule.' Vivian looked at him, scared.

'Don't worry. They think you're my niece.' Again Vivian recalled *Pretty Woman*, which seemed to have a common thread with her life now.

'Ah, that means family is allowed.'

'Yes, of course, but only when I'm free.'

'Oh, so that's how it is. Do you often invite Ferris here?' She tried to sound nonchalant, as she didn't want to reveal her feelings about Ferris.

'We rarely meet.' Thomas noticed that her face became gloomy. 'Why do you ask?'

'Oh, no reason.'

'Vivian, I'm older than you, and I have more life experience. I know you have feelings for my nephew.' Her cheeks flushed red. How did he know? Thomas continued, 'Every time Ferris's name is mentioned, your eyes shine.' Vivian couldn't deny it anymore. She had to confess. 'Is it that obvious?'

'Yes, I'm afraid it is.'

Vivian fretted. If Thomas could see it, then what about Ferris? How could she face him when it was so obvious to everyone she had fallen for him?

'I'm not able to tell you much about Ferris, to be honest, as I don't know much about him. His mother is my step-sister, and we rarely keep in touch. The only thing I can say is... and I hope this stays between us... he was devastated by his last relationship and since then always avoids women.'

She gaped, shocked by what Thomas had said.

'But what happened?'

'Unfortunately, I can't tell you, Vivian.'

'But you do... know, right?' Vivian prodded him gently.

'Yes, I do know, but it's not my place to tell. It's something Ferris needs to explain. However, I doubt he ever will.'

Thomas accompanied Vivian back to her room, and she thanked him for the delicious meal. Alone in her room, she went over her conversation with Thomas. Something terrible must have happened to Ferris. Vivian spent the weekend in her room. She ordered room service because she didn't want to eat alone in the restaurant.

When Monday came, Vivian felt grateful. Finally, she was occupied with her work again. With her work bag and iPad in hand, she went out with her rented car to the project site. In the middle of her journey, her phone rang. Her heart jumped when she saw it was Ferris calling. She pulled over on the side of the road before taking the call.

'Vivian Foster.' She formally opened the conversation, just like Ferris normally did.

'Good morning, Vivian.' Although his voice wreaked havoc

on her heart and mind, she tried to sound relaxed.

'Hi Ferris, everything okay?' For a moment there was no sound on the other line. Then she heard Ferris's voice and took a deep breath. Vivian felt anxious, had Thomas revealed her secret?

'Vivian, I sent Trisha over there. She's already on her way.'

'What?' shouted Vivian. 'For what, and why?'

With a curt tone, Ferris continued. 'Something has happened here. Sean Frenay and Clive Iams will be waiting for you on Wednesday to discuss it.'

She felt her blood boiling with anger. 'But why? Did I do something wrong?'

'No Vivian. You didn't do anything wrong. Be sure to pick up Trisha at the airport and get her up to speed with the project's development. Make sure you're there for the meeting on Wednesday.' Vivian was stunned.

'All right.' They were the only words she could muster.

'Great, I'll email you Trisha's flight details. I'll call Thomas to see if he can arrange another room for Trisha.'

'No need. The suite is big enough for two. We can share it.'

'Fine, I'll send you the email and see you on Wednesday.'

Again Vivian's face flushed red as she asked, 'You'll also be at the meeting?'

'Yes.' She was filled with joy and trepidation.

'Do you know what the meeting will be about?'

'Yes, I know, but I won't tell you now.'

Vivian was annoyed, and while glaring at the car's dashboard said,

'Come on, Ferris, you can fill me in at least a little.'

'No, I can't. It's for the best if you wait until Wednesday, Vivian. Oh, I've just emailed you Trisha's flight details.'

'Fine, thank you. I'll pick her up. See you on Wednesday.'

'See you then, Vivian.' He ended the call. For a while she sat there in the car on the side of the road with thousands of questions and no answers.

CHAPTER 4

Vivian was seated in the same room where she was interviewed by George Maldini six years ago. Time had flown, and her life had changed dramatically. Six years ago she sat there as a timid girl, and now she had evolved into a successful woman full of professional self-confidence. Vivian was rarely at the office. She only met George and Ferris on project locations, or for official business lunches or dinners in one of the city's grand restaurants. Vivian looked around the office and noticed not a lot had changed since the last time she was there, except that George was absent.

How was he? They were always close, but in the last few months, Vivian had heard nothing from him. His cellphone was disconnected, and all his communication went through Ferris. She started to feel uneasy; something was wrong. But what was it?

The door opened, and Sean Frenay and Clive Iams entered the room. Both men, in their sixties, were still very attractive. Her nerves tensed. Though she respected them both, she never got a chance to talk to them. They always kept some distance from the other staff and stayed behind the scenes. But George always said good things about them, so Vivian felt as if she knew them well.

Sean Frenay was the first who held out his hand to greet Vivian, soon followed by Clive Iams.

The three of them sat at the large oval conference table. Clive inspected some documents, and Sean turned toward Vivian.

'Miss Foster, I'm sure you must be wondering why you're sitting here now.'

'Yes, to be honest, I'm confused, but it seems there's an urgent matter going on. It must be extremely urgent for me to have been withdrawn from my current project.'

'Yes, yes, your project, I heard from Mr. Austin that the project is massive. Have there been any significant developments?'

'Yes, it's begun to take shape already. We're actually ahead of the project's timeline,' she replied proudly.

'That's good. Very good. The client must be thrilled about that.' Vivian paid attention to Sean who often repeated his words, while Clive was still busy with the documents in front of him. Didn't Ferris say he would attend this meeting? Where was he? Vivian was still confused, and had no idea what to expect.

'Miss Foster. Yes, Miss Foster. I will explain the reason for our meeting today.'

Vivian tried hard to calm herself, even though she'd grown weary from hearing Sean repeat his words.

'We have some bad news regarding Mr. Maldini.' Vivian suddenly found it difficult to breathe, and her stomach tightened.

'What do you mean by bad news?'

Sean cleared his throat and peered at Clive who was still distracted by the documents, and then continued.

'Mr. Maldini is struggling with incurable cancer. Right now, he's in the final stage, which means he won't be returning to work again. He wants to spend the rest of his remaining time with his partner.'

Vivian's eyes welled with tears, and her mouth dropped open slightly. She couldn't believe what she'd just heard.

'No... it's not possible. This can't be happening!' Tears flowed down her cheeks. Sean gazed at her sadly.

'The last time I saw him, he was just fine.'

'I'm sorry. Yes, I'm sorry, this news is terrible for all of us. But Mr. Maldini has been suffering from cancer for a long time. Only Clive and I know about it, and no one else must know. That's his request. His illness has now reached the final stage, and he wants to spend time at home. At least that's what he said.'

Vivian pulled a tissue from her bag and wiped the remnants of her tears. She couldn't say a word, while Sean continued to speak.

'We Clive, Mr. Maldini, and me have talked for a long time about how to manage the internal operations of the firm when Mr. Maldini is longer active. No matter how terrible this is, the work must go on. Mr. Maldini has informed us that he wants his position to be filled by both you and Mr. Austin.'

Vivian didn't hear a word that Sean said.

Devastated by sadness, everything that happened around her seemed to pass like fog. Her body was in the room, but her mind had drifted somewhere far away. It took a while until she finally returned to reality and could actually listen to Sean Frenay's words.

'I suggest you take a leave of absence for the rest of this week and process this information. Then you will report on Monday to Mr. Maldini at his home, and confirm that you and Mr. Austin will fill his position. You can get the address from the receptionist's desk.'

'No need. I know where George lives.'

'Well, that's good. That's all we wanted to say. Do you have any questions?'

Vivian's mind was racing with questions, none of which Sean nor Clive could answer. She couldn't tell them that she doubted she could work closely with Ferris, the man she loved but who didn't like her at all.

'No. For now, I don't have any questions.'

'Great... Great. If you have questions, please call either myself or Clive.'

'Yes, if you have questions, you can always call us.' Clive looked at Vivian with concern.

'Are you okay, Miss. Foster? Should I call Mr. Austin to escort you home?' asked Clive.

The last thing she needed was to meet Ferris. She really couldn't face him right now.

She needed to process this terrible news first and calm herself down.

'No, thank you, Mr. Iams, I will take a taxi. Everything is fine.'

She said goodbye politely and fled from the office. With eyes brimming with tears, she hurried down the long corridor, which was still decorated with white orchids on pillars, toward the lift. Because her eyes were wet with tears her vision was blurry, and she crashed into someone. It was a man, and he held her tightly. Then Vivian heard his voice, and knew immediately who it was.

'Vivian, Oh my god! Are you okay?'

She tried to pull away from his grip, but he held her tightly. She felt slightly crushed by his tight grip, and his touch felt like it burned her. Once again she tried to break free, but it was no use. Finally, he pulled Vivian into an embrace to calm her down. She surrendered.

'Ssshhh... it's okay, calm down.' He rocked Vivian softly in his arms.

'I know you were close with George.' Vivian clenched her fists in front of his chest.

'Right… I *am* really close with him. You said that as though he isn't here anymore, but he's still alive!'

Despite her deep sadness, she couldn't deny she was enjoying this warm, tight hug.

This was what she missed, despite the awful situation.

In Ferris's arms, she felt safe and comfortable.

The scent from his aftershave and arms that held her tightly made her forget the real reason she was sobbing.

The sound of approaching footsteps made Vivian's imagination fade and reluctantly step out of the embrace. It was Sean and Clive. Clive looked at her worriedly and turned to Ferris.

'I think it would make sense if you took Miss Foster home.' Ferris nodded in agreement.

'No, no need, I'll take a taxi,' Vivian refused.

'Miss Foster, I don't think you want to get into a taxi in this condition. You look like a panda bear.' Vivian was mortified. She didn't realize her tears had made her mascara run severely. In this bedraggled state, she just wanted to lay herself down in Ferris's arms. Sean and Clive walked into another room and disappeared, leaving just the two of them. Vivian and the man she wanted to make love to. Her imagination was ruined when she realized she looked disheveled. Vivian frowned. 'Ferris, do I look like a panda?'

She looked painfully hurt and deeply sad. Ferris gently placed his hand on her lower back and steered her to the lift.

'Yes, but a very slim panda bear.' She laughed.

'See, you can laugh again. It's better like this. Come on, let me take you home.'

Ferris parked his luxurious Range Rover in front of Vivian's apartment.

'Can you walk by yourself? Do you need me to accompany you upstairs?'

Vivian tried to think fast. If Ferris took her inside, she might get him to open up and talk, and who knows what else could happen. But she shot down all those dreams. No, she couldn't allow this man to go inside because she knew her hopes would end up in disappointment. She needed to be strong, and resist her desire to be with him.

'No, thank you, I can walk by myself. Thank you for bringing me home.'

With her right hand, she pulled the handle to get out and head inside. A second after the door opened, Ferris took hold of her left hand.

'Vivian, I know the news you've heard is upsetting. I know you have a special bond with George.' Vivian could feel her tears roll down again and tried as hard as possible to stop them.

'I consider George to be my father, and I still can't completely understand and believe it.' Tears streamed down her cheeks.

'I can come a bit later on Monday, to give you some time alone with him.'

'You really don't mind? Because I would appreciate that.'

'Of course I don't mind, otherwise I wouldn't have suggested it.'

Vivian was flooded with relief. 'Okay. Thank you. And thanks again for bringing me home.'

'If you need a friend, you can call me anytime Vivian, okay?'

'Okay. Thanks... see you later Ferris.'

She quickly went outside and disappeared through the door of her apartment block. The minute she set foot inside her apartment, Vivian let go of all her anxieties and grief. She burst into tears. Her body shook as she cried, until she fell asleep on the couch. She woke up because of cold air coming in from the windows. She saw that it was dark outside already. How long had she been asleep? Her stomach rumbled loudly. She realized she hadn't eaten anything that day. She decided to take a hot shower, and after that, she would satisfy her hunger. Then she would call her mom and her friends.

She padded to the bathroom, opened the shower cubicle, and let the hot water flow down. She was shocked when she saw her reflection in the mirror.

Her eyes were swollen. Beneath them there were dark patches framed by blackish blotches from the running mascara. She stared in the mirror, and had to admit what Clive had said was true. Her eyes did look like a panda's. She loosely tied up her long brown hair.

Wearing only a bathrobe, she sat at the bar table and stabbed at the salad which she barely ate.

Her mind drifted to the conversation with Sean and Clive and the moment when Ferris hugged her.

Each time she closed her eyes, she could feel his strong arms hugging her and the scent of his aftershave. It quickly aroused her. His strong body was so close to Vivian's, and once again she imagined how they would make love, caressing every inch of each other's bodies.

Vivian would carefully take Ferris's cock in her mouth and suck and lick it until Ferris came. Ferris would satisfy her with his fingers and tongue, and when she reached orgasm she would shout his name as loudly as possible. She also imagined him stroking his cock with lubricant and little by a little edging it into Vivian's ass. Inside her mind, she could even imagine the pleasure of being stimulated from behind, even if she'd never tried it. With Ferris, she would do anything. She wanted to feel everything with him. The cold air sweeping her back made Vivian return to the real world. She tightened her bathrobe. Her appetite was gone. She threw away the rest of her salad and lay down on the couch with the phone pressed to her ear.

'This is Ellis Foster's voicemail. I can't answer your call right now. Please leave a message after the beep, and I'll call you back as soon as possible... beep.'

Vivian hated leaving messages, so she simply hung up the phone. She searched for Genieva's contact, and pressed the dial button to call her friend.

'Hi, Vivian.'

'Hi Nieva, How are you doing? What's the story about your broken leg?'

Genieva laughed out loud. 'If I tell you, you must promise you won't laugh at me.'

'How can I do that if you're already laughing now?'

'Hahaha, yes, you're right. But this is embarrassing.'

'Just tell me,' urged Vivian.

Genieva still roared with laughter.

'Okay, so here goes. Are you ready?'

Vivian waited with full enthusiasm.

'Yes, yes I've been ready since yesterday!'

'You know that I can't walk in high heels, right?' Vivian exploded with laughter.

'Oh no... no Nieva, don't tell me you busted your leg because of high heels!?'

'Hahaha yeah, it's bad, right? No more high heels for me.'

'Gee, an accident like this could only happen to you!' Vivian thought for a second whether she should tell her friends that she was back home, but decided not to.

They would insist on getting together, and she didn't want to see anyone right now.

'Luckily, Sal is here to help me out, because I can't get around with the cast on my leg. It's handy to have a personal assistant. Right now she's buying me a meal. I could get used to it.'

'Yeah, I can imagine that.' Vivian decided to cut the call quickly before Genieva asked her about the project in Vegas, which might force her to admit that she was at home.

'Okay Nieva, make the most of your assistant. I've got to go. We'll talk later. Oh, don't forget to kiss Sal for me.'

'Alright, Viv, I'll tell her later. Bye-bye.' Vivian was relieved she didn't need to lie directly to her friend.

Early on Monday morning, Vivian prepared to go to George's house. She studied herself in the mirror, assessing the combination of her navy pants and light blue blouse. Her ensemble intensified her blue eyes. She wore light make up; only mascara and thin lip gloss. Her long hair was tied chicly at the nape of her neck, completing her elegant look.

She checked her bag to make sure she had tissues as she might need them later. From the refrigerator, she took chocolate truffles which she'd bought for George in Vegas. He loved this type of chocolate.

With her bag on her arm and the fancy truffles in hand, Vivian walked to the corner of her street to hail a taxi. If her position at Frenay & Iams was going to change, she would buy a car. Up until then she didn't need one because she was always away on business trips.

The taxi driver stopped in front of a tall apartment complex. She paid for the trip and stepped into the apartment's entrance. The employee at the guard's desk recognized Vivian, so he immediately welcomed her and walked with her toward the lift.

'I will tell him you're heading up, Miss Foster.'

'Thank you, Ralph.'

Before she knocked on the door, Edward, George's partner, opened the door for her.

'Hi, Vivian, you look beautiful as always. Please, come in.'

'Thank you, Edward.' As usual, he warmly welcomed Vivian with a kiss on both cheeks. Edward had a friendly face.

His eyes were green, sharp nose slightly slanted, and his lips were thin. His short blond hair shined in the sun. As well as these intriguing features, his tall and slender figure made him look much younger than his age.

'How are you, Edward? I'm so sorry. Why did I have to find out this way, why didn't he tell me?'

'He's been sick for a long time, Vivian. He didn't want to tell anyone because he didn't want people to treat him with pity.'

Vivian wiped her tears. 'I understand... but...'

Edward cut her off, 'I know, honey, you have a special bond that will be there forever. Come on, let me take you to him. He is waiting for you. He's in the library now.'

Vivian followed Edward through the opulent hallway. Vivian had to walk quickly to keep up with him. They stopped at a towering carved wooden door, and Edward turned around to Vivian.

'You can go inside. He is waiting for you. I'll make tea and bring it to you a little later.'

Edward went to the kitchen. Vivian took a few deep breaths to prepare herself. She took the door handle with her right hand, but quickly let go. What would she see inside? What could she expect? She didn't know what she should she say, and the last thing she wanted was to burst into tears. She gathered her courage to open the door without knocking first.

The library was vast, with the walls on each side stacked from top to bottom with books.

Just like in old libraries, there was a special ladder on wheels to reach the upper shelves. The large floor to ceiling window looked out onto the Hudson River an almost perfectly mirrored view as the one that could be seen from the Frenay & Iams Office.

The view was so beautiful, and the sun lit up the room. George was sitting down with a book in hand. He was reading, and hadn't noticed that Vivian was standing there observing him.

'George?' He was surprised, and let the book fall in his lap. His face brightened when he looked at Vivian.

'Vivian! It's been so long since I've seen you. Come here.' He gestured for Vivian to come closer. Vivian knelt beside George. She held his thin hand that was resting on his lap and burst into tears with her head on his knees.

'Calm down, sweet child… calm down. It's okay. I'm at peace with all of this.'

'Ho… how can you say that?' George gently squeezed Vivian's hand.

'It is what it is, my dear. I can't complain, because my life has been wonderful and fulfulling. Come on, get up and take a chair. You'll ruin your pants if you sit on the floor like that.'

'I don't care,' she said softly. She stood up and sat beside George while looking for the tissues in her bag. She took one from the pack, dabbed at her eyes, and looked at George closely.

'Let me guess. I must look like a panda again?'

He laughed and shook his head. 'Like a panda? No. What gave you that idea?'

'Clive told me the other day that I looked like a panda, after my mascara has run down my cheeks. I'd been crying.'

'Typical Clive. He's always awkward when speaking with a beautiful young woman. But if you did look like a panda, I bet you'd be a very pretty panda.' Vivian dabbed at her nose with a tissue.

'So my mascara is still intact, right? It hasn't streaked down my cheeks?'

'Trust me. You always look charming and exquisite.'

Edward entered the room with a tray carrying a porcelain teapot and three matching cups and saucers. He winked lovingly at George then placed the tray on the table and poured tea into each cup. Vivian took the box of truffles from her bag and handed it to George. With raised eyebrows, he opened the box carefully. He smiled when he saw what it contained.

'Did you buy these for me?'

'Of course. I know they're your favorite.'

'But you can't buy these anywhere in the city!'

She shrugged her shoulders and smiled. 'Only the best for you, George.'

George and Edward chuckled in unison. Edward then sat on the armrest next to George.

'This woman has good taste, George, when it comes to fine delicacies.'

'Not only delicacies, honey. Vivian has a good taste in everything.'

Vivian noticed how lovingly the two men looked at each other.

'Edward, have you contacted Ferris to come tomorrow and not today?'

'Of course. I know how much you just want to spend time with Vivian today.'

'Thank you, darling. Can you get that photo album in the bedroom for me? Then I can show Vivian something.'

'Alright, I'll be right back.' He kissed George on his bald head and then left the library. George turned his head with a severe expression. 'Vivian, I have an important matter to discuss with you. As you already know, I don't have much time left. The doctors estimated that my life expectancy is around six months to one year.' Vivian wanted to say something, but George gestured for her to listen first. Although he was seriously ill, he didn't look like dying. He did look thin, but apart from that, he still looked healthy. Others might not believe he was terminally ill. Vivian channeled all her strength into ignoring the thought that George only had half a year to live. She didn't want to suffer the loss of a father a second time. Her own father died suddenly and unexpectedly due to a heart attack. She didn't have time to say goodbye to him. But she would try to spend as much time as possible with George. His voice disrupted her thoughts. 'What I'm about to say I should have told you a long time ago.'

CHAPTER 5

Vivian looked at him questioningly. 'What is it, George?'
Edward stepped into the library with a big photo album and
gave it to George. 'I will leave you two alone,' he said gently.
George nodded his head. Edward took his cup of tea from the
table and left the room. George gripped the photo album tightly
with both hands as if someone might take it away from him.

'Vivian, do you still remember your job interview?'

'Yes, I still remember it. Throughout my entire life, I've never
felt that nervous.'

George nodded, satisfied.

'You know, Vivian, I would never actually interview
candidates. Usually Evelyn from Human Resources would
conduct all the interviews.' Vivian looked at George
quizzically.

'By chance I saw your CV with your photo attached. Back
then, I knew you had to be the one who would get that job,
even though you had no experience at the time.'

'But why?'

George opened the photo album and pointed at a photograph.

'Because of this.' Vivian stared at the photo, her eyes and
mouth wide open.

'Wh... Who is that?' Vivian stuttered and kept her eyes fixed
on the photo. The woman in the photo looked exactly like
Vivian.

The only difference was that her hair was blonde, and she had a beauty spot above her top lip.

'This was my daughter, Victoria. Unfortunately, she is no longer with us.'

'What..?! George, I had no idea you had a daughter. When did she pass away? Was she sick too?'

George closed his eyes and took a deep breath. 'Victoria committed suicide eight years ago.' When George opened his eyes, he saw Vivian was shocked. 'You know, Vivian. This is no coincidence.

When I saw your photo, it was two years after my Vic had died. I felt like I saw Victoria in you. Even though there were slight differences in your physical characteristics, both of you were like two halves. Even your names are similar.'

Vivian listened carefully and shifted closer so she could hold his hand.

'I don't know, Vivian, do you feel that we just clicked when we first met?'

'Yes, I felt it. The first time I met you, I felt comfortable, and like we already knew each other.'

'See. This was destiny. I usually don't believe in this kind of thing, but I believe it was Vicky who brought us together.'

Vivian bit her bottom lip and considered asking why Victoria decided to commit suicide, but chose not to.

'Oh my god, George. I don't know what to say. What does Edward think about all this?'

'Edward was dumbfounded when he saw you for the first time. He also said this can't be a coincidence.'

'I just want to say that I'm glad if Victoria was the one who brought us together, because if you see your daughter in me, I see a father figure in you.'

George's eyes welled with tears, and Vivian held out her arms to hug him. They cried softly in each other's arms.

Edward walked into the room, this time carrying bagels with smoked salmon and cream cheese. He sat beside Vivian and held her hand to his while asking, 'Were you surprised, dear?'

'Yes, to be honest, I was completely amazed.'

'I understand... I was also shocked when I first saw you. You and Victoria were so similar. I'm sure if she were alive, you would be the best of friends.'

'Yes, I think so, too,' George agreed.

They ate the bagels in silence, their minds drifting. Not long after they'd finished, George's said, 'That was delicious, honey. Thank you.'

'You're welcome.' Edward answered.

'George?'

'Yes, dear?'

Vivian shifted to look at him. 'Why didn't you tell me you were sick?'

'I didn't want people to pity me. If I said I had stomach cancer four years ago, then for the last four years I would have been treated as someone who was dying.

I didn't want that, and I still don't.'

'But you should have told me, George, I'm not just anyone…
I mean… ah, you know what I mean.'

'I get what you're trying to say, dear. Yes, you're right. I
should've told you, not just Sean and Clive. I'm sorry. What
else did Clive and Sean say to you?'

Vivian revisited her memories. During the conversation she
was so consumed by grief she didn't notice everything Sean
said to her.

'Uhh, that Ferris and I will jointly take over your position and
you will transfer all responsibilities to both of us.'

'Correct. How do you feel about that?'

Vivian knew what George was trying to say but acted
innocently. 'What do you mean?'

'Come on, Vivian. Only a fool couldn't see what Ferris means
to you.' Vivian's cheeks blazed red.

'He obviously doesn't share my feelings. You know it too. So
there is nothing left for me to do but do my job as best I can.'
His fine wrinkles deepened as he smiled. 'You're always so
dedicated.'

'George... you've always worked with him, right?'

'Yes.'

'Do you know what happened in his past? What happened in
his love life that made him the way he is?'

George took a deep breath, rubbed his bald head and then
stroked his neatly trimmed beard.

'Yes, Vivian. I know what happened, but I can't tell you. Ferris trusts me with his story, and I won't betray his trust. All I can say is, it was not pleasant for him, and it had a deep impact on his life. If one day he tells you, I hope you won't judge him or change your view toward him. Promise me, Vivian, that you wouldn't do that.'

She wasn't sure what she should say except, 'Yes, I promise.' Edward returned with a slight look of concern.

'George, honey, you must take your medicine and get some rest.'

'Yes, you're right. Vivian, tomorrow I'll explain to you and Ferris about your new positions at Frenay & Iams.'

'Yes, all right.' She stood up and peered at George's tired. She kissed him on his forehead and asked, 'What time tomorrow?'

'Come here at eleven o'clock, dear.'

'All right, I'll be here. Is there anything I can bring you?'

'No, I don't need anything. Thank you for being so caring.'

'Okay, see you tomorrow, George, and please don't forget to rest.'

'See you tomorrow, dear.'

Edward walked Vivian to the doorway and kissed her cheeks.

'Vivian, if you don't mind, please come at noon tomorrow, so I can make sure he can rest a little bit longer. He really needs it.'

Vivian looked at him with concern and said, 'I understand. It must be so difficult for you. How're you holding up?'

'It is hard. I don't want to leave him alone, so I've taken leave without salary. Thank god that the company I work for understands our situation.'

'Edward... if you need my help, let me know. I can get the groceries, give him medicine, buy him truffles, anything. Call me even if it's the middle of the night, okay?'

Edward hugged her. 'Thank you, sweetheart. If I really can't take it anymore, I'll call.'

Vivian pushed the lift button, and the door opened. On her way down she realized it was still early, so decided to take a cab to her mother's office.

She pushed open the big glass doors of her mother's architecture firm on the forty-fourth floor. Melanie, who was sitting behind the receptionist's desk, greeted her warmly.

'Hi, Vivian. It's been a long time since I've seen you here.'

'What can I say… I've been so busy, and I'm often away on business trips.' Vivian exaggerated her answer. Melanie smiled revealing a row of perfect white teeth.

'I'm jealous of you. You must have a great job.'

'Yes, if you like traveling. Is my mother in?'

'Yes, she is. They just finished a meeting, so hurry inside before the next meeting starts.'

Vivian waved once more at Melanie before she went inside.

'Honey, what a surprise! I thought you were still in Vegas!?'

Vivian kissed her mom's forehead and sat across from her.

'I've been back since Wednesday.'

'Oh, how fast three weeks have passed.' Vivian and her mother were the complete opposite. She didn't hate her mother, but she wasn't too close to her either.

'No mom, I've only been gone for two weeks. A colleague took over my project because headquarters pulled me back.'

'What's the reason behind all of that?'

Vivian told her mother all about George and the change in her position at Frenay & Iams. Upon hearing this, her mother viewed the situation only along business lines, immediately seeking self-benefits. From the beginning, her mother didn't like Vivian working there. She wanted her child to work for her.

'You know, baby. If you don't like it there, you know you're always welcome here.'

She regretted going. Vivian should have known that her mother would use this opportunity to try to entice her to work for her company. She wanted to tell her mother to stop being so heartless because she couldn't even empathize with what happened to George, but Vivian knew it was a waste of time.

'I know, Ma, but I still want to work for Frenay & Iams.' Vivian looked at her watch and acted surprised. 'I'm sorry, Ma, I have to go, otherwise I'll be late for my next appointment.' She walked around the table and kissed her mother's forehead. 'I'll call you later. Goodbye.' Vivian left her mom's office and Melanie noticed her gloomy face.

'Was she being annoying again?'

Vivian glared. 'Ah, that woman has no heart.' They both giggled.

'Easy for you to say, it's your mother. I'm not brave enough because she's my boss!'

'I admire your ability to put up with her. See you later, Mel!'

'See you.'

Vivian returned to her apartment with a bag of Chinese food. She put a plate on the dining table and took her favorite drink from the refrigerator, ginger ale. She arranged the noodles on the plate and tucked in with chopsticks. Her phone rang, and she was startled when she saw who was calling. With a trembling hand, she deliberated on how she should answer. Formal or relaxed? She chose the former because Ferris was always formal with her.

'Vivian Foster.'

'Hi Vivian, it's Ferris.' Why did his voice always affect her so strongly. His rich flowing voice almost made her heart flutter.

'Oh, hi Ferris.'

'Vivian, I'm calling to ask how it went at George's?' Of course that's what he wanted to ask. There was no way Ferris would call her just to find out how she was.

'It was very emotional, and no matter how hard I tried, I couldn't stop myself from crying.'

'Did you morph into a panda bear again?'

She heard Ferris laugh, and was amazed that this rigid man

was finally starting to joke a little. His words also made Vivian chuckle.

'No, George assured me that I didn't look like a panda.'

'All right. What time is George expecting us tomorrow?

'Twelve o'clock. Edward will serve lunch.'

'Okay. See you tomorrow.'

Vivian was a little disappointed that the conversation was so concise. She longed to hear more of his voice. She took a deep breath. 'Yes, see you tomorrow, Ferris.'

'Vivian?' His voice sounded equally lustful and seductive. 'Do you need a ride to George's apartment? I don't mind picking you up.'

Although Vivian wanted to accept, when it came to Ferris, she couldn't help but say the opposite of what she actually intended. 'No thanks, don't bother, I can easily take a taxi.'

'As you wish, Vivian. See you tomorrow.'

Vivian paced back and forth in her apartment. How should she act? Why couldn't she accept the reality that Ferris had no interest in her? Maybe Salfina was right. Did Vivian feel attracted to him because this man was hard to get?

She must discuss this with George tomorrow. Maybe he could offer advice on how to solve this problem.

Her mood darkened throughout the evening.

There was nothing interesting on TV and she didn't feel like talking to her best friends. She decided to prepare her outfit for the next day.

Naturally she wanted to look gorgeous in front of Ferris even though she knew he wouldn't notice her clothes at all.

She entered her neatly arranged walk-in wardrobe. After scanning the racks and shelves, Vivian settled on tight jeans with a white V-neck shirt and black blazer, and on her feet she would wear black Philipp Plein heels. Once she was satisfied, she draped her clothes over her bed and went to the bathroom. She turned on the bathtub faucet and sprinkled in powdered bath soap. A heavenly scent drifted up, and for the first time in a long time, she could rest her tired body for a little while.

Ralph, the reception officer of George's apartment, saw Vivian get out of the taxi and opened the door for her with a wide and sincere smile.

'Good afternoon, Miss Foster. No need to enter your name in the guest register. Please go ahead.'

'Thank you, Ralph. Is Mr. Austin already here?'

'Not yet, Ma'am.'

Vivian sighed with relief. Maybe she could devise a strategy with George before Ferris arrived.

Edward was waiting on the doorstep when Vivian stepped out of the lift.

'Hi, Edward.'

'Hi, honey. Please come in. George is waiting for you with a long face. He's a bit upset with me because I postponed the appointment for an hour.' Vivian giggled.

'Did he sleep well?'

'Yes. Adding an hour's rest did him good, even though he's too stubborn to admit it.'

'Okay, I'll meet him quickly. I want to ask him something before Ferris arrives. Is he in the library?'

'Well, hurry then. I will stall Ferris when he arrives,' said Edward with a wink.

The clack of her high heels echoed through the hall, which had been recently cleaned. She could smell the fresh scent of the cleaning fragrance. Slowly, she opened the door of the library and saw George sitting in the same place as he was the day before. George's face lit up when he saw her.

'Vivian, come here. I want to say something before Ferris arrives.' She immediately went closer and sat on a small chair next to George. 'Yesterday after you left, Edward and I talked a lot about you. Besides the fact you're so similar to Vicky, we also talked about Ferris.'

She opened her mouth to say something but George gestured for her to wait.

'I know you have deep feelings for him, and I'm sorry he doesn't feel the same way about you. But it would be such a shame if you let these unrequited feelings affect your life. Life is too short not to enjoy it, and you're torturing yourself, dear. It's not right. Edward and I believe you're a strong woman and can manage your feelings for Ferris if you just spend more time with him.

Up until now you rarely meet him, and that's why you feel fireworks erupting in your heart whenever you see him. However, I believe if you see him regularly, you'll learn to control these feelings. That's how it usually goes.' Vivian was silent. She was completely absorbed in his words.

'Oh George, do you think I could? Don't you think Ferris would notice how I feel about him?' George squeezed her hand.

'I know you can do it. And no, Ferris wouldn't notice your feelings toward him. He has built a wall around him, so just don't think about that.'

The heavy burden weighing down her shoulders seemed to have disappeared. She sat up straight and adjusted her shoulders, her long braid moving in time with her body.

The library door opened. Ferris stepped in with Edward behind him. Vivian couldn't believe her eyes when she saw Ferris's clothes were matching with hers. Like Vivian, he wore jeans that clung to his slim hips, and a white shirt covered by a black blazer. He looked incredibly charming, and as though he'd just come straight from a magazine shoot.

George, Edward and Ferris engaged in conversation while Vivian enjoyed a cup of tea. She looked at each of them in turn without really hearing the conversation. At the same time, she stole a glance at Ferris without him noticing.

What a heavenly view. Ferris really was good looking. His short black hair was thick and lustrous.

His nose was perfectly sculpted. His lips were extremely alluring, hiding perfectly straight white teeth. His sharp jaw framed his striking good looks. Vivian wondered what had happened during his previous relationship. She just couldn't understand how a woman could dare risk losing this gorgeous man. If Vivian had the chance, she would do anything to please him. Her train of thought was derailed by Edward, who suddenly rose from his chair.

'George, would you like to have lunch here or in the dining room?'

'The dining room, thank you.'

'Okay, I'll go and prepare, and call you when it's ready.'

'Is there anything I can help with, Edward?' Vivian had already stood up from the stool and Edward immediately understood the sign.

'Sure, sweetheart. I'd appreciate that.'

Vivian helped arrange the table. Edward was a great cook.

'Edward, can I ask something?'

'Sure, dear. Shoot.'

Vivian paused slightly before asking, 'Do you think Ferris prefer blonds?'

Edward cackled and gently pinched her cheeks. 'Vivian, my dear, you're very beautiful, so never have any doubt about your appearance. I may prefer men, but I know beauty when I see it. What makes you even more beautiful is that you're unaware of your own beauty. Your humbleness increases your beauty.'

Vivian turned crimson. She never knew how to accept a compliment. She felt sheepish, as she just never felt confident when she looked in the mirror.

'Edward, I'm not fishing for a compliment. I've felt insecure around Ferris since I first met him, and have also completely lost interest in all other men.'

'I know you're not fishing. Ferris enchants you to the point where you never realize how all those men are stunned by your beauty. You must be grateful, dear. So, when it comes to Ferris, you need to think, "It's his loss for not wanting me". Then open your eyes, and you'll see there are a lot more handsome men in this world.'

'Do you know what happened in his previous relationship?'

'No, I don't know. I truly don't know. All I know is that he suffered a lot and that it's had a lasting impression on him.' After a long lunch, Vivian, George and Ferris returned to the library, where they spent the rest of the afternoon exchanging ideas about how to divide the workload. They decided that Ferris would step into George's position, and Vivian into Ferris's role.

Traveling would still be part of Vivian's job but not business trips that would force her to be away from home for weeks. Hearing this made Vivian happy. She could spend more time with George and her best friends. Moreover, if on one of these days she met a man, it would be nice not to be away from home for too long.

CHAPTER 6

Month after month passed by. Thank god George was still alive, even though his condition was declining. Vivian visited twice a week, on Wednesdays and Fridays. Each day, George was getting weaker and more withered. Vivian was afraid that this man whom she considered like own father would lose his battle against the illness. Despite his ailing health, George's face still beamed each time Vivian visited him.

Her collaboration with Ferris was professional and formal, although occasionally Vivian still discretely looked at him lovingly. Deep in her heart, she still wanted this man.

Vivian liked her new position, and clearly this news didn't sit well with her mother.

During each site visit, Vivian and Ferris give sincere pieces of advice to young interior designers and architects. They both genuinely felt that they were running the firm with passion and commitment. Most surprisingly, there were still clients who specifically asked for her to work on projects, and even offered her double the fee. Vivian was pleased with her increased salary.

She bought herself a gift: an Audi Q5 with all the extras. It had crossed her mind to buy a bigger apartment, but she decided against it as she was content with her apartment in the Upper West Side. Together with her best friends, and sometimes with Melanie, her mom's assistant, she often went along to

The Club. Yes, she was satisfied with her life now, even though she didn't have a significant other.

Every time she went out with her friends, she often met a few appealing men, but not one of them could make her forget about Ferris. Each time Vivian went on a date, there was always something that turned her off.

Meanwhile, her friends always had their own love stories. Salfina was in love, and Melanie had just started a new relationship. Unlike the others, Genieva preferred one-night stands. To her, a partner was not significant. Her priority was her career.

It was Friday night, and Vivian was just breaking through a traffic jam. Thankfully, her office and George's house were very close. As usual, Ralph welcomed her with a broad smile. Vivian nodded at him and waited for the lift door to open.

Like usual, George sat on the big seat in the library. He liked reading there while looking at the view of the Hudson, but he seemed miserable. His face was withered and gaunt.

Edward looked just as miserable. Wrinkles appeared on his face and dark circles beneath his eyes. His pants slipped down from his thin hips. Although he'd already tightened his belt, his pants seemed way too big on him.

Vivian walked inside and saw George almost asleep in his chair. Carefully she took off her shoes, worried it would wake him up. She padded barefoot across to the big bookshelf.

Her eyes were fixed on the copy of Shakespeare's *Romeo and Juliet*.

'Hi, dear. You're here.' George rubbed his eyes with his bony fingers.

'I only arrived five minutes ago. You were sleeping soundly. I'd rather look for books to read rather than wake you up.' Vivian looked at him tenderly, but her stomach tightened when she saw that George had turned into a living skeleton.

'Hmm, what did you want to read?'

'*Romeo and Juliet*... do you think I'd like it?'

'Vivian, promise me your life won't end in tragedy like Romeo and Juliet. You are a lovely girl. There's so much more in this world than Ferris.'

She could feel her eyes burning, her tears threatening to fall, but did all she could to contain her emotional tempest.

'Don't worry, George. My life won't end in tragedy. I promise.' Vivian took George's thin hand and gently squeezed it.

'Do you want to eat here or in the dining room?'

'Here. It's too much for me to walk there right now.'

'Okay, then I'll tell Edward, and we'll eat here.'

Vivian saw Edward in the kitchen, he was standing with his back to her. He was busy putting the finishing touches on the pasta before plating it.

'Edward?'

He turned around and looked startled as he hadn't noticed

Vivian arrive. It was her turn to look surprised, as she saw tears streaming down his face. With open arms, Vivian hugged him tightly. It didn't take long before she too started sobbing.

'Oh, Vivian... I'm terrified. I know I'll be the one who's with him when he's crossing over. Or worse, what if I'm not by his side and he passes away all alone?'

Because of her tears, Vivian couldn't say a word.

'I almost can't sleep because I don't want to leave him alone.' With the cloth draped over his shoulder, he wiped his tears. 'Vivian, I'm glad that you come twice a week. You're like his daughter and the days when you're here are the days when he can laugh freely. On the other days he only sits in silence or reads.'

'If you think it's necessary I can come every day, or I can sleep here so I can help you too.'

Edward firmly shook his head. 'No, sweetheart. You're an angel, but that would make George wearier.'

'I understand, but really, Edward. If I could do something to help you, please don't hesitate to call me. I will come anytime, okay?'

'I know sweetheart. You truly are an angel.' He kissed Vivian's cheeks and asked, 'Where would he like to eat? In the dining room or the library?'

'Uhh... George said in the library. What can I help you with?'

'No, it's fine. You accompany George. I'll bring dinner soon.'

'Okay, I just need to go to the bathroom first to get rid of my panda eyes,' Vivian chuckled, and Edward winked at her.

'Darling, you know waterproof mascara exists, right?'

Vivian laughed. 'Oh, really? How do you know that?'

'Oh, Vivian sweetheart, I also read *Vogue* and *Cosmopolitan*.'

Vivian was laughing and shaking her head when she stepped out of the kitchen. The atmosphere in the library was comforting and relaxed. Edward has lit a fire in the fireplace because George felt cold. The sound of wood burning crackled loudly. After they finished their meal, the three of them played cards. Vivian looked at her watch and noticed that it was already quite late.

'Gentlemen, as ever, it's been lovely spending the evening with you, but it's already late. It's time for me to go.'

'Is it already that late?' George looked at Edward with surprise.

'Yes, honey. Also, it's time for you to take your medicine and then after that, a bath.'

Vivian rose from her chair and put on her shoes, preparing to leave.

'See you on Wednesday, George.' When she tried to kiss George's forehead, he lifted his head and raised his eyebrows. 'What do you mean, "See you on Wednesday"? If I'm not mistaken, next week you'll be sitting on a white sandy beach sipping cocktails.' Vivian was baffled.

'Don't forget I was your boss, so I know that this is exactly the time for your vacation. I may be sick, but I'm not senile.

I can still think clearly,' he said while tapping his thin finger on his forehead.

'I won't be going to any white sandy beaches. I will postpone my vacation because I want to spend more time with you George.'

'Ohh no. No no no. Exactly as planned, you will go on vacation. You have worked so hard already, and you deserve to have fun.' Vivian stood up with her hands on her waist and turned to Edward to win his support, but Edward remained silent and shrugged his shoulders.

'But George, I can't go, I want to stay beside you... for...'. Vivian kept her mouth shut. She couldn't say that she wanted to be with him when he took his last breath.

'Don't worry. I promise I will still be here when you're back from your vacation.'

Her tears ran down her cheeks, and she fell to her knees next to him. 'Bu... But...'.

'No buts... I won't go anywhere. I'll wait for you here, okay? I want you to enjoy your vacation, and when you're back, I want you to tell me all about it.'

George swept Vivian's fringe from her face and tenderly wiped her tears, before bowed toward her to kiss her forehead.

'Go now, dear. It's late, and I'm exhausted.'

Reluctantly, she released herself from George's grasp, grabbed her bag, and left the room with her head hanging down.

Vivian rolled over with anxiety in her bed.

She had dreamt that she'd seen a deep hole in the ground. Vivian was standing at the edge of it while bending down. Because she was unbalanced, she fell down the shaft. With her hands and feet, she tried to climb out but to no avail. She opened her mouth and tried to shout for help, but no sound came out. In a panic, she reached into her pocket for her phone, but couldn't find it. She looked up through the darkness, and saw lightning strike.

'NO!' she screamed.

This time the voice came from her mouth. She woke up on top of the bed, drenched with sweat. Her heart was thumping wildly, and she looked around fearfully. She'd just had a bad dream. The clock showed that it wasn't even past seven, but she couldn't get back to sleep.

In the kitchen she brewed a pot of coffee, then sat at her desk and opened her laptop. She might as well finish some work, she thought.

When Vivian tried to access Frenay & Iams' server, she failed. She tried several times, but it still wouldn't connect. Even though the sun had just risen on her Saturday, she decided to call Ray, Frenay & Iams' IT officer.

'Good morning, this is Ray Sheldon from Frenay & Iams.'

'Uhh, hi Ray, this is Vivian Foster.'

'Hello, Miss Foster, what can I help with?'

Vivian brushed her long hair away from her face.

'Yes, I have a problem. I've just tried to access the company server to work from home, but it failed.'

'Hmm, please wait for a moment. I'll check that for you.'

After a few minutes, Ray picked up the phone.

'Yes, I have found the source of the problem.'

'So, what is it?'

'I don't know how to explain this, Ma'am, except that Mr. Maldini has ordered for your access to be blocked for the next three weeks. I'm sorry, Miss Foster.'

Vivian was confused by what she'd just heard. She was speechless.

'Miss Foster, are you still there?'

'Yes, Ray. I'm here. All right, thank you for your help. Goodbye, Ray.'

'You're welcome. Goodbye, Miss Foster.'

Why had George done this? Surely he could understand why she didn't want to go on vacation? There was no choice for her but to take a holiday as three weeks at home without being able to work was not an option.

Vivian searched for vacation destinations online. She tried to find a place not too far away, in case she needed to rush to George. In the end, she decided on a ticket to the island of Aruba in the Caribbean Sea.

She booked a resort with full facilities, completed her personal information and paid by credit card. She'd depart on Monday afternoon. Since she couldn't work, she figured she'd take a bath, have breakfast at Sarabeth and then go shopping. She needed a new bikini and a few other things anyway. At Sarabeth, the queue was way too long. This place was always full, especially on the weekend. She couldn't be bothered waiting so decided to leave. Suddenly she was surprised by someone knocking hard on the window from inside the restaurant. Melanie was waving and signaling for Vivian to join her. She stepped in and strode past the crowd in the queue. Some even shouted unpleasant things at her, but she didn't care. Melanie also signaled to a waiter to bring a café latte for Vivian.

'Ah, this is delicious. I really needed this,' Vivian said while holding the coffee in her hands.

'I figured. Luckily I saw you outside.'

'Thank God for that, when I saw the line I thought there was no way I could stand in that queue. How come you're here so early?'

Melanie took a sip of her coffee before she answered, 'I have to go shopping for a new outfit for tonight, and after that I'm going to spoil myself and go to a spa.'

'Wow, what's your big plan for tonight if you need new clothes?'

Melanie glared at her. 'Duh, Viv, are you hearing me?' Vivian stared at her, not getting it. 'Don't tell me you forgot. We're going to The Club tonight. You know, dancing and drinking and having fun. Remember? Salfina booked a table.'

How could she have forgotten? Recently she'd been so preoccupied with her work and George that she didn't remember anything about this date with her girlfriends. 'Oh my, sorry... sorry... I confess I'd forgotten all about it.' Vivian told Melanie about George and what happened yesterday, and that she was forced to go on vacation. After that, it was Melanie's turn to talk about her love life, which made her also want to dress up for someone.

'We can go shopping together. For my vacation, I need a new bikini and all the rest.'

'Yes, brilliant. Shopping together is so much more fun when you're not alone. If you want, you can also join me at the spa.' As Vivian had nothing else on her agenda, she accepted Melanie's offer. After a few hours at a glitzy mall, they left with many shopping bags then waited for the valet to bring Vivian's Audi to the lobby.

The spa was so quiet and tranquil. For a while, they forgot they lived in hectic and crowded New York. They decide to start with a massage. The masseuses worked quietly while they chatted.

'Where are you going on vacation, Viv?' Vivian, who was lying on her stomach, turned her head to her friend.

'To Aruba. If something happens to George, I could be back in New York in half a day.'

'I got it. You don't mind being alone on vacation?'

'Umm, no. I'm used to traveling alone.

Even though it's better if there's a friend with me. You want to come?'

'I would love to. But I can't take time off right now, and besides, your mom would have a stroke if I ask for another day off. I've only just worked for a week after returning from vacation myself.'

Vivian thought for a second. 'Come on, I'll arrange it with my mom later, and I'll pay for your vacation.'

'Thank you for the offer, Viv, but no thanks.'

'Think about it. You have until Monday.'

That afternoon they were pampered with various treatments including waxing and a manicure. Vivian took care of the bill by charging it to her credit card as she knew her friend wasn't earning as much as she was.

At The Club, it was crowded as usual. The music was its regular deafening level. Fortunately, Salfina had booked a table away from the dancefloor so they could still talk without having to shout. Melanie couldn't sit still. She wanted to go to the dancefloor to show off her new dress.

'Who wants to dance with me?'

'I want to, but may I remind you I have a cast on my leg. I'd break my other one if I joined you,' Genieva said with a laugh.

'Me, me!' Salfina shouted while jumping out of her seat. Vivian and Genieva giggled as they watched their friends dancing.

Genieva looked at Vivian and asked, 'Is everything okay?' Vivian knew exactly what she meant. 'Yes, of course. Everything is okay.' She tried to find another topic because she didn't want to talk about George, which would make her depressed. 'I tried to convince Mel to go on vacation with me, but she didn't want to.'

'Well, of course... I know what it feels like to work with someone like your mother.' Vivian cackled when she heard that. 'Yeah, that's why I don't want to work with her. There would be a war every day.' Genieva nodded in agreement. Not long after, she signaled for Vivian to turn her head toward the man who was standing across from them. 'Do you see that man?'

'Yeah, why?' Genieva motioned for her to come closer.

'He's been standing there since we sat down here.'

'Yeah? What's so strange about that?' Vivian didn't understand.

'Look closer. There's something strange about him. He definitely doesn't fit in this club, and he's been busy texting on his phone the whole time.'

Vivian looked at him closely. Indeed, he looked completely out of place at The Club.

'What do you think he's doing here?' she asked.

'I don't know, but I have a bad feeling about this guy.' Vivian exploded with laughter. 'You should be a detective, Nieva. You've denied your destiny.'

Genieva looked at her friend sourly. 'Yeah, go ahead, laugh it up. But I'm sure I'm right.'

The waiter brought the next round of drinks and snacks. Melanie and Salfina returned to the table with sweat glazing their brows and temples. Salfina raised her glass and shouted, 'To Vivian in Aruba, where you'll be relaxing under a coconut tree on the seashore on Monday!'

They toasted each other, and knocked back their drinks.

'Woah, this is really good!' Salfina cried, then signaled the waiter to bring another round. They drank and nibbled on the snacks until late, laughing and enjoying the night together. For Vivian, this was the first time she could completely relax and forget about George for a while. This was exactly what she needed; to let go of all her sadness for one night and get back to having fun like someone her age should be doing. Even so, her interest was triggered by the man who made Genieva suspicious. It was indeed bizarre. All night he'd been standing there, texting on his phone. Ah, to hell with it. What did it matter now she was with her friends having fun?

Salfina and Melanie were loud as they'd had a lot to drink. They chatted with increasingly loud voices about erratic topics. Genieva's eyes began to droop, and she tried hard to keep her eyes open. Vivian was the only one who hadn't drunk too much. Her alcohol tolerance was very low, and since the Las Vegas accident, she'd promised herself never to drink too much. With difficulty, Vivian tried to get her friend's attention to persuade them to go home. It was Vivian's job to make sure they got home safely. It was a wearisome job leading these three out of The Club. Melanie and Salfina walked ahead. They always wanted to chat with everyone they met on the way to the exit, and it took a long time for Genieva to walk on crutches with her leg in a cast. It took Vivian almost an hour to get the girls safely in a taxi. The taxi driver was entertained by Melanie and Salfina who sang a lullaby in the back seat, while Genieva immediately fell asleep on Vivian's shoulder and snored.

'Must've been a great night?' The driver asked Vivian.

'Yes, you could say so. It seems like I'm the only sober one.'

'No, no. I'm sober too,' Melanie said. 'Look, I can still touch the tip of my nose with my finger.' She tried to prove it but it ended with Vivian and the driver laughing at Melanie as she almost poked herself in the eye, while Salfina, busy with her solo concert, was now singing the national anthem.

'Yes, I know you're conscious,' said the driver who then joined Salfina to sing.

'I'm sorry. I'm really sorry,' Vivian apologized to the driver.

'No, it's fine. I'm the one who's entertained. It's much better than drunk passengers who are pissed off or aggressive.'

'Yeah, you're right.'

It was then Genieva's turn, the last passenger to be delivered home. The driver was very friendly and helped Vivian to carry Genieva to her floor, and then dropped Vivian in front of her apartment. She paid the taxi fare and gave him a large tip for his patience and assistance. The moment she was in her apartment she threw off her shoes, sat at her desk and turned on her laptop. Vivian stared at the bright screen, then promptly turned it off again. She still couldn't access the Frenay & Iams server. She'd better go to bed. The next day she'd be busy preparing for her vacation. The next morning, Vivian opened her suitcase on her bed, and walked back and forth between it and her wardrobe. She was very well versed in how to pack a travel bag. She arranged all her belongings neatly and efficiently, and packed a few books to read on the beach or by the pool. The only thing she hadn't packed was her toiletries, which she'd place in her suitcase tomorrow before she left. She walked toward the refrigerator and took out some cold grapes and a piece of camembert cheese. Suddenly Vivian remembered she needed to tell Ferris that George had forced her to go on vacation for the next three weeks.

She looked for Ferris's name and pressed the dial button.

'Hello, Vivian.'

Vivian was surprised because Ferris usually picked up the phone with a formal greeting.

'Uhh... Ferris, I'm sorry to interrupt you on a Sunday morning, but...'

She hadn't finished when Ferris said, 'No need for an apology. I'm not busy. So tell me, what do you need me for?'

Vivian could think of about a hundred things she needed him for, none of which she could confess to him. Without realizing it, she closed her thighs tightly to stop the tingling she felt between them.

'I want to tell you that George has sent me on vacation. He even ordered Ray to block my server login code for the next three weeks, to make sure I won't be preoccupied with work.' Ferris laughed out loud. Vivian instantly flushed hot and cold.

'Yes, I know. George called me yesterday to explain. I've been waiting for you to call me.'

'I'm sorry I'm late telling you.'

'You don't have to apologize to me. You deserve to go on vacation. I hope you enjoy it.'

'What about you? You're not going on vacation too?'

'Later in the fall, I will take a week off.'

'Oh, okay.' Vivian didn't know what to say next. She still desperately wanted Ferris.

'I'll still carry my phone, so if there are any changes, you can reach me.'

'Enjoy your vacation. We'll meet again at the office in three weeks.'

Yes, of course, in the office. Where else would it be? Vivian thought sarcastically. After they chatted a little, he ended the call. Her mood worsened throughout the day because of him.

CHAPTER 7

At the side of the palatial resort's swimming pool, Vivian enjoyed the intensity of the sunlight and the gentle breeze caressing her body. The day before, after she'd arrived at the hotel, she decided to go to one of the restaurants the hotel's front desk recommended. Its cuisine was so delicious she was already looking forward to dining in the same restaurant that night.

Vivian had applied sunscreen twice to her body. She took several brochures from reception to see what kind of activities the island offered. There was plenty to do, like walk along the cruise ship dock, visit the butterfly park, or explore an ancient gold mine.

Suddenly Vivian realized she needed to let George know she'd arrived safe and sound at her resort. She called Edward's number as George's was no longer active.

'Edward Evans here.'

Vivian smiled. 'Hi, Edward.'

'Hello sweetheart, are you on vacation?'

'What else could I do? George really made it impossible for me to stay. He blocked my access to the work server to make sure I couldn't work at home.' She sighed.

'I'm sorry to hear that, sweetheart. I'm also sorry I couldn't help you last time you were here.

George insisted you go on vacation. There was no point arguing with him.'

Vivian's thoughts returned to the night she gazed at Edward to beg for his support to let her stay at home. She shivered suddenly, despite the warmth of the sun.

'It's okay. I just want to let you know I arrived safely at my destination.'

'Ah, thank God. Where are you now?'

'Aruba.'

Edward whistled through his teeth. 'Ah, so glad. Enjoy your vacation, dear. As George said, you deserve a nice vacation.'

'Thank you, Edward. Even though I would prefer to stay at home,' she said sullenly.

'My dear, come on... by the way, I can't talk too long on the phone. I hope you don't keep your phone too close to you during your holiday, and just try to enjoy the time there.'

Vivian was surprised to hear that.

'Uhm... It's tough to say this to you Vivian, but I promised George I wouldn't answer your calls until your vacation is over.'

Vivian's face flushed at Edward's explanation. 'Why did he do that? I can't work, I can't call. Edward, what is going on? I don't have a good feeling about this!'

'I can't do anything, Viv. I can only do what George wishes. I promise you, if anything happens, I will call, okay? I must go now, he's calling for me.'

Before Vivian replied, the call was cut off. In tears, she sat alone on the island. Angrily, she got up from her comfortable chair, threw her sunglasses on it, and plunged into the pool. Vivian hoped the cold water would cool her head. She swam from one side to the other side to quell her uneasiness. It didn't help at all. After she'd run out of energy, she got out of the pool, grabbed her belongings, and walked to her room. Vivian threw down her things and flung herself on the couch. She was ready to pack her luggage and fly back to New York that day. However, she knew it didn't make sense because she had no home at the moment. She couldn't work, nor could she visit George, and her friends were busy with their jobs. Vivian felt she'd been punished for the next three weeks. She had no choice but to enjoy her time there.

Fortunately, she'd booked a lavish room with an ocean view. It was not as fancy as a suite at Bellagio, but yes, this room was still impressive.

On the balcony, there was vast day bed with a view looking down to the beach. She slid open the balcony door and lounged on it with a book. After five minutes she threw the book aside because she couldn't concentrate, but the roar of the waves seemed to grant her the peace she desired while enjoying the view.

In the distance, she saw a flock of seagulls flying in circles. Vivian narrowed her eyes, and a smile appeared on her lips when a dolphin rose to the surface of the sea.

What a beautiful sight was offered by her balcony.

After her bad mood caused by George's wishes and fatigue after swimming, Vivian began to feel extremely hungry. She decided to eat early and try to rest because tomorrow she would spend her day shopping at Oranjestad. Vivian looked at her reflection in the mirror. She saw slightly tanned skin and a bikini line across her chest. Her perky round breasts were brighter than the rest of her light brown skin. Fortunately all her bikinis were the same model, only in different colors, so her bikini tan lines wouldn't show.

After a long bath she wore a white summer dress, which made her brown skin glow. Her white shoes coordinated beautifully with her dress, and she adorned her messily tied up hair with a fresh white frangipani flower.

Although the fresh grilled shrimp and salad she'd ordered were delightful, she couldn't enjoy her meal. What's more, she noticed almost everyone was watching her. The men couldn't take their eyes off her, and the women took turns glancing at her with looks of annoyance. Never before had she realized she was being watched and it made her feel extremely uncomfortable. She hadn't even finished half her meal when she decided to leave the restaurant. Everyone staring at her had made her lose her appetite.

Vivian walked back along the beach, which was still crowded even though the sun had set.

Dozens of couples walked along holding hands, the shallow

waves smoothly rolling toward their feet. Vivian took off her shoes and walked into the water until it reached her ankles. Its sharp temperature made her shiver, so she decided to return to her room.

The next day, the taxi driver dropped Vivian in the center of Oranjestad, and her eyes immediately lit up when she saw a row of colorful houses. The dozens of cute boutiques seemed to lift her spirits, giving her stamina to shop without stopping. In one of the boutiques, her eyes were drawn to a pale yellow dress with wide shoulder straps. The short knee-length dress looked simple, but the cut of the A-shaped dress was divine. She also found a cute bandana and flip flops with floral accents. Soon after, an employee encouraged her to try it on in the dressing room. When Vivian came out, she was surprised by her reflection. The color was perfect on her.
The shopkeeper helped her put on the bandana and asked her shoe size, and soon returned with the flip flops in her size.

'Believe me, Ma'am, this is not a sales pitch. I've seen many women try on this dress, but none of them could wear it as beautifully as you. This dress was made for you!'

'Thank you... I think it suits me quite well.'

'Ma'am, this dress is only eighty Aruban Florin. It's not a designer dress, but when you wear it, it looks like one!'
Vivian calculated the exchange rate in her head. Eighty Florins wasn't even forty-five dollars.

She'd never bought such cheap clothes. In her wardrobe there were only designer clothes.

'You're convincing. I'll take the flip flops and the bandana too. Do you have anything else in the same color?'
The employee thought for a moment, walked away, then returned with a blouse. Vivian thought the blouse would go well with black pants, making a great work ensemble.

'Yes, I'll take this too.' The female employee looked happy and enthusiastic when she heard that. At the cashier, Vivian paid and chatted for a while. They also gave Vivian a shop address which sold designer bags.

With a total of sixty dollars, Vivian had managed to get a dress, blouse, bandana, and flip flops. She was amazed and wondered, how could that be possible? This place was just right for her.

At a store selling souvenirs and gifts, she bought various trinkets for her friends and mother. After glancing at her watch she realized it was lunchtime so she looked for a restaurant with a seat on the terrace.

After exploring a little, she chose a gorgeous restaurant which still had one table left on the patio. After ordering a mineral water and café latte, she studied the menu. Her attention was then drawn to the two women sitting at the table next to hers. Without meaning to, Vivian overheard their conversation while her eyes were still fixed on the menu.

The women were discussing various men they had slept with,

and in particular, their penises! Vivian was amused and couldn't help but giggle. The women heard her and looked at Vivian with a surprised smile.

'Ah... sorry, I wasn't eavesdropping, I just couldn't help but laugh when hearing your conversation,' Vivian said with an apologetic shrug.

'Oh, no problem, I don't mind, I'm just very upset. I was just complaining about the fact that I always seem to meet men with small cocks. I must be subconsciously attracted to them!' Once again, they burst out laughing. These two women were enjoying an entertaining conversation indeed, and Vivian gladly accepted when one of them invited her to shift her seat to their table.

Vivian introduced herself, as did the women. The short curly-haired woman was Angie, and her tall friend with short black hair was Patty. They explained that they often spent time together, they worked together, traveled together, and sometimes even shared the same man! Vivian was shocked to hear that.

'You share the same man? So, one night he'll be with one of you, and the next he'll be with the other?' Vivian asked. Patty replied with a laugh, 'No, sweetie. It means the three of spend time together. You know, a threesome?'

Vivian, who was sipping water, coughed a little. Angie patted her back and continued, 'Trust me, it sounds much more vulgar than it is.'

A waiter interrupted the conversation when he brought their dishes, and the topic shifted to the island's best shopping destinations.

Angie and Patty were staying at the same hotel as Vivian, and they agreed to meet to have dinner at the hotel. Vivian was delighted with the food at the hotel restaurant the day before. After lunch, they split up, and Vivian went to the designer bag store which had been recommended to her.

There she purchased a Louis Vuitton bag and a Hermès belt. Vivian then walked to an opulent boutique and bought a tight black short skirt that was suitable to wear to the office. Then she hailed a taxi and returned to her hotel. In her room, she neatly hung all her recently purchased items in the closet, and put the bag and belt in her suitcase. She then took a bath before strolling down to the lobby to meet Angie and Patty.

When she arrived in the lobby at six-thirty, Vivian saw Angie and Patty sitting on a red velvet lounge. They were watching someone walking in the distance. Vivian approached them with a smile.

'Have you already identified someone appropriate for you?'

'Yes, Vivian. Honestly, I could spend the night here without being bored,' Patty replied excitedly. She then leaned on Angie while trying to keep an eye on the man who'd almost disappeared from her sight.

'What a shame, he's almost vanished.'

'Don't you meet handsome men here?'

'Hmm, nope.'

'Goodness. I think you need glasses. There's something wrong with your pretty blue eyes.'

Vivian laughed and said wryly, 'Thank you for your optometry advice.'

Patty jumped off the couch while shouting, 'Let's hit the restaurant. I'm starving!'

The restaurant served a wide variety of local specialties, such as fresh fish soups and creamy chowders. After they ordered, Patty and Angie's attention went straight back to the men who were strolling by. Vivian could only laugh at them internally; she'd come to the conclusion that they weren't compatible as friends. Their eyes seemed to strip every man who walked past their table.

Even their drinks waiter caught their attention. He had a particularly large nose and chunky hands. Angie and Patty observed the waiter and shortly after he left their table, Patty declared matter-of-factly, 'I'm certain.'

'What do you mean?' asked Angie curiously.

Haven't you heard what people say about men with big hands and a big nose? It means his manhood is big too! Didn't you see the bulge in his pants?'

'Yes, of course I've heard that, but I'm sure it's just a myth. You still remember Erick?' Patty squinted her eyes, trying to recall this Erick.

'His hands and nose and even his feet were enormous, but his goods were hard to find.'

'Oh, yes, that's true. I'd forgotten about Erick because obviously his package hadn't made an impression.' They threw their heads back, cackling. Vivian was amused, but she also felt sorry for Erick. Their conversation moved on when their steaming soups arrived.

'So, what do you do for a living, Vivian?' asked Patty. Vivian was relieved. Finally, a topic other than men. She described her job enthusiastically.

Patty teased her, 'Wow, you sound perfect, so why don't you have a partner?'

Vivian was reluctant to share the story of her unrequited love for Ferris. If she told them, she was sure they'd make fun of her.

'Because I used to travel a lot for work, and had no time to find a partner. I was always traveling from project to project. But now that I've received this promotion, I'll be in New York much more. Hopefully, I'll find the right man.'

'Ah, so that's why you're on vacation, you're on the hunt for Mr. Right?'

'No. My boss forced me to go on vacation because apparently I'm a workaholic.'

Angie chimed in, 'That's too bad. The day after tomorrow we're heading home, otherwise we could have stayed and helped you snag someone here.'

'Yeah, too bad,' Vivian feigned disappointment. She was relieved, because she couldn't imagine spending her vacation with these two women and putting up with their nonsense. If it was only two days, she could survive, but any longer than that would seriously get on her nerves.

After dinner, Vivian made up the excuse that she had some important phone calls to make. They arranged to meet in the lobby for dinner the next night at seven-thirty. When she reached her room, Vivian leaned on the door and took a deep breath. She was thankful she only had one more dinner with them, but even that seemed too much. One day with them was enough.

The next day she woke late, at a quarter past ten, which was very unusual. Because she'd overslept she had a headache. She needed coffee. She whipped up an instant coffee and gulped it down. She felt a little better, and her headache began to disappear.

Vivian planned to spend the day at the pool. An hour and a half later, she was lying down in a comfortable deckchair with her upper body shaded by an umbrella and her feet bathed in sunlight. She placed her book, sunscreen, iPad, and mineral water bottle on the table next to her. Vivian applied sunscreen and put on her sunglasses so she could watch people without being obvious.

There weren't many guests at the pool because most of them had gone to the dock to see the cruise ships on display.

Not far from where Vivian was lounging, an older couple were taking a nap on matching deckchairs. There was a couple who looked about the same age as her splashing in the shallows of the pool with their chubby little girl. Vivian quickly grew bored, and she wasn't in the mood to read. She felt restless, flat, and didn't know what she should do. She looked at her watch it was only twelve-thirty. She began asking herself, could she really spend the whole day by the pool? Vivian just wasn't the kind of person who could happily while away a whole day doing nothing.

What exactly what she doing there? She didn't want to be there. She should have gone home to her apartment. She reached for her phone and called Edward, but there was no answer. When she heard the voicemail message she hung up. She couldn't ignore the urge to just pack her belongings and go straight back home.

She was lonely. Yes, she could go to dinner with Angie and Patty, but she didn't want that. She knew exactly what would happen if she went. Minutes passed by, her boredom and restlessness increasing. She gathered her things and went back to her room. She'd sit alone on the balcony, so no one would see her in despair.

She stood on her balcony gazing at the ocean.

'Spectacular view, isn't it?'

Vivian was surprised by the voice. On the next balcony stood a tall and strikingly attractive man.

Not as handsome as Ferris, but he was blessed with good looks. He was bare-chested, his muscles not excessive but still well-toned. The sea breeze tousled his blond hair that fell over his brown eyes.

'Yes, it's stunning. I saw dolphins from my balcony yesterday.'

'Really? Then I might spend more time on the balcony.'

Vivian saw his strong white teeth when he smiled. He had a dashing smile. She was immediately attracted to this man.

'When I checked in, I saw some tour packages advertised in brochures. But if I could see dolphins from here, then I don't need to go anywhere. Have you seen much of the island?

'I went downtown for a day, it's a pleasant trip.'

The man smiled. 'Maybe we could go together unless you're here with your husband or boyfriend.'

Vivian was surprised by this comment it meant he was alone here too. 'Yes, that would be nice. We could go together, unless you're here with your wife or your girlfriend.'

He laughed. 'Checkmate!' He held his hand across the railing to introduce himself. 'I'm Ethan.'

His touch made her a shiver. 'I'm Vivian.'

'Vivian, I know we've just met, but would you like to go to dinner with me later?'

Vivian thought for a second. Of course she wanted to, but she didn't want to run into Angie and Patty.

She imagined how the two women would glare at her if they

saw her with this man, so she quickly invented an idea.

'Tonight I want to eat on the balcony while looking at the dolphins.'

Ethan tilted his head and looked at Vivian with a charming smile. 'May I accompany you then on your dinner date with the dolphins?'

Vivian felt her stomach flutter and her cheeks flush pink. 'With pleasure,' she said with a small smile. 'What would you like to eat? I can recommend lobster. It's wonderfully fresh.'

'You decide. I'll go to your suite in half an hour.'

'Okay, Ethan. See you soon.'

Vivian went inside with a huge grin on her face. Ethan was not only handsome, but funny too. She'd enjoyed their small chat, and found it extremely refreshing. She walked quickly to the closet and thought about what to wear. Something casual, but not dull. She chose a red wraparound dress with white hibiscus flowers, and white sandals. She called reception and ordered an array of appetizers and a whole grilled lobster. In the bathroom she couldn't stop smiling. She couldn't remember the last time she felt attracted to someone except Ferris, the man she couldn't have. Ethan seemed to be doing something magical to her. She was starting to feel alive again. To complement her blossoming excitement, she chose black lace Victoria's Secret lingerie. Not that Ethan would ever see it, but it made her feel more sensual.

Normally she always wore her hair up, but that night she let her long brown hair cascade onto her shoulders. There was a knock at the door. Before opening it, she quickly glanced in the mirror to give herself a boost of confidence. She had hoped the room service would be delivered before Ethan arrived, but there he was, freshly showered in ivory linen pants and a tight blue V-neck shirt. Sexy and sophisticated. Vivian didn't know where the feeling came from, but she felt like dragging him straight to bed. This wild thought turned her cheeks rosy pink.

She opened the door wide. Ethan walked in carrying a bottle of rosé champagne. Vivian followed him, steeling glances at his tight butt. 'The room service hasn't arrived yet.' Vivian didn't know what else to say.

'No problem, we're in no hurry, right?' Ethan said with that charming smile of his. 'How about I open this bottle while it's still cold?' His eyes drifted over Vivian from top to bottom, and Vivian felt her nipples stiffen with his gaze.

'Thank you, that would be lovely,' she said with a sultry voice. They stood side-by-side on the balcony, close, but not touching. She could feel the electricity buzzing between them, which made the fine blond hair on her arms stand up. Ethan poured the champagne into two glasses and passed one to Vivian, then raised his glass.

'Cheers to the dolphins, and to you, Vivian.'

'To the dolphins,' Vivian repeated. She sat down and sipped her champagne. 'Thank you, it's delicious.'

Ethan sat next to her and placed his hand on the back of

Vivian's chair. 'I'm glad you like my choice.'

She wanted to lean back so she could feel Ethan's hand on her shoulder. Even though she resisted, she was starting to relax in his presence.

'Tell me, Vivian. How is it possible for an exquisite woman like you to not be in a relationship?' With his thumb, Ethan slowly played with Vivian's long hair.

'Why do you assume I'm single? Maybe there's someone waiting for me at home.'

Ethan gave a half-smile. 'Well, I don't see a ring on your finger, and if you do have a husband or boyfriend, surely that guy is crazy for not being here with you right now. He could he bear to be apart from you?'

'I also want to ask you the same thing, Ethan.'

'My answer is simple, Vivian. I simply haven't met the woman of my dreams, that is, until an hour ago.' Vivian looked at Ethan with wide eyes. Her skin flared hot, and her cheeks flushed red. 'You don't need to feel shy, Vivian. I think you are mesmerizing.

'Ethan, you're making me blush.'

'Sorry, I didn't mean to embarrass you. I just said what's on my mind.' For a moment, their eyes locked in silence, their faces inching closer. Vivian tilted her head up, wanting to be kissed, but then there was a knock at the door.

'Ah... that must be the room service.' Vivian got up to open the door, hiding her disappointment at the interruption.

CHAPTER 8

The aroma of the dishes was tantalizing. 'Where would you like your dinner, Ma'am?' the waiter asked politely.

'On the balcony, please.' Vivian led the way, and the waiter followed. Ethan stood up and leaned on the railing looking out at the ocean.

'Is everything to your satisfaction, Ma'am. Is there anything else you require?'

'Can you please bring another bottle of champagne?' Ethan said.

'Certainly, Sir.'

In a few minutes the second bottle arrived, and it complemented the lobster perfectly. Ethan ensured their glasses remained full.

'It's gratifying. A beautiful woman, delicious food, and spectacular scenery. What else does a man need?'

Vivian laughed loudly. Ethan had comically pointed at her, the food, and the ocean as he delivered his cheesy line. Suddenly she jumped up excitedly and pointed toward the sea.

'Look, Ethan, look! Dolphins!'

Ethan stood behind her. He was so close she could feel the warmth of his body and breathe in the woody, spicy scent of his aftershave. Ethan turned Vivian around until her back pressed against the railing. He stared at her lips lustfully, softly gripped.

He was standing so close she could feel the length of his hardened cock pressing against her. Vivian wanted this man. She wanted to taste him. It had been too long since someone had touched her this way. Her body screamed to be touched. Ethan recognized the desire in her eyes. He held her face with both hands and kissed her passionately. Their tongues collided. Ethan's hand slid to her dress straps and he released the knot. With one deft movement he unraveled the dress, then took a step back to admire her body. She was grateful she'd selected her sexiest lingerie.

'Divine.' His deep tone was almost a whisper. He hungrily kissed Vivian's neck and stroked her breasts. Vivian sighed heavily. Ethan gently took off her dress and dropped it on the floor. She was standing on her balcony with a man, wearing nothing but lingerie. She didn't care if someone saw them, and this thought aroused her even more. Would she dare to make love out in the open?

Ethan unclasped her bra, then cupped her creamy breasts. He sucked on her left nipple, then nibbled it gently. Vivian was still leaning on the railing and she gripped it tightly with both hands. Ethan sucked her other nipple, and with her breath quickening, Vivian moaned.

Ethan knelt in front of her and slowly pulled down her black lace panties. Now she was completely naked.

'Do you want to go inside?' asked Ethan.

'No, I want to do it here. Now.'

Vivian's eyes were filled with desire. Ethan, still kneeling in front of her, gently parted her moist labia, then dipped in his tongue.

'Hmm, Vivian. I'd like to taste you every day.' Ethan's tongue explored deeper, then moved up and down, increasing in speed. The tip of his tongue found her swollen clitoris quickly, then circled around it. Her thighs were trembling.

Ethan picked Vivian up and positioned her on the chair with her legs over his shoulders. Again he licked her slick, wet folds, flicking and teasing her clit. Her moans grew louder when he slowly inserted two fingers inside her, while his tongue kept circling her clit. She flicked her hips back and forth for more friction.

'Ethan stop, stop, I'm almost there!'

He pulled back and stood in front of her. Vivian quickly unzipped his pants and his rigid cock sprung out. Vivian gasped at the size of it, then glanced up at him lustfully before opening her mouth wide to wrap her lips around it.

'Vivian… your mouth, your lips… oh God it feels good.' Feeling challenged, she opened her jaw wider and lengthened her neck so she could take in more of him, then quickened her pace while staring wickedly up at him.

Now it was Ethan's turn to moan. 'Vivian, where have you been all my life?' Her mouth and hands were perfectly synchronized as she sucked and gripped his swollen cock.

'Vivian, oh... yes... keep going... it feels so good.'

He held the back of her head steady so he could slide in and out of her mouth. 'I don't want to come yet.' He stood up and picked her up from the chair then kissed her ferociously, his driving need pressing into her thigh. 'What do you want? What's your favorite position?'

Vivian couldn't think straight anymore. 'I don't care, just take me now!'

Ethan pulled Vivian back to the railing and turned her around toward the ocean. He widened her trembling thighs and she tilted her hips up. She was wet and ready. In a flash he entered and pushed to the hilt. Vivian screamed with pleasure. He told her to hold the railing tightly as he gripped her hips from behind. Ethan thrust his swollen cock in and out, faster and faster. Vivian panted and groaned with delight. She could feel his balls bouncing quickly between her thighs.

She had wanted this for such a long time. Ethan's breath became heavy. Suddenly he pulled out and turned Vivian around and started to grope and kiss her breasts. She grasped the railing with one hand while squeezing his balls with the other.

'Vivian, I can't hold it anymore. I almost came.'

'Then come, Ethan, come.'

He parted her wet folds with one hand then thrust deep inside her, shuddering as he came. Vivian's legs felt weak. Ethan carried her to the bathroom. He placed her gently on the edge of the bathtub and turned on the faucet.

Steam filled the room. He then lifted her into the bath, then climbed in next to her, their legs entwined. Vivian leaned on him and embraced him. Ethan let go of her arms and began to gently bathe Vivian. He soaped her all over, and when he reached her breasts, her nipples hardened. She sighed heavily, pressing her thighs together tightly. She was horny once more. Vivian stroked Ethan's chest, her hand slipping down his chiseled abdomen to his groin. Even when it wasn't erect, the size of Ethan's cock was still impressive. With Vivian's touch, he got a hard-on immediately. Vivian leaned down, and tingling with desire she started licking and kissing the tip of his erection.

'Vivian, what are you doing to me?' With her lips, tongue, and hands, Vivian worshiped Ethan's pulsating cock until he climaxed. His cum slipped from the corner of her mouth. Ethan helped her to stand, placed his arms around her, then held her against his chest. They stood there embracing until their breathing became regular again.

Ethan lifted her up and held her against the wall. Vivian wrapped her legs around his torso and her arms around his neck. Her clit throbbed in anticipation. He thrust his cock up and deep inside her. She angled her hips so his hard-on pressed against her G-spot, sending her into convulsions of pleasure. She could barely remember to breathe.

'Vivian, you have the sexiest body,' he panted into her ear. 'I will never stop wanting you.'

Ethan thrust even deeper and faster. With each thrust she groaned. He was on the verge of climax. Vivian's arms wrapped tighter around his neck, and her legs tighter around his torso. She was also on the verge of orgasm. She panted and moaned.

'Oh, yes... Ethan... keep going... I'm coming!' He pushed even harder and faster, until they both came together, shuddering against each other.

'Vivian, I don't know what you're doing to me. But it feels like I could never be satisfied without you.'

'Me too. I've never felt like this before either.'

Ethan kissed her tenderly.

Vivian stretched out on the bed while her hand searched for the man next to her. Surprised, she rose. He wasn't there. Her heart started pounding. Was it possible she was dreaming again? Vivian glanced around. On the bedside table she saw a small note:

Good morning, Vivian. Stay in bed. I went jogging and will return a little later with breakfast. Love, Ethan.

After reading the note her mind raced with questions. So it wasn't a dream.

The erotic scenes from the night before flickered through her mind. It was wild. It was hot.

Vivian had never had such an intense night of sex and multiple orgasms. In the middle of her racing thoughts she suddenly panicked. What made her so bold as to have unprotected sex with a stranger? Vivian only knew his name. She jumped out of bed. She felt dirty.

She rushed to the bathroom and brushed her teeth. She stared hard at her reflection in the mirror and felt disgusted. She bent down to rinse out her mouth several times. When she raised her head and looked in the mirror, she was shocked. For a split second, she didn't see her reflection. The woman in the mirror looked like her, but it was not her. The reflection had long blond hair, big blue eyes, and a beauty spot above the upper lip. It took a few moments before Vivian realized the reflection was Victoria, George's dead daughter.

Tears burned her eyes. Had something terrible happened to George? Was this a sign? She quickly ran back to the room and frantically searched for her phone. With a trembling hand, she called Edward. She heard the dial tone but it soon switched to voicemail. Even though she hated leaving a message, this time she did.

'Edward, this is Vivian. I know I'm not supposed to call you, but I really want to know that everything is okay with George. Please, Edward. Just let me know.' She ended the call. Dazed, she stared at the phone in her hand. Had she gone crazy? What had she seen in the mirror? Why did she have sex with a total stranger? She had no answers to these questions.

All she knew was that she had to get out of there before Ethan returned. She couldn't and wouldn't meet this man again. Vivian rushed to take a shower and put on clean clothes. She grabbed her bag and phone then searched for her room's keycard. She couldn't find it anywhere. Ethan must have taken it. She decided to leave without the damn card.

Before stepping into the hallway, Vivian looked around to make sure Ethan wasn't around. What she was most afraid of now was running into him and having to explain why she was running away. After she'd made it out of the resort, she sighed in relief and immediately hailed a taxi.

The driver turned and asked Vivian, 'Where to, Ma'am?'

Vivian looked around. She really didn't know where to go. 'I don't care, just take me somewhere quiet please.'

The driver shrugged in astonishment and stepped on the gas. She leaned back and closed her eyes. She had to calm herself down. This was not the first time she'd had sex with someone of course, but usually they weren't complete strangers. She'd never had a one-night stand before. She hated the idea of them. She was different from Genieva who never wanted more than sex. Her friend's motto was: 'Once you're satisfied, you should be free to have fun with others later.'

The taxi stopped suddenly and she opened her eyes. She looked around and saw the driver had taken her to a chapel on the shorefront. Vivian paid the fare and got out.

There was no one around. It was still quite early.

Vivian walked to the small chapel, and felt calmer as soon as she walked inside. She sat on a pew and gazed at the flowers, candles, and statues of Christ. Vivian put her bag on her lap and heard her phone ring twice, meaning she'd received a text message. She grabbed it and saw Edward's name on the screen:

My dear, George's condition is fine. No need to worry. See you when you're back. Love, kisses, Edward.

Without realizing it, tears started rolling down her cheeks as she read Edward's message. She felt deeply relieved. The message came at the right time and place. Vivian had been terrified after seeing Victoria's reflection in the mirror and thought it was a bad sign, but thankfully there was nothing to worry about. She wiped her tears, stood up, then lit a candle for George. Kneeling, she made the sign of the cross, then left the chapel.

Vivian sat on the sand and a street vendor approached her. He was selling beach towels and sunscreen, but Vivian was only interested in the water he carried. She bought two bottles, then the vendor continued south towards the resorts. Vivian sat quietly on the deserted beach and her troublesome questions returned. How could she have been so reckless as to have unsafe sex? Even though she was on the pill, she should have been wary of STIs. They should have used condoms. The minute she arrived back in New York she would get tested.

Even though it was unsafe, Vivian had to admit it was the best sex she'd ever had. What this man had done to her made her flare with desire. It was so different to what she had experienced before. Even just thinking about she started to feel aroused. She pressed her thighs together tightly to suppress the tingling.

What should she do now? Vivian didn't want Ethan to think she was someone who slept around. But for the first time in a long time she was able to forget Ferris, although she knew nothing about Ethan. She didn't know where he came from, what he did for a living, and whether he was seriously interested in her or just playing around. She sincerely hoped he wasn't, because she liked Ethan and wanted a man like him in her life. Vivian had to face him and find out his intentions. She got up and brushed off the sand. She decided to walk back to the resort so she'd have time to think things through.

It was almost dark when Vivian finally made it back to her. She had lost her way several times, but finally found it. She knocked on the door because she didn't have her keycard. No answer. She walked to Ethan's room and knocked on his door. After a short time she decided to walk down to the lobby to ask for a replacement card, but then Ethan's door opened. His face was a mess of emotions: shock, anger, concern, and fear.

He grabbed Vivian's arms and pulled her into his room.

'Where have you been? Do you have any idea how worried I was?'

Vivian looked down, unable to look him in the eyes. She couldn't find any words to say. She was exhausted. Her knees felt weak and started to fall. Ethan tightened his grip on her arms and noticed her pale face. He picked her up and carried her into his bedroom. He lay her down gently on his bed, then placed a cold towel on her forehead. Her eyes opened slowly, and she stared straight into his worried brown eyes.

'I'm sorry,' Vivian said softly.

'Where were you? I was worried sick about you! You've been gone all day!'

Vivian realized she owed him an explanation, but she was still too exhausted to speak properly. 'I'm sorry I made you worry, but I needed to think about a few things. I'll answer your questions, but not right now. I'm exhausted and my head and legs hurt like hell.'

Ethan looked at Vivian's feet and saw how red they were. He looked at her angrily. 'Have you had anything to eat or drink?'

'Only two bottles of water.'

'Are you out of your mind Vivian? How could you be so irresponsible? How could you walk such a long distance in this heat without eating or drinking anything? Imagine if you'd fainted in the middle of the road, what could've happened to you. You could have been robbed, or worse, raped!'

'I know. I'm sorry, okay. I didn't think twice. You don't have to bite my head off.'

'Forget about it. I will draw you a bath and order some food.

You'll stay here tonight so I can look after you, and you can explain everything in the morning.'

Vivian grimaced at his raised voice, but at the same time she was enjoying being cared for. Vivian's eyes followed Ethan when he went to fill the tub. He was genuinely concerned about her. He was even still wearing his jogging shorts. His hair was tousled, and he hadn't shaved.

Ethan stepped out of the bathroom with a bathrobe in his hand, which he placed on the bed. He sat at the end of the bed, and gently removed Vivian's shoes.

'Oh my god, Vivian, how long have you been walking?'

'I don't know. I didn't keep track of time.'

'How is your headache now?'

'Quite severe. I'm dizzy and a bit nauseous.'

Ethan peered at her with a deeply worried expression. 'Hmm, that's not good. Come on, let me take you to the bathroom.'

When Ethan went to open her shirt buttons, Vivian pushed his hand away and looked at him sheepishly.

'Come on, Vivian, what's the matter with you. I've seen you naked before. You slept with me last night, remember?'

Vivian looked at him in silence. He was right. Ethan gently undressed her, lifted her from the bed, carried her to the bathroom and carefully placed her in the warm water.

'Is the water too hot?'

'No, it's perfect. Thank you.'

Ethan observed her face thoroughly and noticed she was still pale. 'Wait a minute. I'll be right back.' He left the bathroom. Vivian started shivering even though she was half submerged in warm water. Ethan returned with a pair of his shorts and a shirt.

'When you're ready, you can wear this.' He walked out of the bathroom, and she heard a conversation on the phone. Vivian got out of the tub and washed herself in the shower. She had to steady herself with her hand on the wall because of dizziness and nausea. Before she put his clothes on, Vivian sniffed them to inhale his scent of expensive perfume which clung to them even though they were freshly washed.

Vivian combed her hair and braided it before she walked back to the room. She was relieved she could walk to the bed without falling. Every step, Vivian felt her head throbbing. She couldn't Even call Ethan and ask for aspirin. She sat on the bed and there was a knock at the door. Why did he knock? Vivian was confused.

'Yes?' Vivian asked softly. The door opened slowly. Ethan entered the room followed by a man carrying a medical bag. Vivian looked at it questioningly, but before she could ask, Ethan already began to explain.

'Vivian, this is Doctor Moreno. I asked him to check your condition. Are you okay with that?'

Vivian hadn't expected this. 'Ah, yes, fine.' She immediately felt grateful. The doctor started to examine her and ask some questions which she tried her best to answer.

'Ma'am, I'm sorry to tell you this, but you have heatstroke.'

'Heatstroke?' she repeated in disbelief.

'Yes, make sure you have plenty to drink and lots of rest.'

'I'll make sure she gets enough fluids,' Ethan responded to the doctor's advice.

'Alright then, I have to go now. I have an appointment.' After he gently shook Vivian's hand, Doctor Moreno left the room with Ethan.

Not long after, Ethan returned with a tray carrying a glass of water and an aspirin. He sat beside her. She shyly looked up at him and he winked at her. She was deeply moved by the attention he was giving her. Without realizing, tears sprung to her eyes.

'Hey, hey, don't cry. Everything's going to be fine.'

Vivian couldn't resist the urge to put her arms around his neck tightly.

'Come on, no more tears. There's someone else here to see you.'

She wiped her eyes and looked at Ethan quizzically. 'To see me? Who?' She panicked a little, thinking it might be Angie and Patty. But that wasn't possible they'd left two days before.

'Now, take the aspirin first. Are you cold?'

She took a sip of water and swallowed the aspirin. 'Yes, a little.'

Ethan went to his closet and took out a gray sweater.

'Thank you.'

Ethan winked again, this time more playfully. 'My clothes look good on you.'

Vivian gave him a little smile before Ethan left the room and returned with a young woman in a white uniform with pink stripes. She was pretty and had a friendly face.

'Hello, Ma'am. My name is Grace, and I'm here to give you a pedicure.'

Vivian looked at Ethan with surprise, and her heart thudded with fondness. Vivian was almost sure she was willing to spend her life with this man. Not only was he handsome, but he was a wild animal in bed, and so attentive.

'I'll leave you to it.' He left the room with a smile.

Grace gave her an extremely professional pedicure, but she didn't stop talking.

She talked about many things; her husband, her three children, her mother and her grandmother, who were also beauty therapists. Vivian couldn't keep her eyes open, and even though Grace was still busy talking, she fell asleep.

At midnight, she woke up feeling hot. She was lying down on Ethan's bed, still wearing his gray sweater.

Ethan was lying next to her with his arms and legs embracing her.

With difficulty, she managed to break away from Ethan's arms without waking him up.

Vivian still didn't feel well yet, but Ethan had prepared another aspirin and glass of water beside the bed.

Full of gratitude, she took it and swallowed it with water, then went back to bed. With her eyes closed, she listened to Ethan's slow and steady breathing.

A smile spread across her lips when she thought about how sweet, caring, and attentive this man was.

When Vivian's father died, she had learned to take care of herself because her mother was too busy with her career. Now, for the first time, she was experiencing what it feels like to be taken care of, and she enjoyed every second of it.

Vivian wondered… was this love? Everything felt so real, so comfortable, and so genuine, even though she almost didn't know Ethan at all. Vivian was almost certain this man could be her true love.

CHAPTER 9

The next morning, Vivian awoke next to Ethan. He was lying on his side while gently kissing her eyes and the tip of her nose.

Vivian rubbed her sleepy eyes and looked at him with a smile.

'Good morning, angel. How are you feeling?'

Vivian stretched out her body. She felt much better than the day before. 'I feel fine! It's just, I'm completely famished.'

Ethan held out his hand to help Vivian get up and said, 'Good, because I ordered breakfast for us.'

This man was like a lottery ticket! Vivian felt fortunate to be with him.

'Ethan, you spoil me too much.'

'There's nothing too much for you. A woman like you must be treated like royalty.' He put his arm around her waist and helped her walk to the balcony where the breakfast had been served. Vivian was touched by what she saw: coffee, tea, milk, fresh orange juice, tropical fruit, pastries, toast it was way too much for the two of them.

'Gosh, Ethan. You could feed an entire orphanage with all this!'

'If you want, we can pass on breakfast and bring the food to the orphanage.' Vivian sat down and looked straight into Ethan's eyes. 'Ethan, I want to thank you for taking care of me last night Sorry if I had you worried.'

Ethan poured her a coffee, then sat down next to her, returning her gaze. 'Why did you run away like that?'

Vivian sipped her coffee and shifted her position. She knew she owed him an explanation. 'I don't know where to start,' she bit her lower lip nervously.

'Don't do that.'

'Do what?'

'Bite your lip, it turns me on,' Ethan said, softly rubbing Vivian's lips with his thumb.

'I panicked when I woke up. I thought what happened the other night was just a dream. I have been yearning for a certain man for such a long time, but he was... out of reach. I dreamt about him almost every night, so I was afraid that it was all just another dream. When I saw your message, I realized it was real. I left because I'm ashamed.'

'Ashamed? What do you mean?'

She cleared her throat, took another sip of coffee, and continued. 'I'm ashamed of myself because I'm afraid you'll think badly about me. I'm afraid you'll see me as a cheap girl who sleeps with anyone. Because Ethan, that's just not true. I've been alone for years. I was also angry with myself because I had unprotected sex with someone I barely know, with all due respect.'

Ethan looked surprised. 'Don't you take the birth control pill? I saw them in your bathroom near your toiletries.'

'Yes, I take the birth control pill, but that's not the point. We should've used condoms for protection against sexually-transmitted diseases.'

Ethan laughed suddenly and played with Vivian's braid. 'You don't have to worry about catching a venereal disease from me, Vivian. When I am actively having sex, I have routine my check-ups. You only have one body, so I strongly believe you must take good care of it. So in this case, you have nothing to fear with me.'

She glanced at the table, took a slice of toast, and spread pineapple jam on it. It was tart and not too sweet. She had to admit that the food at this hotel was delicious. She chewed her toast while her mind prepared the question she could no longer avoid. She wanted to know the answer now, rather than continue in in the dark. If Ethan only thought of this as a vacation romance, and not something with potential for a long-term relationship, she wanted to know now before she fell in love with him.

'Ethan?' She took a deep breath.

'Yes?'

'I'm scared.'

Ethan placed his cutlery on his plate and looked at her. 'What are you afraid of, Vivian?'

Now or never, she thought. 'I want to know what your intentions are. If I'm just your holiday plaything, then I can't continue like this.'

Breathing deeply, he looked at her with a frown. 'Vivian, I'm not playing around with you. I don't know what you think about me, but I'm not the type of person who, after a brief introduction, immediately goes to bed with a woman. This is all new for me too. I've never felt like this before.'

Vivian listened carefully and absorbed what Ethan had said.

'I'm the type of man who respects women, but you're different from all the women I've ever met. You're special. You do something to me that I've never got from any other woman. I want to protect you, take care of you, and spoil you. Believe me. I'm not playing with you.'

He took a sip of coffee and continued. 'To be honest, I'm also afraid, Vivian. You just told me you have feelings for another man, whom you can't reach. Can I compete with this man? I mean, am I good enough for you? Who knows, perhaps later you will also break my heart.'

With mixed emotions, Vivian processed his words. She was relieved that she wasn't just an outlet for his lust, but she didn't know how to convince him that she now thought he was the one not Ferris.

Now that they'd both confessed their true feelings to each other, Vivian wanted him even more. She wanted to grow old with this man.

'Ethan, you're the first person who has made me forget about that man. When I first saw you, I wanted to be yours. So yes, you're more than enough for me.'

Vivian bit her bottom lip and gazed at the man in front of her. She'd forgotten that Ethan became aroused when he saw her biting her lip. Before Vivian realized, she was in his arms, and they were kissing passionately.

Ethan embraced her gently. His eyes were dark, and his breathing was hot. 'How's your condition now?'

Vivian licked her lips. 'Fine.'

'Thank God, because I want you now. I need to drown myself in you.' He lifted her up and carried her to the bedroom. He undressed her quickly, then lay her down on the bed. Her nipples hardened, and her chest rose up and down with her heavy breathing. Ethan stood naked at the foot of the bed while watching Vivian closely. Vivian's eyes fixed on his massive cock standing fully erect. She groaned when she saw how Ethan held it and stroked it slowly. Once again, she bit her bottom lip. She was desperate to taste him in her mouth.

'Vivian, do you trust me?'

'Yes.'

'Do you trust me enough to be with me without a condom?'

'Yes. I trust you.'

He smiled and lay down beside her with his head propped up on his arm. Mischievously he said, 'Good girl, now what do you want?'

Vivian pushed him down, and swiftly wrapped her lips around his stiff, throbbing cock. He sighed and groaned with pleasure. Vivian stared up from under her long eyelashes,

133

pleased with how much this man enjoyed her touch. She licked and sucked then gripped his cock slowly at first, then quickened her pace, taking him deeper into her throat.

Ethan was groaning, and his hips were moving in time. Vivian felt his body go rigid, and his cock pulsating in her mouth. He was almost there. Vivian released her mouth and then slowly licked his balls. She licked her fingers, rubbed the tip then sucked on it forcefully.

'God, Vivian. I can't hold it much longer!'

Again she took him deep into her mouth while massaging his balls. He shuddered, and the warm liquid filled her mouth. She swallowed it all.

Vivian crawled on top of him and looked him in the eyes. Tense, she waited for what would happen next. Ethan's cock drooped limply but still looked large. Vivian bent down to kiss it lightly.

It only took a second for him to get hard again.

Vivian sat down while gazing at his virile masculinity. She felt his hands on her waist slowly lifting her up.

'I want to be inside you Vivian.' He held her above him and with her right hand gripped his cock and guided him inside her.

'Ahh… yeah... Ethan... it feels so good.' Vivian began to move her hips up and down, but paused for a moment so she could feel just how deep he was inside her.

Then she started moving her hips again, gradually at first, then she increased her pace.

Ethan's fingers gripping her hips to hold her in position, and with his hips, he thrust back and forth.

Vivian's thirst for this man made her feel crazy. She couldn't control herself anymore.

'Look at me, Vivian.'

She opened her eyes and looked straight into his.

'Let your hair out.' She pulled off her hair elastic, and her hair cascaded down her back and over her breasts.

'You are so stunning, Vivian. You are so beautiful.' Ethan held her hips firmly in place so he could thrust harder and deeper inside her. When he came, he shouted Vivian's name.

Exhausted and satisfied, they lay next to each other and focused on slowing their breathing. They faced each other, their fingers interlaced.

'Let's freshen up and get dressed, what do you say?'

Vivian brushed her hair from her face. 'Where should we go?' With difficulty, she hid her disappointment because she preferred to stay in bed with him.

'We could just grab a cab, and see where we end up.'

'Okay, sounds like a plan to me.'

Under the shower, Ethan knelt in front of her and parted her thighs. With his tongue and fingers he easily brought her to orgasm, her body twisting with pleasure. She could never get enough of his touch.

In the taxi, Ethan put his arm around her, and she laid her head on his shoulder.

Several times the taxi driver glanced at them in the rearview mirror and chuckled at how in love they were.

The taxi stopped, Ethan paid the fare, and they climbed out. They'd come to the ruins of the Bushiribana gold mine. Vivian looked around. There were many tourists taking pictures of the ruins. Hand in hand they walked around, although Vivian didn't know what kind of ruins they were. A tourist approached Ethan to ask him to take a picture of him and his girlfriend with the ruins in the background.

'What kind of building was this?' Vivian asked Ethan after he was done taking their picture.

'It used to be a gold mine.' Ethan put his arm around Vivian's shoulders and shared what he knew about the nineteenth century gold mine which turned out to be a lot. Even the couple who'd had their photo taken by Ethan strolled over to hear his explanation. Vivian giggled inside because he was acting like a tour guide. They then decided to walk along the beach.

'How come you know so much about this gold mine?'

'My father owns a diamond mine in South Africa.'

Vivian stopped, and her face went pale. She suddenly felt violently ill. Was it him? Ethan Stein!? The man her friends warned her about? Her friends' words echoed loudly through her head: dangerous, dangerous, dangerous, playboy, playboy, playboy, stay away, stay away, stay away.

Why hadn't Vivian asked him about his last name? How could she be so stupid!?

She had to get away from Ethan immediately. She thought about the two women who had committed suicide after being in a relationship with him. Vivian had to find an excuse to return to the hotel.

'Vivian, why is your face pale?'

She gathered the courage to sound as casual as possible and hide her panic.

'Suddenly I'm not feeling so well. Maybe I'm not completely recovered from yesterday.'

Ethan looked at her worriedly. 'Should we go back?'

Vivian had to act as if everything was fine. 'You don't mind? I don't want to ruin this day.'

'No, I don't mind. Come on, let's find a taxi and go back to the resort.' He hugged her, and even though she wanted to push him and run away, she had to pretend everything was fine. In the taxi, Ethan pulled Vivian into his arms. There was nowhere to hide. How could she be so stupid? She'd made love multiple times with a man she should be avoiding. She bowed her head, feeling sorry for herself. Why was her life like a melodrama? Why couldn't she just be happy? Vivian planned to ask Ethan for the truth as soon as they reached the resort. She had to face reality. Vivian was furious with herself for neglecting to ask where he came from and for his last name. For the previous few days she'd been completely preoccupied with having sex with him. The lift's doors opened, and they walked together to their corridor.

'Which room, angel?'

'My room.' She did her best to sound as normal as possible.

'Do you want me to stay with you?' Ethan opened the door to Vivian's room before she answered.

She walked straight to the balcony. It was there she had started to fall for Ethan's charm, and there she had made love in the open for the first time. Vivian felt disgusted, and her back shivered. She glanced at the ocean and tried to find the right words.

'Would you like some water, Vivian?'

'Yes,' she replied briefly.

Soon Ethan came with two glasses of water, and stood next to her. Instinctively, Vivian backed away.

Ethan looked at her with raised eyebrows. 'Do you want to tell me what exactly is going on?'

'How long do you think you can hide it from me, Ethan Stein!?'

Ethan looked at her with a smile because he knew exactly what she meant.

'How did you know I was here? And don't tell me it's all a coincidence!'

Vivian looked furious. Ethan shrugged as he answered casually, 'The Club.'

'What do you mean, "The Club"? Were you following me?'

He sipped the water and leaned nonchalantly on the railing with his hand in his pocket.

'The last time you went there with your friends, I sent people to eavesdrop on your conversation.'

Vivian gasped and heard Genieva's voice in her head saying, 'I have a bad feeling about this guy.'

She tried to remember the suspicious man in The Club, who was constantly sending messages on his phone. Vivian's whole world seemed to collapse. She thought she had finally found Mr. Right, but it turned out he was the man she should have avoided. Tears of sadness and anger rolled down her cheeks. Ethan tried to wipe them away, but Vivian shook her head.

'Don't touch me, and stay the hell away from me! Why are you doing this to me?'

'Listen, Vivian. You could have asked me about my last name, but you didn't. What if I'd introduce myself with my last name? Of course you wouldn't have wanted to talk to me. So don't blame it all on me. It takes two to tango, right?'

For a moment, they just stood and looked at each other. Ethan was right. She couldn't blame it all on him.

'Ethan... I want to be alone right now. I need time to think.'

'I understand. I'll be next door if you need me.' Ethan put his glass on the table and left without saying anything or looking back at her.

Vivian fled from the balcony and closed the door because she didn't want to see or hear him. It crossed her mind to call Salfina or Genieva, but this thought shifted quickly. If she did, she wouldn't be able to stop herself confessing that she'd had sex with Ethan Stein. She couldn't and didn't want to tell them. She felt mortified.

On the couch, she fell asleep and woke up in the darkness. She wanted to open her balcony door but halted the thought. Her rumbling stomach reminded her how hungry she was. That morning she'd only had toast with jam, but she knew she couldn't eat right now. In the dark, she walked to the fridge and returned to the couch with a bottle of water.

What should she do? For a moment she thought of going home, but if she did, she would have to tell her friends the reason for returning early from her vacation. What was the alternative? Ask for a different room, or better yet change to a different resort far away from Ethan?

Vivian's thoughts were interrupted by the sound of her room phone ringing. That must be Ethan, she thought. Who else could contact her through that phone? Vivian didn't answer it. The phone rang again. Panicking, Vivian ran over to it and pulled the plug from the socket, then she sat back on the couch and hugged her knees.

When Vivian had finally managed to calm down a little, a knock on the door surprised her. Vivian held her breath, but the knock got louder. She heard Ethan's voice calling her name. Stubbornly she remained on the couch. She didn't answer. Why couldn't he just leave her alone? She heard a rustling sound. A piece of paper slid under the door. Vivian walked silently to pick it up.

She walked to the bedroom, turned on the light, and started to read.

Vivian, I'm sorry we've started out this way. I should have approached you differently, but I didn't know how. I want to know if you're okay because I'm worried about you. We're both adults, and I hope we can discuss this situation and find a way out of it. Vivian, everything I said to you was sincere, and I mean it. This is not a trick. You're too special for that. I'm sure you have heard bad stories about me, but I hope you can at least give me a chance to explain. There are two sides to every story, right? Tomorrow morning at ten I will knock on your door, and if you don't open it, I will know you don't want to talk to me, and I will have to accept and respect that. I will leave you alone, and leave the island. Vivian, please just give me a chance so I can explain everything.
Love, Ethan Stein xxx.

She read the letter many times in a storm of emotions. On one hand, she was still furious and disappointed, but on the other, she agreed there are always two sides to every story.
If she gave Ethan a chance, would that mean she had betrayed her friends? But Salfina and Genieva also didn't know the truth. They had heard the story from other people's gossip. If the story wasn't true, Vivian would lose the man she had just fallen in love with.

After all, it wouldn't hurt to hear Ethan's story. She would decide what she would do after she listened to his explanation. Under the shower, Vivian's mind returned to the intimate moments they shared in this bathroom. She soaped her whole body, and when her fingers slid over her breasts, she felt her nipples harden. Vivian couldn't ignore the quivering between her thighs. Her right hand slid down and she slipped two fingers inside, imagining they were Ethan's. It felt so good. Her left hand twisted her nipples while her fingers danced inside her. She had never masturbated before. She was thrilled with how incredible it felt. Her fingers sped up as she rubbed her clit, while her other hand squeezed her breasts. She threw her head back and slid down the shower wall as she came.

Vivian awoke the next morning after a bad night's sleep. She'd had trouble sleeping because she felt like she wasn't alone in her room, like there was someone watching her. Several times she turned on the lights to look around, but there was nothing unusual. It was now ten past nine. Vivian had to hurry because Ethan would knock on her door at ten.

She opened her closet and carefully considered what to wear. After all that had happened the day before, she wanted to look her best. She fixed her gaze on the pale yellow blouse she'd bought downtown and put it on. She looked gorgeous. The color of the blouse looked perfect with her brown skin, and her breasts looked enticing.

The tight black skirt clung to her slim hips and long legs. Vivian deliberately left her hair down because she knew Ethan liked it.

Right on ten there was a knock at the door, and Vivian padded over to it barefooted. She paused before she opened it. Ethan was leaving, but the sound of the opening door made him turn around.

He stared at her in awe as though it was the first time he had seen her. 'Vivian, you look absolutely stunning.'

She stared at him silently before she eventually let him enter her room.

CHAPTER 10

Ethan walked past Vivian, clutching a bouquet of white roses. He paused in front of the couch and turned toward her. 'These are for you.'

She accepted his peace offering of roses and placed them on the coffee table. 'Thank you.' Vivian saw how he looked like a young boy in an awkward situation. Somehow, this sight stirred her heart. But she mustn't allow herself to be distracted she needed to be strong and restrain her feelings. 'Do you want coffee?'

'Yes, please. Thank you.' She poured the large pot of coffee into two cups. Ethan sat on the couch with his gaze fixed on Vivian. She nodded and sat on a chair opposite him. Vivian felt flutters on her skin as she looked at his sturdy chest. Without realizing it, she tightly pressed her thighs together.

'Ethan, I have decided to hear your side of the story. This doesn't mean I forgive you. I still need time to process all of this before making my final decision.'

'I completely understand. I'm glad you gave me a chance to explain. This further proves how special you are.'

Vivian shifted in the seat and crossed her legs. Ethan's gaze drifted across them.

'Vivian, I can guess the kind of story that you heard about me. That I'm a playboy and I always do everything to get what I want.'

He stood up and began pacing in front of the couch. Vivian watched from her chair.

'I admit I have disappointed many women, and I have also mistreated some of them. But most of the women who've gotten close to me weren't interested in me as a person. They were only interested in my money.'

Vivian scoffed while looking directly at him. 'I'm not interested in your wealth. I'm perfectly capable of taking care of myself, but for God's sake stop pacing, it annoys me.'

'Oh, sorry.' Ethan returned to the couch opposite her. 'I know you're not interested in me for my money, Vivian. That's one of the things that makes you different from all the other women I've been with. I realized the first time I saw you dance at The Club, and then again when I talked to you for the first time, that you are the one for me. You make me feel complete. With other women, I always felt something missing, but I didn't know what. With you, everything feels right. Not to mention how beautiful you are.' Ethan sipped his coffee and played with his cup. He looked clumsy and awkward.

'What about the story about the two women who committed suicide after being with you?' the question came tumbling out of Vivian's mouth.

Ethan's face changed dramatically. He looked like he was struggling to contain his emotions. Vivian could see tears stinging the corners of his eyes.

'I don't know Vivian. Can you try to imagine how you would

feel if everyone blamed you for someone's death? It's had a tremendous impact on my life.' Ethan looked deeply hurt.

'But you fled to Europe afterwards.'

'I left, but I didn't flee. What would you have done? What would you do if everyone accused you of being the reason why someone committed suicide?'

Vivian shrugged her shoulders. She couldn't imagine what she would do.

'I left because I couldn't take it anymore. Trust me, Vivian, it's taken a very long time to recover from all of this. I have absolutely nothing to do with the tragic death of these two young women, but the severity of this guilt will haunt me for the rest of my life. I can't do anything to defend myself.'

Vivian pondered Ethan's words and realized the struggle he faced, because what he said was true. The guilt probably would haunt him for the rest of his life.

'You know, Vivian, I don't know how the story spread around, but really, everything was just coincidence. Maybe they gossip about it simply for the thrill of it. It might just bubble from other people's jealousy toward my family and me. I just don't know. I won't deny I didn't have relationships with those two women who ultimately ended their own lives, but you have to believe me when I say I have nothing to do with their deaths. The worst part of it all is, I now have to defend myself in front of the woman of my dreams for something I had nothing to do with.'

Vivian was deeply saddened when she heard that. She really couldn't imagine how difficult it must be to try to overcome this heavy burden. What if what he said was true? But Vivian also couldn't believe that people who were simply jealous of Ethan's family's success would do such a cruel thing.

'Why did you follow me here?'

'I came here because back in New York, your friends always made sure I could never approach you. I know they've already made their minds up about me.'

'How did you know I was here alone?'

'I sent that guy from The Club over here to make sure you were alone. When he assured me that was the case, I took the first flight over here.'

'But why didn't you say who you are from the beginning?'

'Because I was afraid of how you would respond. That morning when I returned from jogging and you had suddenly disappeared, I was worried you'd already figured out who I was. I hated myself for it, and that's why I finally let on at the old gold mine. Because I wanted you to know who I am.'

Vivian recalled how Ethan looked that day when she returned with heatstroke, how worried and frantic he was, but most of all she remembered how kindly and patiently he'd taken care of her.

'Listen, Vivian. I'm not playing around with you. If I was, I wouldn't have told you about my father's diamond mine, which of course you already knew about from your friends.

147

I'm relieved that you now know, so I can pray you believe my side of the story.'

Vivian rose from her chair and stood with her back to Ethan, staring out the window.

'Vivian, please say something!'

Right when she turned back to him, her stomach grumbled loudly. Vivian was starving.

'When was the last time you ate?'

Vivian's face flushed red with shyness. 'Yesterday on your balcony,' she revealed.

'Come on, I need to make sure you eat something first.' Ethan got up from the couch and held out his hand. Vivian wanted to feel the touch of it badly. 'Come on, Vivian, you have to eat.'

She let Ethan persuade her to have breakfast with him at one of the resort's restaurants, and like the day before he ordered way too much. She thought it was a shame so much of it would go to waste. In silence they began to eat, both lost in thought. Every now and then, their eyes met, but none of them started a conversation.

At the table across from them, there was an old couple which Vivian estimated to be in their seventies. The old woman smiled at Vivian and said, 'You look lovely together.' Vivian wanted to explain that they were not a couple, but the old woman continued. 'Looking at you two reminds me of when we were young.' The old woman looked lovingly at her husband, who gently caressed her cheeks.

'You must, at all times, protect and respect your woman. That's the secret of a good marriage,' the old man said to Ethan.

'I'll keep that in mind,' Ethan replied. Soon both men fell into a friendly conversation. Vivian sat quietly until the old woman moved her chair closer to Vivian and clasped Vivian's hand with her wrinkled hand. She studied her closely as though she was trying to read her mind.

'Honey, don't be too hard on him. I can see how much he cares about you. It's clear that he worships you, and that his heart is in the right place. I can tell by the way he looks at you.' Vivian was touched because the old woman told her this in a tone filled with motherly love. Her own mother never spoke to her this way. She decided not to reveal they were not a couple.

'I will do my best Ma'am and try to not be too hard on him.' The old man slowly rose from his chair and reached out to his wife. 'Come on, my dear Eva. It's time for us to play golf.' The old woman stroked Vivian's cheek and whispered in her ear, 'Enjoy your time together. Life is over before you know it so you should treasure every moment.' Vivian and Ethan watched the couple walk away hand in hand. Ethan wiped his mouth with a napkin and placed it on the table. 'Excuse me for a moment.'

A while later he returned and held out his hand to Vivian precisely as the old man had done for his wife. Hesitantly Vivian took his hand, and Ethan led her out of the restaurant.

Outside, a taxi was waiting.

'Ethan, I really don't think it's a good idea. I want to go back to my room to do some thinking.'

Ethan brushed away a long strand of hair that covered her face. His touch delighted her, but she didn't show it.

'I know, but it's just for a moment. We'll be back soon. Trust me!'

The taxi stopped in front of an old building, and Ethan helped Vivian out of the car. The driver also got out and opened the trunk. Vivian couldn't believe her eyes. It was filled with sandwiches, cupcakes, and other delicious treats. Behind them, another car pulled up, and its trunk opened to reveal dozens of books and toys. Ethan had granted Vivian's wish to give food to the orphanage. She was deeply moved, and gazed at him adoringly.

'Ethan, I don't know what to say.'

'You don't need to say anything. Come on, let's give this all to the kids.' He took Vivian's hand and they walked into the building.

Once they were inside, the staff distributed everything to the children. They giggled with delight. Vivian sat on a bench in the shade and watched the children playing with the toys. She was even more touched when she saw Ethan, who was still speaking with the orphanage's caretaker.

Their eyes met, and Ethan signaled for Vivian to join them. The caretaker led them into a grimy office and told them they could wait for the director there. Vivian looked around the dilapidated office and mold on the walls and peeling paint.

'I hope the children's bedrooms are in better shape than this office, she said warily.'

Soon, the door opened and a heavily overweight man staggered in. The chair creaked when he sat down. The man thanked Ethan and Vivian for their generosity and asked what the reason for this meeting was. Ethan looked at Vivian and gripped her hand.

'The reason for this meeting is that I want to renovate this entire orphanage. I also want to ensure enough food is delivered daily for the children.'

Vivian squeezed Ethan's hand so hard that it hurt. The director of the orphanage was completely startled by this announcement. Ethan continued to describe his project, which impressed Vivian tremendously. All kinds of emotions flooded through her. Even though Ethan had said several times that Vivian was an extraordinary woman, in that moment she felt it was he who was the extraordinary one.

All the terrible stories about him seemed to evaporate into the air. Vivian no longer wanted to think about it. She was convinced that the story had arose from mere jealousy, and she decided to no longer doubt his side of the story.

When they returned to the hotel, their footsteps paused in front of Vivian's room. She was tongue-tied, not knowing what she should do.

Should she invite him in or not? She still needed time to think about everything. Vivian turned to Ethan, who looked hopeful.

'Ethan, I need time.'

He took a step forward, forcing Vivian to take a step back into her door. 'Vivian, what else do I need to do to convince you? Do you know how tormenting it is, to be standing right next to you without being able to touch you? Don't you understand my feelings for you at all? Please, let me explain.

'I'm sure that I love you. I want to be with you. I want to protect you, cherish you, and I want to be there when you open your eyes in the morning. There is nothing I wouldn't do for you. I will never deny you anything. Correct me if I'm wrong, but I'm pretty sure you feel the same way about me. Please, Vivian, don't turn your back on me. Give me another chance to convince you. And important of all, let me show you how a woman like you should be treated.'

Vivian was overwhelmed by his words, especially after seeing a tear roll down his cheek. With both hands, she grabbed his face and kissed his lips. Their tongues intertwined.

Panting, Vivian pushed him away and slowed down her breathing. 'You're right. I can't stay away from you either. But so much has happened in the past few days. I still need to think things through.'

Ethan stroked Vivian's hair and looked at her expectantly.

'Okay, I won't force you. Take all the time you need. I'll be waiting for you next door.'

He kissed her neck and reluctantly let go of her hand as she stepped into her room.

Throughout the rest of the day and night, Vivian weighed her decision carefully. She tried to put herself in Ethan's shoes until she was determined to give a relationship with him a chance.

The worst case scenario was she could be left behind with a broken heart. There was no guarantee that their love would last forever. If she was committed to this relationship, then no one must know about it especially her friends. Salfina and Genieva had already made up their minds about him, and there was no way she could change that.

The only thing she wanted in that moment was to be touched and loved by him, because sex with Ethan was mind-blowing. He made her do things she'd never done before, and she loved it. She wanted to explore what else he could teach her.

After a long warm bath she felt refreshed. She pulled on a satin bathrobe and walked out onto the balcony.

Vivian leaned against the railing and held her breath when she heard the balcony door next to hers open. For a moment, she thought of running back inside, but abandoned the idea. If Ethan didn't lean on the balcony railing, he wouldn't see her. So Vivian decided to stay. She took a deep breath and filled her lungs with the ocean air and stared up at the stars.

'Good evening.'

Vivian was startled by the familiar voice, then looked at him.

Ethan was standing on his balcony bare-chested. His hair was wet. Under the moon and the stars, his stunning, statuesque torso stimulated Vivian's nipples, making them show through her satin robe. He held out his hand across the railing and said, 'What a lovely evening, may I introduce myself. I'm Ethan Stein.'

Again, Vivian was surprised by this man. He seemed to always take her words seriously. 'Hello, I'm Vivian Foster. Indeed it is a glorious night, Ethan Stein.'

'Vivian, what a beautiful name. Almost as beautiful as this view.'

She couldn't help but laugh. Ethan also always seemed skilled in making her smile.

'Thank you.' Her instincts told her she'd made the right choice, and that everything was going to be okay.

'I know it's already late, but may I invite you to have a drink me? I have a bottle of champagne that is screaming to be opened.'

From just behind him, he grabbed the bottle and showed it to Vivian. She laughed and shook her head. When Vivian looked back at him, she noticed his eyes had darkened with desire.

'Open your door, I'm coming right over.'

Wearing only pajama pants, Ethan opened his door, and his eyes flicked down at Vivian's satin bathrobe. His eyes fixed on her breasts and hardened nipples under the thin fabric of her robe.

He tugged off the robe's belt and pulled her to the bedroom. Her robe fell open. She was wearing nothing underneath. Ethan knelt, folded his hands together and proclaimed, 'Thank you, God, for returning the woman of my dreams.' Vivian's heart was beating fast. She lay on the bed, and Ethan crawled on top of her in the opposite direction. He parted her thighs then buried his face between them, licking and lapping her silky folds while she wrapped her lips around his enormous erection.

The loud sucking sounds of their erotic frenzy aroused them even more. Vivian opened her eyes when she felt Ethan's finger tickle her ass. It felt strange, but exhilarating. She wriggled her hips to encourage him. The combination of his tongue licking her clit, two fingers thrusting inside her and another one teasing her behind sent her wild.

She had never tried anal sex, and now she wanted more than just his finger.

'Ethan?' Vivian murmured.

'Hmm, yeah?' Ethan's voice was hoarse.

'I... I want more.'

'What do you mean?'

'I want you to take me from behind.'

He shifted to the side and looked at Vivian. 'Are you sure? Because I don't think you've done it before. You're very tight down there'

Vivian nibbled her bottom lip and looked at Ethan timidly.

'No, I've never done it, but I want you to give me that pleasure.'

'My angel, believe me, it couldn't give me more pleasure and satisfaction than to take you in that position, but I can't just push it in it can be painful. Something like that takes practice. You need to be stretched slowly so I could fit.'

'How do you stretch it?'

Ethan lay down with his head leaning on his hand while staring at Vivian. 'You stretch it little by little. You start with one finger until you get used to it. Then you try two fingers and so on and so on.'

'You said you'd do anything for me, Ethan. Please do this. I want you to give me this pleasure.'

'Are you sure, Viv? I don't want to hurt you.'

Ethan had called her 'Viv' for the first time, and she loved the sound of it. 'I'm sure.'

'Don't move, I'll be right back.' He jumped out of bed, went to the bathroom and returned with a tube of lubricant. 'This is what we need. The lube will make it easier for me to slide into you. Get on your hands and knees.'

Vivian immediately obeyed him, with tension and adrenaline flowing through her body. She watched Ethan over her shoulder as he smeared his fingers with lube.

'Are you ready, Viv? You need to relax.'

She took several deep breaths, while Ethan rubbed her behind with lube.

'Are you ready?'

'Yes.'

Ethan edged a finger slowly inside. He felt her muscles contract. 'Try to relax, angel.' Ethan pushed it in further until his whole finger was inside her. He gave Vivian time to adjust then he carefully pulled it out a little then pushed it back in. Vivian quickly got used to it, her body moving in time with Ethan's finger.

'Does it feel good, my angel?'

'Yes, Ethan, I want more.' Ethan chuckled then started to edge in his index finger. Vivian's muscled contracted again, but she quickly adjusted and relaxed into it.

'Oh my God, Vivian, when I see my fingers disappear inside you like this, I can't wait to slide my cock inside you.'

His lustful words gave her the courage. 'Do it,' she dared. She heard the cap of the lube flick open again. She looked over her shoulder to see Ethan rubbing his huge hard-on with lube. Vivian bit her lip. Ethan parted her cheeks while he gently pushed the head of his cock into her tight ass, inch by inch. He Ethan moved his hips slowly. She tried to relax when she felt him halfway inside her. Vivian felt her muscles tighten. Despite the pain, she felt just as much pleasure. Ethan pushed deeper into Vivian, and she could hear his ragged breath. He pulled out and pushed back inside, this time a little bit deeper.

'Are you okay. Can you handle it?' She sensed the concern in Ethan's deep voice.

'Yes, it's okay. Please don't stop!'

'God it feels so damn good. I love your tightness, Vivian.'

His words made Vivian gently rock her body which made him more eager to push deeper. Ethan grasped her hips firmly and started to thrust even harder. Vivian screamed between pain and pleasure. Ethan pushed his cock in entirely and waited so Vivian could feel the full length of him. Vivian moved forward so his cock slid out of her then quickly pushed back down on it, forward and back until Ethan gasped, groaned and growled. He gripped her hips and pulled her hard. He shouted her name again and again and then shuddered against her. The pleasure and pain made her scream, 'Yes! Yes! Deeper! Give it to me!'

'Vivian, I'm going to come inside you.' Ethan crashed down next to her with cum still dripping out of him. 'How was it? Are you in pain?'

'Yes, it hurts, but it's nothing I can't handle. It felt so good.'

Ethan tucked Vivian's hair behind her right ear and whispered, 'You really are the woman of my dreams. You're mine now. I'm going to make sure that you never leave me.'

CHAPTER 11

Vivian and Ethan were inseparable. Countless times people shouted at them, 'Please get a room!' and they would laugh and answer in unison, 'We have a room.'

Ethan had moved all his belongings into Vivian's room. She'd quickly realized how laidback Ethan was, and everything between them felt completely natural, as though they'd known each other for years.

Ethan was buttoning his shirt when Vivian came out of the bathroom. She'd just finished putting on light makeup. He stared at her, astonished. It was the first time he'd seen her wearing makeup. Her eyes looked larger because of the mascara, and her pale pink lip gloss made her full lips even more sensual. She was wearing the pale yellow dress she'd bought at Oranjestad. Vivian pirouetted playfully in front of him.

'Can I go out with you like this?'

He rose from the bed and walked over to her, stopping just inches away from her. 'Have I already told you how beautiful you are today?'

Vivian looked away while laughing. 'Only four times today.'

Ethan looked at her with an amused smile. 'I love it when you keep track of things.'

Hand in hand they passed through the lobby. People watched them, noticing what a perfect couple they made. Outside, the limousine Ethan had rented was waiting for them. They were driven to a nightclub. Once they were inside, men stared at Vivian's sexy curves, while the women couldn't take their eyes off Ethan. But neither of them cared. They only had eyes for each other. A scantily dressed nightclub employee guided them to their reserved table, where a cold bottle of champagne was waiting for them.

Ethan took Vivian's hand, kissed it, and caressed her wrist while saying, 'Hmm, something is missing here.' He looked at Vivian mischievously, then from his pocket withdrew a small black velvet bag. He opened it and peered inside. 'Here it is, the thing that's missing from your wrist.' Vivian watched him with wide eyes as he took out an exquisite bracelet and placed it on her wrist. It sparkled brightly under the nightclub's silvery lights.

'Ethan, it's beautiful.' She put her arms around his neck and kissed him passionately.

Ethan caressed the bracelet with his thumb and looked deep into her eyes. 'A woman like you shouldn't be wearing anything less than diamonds.'

Vivian was surprised. She thought it was zirconia. 'Diamonds? Ethan, I can't accept this!'

'Why not?' Vivian searched for the right words. 'Because it's too much to give this to someone like me.'

'First of all, you are not just "someone" Vivian. You are the woman of my dreams, and I want to be with you.

160

You deserve it. Secondly, these diamonds came from my father's mine, so the price is no issue. Of course, if a regular customer had purchased it, it would have been extraordinarily expensive. But I designed it and made it myself. It's one-of-a-kind. And now it has found its place on your wrist, which is exactly where it should be.'

Vivian's eyes filled with tears of happiness, love, and joy.

'Ethan, it is beautiful. I will cherish it forever.' He embraced her and kissed her fiercely.

After they'd finished the champagne and some fresh pastechi, a traditional Aruban snack, they walked hand in hand to the dancefloor. Pressed against each other they danced and grinded slowly, and it wasn't too long until Ethan shouted in her ear,

'Vivian, we have to go home now. Something is going to erupt in my pants.'

She laughed. 'Then let's go so I can help you with that.'

Back at the resort, as soon as they'd shut the door of Vivian's room, they undressed each other in a frenzy. Then they both stood naked, in awe of each other's bodies. Vivian could not keep her eyes off his pulsating cock, which pointed straight at her. She bit her bottom lip.

'What do you want?' his voice was dark and heavy. He always asked what Vivian wanted.

'What do you want, Ethan?'

'Do you really want to know?'

'Yes.'

'I want to jerk myself off, and I want you to watch me doing it. After I'm done, I want you to masturbate.'

It seemed Ethan never ran out of ideas. His proposition deeply aroused Vivian because she loved watching him touch himself. Vivian sat on the couch, staring up at him. Ethan gripped his cock and slowly stroked it. Just looking at it made Vivian feel the dampness spread between her thighs. She slowly licked her lips. Ethan's pace increased as he tightened his grip. He stood closer to her, staring at her lustfully as he pleasured himself.

'Vivian, lie down. I want to come on your breasts.'

She quickly lay down and with one foot on the couch he groaned, 'Yes… yes... Vivian!'

His cum splattered over her chest. Vivian rubbed it over her breasts and stomach. Her nipples stiffened instantly and she twisted and pulled on them gently.

Both her hands slid slowly down her stomach. She opened her legs as wide as possible. She wanted Ethan to see every part of her. With the fingers of her left hand she spread her slick folds, and with her right she rubbed her swollen clit, slowly at first, then faster, before pushing two fingers inside her. Groaning with pleasure, she quickened her pace. Her eyes were fixed on Ethan. When she came a few moments later she screamed his name.

'My God, that made me so horny.' Ethan helped Vivian to sit up straight and put her legs over his shoulders. He then buried his face between her legs.

Vivian squealed, still sensitive after her orgasm. Ethan licked and sucked her wet pussy vigorously, and the sounds stimulated her even more.

She gripped the back of his head and widened her legs. With his fingers and tongue in a steady thrusting motion, he gave her exactly what she wanted... another shuddering orgasm.

Ethan kissed her, and she could taste herself on his tongue. Vivian wanted to give him the same pleasure. She pushed him down on the couch, knelt in front of him and took him deep into her mouth. Ethan closed his eyes and threw his head back. Vivian licked his balls, then firmly gripped the base of his cock and wrapped her mouth around its tip, sucking the warm cum out of him. Ethan groaned and sprayed more cum into her mouth. Vivian pulled back and looked at Ethan mischievously.

'What?' Ethan snickered.

She just shook her head. She hadn't swallowed. Vivian grabbed Ethan's face and kissed him.

'Wow, what was that?'

'That was yours. You just tasted yourself.' Ethan kissed Vivian hard.

The next morning at breakfast, Vivian was lost in thought while Ethan read a newspaper. She sighed deeply, and Ethan turned to her. 'What's wrong, angel? You haven't been yourself this morning.'

'This is our last day. Tomorrow I go back home, back to reality.'

Ethan folded his newspaper and looked at Vivian worriedly.

'What are you afraid of?'

'What will happen to us now?' Vivian had managed to completely avoid this topic so far. She was aware that no one could know about her relationship, especially her friends.

Ethan took Vivian's hand. 'Angel, I know you're worried about your friend's reaction. If you face it calmly, we can handle this. No one has to find out that we're seeing each other. You can just come to Dubai every weekend.'

Vivian was relieved that Ethan was aware of her anxiety, and that he approached it calmly.

'Sounds like fun, but it's thirteen hours flight, right? That would mean I could only visit you for a day, and then I'd have to return the next day.'

Ethan raised his eyebrows and thought for a moment. 'You could suggest to your office that they extend your workdays to give you a long weekend every second week. In that case, we would have two full days.'

'I don't know. I'd have to think about it first.'

'You could always just quit your job, Angel. I can pay for everything you need.'

'Oh no, no way. I'm capable of taking care of myself. Besides, I love my job,' Vivian answered firmly.

'Okay, slow down, it was just a suggestion. We will find a solution. If necessary, I can visit you in New York. The only thing is that we won't be able to go outside.'

'I know. Let me talk to the office first and go from there.'
They spent the rest of the day by the pool in a world of their own.

At the airport, they embraced each other tightly.
'You have to go, Angel. Your flight is almost leaving.'
Vivian looked at him through tear-streaked eyes. Holding her face, Ethan wiped her tears with his thumbs. 'Don't cry, my dear. We'll meet again soon.'
'It's still two weeks away!'
Ethan kissed her gently. 'Two weeks will be over before you know it. I'll call you every night.'
'You promise?'
'Yes, I promise. Do you think I could sleep without hearing your voice?'
Vivian smiled and hugged him once more. Their last kiss was passionate and lingering. Vivian walked through immigration without looking back, because she knew if she did, she would run back to him and miss her flight.
The flight was tranquil, as she was one of only four passengers in business class. Vivian refused the champagne because it reminded her of Ethan. She missed him painfully already and felt terribly lonely without him. Now she understood what Ethan meant when he said that with her he felt complete. That exactly how she felt now. Vivian stared out the window of the plane and gently caressed the diamond bracelet on her wrist.

While waiting for her luggage, Vivian turned on her cellphone and a moment later a few text messages from Ethan appeared:

Angel, you just left, but I already miss you so much xxx

And then:
You are the best thing that has ever happened to me xxx.

Followed by:
I put the certificate of authenticity of the bracelet in your bag, keep it safe xxx.

Then finally:
I've never understood what love means... but now I have you in my life I'm starting to understand it. I love you, Angel.

Vivian became emotional. She held the phone close to her chest, and happy tears ran down her cheeks. The baggage conveyer belt started, and soon after she saw her suitcase emerge. Vivian quickly replied to Ethan:

Dear Ethan, I really enjoyed my vacation with you. I just landed and am waiting for my luggage. I also miss you very much, and I look forward to seeing you again. I miss your voice and your touch. You're also the best thing I've ever had in my life... I love you too. I can't wait to visit you in Dubai in two weeks and be in your arms again. Only in your arms, I feel safe and at home. Forever yours, Vivian xoxo

She looked up and realized her suitcase had passed her on the conveyer belt, so she chased after it wanting to leave the airport as quickly as possible.

Vivian opened the door to her apartment. Even though she missed Ethan, she was grateful to be home. She always loved being at home as it was her happy place comfort zone.

Whenever Vivian returned from a trip, she immediately unpacked her bags and washed her clothes, but this time Vivian felt reluctant to do so. She walked to the bathroom and turned on the tap for a hot bath.

After undressing, she went to remove the bracelet Ethan had given her, but decided against it. Ethan had said it was stainless, so there was no need to avoid water. After all, Vivian had promised him never to take it off.

She had just finished her bath when her phone beeped twice. She quickly wrapped a towel around herself and grabbed her phone. Her heart was beating fast, but it wasn't Ethan who'd texted her. The message was from Ferris. She felt both joy and disappointment. Although she was disappointed Ethan hadn't replied to her message yet, she couldn't deny she was excited to see that the words had come from Ferris.

Throughout all the time she'd known this man, he had never sent her a text message.

Her stomach fluttered, and with trembling hands she opened Ferris's message.

Hello, Vivian. Welcome back home. I hope you had a nice holiday even though you didn't want to go in the first place. Have a good weekend and see you on Monday. Greetings, Ferris.

She inhaled sharply, her heart beating wildly. She really thought she was over him after her time in Aruba with Ethan, but that couldn't be further from the truth.
Vivian read Ferris's message again and wondered whether she should reply. She couldn't resist out of curiosity as to whether he'd respond.

Hello, Ferris, thank you! I just got home, and in the end, my vacation was enjoyable.

Vivian hit the send button because she didn't know what else to add. Maybe she should have asked something about work, but it was too late, the message had already sent. Soon, there was a reply.

I'm glad you enjoyed your vacation. Surely the weather down there was good, huh?

Vivian threw off her towel, pulled on a bathrobe and sat on her bed. The butterflies nesting in her stomach danced with joy again. She beamed. She had already forgot about Ethan, and her mind was filled with Ferris's face. She longed to hear his voice.

Yes, the weather was lovely down there. The climate is so much better there. I loved the ocean breeze.

Vivian deliberately didn't ask questions about work because she didn't want their chat to return to its regular formality. Vivian had never made light conversation with Ferris, so she took the opportunity to go on.

Ah, I envy you. Aren't you tired after a long trip?

Vivian couldn't believe he kept asking questions, and was keeping the conversation going.

No, I'm not tired. I just finished taking a bath, and now I'm starving. But my refrigerator is empty.

So you haven't eaten anything yet?

No, I haven't, but I'm feeling too lazy to get dressed and go out to eat. I'm just glad to be home now.

Clutching her phone tightly, Vivian waited for a reply. This time it took a little longer for Ferris to answer.

I haven't eaten yet too. If you'd like, I'll get some take out and we can eat together. It will give us time to discuss work matters because it's going to be crazy during the next few weeks.

With wide eyes, Vivian read the message many times, her heart rate increasing by the second. She couldn't deny she still had very deep feelings for this man. Even Ethan couldn't change that. Could Vivian invite him over after everything that had happened with Ethan? What would Ethan think if he found out? Why was she so confused? After all, Ferris had only suggested they eat take out together, and it wouldn't be the first time they shared a meal. Vivian reassured herself that Ferris wasn't interested in her at all.

 Her phone beeped again, and Vivian almost slammed it down in surprise.

Vivian?

After frantically weighing it up, she decided to take Ferris up on his offer.

I really would appreciate it, if you don't mind taking the trouble.

No trouble at all. What would you like to eat?

Surprise me.

Well, okay then. I'll be there in a half-hour.

Vivian sat petrified on her bed. Her time with Ethan had convinced her she was completely over Ferris. She was also certain she loved Ethan, but now she was beginning to doubt her feelings.

Vivian combed her hair, which was still wet after her bath. She had to hurry because Ferris would arrive soon and she couldn't meet him wearing only a robe. Twenty minutes later, casually dressed and with no makeup and her slightly damp hair loose, Vivian opened the door for Ferris. Her heart raced when she saw this handsome man standing in her doorway, holding two plastic bags of take out.

'I hope you like Italian food?'

Vivian invited Ferris inside while answering, 'Italian is perfect, thank you.'

Ferris followed Vivian to the kitchen and placed the bags on the counter.

'You look good. I've never seen you with your hair down. It suits you.'

Vivian blushed, lost for words. 'Uhh... thank you, Ferris.'

Even though Vivian preferred to sit at the bar,

she wanted a more intimate dining atmosphere, so she chose to sit at the dining table. Vivian set the table while Ferris removed the containers of pasta from the plastic bags. 'Where do you keep your bottle opener?' he asked.

'In the first drawer next to the fridge.'

Ferris placed their dinner on the table, then walked back to the kitchen. He returned to the dining table with two glasses and a bottle of red wine.

Ferris looked completely at ease in Vivian's apartment. He sat down across from her, poured wine into each glass and handed her one.

'Cheers.' They said together while lifting their glasses. Vivian sipped the wine and starred at Ferris in surprise. Two years before, during a business dinner with George and Ferris at an Italian restaurant, Vivian had tried the exact same wine and loved it. None of them knew the name of the winemaker at the time, but it dawned on Vivian that Ferris had remembered she'd been very fond of it.

'You found it!' Vivian exclaimed.

'Yes, I was in luck. I was a speaker at a seminar recently, and this wine was served at dinner.'

Vivian sipped her glass. Even though she'd only drank expensive champagnes during her vacation, she felt this wine was far superior.

'Please remind me to write down the name of this exquisite wine so I can buy some.'

172

'It's a Barbaresco, one of Italy's finest. That's why we're also having Italian food.'

Vivian gazed at him appreciatively. For the very first time she was able to talk with him casually. 'Let's eat before it gets cold.' Everything looked extremely tasty: cannelloni, lasagna, and ravioli. Vivian adored Italian food, and tasted each dish one by one. While Vivian ate, Ferris suddenly lit a large candle on Vivian's dining table, accentuating the intimate atmosphere. During dinner, Vivian discussed many things, including her vacation, but of course she didn't say a word about Ethan. When they'd finished eating Vivian thanked Ferris again.

'That was absolutely delicious.'

Ferris stood up and brought their plates to the kitchen. 'I hope you have room left for dessert.' Vivian watched him as he moved about the kitchen. All she really wanted was to wrap her arms around his neck and kiss him passionately. Ferris returned with two slices of tiramisu.

'Oh Ferris, this will ruin my figure!'

He looked at Vivian closely. 'There is absolutely nothing wrong with your figure.'

The way Ferris said it in his deep, gravelly voice made Vivian's nipples stiffen, and they became visible through the thin fabric of her t-shirt. Ferris's eyes darted toward her chest and then he looked away quickly. Vivian thought she could see a splash of red in Ferris's cheeks, but she wasn't entirely sure because he'd looked the other way.

'This is truly the best tiramisu in town. It's almost the same as in Italy.'

'Yes, it is delicious, Ferris.'

He poured the last of the wine into their glasses, and Vivian began to wonder if he would start talking about work. She really hoped he wouldn't. What she really wanted to ask about were his previous relationships, but she didn't dare to do so. She also wished she could be honest with him and reveal that she had fallen for him the moment they'd met, but of course she couldn't say that either. He looked at his watch, drank his last sip of wine, and said, 'It's late. I'd better go so you can rest.'

Vivian panicked. She didn't want him to leave. 'How could I be tired? I just spent the last three weeks doing nothing,' she lied. 'Should I make coffee, then you can tell me about the busy period in the office we're expecting?'

'No, thank you Vivian. It's better that I go home. Technically it's still your vacation. Work can wait until Monday.' He stood up, searched for his key in his pocket, then walked toward the front door. Vivian followed Ferris's steps as she sank with disappointment.

'Ferris?' He was grasping the door handle when Vivian called him.

'Yes?'

'Thank you so much for dinner, and especially the wine,' she said wistfully, her eyes brimming with hope.

Unexpectedly, Ferris reached out and tucked a strand of hair behind her ear.

'You're very welcome. You must wear your hair down more often. It looks good on you.'

From the window, Vivian watched his Range Rover drive away. Completely confused, she sat on the couch and went over everything that had just happened. During all the years she'd known him, Vivian had never seen him so relaxed and comfortable as he was that night. She was certain he had enjoyed her company as a person, rather than just a colleague. She also suspected he was trying to please her with the delicious dinner and the special wine. What was going on? Vivian didn't want to think about it anymore and went to bed, hoping for a good night's sleep.

CHAPTER 12

Dawn had just broken, and Vivian was already busy. She unpacked her suitcase, did her laundry, and cleaned her entire apartment. She deliberately kept herself occupied so she wouldn't drown in her worries, and sent her friends and Edward a message letting them know she'd returned. Salfina had replied that she would swing by in an hour or two.

Vivian was looking forward to seeing her best friend so she could tell her all about Ferris. Of course, she couldn't say a word about Ethan because her friends would launch into a frenzy if they found out. Vivian was desperate to discuss Ferris with Salfina, so she could help her decide which road she should choose.

'Hey, Viv, you look good girlfriend!' Salfina hugged Vivian and took a good look at her.

'What's up? Is there anything you want to share?'

'What makes you think I have something to share Sal?'

'Come on, Viv, I know you. I can tell by the look on your face something is bothering you.'

Vivian walked into the kitchen to make some coffee. 'Ferris. That's what's bothering me.'

Upon hearing this, Salfina rolled her eyes. 'What about him?'

Vivian told her what had happened the previous night, and Salfina listened gingerly. 'So, correct me if I'm wrong, but that was your first time eating together and chatting casually?'

'Yes and… he looked at my breasts.'

Salfina laughed. 'What's so special about that? All straight men like to look at boobs. They're obsessed with them.'

'Not Ferris,' Vivian defended him. 'I don't know what to do Sal. How should I handle him?'

'You have to face it. The only thing you can do is to be upfront with him. Tell him how you feel. What do you have to lose?'

'Sal! We're colleagues! What if after I revealed the truth about how I feel about it, he rejects me? I still have to work with him, you know.'

Salfina thought for a second. 'If that's the case, I would accept the job offer from your mom, so you don't have to deal with this man anymore and open a new chapter in your life.' Vivian considered her friend's words. She felt Salfina was right, but the problem was, she wasn't sure she could work for her mom.

'That's a nice bracelet.' Salfina's remark startled her.

'Thanks.'

'Where did you get it? I want one too!'

'Uhh, I bought it at the flea market in Aruba,' she lied. Disappointed, Salfina returned to the subject at hand. 'Viv, I think you should tell Ferris the truth. Maybe yesterday he was testing the water, to see if you are also interested in him. It makes perfect sense that because his previous relationship fell apart, he'd be far more wary about how he approached women after that.'

Vivian had never thought about this possibility. Maybe Salfina was right, maybe there was still hope for her.

'Yes, maybe you're right, Sal.'

'Of course I am, Viv. Aunt Sally is always right. If I were you, I would simply wait for the right moment.' Salfina glanced at her watch. 'Gotta go, Viv. I have lunch at Jake's parent's house, and it's almost a two-hour drive.'

'I'm glad your relationship is working out well with Jake, you're glowing!'

'Yeah, me too. It's getting serious now. We decided to move in together.'

'Awesome, I'm so happy for you Sal! I know how much you wanted that.'

They hugged each other tightly.

'Be honest with Ferris, Viv. I'm sure luck will come your way too.'

Vivian had just returned from grocery shopping when her phone rang. No name appeared on the screen.

'Hello, this is Vivian Foster.'

'Hi, Angel.'

Vivian caught her breath when she heard Ethan's voice. She had completely forgotten about him, and was suddenly overwhelmed with guilt. 'Hi, Ethan.'

There was an awkward silence. 'Am I disturbing you?' His voice was gruff and low. Vivian recognized arousal in his tone.

'No, no of course not. I've been waiting for you to call,' she lied. Vivian was aware that she'd being lying a lot lately, and she didn't like it at all.

'I miss you Angel. I feel empty and lonely. My bed is cold without you.'

Ethan's voice made her realize she really did have deep feelings for him.

'I miss you too, Ethan,' she sighed, as her breathing sped up.

'Vivian I need you. I feel numb when I think about you, and hearing your voice hurts.'

In her mind, she pictured Ethan pleasuring himself. 'If I were there, I would free you from that torment.' Vivian heard him breathe heavily, and she pressed her thighs together because she knew exactly what he was doing. Their conversation became tense and lustful.

'Ooohh... Vivian.. oh my God... I'm coming...'

Vivian listened to Ethan climax, which made her tremble. It didn't take long for her to feel how wet she was between her thighs.

'Sorry, Angel. I couldn't help myself,' Ethan apologized.

'No, I enjoyed it. Are you in bed?'

'Yes, I am. I promised you I'd call before going to sleep.'

'Ethan?' her voice was shaking.

'What is it, Viv?'

'I miss you.'

'Are you aroused too, honey?'

'Yes, very.'

'Good to know you feel the same way too.'

She closed her eyes and wished he was with her now.

'It's late here. I need to try to get some sleep. Tomorrow I have an important appointment with a religious leader. I'll call again tomorrow ok, Angel?'

Vivian took a deep breath. She wanted to talk longer, but she was aware of the time difference. 'Okay, Ethan, good luck for tomorrow. Sleep well.' Vivian sat on the soft couch while staring at the ceiling. Was it possible? Was it possible to fall deeply in love with two men at the same time?

During the call, she was certain she had strong feelings for Ethan, but at the same time, she knew how she felt about Ferris. Everything felt so unclear. What were her feelings for Ethan exactly? Was it love? Or did she just enjoy the sex?

For a long time, Vivian hadn't enjoyed sex so much, but with Ethan, everything was wild, rough, and fun. She experienced things she'd never felt before. From her friend's stories and her own experiences, she knew that usually men were satisfied once they'd climaxed, but Ethan was different.

His sexual desire was insatiable. Many times he had woken her up in the early hours because he needed to have her. And then there was Ferris. Both men seemed to be the opposite. Ethan was young and spirited and sociable, while Ferris had a calm and assured aura. The day before Vivian had seen a different side to him which made her feel completely comfortable.

She knew she had to choose.

The next day, Vivian left for work an hour earlier than she usually did, so she could ease into the work rush. Even though she and Ferris were now sharing an office, she hoped she could still enjoy her job. The office was still quiet as her colleagues were yet to arrive. Vivian enjoyed the silence and tranquility. When she opened the office door however, Ferris was already there.

Ferris turned toward Vivian, an enticing smile spreading across his lips.

'Good morning. You're early!'

Vivian walked to her desk and put her handbag in the bottom drawer. 'Yes, my vacation was long enough. I can't wait to get back to work.' She turned on her computer and saw a pile of envelopes on her desk. While waiting for her computer to load, she looked at Ferris. 'Do you want to fill me in now or later?'

'Later, I've got a meeting soon.' Ferris sat opposite Vivian with a large folder in hand. His scent distracted her. Ferris had reverted back to his usual rigid self, and Vivian wondered how she could ever reveal her feelings to him if he always acted like this. She had to be patient, even though all she wanted was clarity. Like Salfina said, she needed to wait for the right moment.

'Vivian, I'm heading off to my meeting now, and won't be back in the office today. You can still reach me by phone if you need anything.'

'Ah... all right. See you tomorrow then.'

Vivian spent the entire day managing her correspondence and replying to emails. Her inbox was filled with messages from dozens of about a huge range of items she had sought out for the designers it was her responsibility to bargain for them. She would call the auction houses the following day.

Her first day back had passed so quickly, and now she was ready to go home. She decided to call Edward first to ask if she could visit.

The distance between George's house and the office was only fifteen minutes by car. Ralph the doorman welcomed Vivian with his usual sincere and friendly smile, and Vivian glowed. She was happy to finally be able to visit George, and she couldn't wait to tell him about Ferris.

Edward was waiting for Vivian on their doorstep when the lift's doors opened. He looked thinner compared to when she'd last seen him.

'Hello, Edward.'

'Hello, Vivian. You look beautiful as usual. The sun in Aruba has blessed you.'

'Thank you. How are things here?'

'Not too good.'

With a pounding heart, Vivian followed Edward to the kitchen, then sat down beside him. He took Vivian's hand and squeezed it gently.

'Vivian, I think it's just a matter of time before he leaves us.'

Her breath snagged in her throat. She looked at Edward but nothing came out of her mouth.

'A few weeks ago, his condition severely declined. Now he's on morphine to reduce the pain. The doctors increase his dose each day.' Tears flowed down his cheeks.

'Edward, I'm so sorry... can I see him?'

'No, I'm afraid not, sweetheart. He's sleeping.'

Vivian got up from her chair and began to pace. She was angry with herself. For two whole weeks she was having fun, and only thinking about herself and Ethan, while she should have been there accompanying Edward.

'But... why didn't you call me? You promised to let me know if George's condition changed?'

He took a deep breath and gazed at her sadly. 'George made me absolutely promise not to. He wanted you to go and have fun, to be around people your own age.'

'That's just wrong. I should have stayed home.'

'It wouldn't have made any difference. You know how stubborn George is. Have you eaten yet?'

She had absolutely zero appetite.

'No I haven't, I've just come straight from the office.'

'I just made some soup. Do you want me to reheat it?'

She knew Edward's intentions were good, but she knew her stomach couldn't handle anything.

'Thank you, Edward, but I'm afraid I just can't eat anything right now.'

'Come on, Vivian. You must eat something.'

'Okay, I will, thank you. In a minute.'

Edward got up and caressed her cheek. 'Good girl, we'll eat together.'

They sat next to each other while enjoying the creamy pumpkin soup, which was laced with nutmeg. It was very comforting.

'You are a fantastic cook, Edward.'

Edward replied with a small smile, 'It's true. Cooking is my passion. I'm actually writing a cookbook containing all of George's favorite recipes, and believe me, the man has so many I'm wondering whether they'll all fit into just one book!'

They spent the rest of the evening sharing their favorite memories of George. When it was ten o'clock, Vivian decided it was time to go home. She promised to return on Wednesday.

When she arrived at her apartment, she saw four missed calls from Ethan. This time his number wasn't anonymous, but he hadn't left any voicemail messages. She glanced at her watch. It was ten-thirty. She calculated the time difference; it was almost seven in the morning in Dubai. Vivian began to feel annoyed by the time difference. They really needed to schedule a fixed time to call, otherwise they'd never succeed in contacting each other. She decided to call Ethan after she'd taken a bath. On her second day back, Vivian arrived earlier than Ferris. As Ferris suggested, she'd worn her hair down with the pale yellow blouse from Aruba and black pants.

Vivian looked gorgeous, even though she'd hardly slept at all the previous night. The office door opened, and Ferris walked in. As usual, he looked extremely handsome. His hair was still wet from the shower. He looked surprised when he saw Vivian and quickly checked his watch.

'I thought I was late, but you're the one who's in early.'

'Yes, I couldn't sleep last night. Yesterday after work I visited Edward. George's condition is getting worse. The doctors are giving him high doses of morphine.'

'I'm sorry to hear that Vivian. But sadly we knew this would happen sooner or later. Can I get you a coffee?'

'Yes please, café latte would be nice.'

Ferris returned with her café latte and a cappuccino. He looked at Vivian the same way he had a few days before at her dining table. Vivian pretended not to notice as she sipped her coffee.

'This is good, thank you.'

'You're welcome,' he said politely. Ferris sipped his and looked at Vivian from behind his cup.

'Did you see him?'

Vivian shook her head and said nothing. Ferris knew that Vivian didn't want to talk about it. Throughout the morning they sat in silence, occupied with their work.

'It's time for lunch.' Ferris stood next to her desk, and she looked at her watch in surprise.

'Oh my goodness, is it that time already?' Vivian took her bag from the bottom of the drawer.

'Where would you like to eat?' asked Ferris.

'I don't care. As long as it's not crowded.'

'I know a nice quiet place.'

Together they waited for the lift. When the doors opened, Ferris put his hand gently on Vivian's back to let her enter first. His hand made her back tremble, the vibrations spreading throughout her body.

He took her to a small restaurant that only served breakfast and lunch. The restaurant's decor was cozy and made her feel warm. Their table was small, so every now and then their knees touched. Vivian ordered a salad and an orange juice while Ferris decided on an omelet.

'It's nice to see that you followed my advice.'

Vivian looked at him questioningly.

'You're wearing your hair down, and the color of your blouse suits you so well.'

Vivian's face flushed. She was pleased because she'd succeeded in attracting Ferris with her hair and her clothes.

'Uhh... thank you.' She glanced around the restaurant timidly while Ferris grew more relaxed, brushing his alluring lips with his thumb.

'You really don't know how to receive compliments properly, do you?'

'No I don't, sorry,' she apologized.

'How come?'

'I don't know. I guess I'm just never sure how to respond.'

Vivian was secretly happy that their conversation was flowing smoothly again. She was confident he was trying to lure her. Was this the right time to express her feelings to him? Maybe the timing felt right, but it wasn't the right place to do so. Vivian searched for other conversation topics. 'By the way, I bought a case of that delicious Barbaresco yesterday.'

Ferris smiled at her. She knew that he knew why she'd attempted to change the subject. He was being a gentleman and didn't say anything further about it.

On the way back to the office, Vivian asked Ferris if they could drop by the William Doyle auction house to inspect some of the items one of the designers had requested. When they'd arrived, Vivian couldn't find what the designers had asked for, but a large Renaissance painting of a half-naked woman surrounded by angels caught her eye. She gazed at it in awe, and thought it would be perfect for her apartment. She would return later to purchase it.

When they returned to the office Vivian's happiness quickly subsided, because Ferris returned to his usual rigid self.

'Vivian, clear your agenda for this weekend because there is an important meeting in Shanghai.'

'Shanghai? This weekend?' Vivian panicked. She'd already promised to visit Ethan in Dubai and had completely forgotten to schedule an appointment with Sean and Clive to negotiate an adjustment to her working hours.

'Yes, we're about to launch a major project there.'

She'd never been to Shanghai. This city was on top of her list to visit someday.

'I have nothing planned for this weekend, so my schedule is clear.' Another lie.

'Terrific. If you'd like we can extend the trip by a day for sightseeing. I've heard so many wonderful things about Shanghai. What do you say?'

Her choice was easily made. 'That would be great. I've wanted to visit that city for such a long time, so I'm really excited!'

As the week went by, Vivian often sat in silence for hours next to George's bed. She was no longer able to communicate with him as he slept most of the time. She called Ethan each night, who was disappointed because she kept delaying her visit to Dubai. Vivian's work relationship with Ferris was going well he was no longer stern and overly formal with her. After visiting Trisha in San Francisco, Vivian realized she missed her old position. In the new role her freedom and opportunities to use her creativity had been lost. After proposing new working hours with Sean and Clive, she got what she wanted, which made Ethan happy. He suggested coming to New York on her short weekends, but she wasn't sure how she felt about it. Vivian was browsing auction house items online one morning when the phone rang.

Without looking at the screen she answered, 'Good afternoon, Frenay & Iams, this is Vivian Foster.'

'Vivian, this is Edward.'

'Edward?' her eyes widened, and Ferris looked up at her.

'Vivian, George is conscious, and he asked about you. I know you're working, but if you want to see him and talk to him, you should come now.'

'Now?' Vivian repeated and peered at Ferris, who nodded in agreement. Without hearing the conversation, he had guessed what had been said. 'I'm on my way.' She stood up and glanced at Ferris.

'Go on, take all the time you need. I'll see you tomorrow.'

'Thank you, Ferris. I owe you one.'

He smiled at her. 'You're welcome. Call me if you need me.'

CHAPTER 13

Vivian exited the lift and ran toward Edward, who was waiting by the door.

'Come quickly, my dear. I don't know how long he'll be awake.' Vivian followed Edward across the polished wooden floorboards. The clack of her heels was too loud in her ears, and it irritated her. Edward opened the bedroom door carefully, and Vivian stopped at the door in shock. George looked awful. He was skin and bone, he was completely emaciated. Vivian tried to control herself. It was not the time to show sadness and pain. She had to be thankful she could finally see him again while he was conscious With her shoulders back, she walked to his bedside. He looked drastically different from the last time she saw him. His eyes were sunken, and his cheekbones protruded through his sallow skin. Vivian watched him struggle to sit up and smile.

'Hello, dear. It's so nice to see you again,' he touched Vivian's hand. 'How is it back at work?'

Vivian wanted to be as casual as possible with him and not focus on his illness. 'Ah, you know what it's like, always busy, busy, busy.'

'Yes, I know dear. You know I've put in my time there. What are you focusing on now?'

'Ferris and I will go to Shanghai this weekend to meet clients.'

'Wow... Shanghai sounds exciting.'

Vivian then updated George on all the latest gossip, and she could see how it was a welcoming distraction for him. She didn't mention Ferris or Ethan – the last thing she wanted to do was to make him worry about her. Edward entered the room with tea, and Vivian told them about Aruba's glorious climate and local cuisine. She could see George started to look exhausted, but she knew he wouldn't send her away.

'Oh my, it's already this late? I'm afraid it's time to go home.' Vivian noticed Edward's relieved face.

'Wait a minute,' George took her hand and turned to Edward. 'Honey, can you get that velvet bag in the drawer?' Edward did what George asked.

'Vicky also had a room here, even though she rarely stayed in it. When we cleaned up her room, I found this.' George lifted the velvet bag and gave it to Vivian. 'I want you to have this.' With trembling hands she accepted the little black bag, and opened it. It was a silver hair ornament adorned with crystals.

'This is lovely, George. Are you sure you want me to have it?'

'Yes, I'm sure Victoria would agree.' Vivian hugged his frail body with utmost care.

'Thank you, George.'

'I'm sure this will look good against your brown hair. It might be even more suitable than Vicky's blond hair.' For a moment, Vivian didn't know what to say. She gently kissed George's forehead.

'I will wear it proudly and treasure it forever.' Vivian said goodbye and walked with Edward to the lift.

'When I could visit again, Edward?'

'Come Thursday night. We can have dinner together then we'll see if George is up for a chat.'

'Okay, I'll come straight after work. Thank you Edward. See you.' They parted, and Vivian entered the lift. Before the doors closes, Edward winked at her. On her way home, Vivian called Ferris to let him know she wouldn't return to the office that day, and asked him the name of the Italian restaurant where he'd bought their take out.

Vivian dropped by William Doyle's auction house to buy the painting she wanted. When she found out someone had already purchased it, the disappointment was crushing. It hit her hardest when she sat at the dining table, staring at her salad which she stabbed with her fork.

For the very first time, Vivian felt uncomfortable living alone. She desperately wanted to share her life with someone, but with whom? She had feelings for both men and knew she had to make a decision very soon because she couldn't go on like this.

Working was the best remedy to take her mind off her anguish. After a few hours, Vivian left her computer and filled the tub with warm water. It was late, and Vivian wanted to take a bath before she called Ethan. The relaxing aroma of bath salts filled the room.

Vivian stood in front of the mirror and removed the hair ornament from its velvet bag.

With one hand, she combed her hair to one side and with the other, she clipped in the silver piece. George was right. The sparkling crystals looked stunning in her brown hair.

She admired the ornament until she saw a glimpse of Victoria's reflection, who stood smiling behind her. Vivian was astonished, but she wasn't scared, as this wasn't the first time Victoria had appeared in the mirror. Her astonishment came from the fact that Victoria's reflection seemed so real. She thought about what George had said that day, and felt quite sure that she was resting in peace.

With her fingertips wrinkled from the bath, she sat on her bed with her phone in hand. She took several deep breaths before she decided to call Ethan. After a few moments, he picked up.

'My Angel. You called at the right time. I'm so turned on. If you were here, I'd fuck you hard and deep over and over, until you begged me to stop. Tell me that turns you on. Say it to me!' His aggressive tone was new to her.

'Yes.'

'Yes what?' She could hear the dominance in his voice and she kind of liked it.

'Yes, Ethan, it turns me on.' Her voice sounded weak, and she pressed her thighs together firmly.

'Good girl. Now tell me, what are you wearing?'

She swallowed hard before answering, 'Just a bathrobe.'

'Hmm, nothing else?'

'No, I just took a bath.'

'Open your bathrobe.' Ethan was showing his dominant side and Vivian obediently did what he said.

'Touch your breasts.'

Vivian panted and moaned as she did what he ordered. Her breathing became faster as she massaged her breasts.

'I can picture your hard nipples and the way you bite your sexy lips.'

Vivian was no longer able to speak. She could hear Ethan pleasuring himself on the other end of the phone. His breathing was just as irregular as hers.

'Touch yourself, play with yourself. Let me hear your voice. I want to hear you.'

With her right hand, she squeezed her breasts and tugged her nipples, then her hand slid down her stomach. She lay back, spread her legs wide, then with two fingers began rubbing her glistening clit. When her whole body was tingling, she plunged her fingers in, then vigorously sunk them in over and over, a little deeper each time. She moaned loudly, then sighed and groaned while Ethan did the same.

Her fingers moved rapidly, and she realized she'd soon reach her climax. Even though she was enjoying it, she yearned to feel Ethan inside her.

'Vivian... have you come yet? I'm almost there...'

'Oh yeah... God... Ethan... I can't hold it anymore.'

It took a while for their breathing to return to normal. They talked a little and Ethan told her how much he was looking forward to seeing her again. He also said he had a small surprise for her. Vivian tried to guess what it was, but Ethan wasn't revealing anything. Finally, they ended the conversation because Ethan had to prepare for work. Once again, Vivian was annoyed by the time difference, even though in the end she could sleep soundly.

The rest of the week passed by quickly. Vivian and Ferris worked hard to prepare for their presentation in Shanghai. She looked forward to their departure. Vivian was reading her last email while Ferris tidied up his desk then shut down his computer.

'Do you want to grab a bite to eat together?'

Vivian looked at him in surprise. She had no idea where the question had come from. 'I have an appointment,' she said hastily. Vivian thought she could see disappointment in Ferris's eyes, but she wasn't sure. 'Let me see if I can delay it.'

'No, that's not necessary. See you later at the airport. Actually, it's probably easier if I pick you up, so we don't have to park two cars.'

'Yes, that's a good idea,' Vivian agreed.

'Fine then, I'll pick you up at three. Good evening, see you later tonight.'

'See you later.'

Ferris left, and Vivian stared at the closed door.

Lately, she had received varied signals from Ferris, making it even more difficult for her to read him.

Vivian battled heavy traffic on the way to George and Edward's, so it took much longer to reach their home than usual. Ralph opened the door for her and smiled. When she exited the lift, George's apartment door was open for her. She walked inside, and her stomach immediately rattled because of the tantalizing aroma wafting from the kitchen.

'Edward?'

He was busy stirring something in a skillet. 'Hi, sweetheart. Please sit down. I'm still busy with dinner, I can't leave it.' He turned and winked at Vivian. 'If you want something to drink, please help yourself.'

'Okay.' Vivian opened the fridge and took a ginger ale then returned to the kitchen table and sat down.

'How's George?'

'He's exhausted and went to sleep. Today his ex-wife visited. She didn't know that George is sick. She found out from someone or other and immediately came here. After Vicky's death, they haven't kept in touch.'

'Goodness, was he surprised?'

'Yes, of course.' Edward turned around with a spoon in his hand.

'Taste this. I'm just experimenting, so don't ask me what it's called.'

Vivian took the spoon and tasted it. 'Edward, this is yummy…

No, that's not right, this is heavenly! What's it called?'

Edward chuckled. 'I told you, don't ask what it's called. I combined a nice cut of beef with various seasonal vegetables and my favorite Middle Eastern spice blends, and this is the result.'

'I really like it. I hope you still remember all the ingredients because I want the recipe.'

'Of course, I'll write it down for you later.'

After they'd finished eating and done the dishes, Vivian and Edward drank coffee together.

'Edward, I'm anxious.'

'What's bothering you, sweetheart?'

'Ferris.' She took a deep breath, 'Lately I've been getting mixed signals from him. I don't know how to deal with it anymore.'

She told Edward everything, including what had happened after her vacation when Ferris brought over take out and stole a glimpse at her breasts. She explained that he was suddenly showering her with compliments and had even asked her to dinner earlier. Rubbing his chin, Edward listened attentively.

'I don't know what happened in his past, but I think he is meticulously trying not to get hurt again. Maybe he is considering a relationship, but he wants to see how women react to him. However, it's just a wild guess.'

Vivian shifted in her seat. 'My friend recently suggested that I should just come clean and express my feelings for him.

What do you think?'

Edward thought for a moment and sipped his coffee. 'To be honest, I don't think that's a good idea. For a fact, we don't know exactly what happened to him. Maybe because of you, he's starting to feel more comfortable around women. If you declare your feelings to him now, perhaps the wall that he is slowly tearing down will be built right back up again, only this time higher than before. Give him space and time to explore these new feelings. If I were you, Vivian, I would do nothing. Let him heal.'

Vivian listened earnestly to Edward's advice. 'I've never thought of it this way. You might be right, Edward.' Vivian felt quietly relieved and cheerful. Maybe there was still hope.

Later at home, she prepared for her departure to Shanghai and checked her luggage for the last time. If she called Ethan now, she could lie down for an hour and a half before Ferris picked her up. The dial tone rang, but then went to voicemail. Even though she hated to, Vivian left a message saying she would call again as soon as she returned from Shanghai.

Vivian lay down on her bed and stared at the ceiling. Edward's words about Ferris echoed in her mind, preventing her from falling asleep. He was right. She had to give Ferris space so he could heal.

Because she couldn't sleep, Vivian browsed Shanghai's tourist attractions and made a list: the Bund, the Oriental Pearl Tower, Waibaidu Bridge, and the Jade Buddha Temple.

There were so many places she wanted to visit, but she knew they couldn't see them all in one day. Vivian stood at the window and looked down to the street. It was almost completely still. Occasionally a taxi passed, but no more than that. Suddenly she saw a Range Rover appear, making her heart pound. She glanced at the clock; it was only two. Didn't Ferris say he would come at three?

Vivian opened the door and invited him in. Ferris gave her a warm smile that made her skin flutter.

'Hello,' he said softly. It was almost a whisper.

'Hi, you're early,' Vivian whispered too to tease him. He followed her into the kitchen and looked at her from head to toe. Vivian loved having him in her home; it felt so natural, like he belonged there.

'Would you like some coffee?' Vivian asked, still in a whisper.

'If it's not too much trouble.'

'No trouble at all. Tell me, Ferris, why are we whispering?' Ferris laughed. 'I don't know, maybe because it's the middle of the night.'

Vivian laughed too, poured the coffee, and passed a cup to Ferris. Their fingers touched, and she felt tremors all over her body. With his coffee in hand, Ferris strolled around Vivian's apartment, looking intently at her artwork and various objects. Vivian had acquired her collection during her business trips over the years.

'Your apartment sure is cozy. How long have you lived here?'

'Thank you. It's been six years now.'

Ferris faced Vivian while leaning casually against a wall. 'Is this the original layout?'

Vivian sipped her coffee and turned to Ferris. 'No, it isn't. My mother is an architect. She did a whole new layout.'

Ferris placed his cup on the dining table. When he passed her, his sharp, woody aftershave tickled her nose, and she noticed his hair was still half wet, which she found incredibly sexy.

'I'm still looking for someone who wants to work on my apartment.'

'You're looking straight at her. Renovation or redesign?'

'Redesign. I like the layout of my apartment but I need a new interior.'

Vivian was thrilled by this news. She didn't even know where he lived and whether he'd lived with his former lover. There were so many details to discover.

'If you like, you can come and take a look after Shanghai.'

'With pleasure.'

Ferris glanced at his watch. 'It's time to go.'

'Give me a minute. I'll just rinse these cups real quick.'

Ten minutes later, they were on their way to the airport.

The streets were empty so they arrived with plenty of time to spare. On their flight there was only one other passenger in business class, while economy was packed. Once the plane was cruising, an attractive blond flight attendant brought them champagne. Vivian noticed how she vied for Ferris's attention, but he didn't seem to take any notice. He just took the two glasses and gave one to Vivian.

'Cheers to Shanghai!'

'Cheers,' Vivian said before sipping her champagne. Over the next few hours they discussed various documents required for their presentation, but when the lights dimmed they figured they'd better try and get some sleep.

They tidied up the documents and began to relax. On his personal screen Ferris watched a nature documentary, while Vivian watched Marilyn Monroe's classic film, *Some Like It Hot*.

Even though their business class seats were spacious, their arms and hands brushed several times, and each time Vivian's skin tingled even more. Although she was trying to watch the film, Vivian's mind drifted and she soon fell asleep.

Not long after, she awoke because her shoulder ached. She tried to move, but it was difficult. She opened her eyes and saw what was causing the slight pain. Ferris was sleeping soundly on her shoulder. She could smell his woody aftershave. All she wanted was to stroke his thick black hair, but she didn't dare. Ferris slept peacefully. After a few moments she shifted his head slightly back so she could see his desirable lips. Because he was sleeping soundly, his slightly parted lips quivered with every breath. His mouth was so close to hers she could easily kiss him, but once again, she didn't dare.

She could only stare at him with fascination, admire him without him knowing.

She wondered how someone could ever hurt him and break him like that. What kind of person was she? Did she regret it now? Vivian realized she was angry with this woman, but at the same time, she knew it was a waste of energy.

If Vivian had the chance to be with this man, she would do everything to make him happy and help him forget the past. As if Ferris could sense that Vivian was watching him, he slowly opened his eyes and gazed intensely at her for a few seconds. He quickly apologized and sat up straight while looking at his watch. 'We're almost there. I've slept too long, did you get any sleep?'

Vivian looked at hers. It was three hours until they'd land.

'Yes, I just woke up,' she lied. The flight attendant brought breakfast, and Vivian was annoyed because she'd deliberately unbuttoned the top button of her uniform. Fortunately, Ferris didn't show the least bit of interest.

CHAPTER 14

At the Pudong Airport international arrivals terminal, a driver stood waiting with a sign that read 'Vivian and Ferris.' As VIP guests, they were both welcomed to exit from a side door where a luxurious Bentley was waiting. The driver politely opened the door, and they both slid into the plush back seat.

'What a gorgeous car,' Vivian remarked, 'But a little bit over the top for my taste.'

Ferris chuckled. 'I get the feeling that everything will be a little bit over the top.

Our billionaire client likes to show off his money. He's invited us to have dinner before we start the negations tomorrow.

'I'm already curious about his restaurant choice,' Vivian said playfully.

'When we arrive at the hotel, we can rest for a bit if you want.'

'Are you kidding? I don't want to waste a second of my time resting. I want to go out and explore. I don't know which hotel we're staying in, but there must be something to see around.'

Ferris laughed. 'I'm sure there will be a lot to see.'

'You know which hotel we're staying in, right?'

'Oh yes, I know.'

'Really?' asked Vivian in disbelief.

'Yes.'

'Tell me. Maybe I'll know some of the surrounding attractions.

I've already googled some interesting ones, such as The Bund and Oriental Pearl Tower and the bridge – I've forgotten its name.'

Vivian was so enthusiastic that Ferris laughed at her.

'Come on, Ferris. Tell me, where are we staying?'

He gave in. 'Waldorf Astoria on the Bund.'

Vivian's eyes bulged. 'Are you for real!?'

'Why would I lie? It's on The Bund, so there are three tourist attractions that we can easily visit.'

Vivian could barely contain her happiness. The car stopped in front of the majestic hotel its facade alone was worth the visit. A porter opened the door of the Bentley, helped them out, and placed their belongings on a trolley.

In the lobby, Vivian's eyes feasted on the magnificent neo-classical building. Its rich historical architecture had been meticulously restored and combined with breathtakingly elegant sophistication. Even though Vivian was an interior designer herself, she wouldn't change a thing. Her eyes drifted over to Ferris at the reception desk. Vivian noticed that all the female employees couldn't keep their eyes off him. Of course, Vivian couldn't blame them, because she also enjoyed looking at this man. Ferris returned to her with their keycards.

'We're on the top floor. River view.' He placed his hand on Vivian's back to guide her to the elevator. Again, her body trembled. She was dying to make love to him.

Thank God she was now able to control herself,

otherwise it would've been impossible to be near him.

Their rooms were next to each other. Ferris opened the door for her, and they entered. Her room was tastefully adorned with antique wooden furniture, which she guessed was elm or chestnut, and a few ornate vases. Vivian walked to the window and turned to Ferris who was behind her.

'Oh Ferris, what a beautiful sight! I'm sure it looks even more spectacular at night.'

'We'll find out in a few hours.' Ferris looked at his watch before he continued, 'Let's freshen up and see what's out there before dinner, shall we?'

'Will we come back here before dinner?'

'Yes, I think so. We'll be picked up at eight, so we'll still have time to change.'

With a wide smile, Vivian said, 'Well, what are we waiting for? Let's get ready.'

After taking a quick shower, she stood in front of the mirror and looked carefully at her reflection. She was content with her choice of clothes; stonewashed jeans, a dark blue blazer, a white V-neck shirt, and navy blue wedge sneakers. For dinner, she'd prepared a black Yves Saint Laurent dress with matching shoes and bag.

A moment after she was ready, Ferris knocked on her door. As usual, he looked incredibly dashing. Vivian imagined what it would be like to make love with him in the shower. The thought alone made her blush, and she quickly looked away.

'I'm ready, just let me grab my bag.'

Ferris waited for her at the door. 'Ready?' he asked with a teasing smile.

'You bet I am.'

A few minutes later, they were walking together along the Bund. 'Look! Ferris look!' With her slender, freshly manicured finger, Vivian pointed to the Oriental Pearl Tower on the other side of the river. 'There it is! The Oriental Pearl Tower! Can we go there? I want to see it up close.'

Vivian looked at him pleadingly, and even fluttered her long eyelashes at him several times.

Ferris gazed at her and said, 'How could I refuse when you look at me that way?' His voice was low and slightly hoarse.

Embarrassed, Vivian turned her face away. She was lost for words. 'I'm sorry, I didn't mean to embarrass you. I forgot you have difficulty receiving praise. I really am sorry.'

Vivian forced herself to smile. 'Apology accepted. Come on, let's go.' Vivian turned and walked in the opposite direction, away from the tower.

They walked to the end of the Bund, and studied the architecture of the buildings. Vivian was surprised because it turned out that Ferris knew a lot about Shanghai's architecture. Vivian listened attentively as he pointed out the various neo-classical and art deco styles.

Upon their return, they had enough time for a drink in the hotel bar. Ferris ordered a pot of oolong tea.

They had just taken a seat when Ferris's phone rang. He looked at its screen and apologized. 'Sorry, I have to take this.'

Vivian watched him as he walked out of sight. Her thoughts drifted to the awkward moment earlier that afternoon when Ferris praised her. Where did that come from? Her thoughts were interrupted by the waiter who brought the pot of tea and two small cups. He placed the pot on the table, poured the tea, and left immediately.

Vivian looked around the bar, which was full of foreign businesspeople. Her attention was drawn to several women standing at the bar's entrance. They were all watching someone. Vivian already knew who. Ferris must have entered the room. She turned around, and her guess was confirmed. His gaze was set firmly on Vivian. She wondered if Ferris was aware of the effect he had on women.

'I hope Zheng doesn't drag us to a karaoke bar.'

Vivian's eyes widened. 'Karaoke bar?'

'Yes, from what I've read, it's one of his hobbies.'

'My God... I hope he doesn't, because my singing voice is totally flat.'

'Huh, so is mine, but according to Chinese tradition, it's impolite if we reject our host's offer.'

'Then let's just hope he isn't in the mood for karaoke today.'

Ferris filled their cups once more, and Vivian admired how elegantly he did so. Without a doubt, he was Vivian's dream man. Everything about him seemed perfect to her: his appearance, his voice, the way he spoke, his dedication to his work. Vivian and Ferris stood in the hotel lobby while waiting for Mr. Zheng's driver. Precisely at eight o'clock, the luxurious Bentley stopped in front of the hotel.

About ten minutes later, the car pulled over, and a valet opened the door for them. Vivian stepped out and looked at Ferris with surprise. They were standing in front of The Oriental Pearl Hotel.

'We're having dinner here?'

Ferris smiled warmly and sincerely. 'I guess we are!' He glowed, and Vivian noticed he was watching her closely.

'Didn't you say you wanted to look at this building up close?' Ferris's deep voice sent sparks through her entire body.

'Yes, I did. Did you know that we were going to be dining here?'

'No, I didn't. What I do know is that Zheng has beaten me to it because I wanted to take you here on Monday.'

Vivian's face flushed, suddenly shy.

The elevator doors opened. Mr. Zheng was standing with his assistant, waiting to welcome them. The dinner took place in a dimly-lit, opulent restaurant with a breathtaking view of the Huangpu River. Ferris sat on Mr. Zheng's left, and Vivian on his right. Soon after they were seated, a lavish array of dishes were brought to the table; steamed crab, grilled oysters, xiaolongbao, braised eggplant, and a whole steamed fish piled with ginger and garlic.

Vivian quickly became involved in a riveting conversation with Mr. Zheng's assistant about Shanghai's architectural history, while Mr. Zheng described the history of the Oriental Pearl Tower to Ferris. The atmosphere was very relaxed, and Vivian was amused to see Ferris enjoying himself.

Vivian watched Zheng closely. He was tall and slim with a sharp jaw. Ferris was right. Zheng did like to show off his wealth. She could tell from the solid gold ring on his finger, which encased a tablet of white jade with a dragon engraved in it. Zheng turned to Vivian. 'Did you enjoy your introduction to Shanghainese cuisine, Vivian?'

'What can I say, Mr. Zheng. If I said it was exquisite, that would be an understatement.'

'Please, call me Ming. I'll make sure our Executive Chef receives your compliments.' Ming filled Vivian's glass with red wine while giving her a brief history of his family history. The restaurant was emptying, and soon they were the only ones left. The red wine kept flowing, and the party of four grew even more relaxed and convivial.

In the middle of her conversation with Ming, Vivian suddenly noticed Ferris was no longer at their table. She saw him speaking with Feng, Ming's assistant, at the bar. Vivian had the urge to be close to Ferris, but didn't want to be rude to Ming by interrupting their conversation. Thankfully, Ming was called away. Vivian took her wine and walked toward Ferris. She felt a little tipsy, and promised herself that that would be her final glass for the evening. Feng nodded deeply toward Vivian, and she nodded in return.

'Ferris just told me you have an extra day in Shanghai?'

'Yes, we do. I'm excited because Shanghai has long been at the top of my list of cities to visit. Do you have any suggestions for where we should go?'

A waiter passed by silently and without Vivian noticing her glass was refilled.

'There are countless things to see and do in this spectacular city of ours. I recommend visiting the pearl and jade market. However, you mustn't leave Shanghai before taking a cruise on the river at night. The city is at its most spectacular then.' Feng pointed toward the windows. Tourist boats sparkled on the calm river below. Before Vivian and Ferris could respond to Feng's suggestion, they were startled by a blast of music from the back of the restaurant confirming their fear. In a darkened corner of the restaurant stood a tall karaoke machine, and Ming had switched it on. Vivian glanced at Ferris in surprise. He could only reply with a shrug of his shoulders. They had no choice but to join Ming and Feng at the karaoke machine.

'Come on, Viv. We can do this.' Ferris had called her Viv for the first time. It gave her goosebumps. Ming sang Frank Sinatra's *My Way* with all his heart, and Vivian was relieved because she thought his voice was just as off-key as hers. The waiter ensured their wine glasses remained full, and despite her promise to herself, Vivian didn't refuse it.

She needed it to give her the courage to sing. Vivian felt
Ferris's presence behind her. She could feel the warmth of his
breath on the back of her neck. Vivian glanced over her
shoulder, straight into his eyes. The moment was interrupted by
Ming, who asked her to dance. Ming was an excellent dancer,
and Vivian easily followed his lead.

'Have you been a set for a long time?'

Vivian was startled. 'A set? What do you mean?'

'You and Ferris. Have you been dating for a long time?'

Vivian's face suddenly turned red. 'No, we're not a couple.'

Ming raised his eyebrows and continued. 'Are you sure?'

Vivian laughed. 'Believe me. I'm sure.' Vivian immediately
understood why Ming had asked her about Ferris. His hand slid
down her back and squeezed her ass. He even pulled Vivian
closer so she could feel his erection. Vivian instantly felt
nauseous, embarrassed. She didn't know how to escape.
For the second time that night, Feng came to her rescue.

'Would you do me the honor of a dance too?' he asked
formally.

'The honor would be all mine.' Vivian was overwhelmed with
gratitude. Feng looked at her apprehensively. 'Are you all
right?'

'Yes. Thank you.'

Feng glanced around furtively, ensuring no one could hear him.

'I apologize for his behavior.' Vivian looked at him in surprise.

'My boss loves beautiful women, and if he's been drinking,

he can be very annoying.'

'Thank you for saving me from that situation.'

The song ended, and Feng led her back to Ferris.

'What's wrong, Vivian? Did something happen?'

'No. Everything is fine. I'm just a little tired, that's all,' Vivian lied. Ferris looked at his watch. 'It's already twelve-thirty. If you like, we can go back to the hotel now.'

Vivian hesitated. She didn't want the night to end, but she also didn't want to remain in Ming's company. 'Okay, let's go back to the hotel.' When they'd arrived back at the Waldorf Astoria, they walked directly toward the lift. Vivian grabbed Ferris's arm. 'Ferris, I want some of that tea we had this afternoon. I wonder if we can still order it?'

Ferris raised an eyebrow. 'Aren't you tired?'

'Yes, I'm tired, but there's something I need to tell you.'

'Okay, would you like the tea in the bar, or upstairs?'

Vivian bit her lips. 'Upstairs, please.'

They continued in the elevator in silence. Without saying a word, Ferris walked to Vivian's room, then waited for her to open the door with her key card.

'Do you mind if I take off my shoes?'

Ferris smiled at her. 'No, do whatever makes you feel comfortable. After all, this is your room.'

Vivian sat down on the dusky pink couch and admired Ferris as he removed his jacket, loosened his tie and undid the top button off his shirt. 'What is it you wanted to tell me, Vivian?'

Before she could start, there was a knock at the door. Ferris answered it, then set the tea tray down on the low chestnut wood table in front of them. He poured the tea as elegantly as he had earlier that day in the bar. They sat across from each other and Vivian warmed her hands with the tea.

'What do we know about Ming Zheng?'

Ferris looked at Vivian in surprise. 'Well, we know that with his family's long history in Shanghai, and because of his family's business dealings, that he is is an extremely influential billionaire. Why do you ask?'

'In my opinion, if we're going to engage him as a client, we need to be careful about the safety of the designers we send here.'

'I don;t understand what you're saying, Vivian.'

Vivian took a deep breath. 'When we were dancing tonight, he started asking personal questions.'

'Such as?'

'He asked if we were a couple, and after I told him we aren't, he grabbed my ass. He even pressed himself against me so I could feel his hard-on.'

Ferris looked at Vivian in disbelief.

'Luckily Feng noticed and immediately interrupted by asking me to dance. He apologized for his boss's behavior and told me that Ming is usually like that with women when he's been drinking. That's why we need to be careful if we send staff out here.'

213

Ferris ran his hands through his hair several times while pacing back and forth. 'What a terrible situation. I never expected something like this would happen.'

'I didn't want to tell you, but if the project goes ahead, I thought about the designers who'd be sent here. I'd be concerned about their safety.'

'Yes, of course, their safety is of upmost importance. I'm glad you told me.'

Ferris sat back down and refilled their teacups. 'I am so, so sorry this happened to you Vivian. I can't imagine what would've happened if Feng didn't intervene. I'll report this to Sean and Clive first thing tomorrow.' Ferris rose from his seat, walked to the window, and gazed outside. He turned back to Vivian. 'Have you seen this sight at night yet, Vivian?' His voice was low and husky. Vivian slowly got up from the couch and walked over to Ferris at the window.

'It's breathtaking,' she whispered. Vivian could feel his eyes on her, and her heart started beating wildly.

For a moment, their eyes met.

Ferris broke the silence. 'It's late. We need all the rest we can get before our presentation tomorrow.'

'Yes, you're right.' Vivian struggled to hide her disappointment. She walked Ferris to the door.

'Goodnight, Vivian.'

'Goodnight, Ferris.'

CHAPTER 15

After a terrible night's sleep, Vivian woke early to prepare for their presentation. She decided on comfortable designer trousers with the pale yellow blouse she'd bought in Aruba. Normally, working was the best way to distract herself, but that morning she found it difficult to concentrate. Her mind continued to drift back to Ferris, and the mixed signals he'd been giving her recently.

She still couldn't figure out what was going on. There were times when he kept his distance, but then the following day she'd catch him staring at her longingly. Maybe she was just reading him all wrong?

Vivian had been working with him for quite a few years now. She never saw him looking at women he never seemed to show interest in anyone. What happened in his past to make him so immune?

A knock at the door startled her. She slowly opened it to find Ferris standing in her doorway. How was it possible that he could look so fresh? The entire time she'd known him, he'd never had a single bad hair day.

'Oh good, you're awake. I was afraid you might still be sleeping.'

'I've been up for a while now. I just went over the presentation.'

Ferris stepped into Vivian's room.

'Leave the presentation for a moment. Let's have breakfast first.'

'Great idea. I'm ravenous.'

They took the elevator down to the breakfast restaurant. The walls were lined with an extravagant buffet of regional breakfast dishes from across China, as well as Western style dishes. Vivian sampled the scallion pancakes while Ferris tried ci fan gao, which were like sticky rice hashbrowns.

They ate calmly and quietly, before Ferris broke the silence.

'This morning, I called Sean to fill him in on yesterday's incident.'

'Oh, how did he react?'

'He was very worried about you and deeply regretted that this happened to you.' Ferris sipped his cappuccino while staring directly at Vivian.

'I'm glad he's taking the harassment seriously.'

'Listen, Vivian, if you're not comfortable doing the presentation, then I can do it myself.'

'No, no. We'll continue as planned. I won't be defeated by his disgusting behavior!' Vivian stared at Ferris with a fiery expression.

Ferris raised his hand while saying softly, 'It was just a suggestion.' After a slight pause, Ferris continued. 'Sean said we should go ahead with the presentation.

If Zheng decides to choose Frenay & Iams for the project, we will take extra precautions to ensure the safety and comfort of the employees we send to Shanghai. Just like you said.' Ferris leaned back in his chair. 'It might sound strange, but in my opinion, it's fortunate we found out about Zheng so early. Now we can ensure that that kind of incident never happens again. It's clear that Sean is taking this matter very seriously.'

Their presentation took place in one of the hotel's grand, high-ceilinged conference rooms. Vivian and Ferris were going over some final details when Ming entered the room flanked by several colleagues. Vivian greeted Ming calmly, and was strengthened by the fact that Ferris was keeping a close eye on her.

Vivian commenced the presentation with her concept for the Waldorf Astoria's new X, and as she expected, Ming gazed at her hungrily. Naturally it made her uncomfortable, but she didn't show it. After Vivian's part of the presentation, they adjourned for lunch. Dozens of trays of various dim sum were served while Vivian shut down her laptop. Ferris walked toward her and she smiled at him.

'Are you alright?'

Vivian sighed. 'Yes, I'm fine. Thank you. I'm glad my part of the presentation is over. They seemed quite interested.'

'You did very well Vivian, considering the circumstances.'

'Thank you, Ferris.'

'You're welcome. Let's try the dim sum.' They walked back to the table. Two seats remained, both of them to Ming's left. Ferris swiftly sat down next to Ming and Vivian next to Ferris.

Vivian busied herself with her chopsticks while Ming was still staring at her hungrily, leaning forward so he could see past Ferris. Every time their eyes met, Ming winked at her. She ignored him.

Ferris finished his presentation, and Vivian was flooded with relief because it seemed to go extremely well. After today, she no longer needed to meet Ming. To avoid him, she stayed close to Ferris as they tidied up their documents and designs.

Suddenly Ming strode briskly towards Vivian. Ferris realized instantly and stood in front of her.

'Excellent presentation, especially your part Vivian. I'm thoroughly impressed.'

Vivian calmed herself. 'Thank you, Mr. Zheng.'

'I think we should celebrate tonight with a traditional Shanghainese seafood banquet. What do you think?'

'Thank you for the offer, Mr. Zheng, but unfortunately we already have plans for tonight.'

Ming stared irritably at Ferris and turned his gaze towards Vivian. 'You do realize it's impolite to deny your host's invitation,' he said dryly.

'We do realize this, Mr. Zheng, and we are grateful for your hospitality. It's not our intention to be impolite, but we simply have another appointment which we're unable to cancel as our time in Shanghai is limited.'

'Hmm, all right then. I will inform you of our decision before the end of the day. Goodbye.'

Before Vivian and Ferris could respond, he'd turned toward the door. Vivian shrugged her shoulders. 'What a vile man. Thank you, Ferris, for refusing to have dinner with him.'

Ferris smiled mischievously. 'Technically, I didn't lie. We do have an appointment tonight.'

Vivian raised her eyebrow. 'We do? With whom? I thought we were only here on business with Zeng.' Ferris unbuttoned his blazer and removed two slips of paper from his shirt pocket. 'This…' He showed two tickets to Vivian, 'Is our appointment tonight.'

'What is it?' Vivian could barely contain her curiosity.

'These are our tickets for the night cruise.'

Vivian was shocked and giggled in amusement. 'No way! When did you make the booking?'

'This morning.'

'Oh, how wonderful.' Vivian's face beamed and all her feelings of frustration vanished. Vivian was grateful for her warm clothes as it was a chilly night in Shanghai. The boat had just left the dock when a man selling individual white roses approached Ferris and Vivian. 'Sir, would you like to buy a rose for your beautiful wife? The funds go towards a charity working to protect China's dwindling giant panda population.' Vivian burst out laughing. Not only because the seller assumed they were husband and wife, but also because since she found out about George's condition, the panda had become a prominent feature in her life.

Ferris seemed to enjoy the misunderstanding and continued speaking with the seller. 'Of course I would like to buy a rose for my beautiful wife. As a matter of fact, she loves panda bears, now isn't that a coincidence!' Ferris handed the seller some yuan.

'Thank you, sir. Goodnight, and I hope you both enjoy your river cruise.'

Vivian and Ferris continued watching the seller offer the roses to the other passengers.

It was after midnight when they returned to the hotel. 'Would you like some tea or something else before we go upstairs?'

'Tea would be nice. I'm a little cold,' Vivian said.

The hotel bar was charming and warm, and soft jazz played in the background. They almost had the place to themselves except for few businessmen who were sitting at the bar.

'You could try some cognac to get warm.'

'No, thank you. I'd prefer tea.'

Ferris ordered a pot of oolong tea and a glass of cognac for himself.

'Do you often drink liquor, Ferris?'

He thought for a while before answering. 'No, I rarely drink liquor. However, I do like a glass of wine at dinner.'

Vivian was mesmerized by Ferris as he slowly spun the liquid in his glass before sipping it. Her reverie was interrupted by a loud laugh from a man at the end of the bar. Vivian glanced toward him and immediately regretted her decision, as one of the men raised an eyebrow and nodded at her suggestively. She looked away, her cheeks flushed red.

'Do you want to go upstairs, Vivian?' Ferris's voice was filled with concern because he knew she couldn't handle this kind of attention.

Vivian had barely touched her tea, but she couldn't stand being there a moment longer.

'You don't mind? You haven't finished your cognac.'

'It's no problem.' Ferris stood up and put his arm around Vivian's shoulders, and pulled her body closer to his protectively. They walked out of the bar, and as they passed the group of drunk businessmen they whistled and shouted obscenities.

On the way to their rooms, Vivian's heart sank as Ferris let go of his embrace. They stopped in front of her door, and without realizing it, she sighed deeply.

'Are you tired?' he asked.

'No. Not really.'

'Then why did you sigh like that? Is there something bothering you? Is there anything you'd like to talk about?'

Vivian looked up at Ferris, and felt tears roll down her cheeks.

'Hey, hey... what's wrong? What's bothering you?' Ferris wiped Vivian's tears with his thumbs.

'It's nothing really. It's just the Ming thing and the guy from downstairs. I'm just over it, I guess,' Vivian lied. She was tormented because she longed for the man in front of her.

221

In that moment Vivian thought she wanted nothing else in the world but him.

'I understand. You know, Vivian, some men just don't know how to behave when they see a beautiful woman. They revert back to being boys and try to do everything to attract the woman's attention, but they don't realize they make a complete fool of themselves and that their behavior is actually harassment.'

Vivian forced a smile even though tears stung her eyes.

'Try to get some sleep, Vivian. I'll knock on your door tomorrow at ten.'

Ferris kissed Vivian's cheek quickly and disappeared into his room. Vivian stood silently in the corridor while holding the cheek that he had just gently kissed. After taking a long hot shower, Vivian lay on the bed staring at the ceiling. Her hand caressed the cheek that had just felt the softness of Ferris's lips. Even though it was an innocent goodnight kiss, for her, it was still meaningful.

She replayed various scenes of the evening in her mind. Ferris seemed so calm and relaxed on the cruise. It felt like he genuinely enjoyed spending time with her, she'd seen a completely different side to him.

Vivian grinned when she thought of Ferris's words to the flower seller: 'Of course I would like to buy a rose for my beautiful wife.' She finally drifted off to sleep, her face fixed in a dreamy smile.

The next morning Vivian awoke at seven. She packed her suitcase as that night they would fly back to New York. She then checked her email on her phone. There was an email from Ethan.

Angel,
There is an important matter we need to discuss because I can't take it anymore. I miss you too much. We have been separated for three weeks now. This is not what I expected for our relationship. I hope you can make a decision and make sure there is a place in your life for me. It would make me happy if you quit your job and came to live with me in Dubai. I hope you consider it. I'm expecting an answer this weekend.
I love you, angel.
Love, Ethan xx

Completely stunned, Vivian reread the email. It infuriated her that Ethan had brought this up this way. Couldn't he wait until they met face to face? On the other hand, she had to agree that it wasn't a good way to start a relationship.

The fact that Ethan lived on the other side of the world in a different time zone was taking its toll. This situation was very unhealthy for them both. She had to be honest about what she really wanted. Vivian knew Ferris already had her heart, while Ethan took second-place. In that moment she felt that sex with Ethan was his only drawcard.

What would Ferris be like in bed? Would he also pounce on her like a wild animal, and wake her in the middle of the night raging with lust?

Vivian rid her mind of all those thoughts. It was her last day in Shanghai with Ferris, so she could think about everything when she was back home. She decided not to reply to Ethan's email as she wanted to calmly consider it first.

Their last day in Shanghai passed quickly. They visited the pearl and jade market and the Nanjing Road shopping streets. At the end of the road stood the Jing'an Temple, and together they gazed up at it completely awe-struck.

Ferris and Vivian chatted casually throughout the day. When the conversation turned to family, Vivian found out that Ethan was also an only child who had been raised by his mother. His parents were divorced, but kept in touch.

'Do you want to return to the hotel to rest before we fly home tonight?'

Vivian looked around. It was getting dark, and the wind began to blow hard. 'No, I don't. I can sleep on the flight back. I want to enjoy Shanghai while I still can. Maybe I'll never return.'

'All right, in that case, let me find us a good restaurant. Ferris took out his phone. 'I think I've found the one: M on the Bund, it's called. Let's eat there then go back to the hotel.'

'Okay, let's go,' she said with a smile. A few minutes later, they sat in a taxi on their way to the Bund. Strong winds and heavy rain lowered the temperature immediately.

When they got out of the cab and ran toward the restaurant, the heavy rain saturated them both. A waiter greeted them with warm towels, then guided them to a table.

Before sitting down, Vivian decided to use the restroom so she could let her hair down so it would dry faster. When she returned to the table, Ferris looked at her in amazement. She smiled shyly but appreciatively at him.

Ferris ordered a rich seafood stew, while Vivian had Hokkaido scallops. As they ate, Vivian couldn't get warm.

Ferris called the waiter and ordered a glass of cognac. Vivian looked at him with raised eyebrows, 'No wine?'

Ferris laughed, 'This time, no, no wine.'

The waiter quickly returned with the cognac. Ferris spun the glass gracefully, sipped it, and passed it to her. 'Here... try a little. You'll feel the warmth of it immediately.'

Vivian reached out for the glass slowly. The fact that he offered her a drink from his glass made her warm enough. She took a sip, felt the liquid glow in her mouth, then swallowed. Ferris watched her closely, and Vivian felt a tremendous warmth running through her body. She wasn't sure whether it was from the cognac or from the look in Ferris's eyes.

'How is it? Do you like it?'

Ferris's deep resounding voice was irresistible. Before answering, Vivian subtly licked her lips, which made Ferris narrow his eyes.

'It's delicious. You're right. My body is warming up.'

Vivian suddenly realized she'd teased him by touching her lips with her tongue, but it seemed Ferris didn't care. His indifference gave her courage. She returned the glass, and Ferris immediately drank from it. Vivian enjoyed the sight of him swallowing the amber liquid. She couldn't keep her eyes off him. He handed her back the glass, and they continued sharing sips of it until it was empty.

After the third glass, Ferris called for the bill. Vivian's heart sank she didn't want this moment to end.

Ferris helped Vivian to get up. The cognac had made her tipsy. Ferris supported her body and helped her to walk. She started giggling and talking rapidly. 'Ferris, I told you I couldn't handle strong liquor.'

He smiled at her while helping her to keep her balance.

'Yes, you did, but I didn't expect it to go to your head so fast.' The rain was still heavy, but the wind had dropped. Ferris held her hand tightly so she wouldn't fall.

'We better take a taxi,' Ferris sounded concerned.

'No, please. Let's walk. I love to walk in the rain.'

'Are you sure? I don't want you to get cold again.'

Vivian laughed happily and stared at him with red cheeks.

'But now I know how to warm my body. Cognac!' she laughed excitedly, while Ferris tried desperately to keep from laughing at Vivian's behavior.

She could hardly walk straight, so Ferris had to support her all the way back to the hotel. In the elevator, they stood very close.

Vivian held herself against Ferris because she was afraid of falling. They were both still wet from the rain, and Vivian's body felt as cold as ice.

Ferris guided Vivian swiftly to her room, but it took a long time for her to find her keycard in her bag. Gently, he sat her down on the couch. 'Wait a minute. I'll get a towel for you.'

When he returned, he found Vivian fast asleep. Distantly she heard his voice calling, 'Vivian, Vivian, wake up…'

She opened her eyes and their stares collided.

'How are you doing now?' Ferris asked in deeply worried tone.

Vivian closed her eyes again for a moment, then tried to open them widely. Slowly she realized what had happened. With false courage from the cognac, she had flirted with Ferris. How could she have drunk too much? Had she embarrassed herself? Vivian tried to sit up straight and suddenly felt a severe pain in her forehead. Embarrassed, her cheeks blazed red, as she slowly pulled up the blanket that had been covering her body.

'I'm so sorry,' Vivian said softly.

'No. I'm the one who needs to apologize. I shouldn't have offered you so much cognac. I should have known better.'

Vivian pursed her lips and looked sheepishly at Ferris. 'Did I do anything embarrassing?'

He reached out, brushed back the hair that was covering part of her face, and said, 'Not at all. When we arrived I put you on the couch then went to get a towel, but when I returned you were

227

sleeping soundly. I covered you with the blanket, and then went to my room to take a shower and pack.'

Their conversation was interrupted by a knock at the door. A waiter entered carrying a pot of jasmine tea and two aspirins. Ferris took two bottles of mineral water from the fridge.

'Here, drink this. You'll feel much better.'

Vivian took the aspirin and swallowed it with a sip of water.

'We'll leave for the airport in two hours. I assume you'd like to take a shower first.'

'Yes.' Vivian drank the tea and her headache began to subside a little. Ferris got up and walked toward the door.

'I'll be back in a little while.'

'Thank you for taking care of me, Ferris.'

'You're welcome, Vivian.'

When they were quietly settled into their business class seats, the lights dimmed. Ferris adjusted his chair so he could lie back. Vivian noticed that Ferris once again put some distance between them. She knew that when they'd returned to the office, they'd bury themselves in work. She was grateful that it would distract her troubled mind, and her agonizing confusion about the man sleeping next to her.

CHAPTER 16

The minute Vivian arrived home, she kept herself extremely busy, otherwise she'd torment herself by thinking of Ferris and their time together in Shanghai. She unpacked her suitcase, washed her clothes, cleaned her apartment and shopped for groceries. When it was time to eat, she put a lasagna in the oven and did some ironing while waiting for it to heat. She should have called Ethan, but was reluctant to do so because she still needed time to think about the situation.

Her phone rang and when she saw the name on the screen, a wide smile spread across her face.

'Hey, Sal.'

'Hey, Viv. Did you just get back from Shanghai? How was your trip? Did you finally succeed with Ferris?'

Vivian heard her friend's giggling and rolled her eyes in annoyance. 'As a matter of fact, I did.'

'No way! You didn't. Tell me all about it in five. I'm almost there.'

'Sure, I was just about to have some lasagna, you want some?'

'You know me girl, I never pass on free food. See you in five!'

Ten minutes later, they were sitting at the bar while enjoying the lasagna.

'Well, tell me! What happened in Shanghai?'

Vivian told her friend the whole story.

How relaxed and laid-back Ferris was the entire time. She even told Salfina about the rose seller and of course about the cognac disaster.

'From what I'm hearing, it sounds like your Ice King is starting to melt Viv.' Vivian sipped the Asti in her glass.

'I'll have to see about that. The moment we left Shanghai, he immediately put his guard back up.'

'I still maintain that he just doesn't want to be too reckless because of his past. You have to give him time, Viv.'

'Time?' Vivian stood petrified in her kitchen. 'How much time does someone need? I've been waiting for six years!'

Salfina thought for a moment before answering, 'Listen Viv. You need to stop to play the victim here. You are in a position to express your feelings to him, but you choose not to do so. He can't read your mind, so if you don't tell him, he won't know. He is the one with a nasty past, so if you ask me, Ferris is the victim, not you. Also, please Viv, stop hiding behind the excuse that you still have to work with him.'

Vivian looked at her best friend with her mouth open.

'That's so easy for you to say, Sal. Now that you've got a boyfriend, it doesn't mean you have to lecture me.'

'Jake has nothing to do with this, and you know it, Viv. You need to take control of your own life. If you don't, then in a few years you'll regret it, because the best years of your life would have flashed by, and you'd still be in the dark about how he feels. Is that how you want to look back on your life?'

Vivian looked at Salfina and her face flashed with concern, because after speaking at length her best friend's face suddenly went pale and she ran to the bathroom. Vivian followed her and watched as Sal vomited into the toilet. 'Sal, what's wrong, do you need a doctor?'

'No, no. I'm fine, just give me a minute.'

They sat back at the breakfast bar, and Vivian rubbed Sal's back.

'Are you going to tell me what that was all about?'

Salfina beamed. 'I'm pregnant.'

'What!?'

'I'm pregnant.'

'Yes, yes, I heard you the first time. Pregnant? How many months?'

'Ten weeks. No one except you and Jake knows because it's still under twelve weeks, so it's still too early to tell anyone. You understand, right?'

'Yes, I understand. How did Jake react?'

'He's over the moon. He can't wait to tell his parents. If it was possible, he'd tell the whole world!'

'Ohh, Sal. I'm so happy for you. Congratulations!' Vivian hugged her best friend tightly.

'If the pregnancy goes smoothly, Jake and I want to ask you to be our child's Godmother.'

'Me?'

'Yes, you.'

'Oh Sal, of course I'd love to. I'm honored.'

'Okay, that's settled then.'

Vivian watched Salfina pick up her wine glass, but Vivian quickly grabbed it from her hand.

'Oh no, Miss. There will be no more wine for you over the next six and a half months.'

They laughed, and spent the rest of the evening discussing baby names. Sal also insisted that Vivian should design the nursery. It was almost half-past eleven when Sal decided it was time to go home.

'How about a girl's night out at The Club this Friday or Saturday, what do you say?'

Vivian thought for a moment. This weekend she would visit Ethan in Dubai. 'I'd love to, but unfortunately I can't. I leave for Dubai on Thursday night.'

Salfina raised her eyebrows. 'For work?'

'Yes, for work. You know I travel a lot for my job,' Vivian lied. She quickly changed the subject. 'But you also shouldn't go to The Club, Sal. You're pregnant.'

'Yeah, I know. God, how lucky am I to have another Jake banning me from all the fun.' They dissolved into laughter yet again.

After Sal left, Vivian snuggled into the couch and returned to weighing up her situation. Deep down, she knew that Salfina was right about Ferris. She also had to admit that Ethan was her second choice, but was that fair on him?

What if she never stopped longing for Ferris for the rest of her life, despite being with Ethan?

It was so easy to love Ferris because of his calm and humble character, while Ethan was the opposite. Despite her love for Ferris, she couldn't deny she had feelings for Ethan too. But were they real? Maybe she simply had feelings for him because she desperately wanted someone in her life?

For a split second, she felt jealous of Sal. The thought of that scared the hell out of her. Vivian made it her mission this weekend to see just how deeply she felt about Ethan. She would use this time in Dubai to find out what she really wanted.

Vivian looked at her watch. It was time for her to call Ethan.

'Hello, Angel.'

'Hey, Ethan.'

They were struck by silence.

'Didn't you received my email?'

'Yes, I've read it.'

Vivian heard Ethan scoff.

'You didn't find it important enough to reply?'

'Look, Ethan. I was in Shanghai for work, not for fun, and there was no chance to sit down and calmly compose a reply.'

Vivian felt stupid for having to defend herself like this.

'What am I to you?'

'Ethan don't be like that.'

'Don't be like what, Vivian?

It's a reasonable question. What we're doing isn't going to last. You need to quit your job and live with your partner as every woman should.'

Vivian was shocked at Ethan's anger and ferocity, let alone his chauvinistic statement. His words flared her emotions.

'If this is setting the tone for our weekend together, then I'd rather stay home. I've told you many times now that I love my work. If you can't accept that, then there is no point continuing this relationship.'

Ethan said nothing.

'Are you still there, Ethan?'

'Sorry, Angel, that was completely out of line. I'm just worked up because I miss you so much and I want you by my side. Let's stop arguing. I'm so looking forward to seeing you. I want to hold you, kiss you. God, I really miss making love to you.'

'You're right. Let's not fight. I also can't wait to see you.'

Vivian was deeply concerned by Ethan's overreaction. He revealed an aggressive side that made her uncomfortable. Was this the real Ethan? Could Vivian live with an aggressive man like that? She tried to erase the conversation from her mind.

The next day, she woke very early and drove to the office. By the look of his desk, Vivian knew Ferris wasn't in yet. She turned on her computer and saw a pile of envelopes waiting for her.

Vivian began tidying up the Shanghai presentation documents in one folder. A dry white rose petal fell from one of the documents. It was from the rose that Ferris had given her on the boat. She peered down and picked up the petal carefully, afraid to crush it. Vivian gazed at the petal, and a smile spread across her lips. She stood up and held the petal close to her heart, and then jumped a little when she saw Ferris standing in the doorway. She didn't hear him come in. With raised eyebrows, Ferris stared in surprise at Vivian whose face had turned bright red.

'I didn't hear you come in,' Vivian stammered as she tucked the petal under an envelope.

'I just wanted to get coffee. Do you want a cappuccino?' Vivian had to escape the room. She looked like a schoolgirl who'd been caught cheating.

'Yes, thank you.' Ferris continued looking at Vivian curiously. As she walked to the coffee counter she could barely control her breathing. Did Ferris see her place the flower petal on her heart? Her face was still red with embarrassment.

When she pulled herself together, she walked back to the office with her head held high, clutching two cups of coffee. She pushed the office door handle down with her elbow, while her hip pushed open the door. Vivian was relieved to see that Ferris was busy on a call. He nodded in gratitude as Vivian placed the cappuccino on his desk.

After the call, Ferris left the room.

It was already late afternoon, but he still hadn't returned. His car key was still on his desk, meaning he hadn't left yet. Evelyn, Sean's secretary, disrupted Vivian's thoughts.

'Hello, Vivian. Mr. Frenay is ready to see you now.'

Vivian had completely forgotten that Sean wanted to talk to her about the Shanghai incident.

'Thank you. I'll be right there.' She walked along the wide corridor lined with white orchids.

Evelyn greeted her with a smile. 'You can go straight in. He's expecting you.'

'Thank you, Evelyn.' Vivian opened the door to Sean's office. He was on the phone, but gestured for her to sit in front of Sean's vast desk. It was the first time Vivian had visited his office. To her left was a grand fireplace. The entire office's design was very masculine, with a few graceful touches, such as a tall black vase containing crimson orchids. Vivian glanced at Sean, who was still busy on the phone. Despite his years, he was still very handsome.

He was tall and slender. His eyes were gray, almost the same color as Ferris's. She could tell his gray hair used to be black, and noticed he didn't wear a wedding ring. Suddenly she realized that every time she met a man, she was accustomed to glancing at his hand to check if he was wearing a wedding ring. Vivian didn't know where the habit came from.

Sean ended his call, put his elbows on the table, and folded his hands.

'So sorry to keep you waiting.'

'No problem.'

'So, can you please explain to me what happened in Shanghai?'

Vivian shifted in her seat and told Sean the whole story, which he listened to attentively.

'I'm sorry you had to go through that. Yesterday afternoon I called Ming Zheng.'

Vivian looked at Sean with wide eyes.

'It looks like this man has done his homework. He found out that you are an experienced designer. He gave us this project on one condition: that you be the project lead. He even doubled the fee we requested.'

Vivian gasped, but before she could say anything, Sean continued. 'Of course, I refused the offer because I know what his motive was. For me, the safety of our staff and the reputation of this company are far more valuable than prestigious projects.'

Vivian sighed with relief. 'Even so, I feel guilty that Frenay & Iams has to miss out on such an advantageous opportunity. I hope you believe me when I say I did nothing to encourage Mr. Zheng's behavior. However, I'm glad I told Ferris about it and that he took immediate action.'

'Ferris,' Sean repeated. 'Do you like working with him?'

Vivian blushed. She didn't understand why Sean had asked her this. Did he suspect that she had feelings for Ferris?

237

Maybe George had said something about this?

'Yes. I enjoy working with Ferris. He is very professional and driven when it comes to work.'

'Good. I am glad to hear that. I want to thank you for your honesty, but please don't feel guilty. There's absolutely no need.'

'You're welcome, Mr. Freany, and thank you.'

When she returned to their office, Ferris's desk was empty, and his car key was gone. Vivian hadn't seen him since the rose petal incident. During their time in Shanghai, Vivian saw how Ferris loosened up and how relaxed he was, but the minute they got on the plane, he just built his wall up again.

She started questioning herself. Did she make him do that? Did she do something to offend him? Vivian wasn't sure about anything anymore. The only thing she knew was that she was afraid that the closeness they had shared had completely vanished.

The next day, Ferris did not come to the office. He hadn't informed her of an outside appointment. Vivian still felt strange about Sean asking whether she enjoyed working with him. What Ferris avoiding her?

Vivian threw herself into her work so she could complete most of her tasks before leaving for Dubai. For a moment, she thought about her last telephone conversation with Ethan, and how he'd erupted and revealed his overly dominant side. A feeling of deep discomfort returned to her mind.

Even though it was late at night, the airport was still crowded. People shouted and pushed past each other. For a second she began to doubt her decision to visit Ethan in Dubai. Her heart told her she was making a mistake, but she quickly quashed that emotion. She needed to go there to sort out her feelings, even though she knew deep down inside to whom her heart belonged.

After a horrendous thirteen-hour flight wracked by turbulence, she finally arrived at Dubai airport. Vivian descended the escalator to the arrivals terminal, and in the distance, she saw Ethan. With an enthusiastic stride, he approached her and hugged her tightly. She smelled his scent and immediately felt weak.

Once they were outside, she was overwhelmed by the heat. Ethan took her hand and led her to his car, while his chauffeur put her luggage in the trunk. They climbed into the back, and the car pulled out into the traffic.

Ethan gazed at Vivian closely, then suddenly his hands were all over her body, from her face to her breasts and between her legs. He forced Vivian's thighs open and unzipped her pants.

'Hmm... I missed you!' Ethan pressed his fingers into Vivian's pants.

'Ethan!' Vivian looked at him angrily and then at the driver. They were stuck in the hectic traffic of Dubai.

'Don't worry. He's not watching.'

Ethan ignored her.

239

He forced Vivian to lift her ass so he could pull down her pants. She tried to push his hands away, but he was too strong for her. Ethan pulled her legs apart, and with brutal force, he stabbed two fingers inside her.

His head sank between Vivian's thighs, and his tongue greedily licked her cleft. The sound of licking and sucking repulsed her. Completely in shock, she didn't know what to do. She felt humiliated. With all her strength, Vivian tried to fight off his fingers and push his head away.

Ethan unbuttoned then unzipped his jeans, then pushed Vivian's face onto his hard cock and forced it into her mouth. It wasn't long before his cum flooded her mouth. She swallowed it all.

'Welcome to Dubai,' he said with an arrogant grin.

'Uhh... thanks,' Vivian replied, still in shock.

'When we get home, we can have some quality time together, and then later tonight we're attending a party held by my friend, a wealthy sheikh.'

'A sheikh? I've never met a sheikh before.' Vivian tried to sound as calm as possible, even though on the inside she was trembling.

'I think you'll like Yasar.' Ethan then said something in Arabic to the driver.

'I didn't know you could speak Arabic.'

Ethan laughed. 'There's a lot you don't know about me, Vivian.'

The way he looked at her deeply troubled her. It didn't feel right at all.

The driver stopped at a towering luxury villa with a row of tall palm trees in the front yard.

'Welcome home, Angel.' Ethan helped her get out of the car while the driver carried her luggage. After what had happened in the back seat, Vivian was still upset and didn't say much. Once they were inside the villa, Vivian glanced around. Behind a sliding door, she saw a long lap pool.

The driver spoke in Arabic with Ethan before leaving the room. Ethan stood close to her and gazed into her eyes. 'Finally, we're alone.' Vivian looked at Ethan with a confused expression.

'What's wrong? You don't like to be alone with me, Vivian?'

'Of course I like it. It's just that I'm still embarrassed by what just happened in the car.' Ethan leaned close and lifted Vivian's chin with his finger, so she was looking directly into his eyes. 'I will fuck you whenever I want, wherever I want. Also, I don't give a shit about who is watching. You got that?'

Before Vivian could react, Ethan tore open her blouse and dropped her down onto the Persian carpet. 'Now I'm going to fuck you long and hard to make up for all the weeks you made me suffer.' His lips crashed onto Vivian's mouth. She didn't dare to reject him. It was the first time she'd seen him like this. At first the kiss was exciting, but it quickly turned rough and wild. Ethan lifted Vivian up and carried her to his bedroom.

He lay her down on his bed and removed his clothes. Naked, he stood beside her with a throbbing erection.

'Take off your clothes!' Vivian did what she was told without saying a word. He pushed her back down on the bed and opened her legs wide. With one hard thrust, he buried his cock into Vivian. He pumped his hips violently while constantly shouting her name. He grunted and groaned while grinding into her so hard his balls slapped her ass. Then he quickly pulled out, flipped her over, forced her onto her hands and knees and forced his cock into Vivian's ass, which was so tight he growled even louder.

'Oh yeah... I missed this. Can you feel it? Do you feel what I feel? You are mine, you are no one else's. Say you are mine!'

'Yes... yes, I am yours.' Vivian hid her fear.

She allowed Ethan to ravage her, even though she wanted to scream in pain and anger. Ethan continued to pump like a wild animal until he finally reached his climax. Vivian felt the warm cum trickle from her ass. In the bathroom, Vivian cried silently while looking at her reflection in the mirror. She felt like a whore who'd just had sex with a stranger. What just happened? Who was this man? Where was the Ethan she fell for in Aruba? Vivian bent down and washed her face. When she looked back in the mirror, she could see Victoria's reflection behind her. She was crying and slowly shaking her head. Vicky's reflection vanished when Ethan knocked on the door.

'Angel, is everything all right?'

Vivian wiped her tears quickly. She didn't want Ethan to know she was scared. 'Yes, Ethan. I'm fine,' she lied.

'Can I come in?' Vivian opened the door for him, and Ethan pulled her into a hug and rocked her body slowly.

'Sorry, Angel, I don't know what possessed me earlier. It's just that I missed you so much. I can't help it. Forgive me. Did I hurt you?' Ethan forced her to look into his eyes, and she couldn't help but give a forced smile. 'Everything is fine. Really.' Ethan kissed her softly and passionately. It was completely different to how he'd kissed her earlier.

'Come on, let's take a shower together. Then we have to go.' Under the shower, Ethan washed every inch of Vivian's body. He started by soaping her breasts. His touch made her nipples stiffen, even though the water was hot. His hand slid into her folds, and he slowly opened her thighs. He rubbed and tickled her clit, and Vivian sighed with pleasure. Ethan knelt before her and pleasured her with his tongue and fingers, and Vivian quickly came. She then knelt before him and took his huge cock into her mouth. She gazed up at Ethan, and seeing him completely succumbing to pleasure encouraged her.
She took him even deeper into her throat while working quickly with her lips and her tongue. She felt him quivering and knew he was almost there. Vivian sucked even harder and gripped the base of his cock until he shuddered. She tried to swallow his cum, but some slipped from the corner of her mouth.

CHAPTER 17

Back in Ethan's bedroom, Vivian unpacked the entire contents of her suitcase to find suitable clothes for the party. She wondered whether she needed something that completely covered her arms. Ethan came in with just a towel around his waist. A smile spread across his face.

'Come on.' He reached out to Vivian.

With raised eyebrows, she glared at Ethan.

'Come on. We still have two hours before we need to leave for the party.'

She hesitantly accepted Ethan's hand, and he led her to the backyard. It wasn't a big yard, but it was well-maintained and bloomed with flowers. The pool's surface reflected the afternoon sun.

'Wanna go for a swim?'

'What? Now? We just took a shower.'

Ethan took off Vivian's bathrobe. She stood before him completely naked. Suddenly, Ethan pushed her into the pool then jumped in after her.

Spluttering, Vivian surfaced. 'Ethan!'

He swam towards her and pushed her against the pool's edge, then put his arms around her like a cage. 'I'm not satisfied yet, Vivian.' He glared at her.

'God, Ethan. You are insatiable.' Vivian tried to smile a little, but she knew for sure that he wanted to have sex again.

'Exactly, I am indeed insatiable, and now I want to fuck you here in my pool. I want to feel your tight ass again.'

She stared at him with pleading eyes, desperately hoping he wouldn't transform again.

'Turn around!' he demanded, his voice suddenly ice cold. He spun her around then slammed into her, and Vivian knew right there that this wasn't love. She became terrified of him, but with a tense body gave him what he wanted.

He felt how tense she was. 'Let yourself go, Vivian,' he snarled in her ear, but Vivian couldn't. Tears flowed down her cheeks.

'I said, let go! I told you that I would fuck you anywhere and anytime!'

'NO! Stop it, Ethan! You're hurting me!' Tears flowed down her cheeks, and her body trembled with crying.

'Oh, Angel, I'm so sorry.' Ethan turned her around gently, and kissed Vivian's tears away. 'I don't want to hurt you. I love you. You know that right? I can't control myself because I missed you so much.' His voice had softened into the voice of the Ethan she knew in Aruba. Vivian hugged him back. He lifted her out of the pool and carried her inside.

'Sorry, angel, I didn't mean to scare or hurt you. From now on I will do my best to control myself.'

She could only nod without saying a word.

'I have to make a phone call. You get dressed in the meantime.' Ethan left the room, and Vivian stood silently, watching him from a distance.

What could she do? Who was this guy? Did he have two completely different personalities?

Sometimes he behaved like the Ethan she knew, and the next moment he'd transform into a monster.

If Vivian rejected him and returned to New York, what would he do? Would he let her go? She could flee to the American Embassy in Dubai, but how would she escape from his villa? No, she had to deal with this very carefully. She had to ensure that Ethan did not grow suspicious of her. Vivian had to shut down all her feelings and emotions. Otherwise, she doubted her ability to escaping.

While searching for something to wear, Vivian realized her passport was missing from her travel documents sleeve. Reality hit her hard, as she realized she was dealing with a dangerous man. How could she be this stupid? She wished she'd never given him a second chance in Aruba. She should have listened to the warnings of her friends.

Luckily she still had her cellphone. Vivian was startled by Ethan entering the room.

'Why aren't you dressed yet?'

Vivian quickly composed an excuse. 'Because I'm not sure what clothes I can wear. Can I go sleeveless or not?'

'Yasar may be a Sheik, but his mind has been opened to the Western world, so sleeveless clothes are no problem.'

Vivian smiled and sighed with relief. She'd dodged that one. 'What are you wearing, Ethan? So I can coordinate with you.'

Ethan smiled affectionately at her, and Vivian forced a smile in return even though she felt disgusted with him.

'I'm wearing a suit. There'll be many important guests there tonight so we need to dress to impress.'

'Fine, then I'll wear a black cocktail dress.'

They continued getting ready. Ethan got dressed in the bedroom while Vivian did her makeup in the bathroom. Just a little mascara and lip gloss, while in her hair she wore the silver ornament George had given her.

For the second time that day Victoria's reflection appeared in the mirror. She looked afraid. It seemed like she wanted to say something, but she didn't know what it was. Again her reflection disappeared as soon as Ethan entered the bathroom.

'Are you ready, Angel?'

'Almost. I just need my shoes, then I'm ready to go.'

'You look stunning, angel.' Her cocktail dress was Dior, which paired perfectly with the bracelet Ethan had given her. The ensemble was completed beautifully with Victoria's hair ornament.

'Spin around,' Ethan told her. Vivian spun gracefully, then his eyes narrowed as he walked behind her. 'Where did you get this?' Ethan's voice was stone cold as he pointed at the hair ornament.

Vivian instantly grew alarmed. She recognized that tone now. It wasn't Ethan's – it was the psychopath's.

'George gave it to me.'

Ethan sat on the edge of the bathtub while still staring up at her sharply. 'Who is George?'

'George is my former boss.' Vivian explained that George was an elderly gay man who was seriously ill. Slowly it dawned on her that the black velvet hair ornament bag was exactly the same as her bracelet bag. Could it be possible that Ethan and Victoria knew each other? Is that what Vicky was trying to tell her?

All the color drained from Vivian's face. Victoria was one of the two women who had committed suicide after being with Ethan.

Vivian felt nauseous. Her legs grew weak. Ethan caught her before she fainted.

When she awoke, it took a few moments before she realized what had happened.

Vivian heard Ethan talking on the phone, but she kept her eyes closed. After realizing that the story about Ethan was true, she desperately needed time to formulate a plan. Her friends had been right, and Vivian had been too naïve. She'd completely swallowed his story.

With great difficulty, Vivian held back the tears that burned behind her eyelids. No, she couldn't cry. If she wanted to get out of here, she had to be strong. Ethan couldn't find out that she was aware of the truth. Otherwise, she might not be able to escape. Vivian heard his footsteps approaching, and felt him sit down on the edge of the bed.

'Vivian, Angel, can you hear me?'

She had to do something. She couldn't keep pretending to be passed out. Slowly and carefully, Vivian opened her eyes. Ethan gazed at her lovingly and caressed her cheek.

'Oh, thank goodness you're awake. Are you all right? Do you remember what just happened?'

'No, what happened?'

'You fainted.'

'I did? Maybe because I haven't eaten anything yet. Oh, and because you completely exhausted me with your insatiability, sir,' Vivian said with a mischievous smile even though she felt disgusted. But Ethan's expression confirmed that he'd fallen into her trap.

'I don't believe any man could ever be satisfied with you, Vivian.' He rose from the bed and held out his hand to her. 'Come on, let's go to the party. We can eat there.' Ethan helped Vivian get up and looked worriedly. 'Are you sure you're all right?'

'Yes. I'm fine,' she insisted with a smile.

On the way to the party, she carefully assessed all the ways she could try and escape, but soon realized it was no use as she was too distracted in the car to plan properly.

The car stopped in front of the Burj Al Arab Hotel tower, the location of the Sheikh Yasar's party.

The function hall was decorated festively with indoor plants and fountains, and all guests were escorted to their tables.

249

Ethan and Vivian were seated at the same table as the Sheikh. Ethan leaned towards Vivian and whispered, 'After dinner, the party will continue in another more intimate room. There'll also be an orchestra playing.'

'Oh, really? I can't wait! I love orchestral music!' Fortunately, it seemed quite easy for Vivian to fool Ethan.

He rose from his chair, smiled broadly, and extended his hand towards a tall, suave looking man who approached their table. His silver hair was trimmed short, and his camel suit was sleek and refined.

'Ethan, glad you could come.' The two men shook hands and embraced.

'Of course I'm here. Have I ever missed one of your parties?' Vivian assumed that the man was Sheik Yasar, but he was completely different to what she'd expected he'd look like.

'Yasar, let me introduce to you the love of my life, Vivian Foster.'

Vivian rose from her chair and held out her hand to him. He kissed the back of it while gazing at her. 'Beautiful,' Yasar said to Ethan, then added something in Arabic which Vivian couldn't understand. Yasar blatantly ogled Vivian's breasts while he talked with Ethan, which made her feel uncomfortable and awkward.

During dinner, Vivian was completely left out of the conversation which continued in Arabic. Yasar also continued to brazenly stare at her chest.

Suddenly, Ethan pressed his lips to hers and forced his tongue into her mouth. With startling pressure, he continued to kiss her and Vivian followed his rhythm. His hand slowly slid down Vivian's chest and into her dress. He played with Vivian's nipples, then abruptly ended the kiss and stared proudly at Yasar, who was clearly enjoying the scene in front of him. Vivian felt deeply humiliated, but in this situation, she felt there was nothing she could do.

'Yasar, my good friend. As you can see, Vivian is a woman who is different from all the others. She is one of the few women who can handle my sexual desires. She always serves me, anytime and anywhere. Even when she sleeps, she still allows me to fuck her.'

Vivian's face turned bright red, and her head drooped and stared at fists in her lap. She fought hard against the tears pricking her eyes.

'I believe you, my friend. I need to get myself a woman like her.'

Ethan answered Yasar in Arabic, and again Vivian was excluded from the conversation.

Ethan, Yasar, and Vivian were the last to leave the function hall. Ethan walked beside Vivian and Yasar behind them. Vivian knew she was being watched, and when she glanced over her shoulder, she saw Yasar's gaze stripping her naked. Vivian felt she was walking into a nightmare. In performance hall, everyone gathered in small groups.

Various men came to chat with Yasar and Ethan, each one of them inspecting Vivian closely.

Champagne flowed endlessly. The sound of orchestral music floated through the hall as the noise of the guests grew louder as more alcohol was consumed.

Vivian scanned the hall. Everywhere she looked, men were kissing women, and groping their breasts and asses. In a darkened corner, two men kissed and groped one woman, and it dawned on Vivian that they must all be prostitutes. Ethan interrupted her horrifying realization.

'Angel, I have to discuss some important things with Yasar. I'll be right back.'

'Ok, dear. I'll be waiting here.' Ethan kissed her while one hand slid to her breast and the other squeezed her ass. He then glanced around sternly at the other men to show them Vivian was his, and left the hall with Yasar. There she stood, alone in a vast room full of men being entertained by prostitutes.

She decided to escape to the restroom. As she was walking along the corridor, she heard Ethan and Yasar laugh. A door was slightly ajar, so Vivian carefully peeked inside. The room was in total darkness, except for a small dim purple light in the middle. Vivian crept silently inside and hid behind a room divider in the corner. What she saw astonished her. Two women were kneeling in front of them, giving them blow jobs. Vivian was devastated but completely transfixed as she witnessed how much they were enjoying it.

Ethan clutched the woman's hair, pushing and pulling her head roughly. When he forced his cock deeper into her mouth she gagged and vomited a little. He pulled her hair back releasing his cock from her mouth and slapped it across her cheek.

'I said suck it, bitch! I want you to suck all the cum out of me. Understood?' The woman obeyed with tears running down her cheeks. Vivian had seen enough. She wanted to escape, but couldn't move.

Yasar was just as abusive. After pumping into the woman's ass several times, he pulled out and rammed his cock into her mouth.

'Oh, yeahhh. Open your mouth so I can fill it up and keep it open, cause I wanna see it!' Ethan yelled. The woman gagged then vomited again. Before Yasar reached his climax, he pulled his cock from the woman's mouth and sprayed cum all over her face. Vivian felt sick to her stomach and finally found the strength to leave. Just before she crept out of the room, she caught a glimpse of Ethan and Yasar snorting white powder, which she assumed was cocaine. With a throbbing heart and racing pulse, she managed to escaped to the restroom, and started vomiting. Vivian was still in the toilet when she heard two women enter.

'How much did you get?'

'Two hundred dollars.'

'What? I only got one hundred.'

'What? That asshole should have paid you three hundred

alone for slapping you in the face like that.'

Vivian held her breath. It was clear that these were the two women who just been abused by Ethan and Yasar.

'The slap on my face was nothing. His cock almost killed me. Did you see how big it was?'

'Yes. I saw it. I wondered what it would feel like to have such a big cock in my cunt. I was jealous of you.'

'Well, you can have him next time. Let's clean up so we can make more tonight.'

'Yeah, I'm sure we can. This party is full of rich men.'

A few minutes later the women disappeared, and Vivian emerged from her toilet cubicle. She looked in the mirror and stared at her reflection, horrified about what could happen. The image of Ethan slapping his prostitute reappeared in her mind. The terrible truth was that he didn't hesitate to beat women. She must be extremely cautious as it was clear he was completely unpredictable: a dangerous psychopath.

Vivian decided she had to pretend to be deeply in love with him, to give the impression that everything was fine. That was the only thing that could protect her from danger. She gathered her courage to rush back to the party because she knew she couldn't stay away too long. When she arrived she saw Ethan and Yasar talking to a group of men. She walked over to them and grabbed Ethan's arm. Ethan kissed her quickly.

'I was looking for you, Angel. Where have you been?'

She smiled sweetly at Ethan and said,

'A girl needs a powder room every now and then.'
Ethan believed her and kissed her cheek. 'Vivian, let me
introduce you to Farouk.'
Farouk kissed Vivian's hand and nodded politely. 'Vivian, it's a
pleasure to meet you.'
'Thank you.' That was all Vivian managed to say. Like Yasar,
Farouk was also very attractive, with dark eyes, long eyelashes,
and a razor-sharp jaw. The three of them continued in Arabic.
Vivian glanced around the room. She saw the two women who
just moments ago had knelt before Ethan and Yasar. They were
propositioning two other men. A man approached Vivian, and
she panicked. Did he think she was a prostitute too? Was it
possible that Ethan also wanted to watch her serve other men?
The man stroked Vivian's arm, but Ethan pulled the man's
wrist tight and stared at him angrily. 'This woman is my private
possession.' The man apologized to Ethan and swiftly left.
Ethan put his arm around Vivian's shoulder, and squeezed
Vivian's breast. Again he slid his hand into her dress and
played with her nipple, which reacted even though she tried
desperately to fight her arousal. Yasar and Farouk gazed
hungrily at the shape of her nipples under her dress. Her face
flushed bright red again, and again she felt deeply humiliated.
The party was getting crowded. Vivian sat with the three men
in a sectioned-off area. From where they sat, she could look out
over the guests. She now understood why Ethan never missed
one of Yasar's parties – they were full of sex and cocaine.

Ethan handed Vivian a cocktail.

'Here, you have to taste this.'

Vivian took a sip. 'Hmm... it's good. What is it?'

'I don't know exactly, but I think there's mango in it,'

'Very tasty.' Vivian took another sip.

'I'm glad you like it, Angel.'

The three men exchanged glances with an expression Vivian couldn't understand, and then continued in Arabic. Suddenly she felt extremely tired, and struggled to keep her eyes open. Vivian didn't know whether she should blame the cocktail or her long flight. Slowly all voices faded, and she could no longer distinguish the faces around her. They became blurry shadows. Ethan gently grabbed her hand, squeezed it, then placed it on his stiff cock. Vivian pulled her hand away when she realized Yasar and Farouk were still with them. Ethan pulled her wrist hard and put her hand back on his erection.

'Can you feel how hard my dick is, Viv? It's waiting for you, so where do you want it, in your mouth or in your cunt?' His voice sounded malicious as he rubbed her hand against his hardened cock. She heard Yasar and Farouk laughing, but she couldn't see anything. Her surroundings had become completely blurred. What was happening? The only thing she felt was Ethan lifting her up and whispering in her ear that they were going home. Suddenly everything turned pitch black.

CHAPTER 18

Sunlight piercing the curtains woke Vivian up. After blinking a few times, she realized where she was – still trapped in a lion's cage. She slowly turned to see if Ethan was still beside her, and was flooded with relief to find the other side of the bed was empty.

Images from the previous night crashed through her mind. Ethan humiliating her. Ethan having sex with another woman. Ethan snorting coke.

The only thing she couldn't remember was how they'd come home and how she'd ended up naked in bed. Her Dior dress lay crumpled at the foot of the bed.

After trying desperately to remember all the events of the previous night and how they'd gotten home, Vivian gave up. She couldn't remember anything that happened after she'd sipped the cocktail.

Frustrated, she threw off the blanket, and was deeply shocked to see purple bruises on her breasts, hips and thighs. The bruises were the size of fingertips. Anger struck her. Had she been abused in her sleep? She recalled how Ethan boasted to Yasar about how she was always ready for him – even as she slept.

Vivian walked quickly to the bathroom. She had to devise some kind of strategy for how to handle all of this. Under the warm water of the shower she carefully soaped the bruises.

fter pulling on one of Ethan's t-shirts, she went looking for him and found him sitting by the pool. It was time for Vivian to wear her mask. She walked over to him with a wide smile and kissed him on his forehead.

'Good morning dear, did you sleep well?' she asked him chirpily.

He looked at her with the faintest flicker of suspicion, but then a smile appeared on his lips. 'Yes, I slept very well. You?' Ethan looked at her closely.

'I can't remember the last time I slept that well.' Vivian took some of the melon from his plate and sat beside him.

'Tell me, did you enjoy the party? And what do you think about Yasar and Farouk?'

'Yasar was very friendly, and Farouk also seems like an interesting man. It's only a pity we didn't get to dance,' she said casually in between bites of melon. In her mind, the scene of Yasar and Ethan sexually abusing the two women reappeared.

'Yes, Yasar certainly knows how to throw a party.' Ethan smiled, and his eyes drifted across Vivian's body.

'What's on the agenda for today?' Vivian tried to change the subject.

'If it were up to me, I'd spend the entire day here so I could keep you all to myself, but unfortunately that's not possible. Yasar has invited us to go sailing on his yacht.'

'Oh, that sounds like great fun!'

Vivian feigned excitement, while in her mind alarm bells were ringing.

She knew she had to be extra vigilant as there was no way she could flee from a yacht. Vivian had to empty her mind and eliminate her emotions, otherwise she wouldn't be able to handle the situation.

The marina looked spectacular, with rows of sparkling white luxury yachts. Hand in hand, Vivian and Ethan walked down the dock. In the distance, they saw Yasar and Farouk standing at the prow of a super yacht.

'My friends, welcome aboard Topaz, one of my super yachts. Today's weather forecast is good – perfect for sailing.'

Yasar shook Ethan's hand, and they embraced. He then greeted Vivian with a kiss on the back of her hand. Farouk did the same, and then the three men glanced at each other and laughed. Vivian knew they were laughing at her, but she didn't know why. Yasar and Farouk stared at Vivian's body. Ethan stepped closer toward her triumphantly, then squeezed and spanked Vivian's ass.

'Come on. I'll give you a tour.' Yasar extended his hand to Vivian, who accepted it and walked beside him. He showed her all the rooms and facilities, which included a cinema, a sauna, massage room, a bar, and an underwater observation room. At the end of the tour, he introduced her to his crew.

After returning to the main deck, Vivian was surprised to see two other women.

They were standing close to Ethan and Farouk, and Ethan was stroking one of the woman's lower back.

'Angel, did you enjoy the tour?' he asked, while continuing to stroke the woman.

Vivian forced a smile. 'Yes, I just told Yasar how extraordinary his yacht is.' She immediately grew seriously alarmed about what would happen that day. The woman next to Ethan did not look at Vivian once, but continued to stand close to him.

They were already on the open water when the kitchen crew presented a lavish seafood buffet, but Vivian had zero appetite. Her awkwardness grew, as no one was speaking to her. Out of courtesy, she tried to start a conversation several times with Yasar and Farouk, but they weren't interested in the slightest. Ethan was engaged in conversation with the other women and completely ignored her. He even kissed one of the women passionately and fondled her breasts while staring directly at Vivian. She saw his eyes had darkened with lust.

The woman placed her hand on the bulge of Ethan's tight swimming trunks. Vivian watched how Ethan stepped towards the woman and started rubbing against her.

A maelstrom of emotions crashed through Vivian's mind. What type of game was he playing, and what did he expect from her? How would he react if he saw Vivian kissing Yasar or Farouk as she let them touch her breasts? With no idea of what to do or how to react, she lay back in her deckchair and closed her eyes tightly behind her sunglasses.

When she opened them, she realized she'd fallen asleep, but she didn't know for how long. The deck was completely empty. After wrapping herself in a shawl, Vivian walked inside and heard noises coming from one of the bedrooms. She knew exactly what those noises were. Even though she tried to resist, Vivian was drawn to the room, whose door was wide open. Once again, she was numbed by what she witnessed.

The woman who had been sticking close to Ethan all day was on her hands and knees, and seemed to be enjoying the thud of Ethan's cock in her ass and Farouk's in her mouth.

On a chair in the corner of the room, Yasar was leaning back with his eyes closed as the other woman was hungrily going down on him. Vivian wanted to flee but Ethan saw her.

'Come here, Viv!'

She didn't obey him but walked away, but in seconds Ethan grabbed her arms.

'Let go of my arms!' She jerked away, and tears sprung to her eyes. 'Let go of me, Ethan!' He didn't release her but gripped them tighter. Vivian tried her best to escape, but his grip was too firm. He then pulled her into a suffocating embrace and slowly rocked her body like a child.

'Shhh... calm down, calm down, Angel.'

In this moment Vivian quickly thought about her next move. She needed to do something fast. In silence, she prayed.

'Please, please Vicky, help me. I need you.'

In an instant she knew what to do.

She needed to sweet-talk him, but not too much so she wouldn't lose her credibility. Behind them, she still could hear groaning and moaning.

'Why are you doing this to me? I thought you loved me. Why Ethan... why? Am I not good enough for you?'
Ethan slowly released her and looked deep into her eyes.
'Angel, you are the best thing I've ever had in my life. I love you so much.'
Vivian looked at him with wide eyes. 'But... but I don't understand.' She stumbled, not knowing what else to say.
'I love you, angel. Never doubt that. What you saw just now has nothing to do with love – it's purely pleasure. I would be thrilled if you joined us. I'm convinced you will love it once you try it.'
Vivian shook her head hard. 'No... no Ethan, I can't. I'm too shy, and I only want you. You are my only man.' Vivian was disgusted with herself for saying these things.
'Come back in and let me make love to you. I won't share you with anyone else. I promise.' Vivian looked at him in disbelief.
'Come on, Viv... they won't watch us. Don't you want to make love to me?'
With flushed red face, Vivian stared at him, stunned. 'Of course I want you, I just told you so, but not in this way.'
Vivian regretted her words immediately as Ethan brutally pulled her into an empty bedroom.
The psychopath was back.

He grabbed a chair and placed it directly in front of a floor to ceiling mirror, then sat down on it. He tore off her shawl then stripped off her bikini, then forced her to sit on his lap facing the mirror. They both stared at their reflections.

Hard and rough, he groped Vivian's breasts, then lifted her hips and rammed his cock inside her. He shook her hips up and down while forcing her to stare straight into the mirror.

'Don't you see how arousing it is if someone is watching you? I want you to give me that pleasure, Vivian.' He continued to bounce her violently up and down on his cock. Vivian closed her eyes. She no longer had the strength to watch this crazy psychopath abuse her.

'Goddamnit, open your fucking eyes! I want you to look at me while I fuck you!' He kept pumping into her over and over. She was certain he was high on cocaine again.

After Ethan finally came with a guttural moan, he led her back to the main deck. He then quickly ducked back into one of the rooms and returned with two cocktail glasses.

'Drink this, angel. You'll love it.'

Vivian took a small sip. 'Mmm, you're right, it's delicious.' Ethan stared lovingly at her. It seemed the psychopath had disappeared, for the moment.

'Angel, you have to clarify something for me. Are you okay with me having sex with other women?'

Vivian searched for a believable answer. 'I'm okay with it as long as I don't have to see it.

But you must promise me that you'll keep your love only for me.' She could tell by the look on his face that he was relieved. Once again, she'd managed to mislead him.

He kissed her passionately and said, 'You really made my day, my Angel. But please, Vivian, think about my proposal to try it once. It would arouse me so much to watch you have sex with other men or women. It would make me extraordinarily happy. I know that I'm asking you too much, but please reconsider.' Vivian was mortified. He genuinely wanted her to have sex with other people. 'I'll consider it.'

Ethan kissed her cheek and returned to the orgy. Vivian tried desperately to focus on the fact that – if everything went well – tomorrow she would be on a plane back to New York. The prospect of never having to see these men again gave her the strength to keep playing this dangerous game.

'Angel... wake up.' With difficulty, she opened her eyes. Her head felt heavy, and she was surprised to see that it was already dark and that they'd returned to the marina. 'Sorry,' she mumbled.

Yasar poured her a cup of tea from an ornate ceramic pot adorned with gold. 'Must be because of the sea air. It has a soothing effect on those who are not used to it.'

Vivian looked around and realized the two women had disappeared. 'Have we been back for a long time?'

Ethan glanced at his watch. 'Oh, about an hour and a half.'

Vivian blinked. 'Goodness, did I sleep that long?'

'You were really knocked out,' Farouk said dryly, while sipping his tea and staring at her full of lust.

Ethan and Yasar laughed. Vivian narrowed her eyes when she saw the three men snorting cocaine.

Yasar turned to Vivian. 'Do you want some?'

Vivian had to remain calm.

'No, thank you. I'm high on life, can't you tell?' The men laughed.

'So, tell me, Vivian. Did you enjoy Dubai?' Yasar asked her. He sounded sincere. She figured this was her chance to fool them. This would be her ticket to get out of Dubai safely.

'I fell in love with Dubai.' Vivian grabbed Ethan's hand and stroked it. 'Ethan once asked me if I would leave my job and move here to be with him. At first, I was against it, but after these last couple of days I've really changed my mind. What a spectacular, exciting city this is! And your hospitality has been so warm and generous. But most of all, I don't want to be apart from Ethan anymore. I love him too much.' Vivian gazed at Ethan, who looked at her with wide eyes.

'Are you serious, Vivian?'

Vivian stroked Ethan's face. 'Of course, I'm serious.'

'But what about your job? You always say how much you love it.'

'It's true, I often comment on that, but there comes a point in your life when you have to make serious choices about your future. So I've chosen to be with you, the man I love.

Tomorrow I fly back to New York so I can start arranging things. I'll resign from my job and sell my apartment.'

Ethan pulled Vivian into his arms and kissed her passionately. 'Oh Vivian, you don't know how happy I am to hear this.'

Yasar and Farouk applauded joyfully. 'This is a cause for celebration!' Yasar ordered his crew to bring out champagne. Vivian observed the three men who had believed her story. Yasar and Farouk talked to each other while Ethan leaned on Vivian, and her heart jolted when she realized she was looking into the dark eyes of the psychopath.

'Do you love me, Viv?' She was scared to death.

'You know I love you, Ethan.'

'So there's nothing you wouldn't do for me?'

'Nothing.' Her heart pounded like crazy. She had a sinking feeling she knew what was going to happen next.

Without words, Ethan untied her shawl. She wore nothing underneath, as earlier he'd destroyed her bikini when he stripped it off her. Yasar and Farouk's eyes devoured her naked body while Ethan sucked Vivian's nipples. Vivian sat naked on a chair with the eyes of the three men hungrily taking her in. In her heart, she prayed for strength. Ethan dropped to his knees, pried open her legs, and plunged his face between her thighs. Yasar began fondling her right breast, while Farouk sucked on her left nipple. Ethan licked and sucked on her clit. Vivian tried to ignore the sensations, but when Ethan's fingers slid inside her, she could no longer hold back.

'Say you like it,' Ethan growled as he licked and sucked her moistening folds with increasing fervor.

'Yes... yes, I like it, Ethan.'

'Good girl.' Ethan got up and glared ferociously at her. 'I share everything with my friends, including you.' Ethan nodded at Yasar, permitting him to dive between Vivian's thighs while Ethan sat on her right. Vivian closed her eyes and tried to block all her feelings and emotions. Soon after, Farouk was now between her legs.

'Open your eyes and look at me, sexy!' barked Ethan. There was nothing else to do but obey him.

After the three men had finished assaulting her, Ethan stood up and extended his hand towards Vivian, who was still sitting on the chair, naked and numb.

'Come on, let's go.' Vivian grabbed her shawl and wrapped it around her body tightly.

'You really are an incredibly tasty bitch, Vivian.' Yasar and Farouk nodded in agreement with Ethan. 'Now, if you gentlemen will excuse me, I must take my wife home and make love to her before she leaves tomorrow. Fortunately, she'll only be gone for a short time. Isn't that right?' Ethan slapped her hard on her ass, and it stung. Through the pain and shame she managed to reply, 'Yes, that's right. I''l be back before you know it so I can satisfy you every day and every night.' Vivian smiled coquettishly. Yasar and Farouk bid farewell to them. While before they had kissed the back of her hand, now both of them kissed her hard on her mouth. When they were back in Ethan's bedroom, he continued screwing her as hard as he could. On his bed, on the floor, and against the wall. Every ten minutes or so he'd snort more cocaine, which fueled his wild and violent behavior. From his closet, he took two large vibrators. Vivian looked at him, terrified.

'You'll like this.' He switched them both on, then up to full speed. 'Open your mouth,' he snapped.

Vivian immediately obeyed. She knew this was the psychopath talking, and she couldn't afford to make a mistake.

'Ah... good! Open your mouth and suck it.' She did everything he ordered.

'Keep going! Suck it harder!' Ethan shoved the second vibrator deep into her pussy. She felt like a cheap whore. 'I can tell you like it. You really are a horny bitch. I love that about you.'

Ethan continued to shove the vibrators in and out of her, before pulling them out and forcing her onto her hands and knees.

'Hold that position,' he yelled. 'Relax,' he commanded. He slowly pushed one vibrator into Vivian's ass and then rammed the other into her pussy. Ethan sat in front of her and forced his cock into her mouth, pushing it deep into her throat. Vivian almost vomited.

'Deeper!' Ethan shouted. Vivian tried but she couldn't. Eventually, he pulled out of her mouth. With a flat palm, he slapped her cheek and shoved his cock back into her mouth.

'Now suck it!' he screamed.

Tears were running down her face. He was managing to break her. Vivian didn't care anymore. She let him do whatever he wanted, but she could no longer pretend to enjoy it. Her unresponsiveness infuriated him. He stood up and kicked her hard in the stomach. Vivian tumbled off the bed and lay still on the floor, curled up in a fetal position, trying desperately to protect herself. The vibrators still buzzed inside her. Carefully Ethan removed them. 'Are you okay, Vivian?' The psychopath had left, and Ethan had returned.

'Yes, I'm fine. I'd like to freshen up now, if you don't mind.' Ethan lifted Vivian up from the floor, kissed the tip of her nose, and carried her to the bathroom. 'Do you want to take a shower or a bath?'

'Shower.' Ethan turned on the faucets, and it didn't take long until the bathroom was filled with steam.

'You take a shower first. I have to make a phone call.' Internally Vivian sighed with relief because Ethan didn't want to shower with her. She stepped into the shower cubicle and collapsed on the tiles, crying loudly. Vivian felt like a prostitute. She let Yasar, Farouk and Ethan violate and humiliate her. What kind of woman had she become? Was she so desperate for love?

She did not recognize herself anymore. Why had this happened to her? With great difficulty, she stood up and saw that her body was covered in bruises. She carefully soaped every inch of herself, then stepped out of the shower and wrapped herself in a towel. Vivian combed her hair and with inflamed red eyes she stared at herself in the mirror. Victoria's reflection joined her, and she was crying with her. Vivian slowly opened the bathroom door and went out into the bedroom. Ethan wasn't in the room. Vivian crawled into bed, pulled the blanket over her body, and cried herself to sleep. The next day she was awoken by sunlight again. Ethan wasn't next to her. Vivian didn't even know if he had slept next to her at all. She didn't care. Today she could finally return home and leave this hellish nightmare. In the kitchen, she poured herself a cup of coffee and walked barefoot into the backyard. There she found Ethan reading a newspaper while drinking coffee and eating toast. With her coffee in hand, she sat next to him and timidly looked into his eyes to discover which Ethan she would be facing this time.

'Why do you look so serious, Angel?'

Vivian sighed with relief. 'I'm sad because I have to go back today. I'll be missing you again.' Ethan intertwined his fingers with hers and kissed the back of her hand. 'Don't be sad. It's only for a few days, right? If I weren't so busy, I'd come with you.'

'Yes, you're right. It's just a few days.'

Vivian knew she needed to be hyper-vigilant with her words so as not to raise any suspicion.

'When you're back we'll throw a big party to celebrate you moving in with me. How about that?'

'I can't wait!' Vivian gushed. Ethan glanced at his watch. 'We have to leave on time. We don't want to get stuck in traffic on the way to the airport. Ethan's words were like music to her ears. Vivian quickly ate some toast, then got dressed in the bathroom. Ethan remained occupied with several phone conversations while Vivian packed her suitcase.

She was just about to pack her hair ornament when Ethan snatched it from her hand while continuing his phone call in Arabic. Vivian stared at him questioningly, but Ethan only shook his head. What could she do? The ornament was extremely precious to her, but she couldn't argue with Ethan at this point. All she wanted was to go home and escape him. In the bathroom mirror, she observed that Ethan put the hair ornament in the drawer of his bedside table. If there were a chance, she would take it back. A few moments later, Vivian was packed and ready to go, but she hadn't had a chance to retrieve the ornament. She pulled her suitcase into the living room. 'So you've got everything, Viv?'

'No. I can't seem to find my passport.'

From the inside pocked of his jacket,

Ethan pulled out her passport.

'I kept it safe for you. It's an extremely valuable document, so I didn't want it just lying around. If one of the maids found it, it might be gone by now.'

'Sorry, I didn't realize that.'

'Ready to go?' He gazed at Vivian affectionately.

'Yes... I'm ready.' She was at the front door. The driver had already put her suitcase in the trunk of Ethan's car.

'Oh, sorry, can you please wait a minute? I forgot my sunglasses!' Vivian ran back to the bedroom. She glanced out the window and saw Ethan talking to the driver.

Vivian had of course deliberately left her sunglasses so she could retrieve her hair ornament. With trembling hands, she opened the drawer, picked it up, and put it in her bag. Vivian clutched her sunglasses as she returned to the car. 'Here they are! I'm ready now.' Ethan opened the door for her, helped her climb in, and sat next to her. The traffic wasn't too bad, and they arrived at the airport with plenty of time. Impatiently, Ethan glanced at his watch because they'd arrived early. Vivian seized the opportunity to free herself from him.

'My dear, you go to work. I'll be fine. I can wait in the business lounge before my flight leaves.'

'Are you sure?'

'Of course.' Ethan hugged and kissed her passionately until both of them were out of breath.

'See you very soon, angel.'

'Yes, see you soon.' Ethan kissed her once more, then Vivian got out of the car. She watched it drive away.

CHAPTER 19

To kill time before boarding, Vivian read a magazine in the business lounge. She usually loved the benefits of business class, especially the plush lounges, but this time she couldn't relax. She was restless. Every sound she heard made her even more tense.

Frustrated, she walked back and forth in the lounge. There was an announcement over the PA system: her flight had been delayed. She was desperate to be home in the safety of her apartment.

The sound of a door opening caught her attention. Vivian started to feel uncomfortable because no one entered the lounge.

An uneasy feeling consumed her. What if Ethan had hired someone to drag her from the airport back to his house? She could end up as a sex slave for him, Yasar and Farouk. None of her friends knew where she was in Dubai, which would make it extremely difficult to search for her.

Vivian remembered that when Ethan left the airport, he was talking to a security guard. He could use that for an alibi if Vivian disappeared. She panicked, grabbed her bag and left the lounge. She had to find a crowd. She'd feel safer if she was surrounded by people

As she walked through the airport, she passed a coffee shop called Segafredo and decided to go in.

It was very cozy and relaxed. A waiter passed her the menu, which was on an iPad, and she quickly realized how hungry she was. She ordered bruschetta and a glass of red wine, and after she ate her body felt a lot better.

When Vivian heard her flight's boarding announcement, she paid the bill and gathered her belongings before striding swiftly to her gate.

Forty-five minutes later, the plane taxied onto the runway, ready to take off. Vivian took a long, deep breath. Now she really was on her way home and leaving her nightmare in Dubai. It didn't take long for her to fall asleep.

In her dream, she saw Ethan put the sparkling hair ornament in Victoria's blond hair. She looked thrilled, and seemed very grateful. The next moment Ethan and his two friends were sexually assaulting Victoria. She tried hard to fight them off, but she wasn't strong enough.

Several times they slapped her hard and pulled her hair. Even though she wasn't strong enough, she kept fighting. The three men tied her to a bed so she couldn't move. They penetrated her mouth, ass, and pussy. Vivian could see tears streaming down Vicky's face. She was completely helpless.

There was nothing Victoria could do to protect herself.

The bathtub was half-filled with water, and the taps were still running. Victoria got up from the cold floor and then walked to the tub. She took something from a small bag and kept it hidden in her hand.

The dream continued. Vivian saw Victoria open her bathrobe and step into the tub. Because the room was filled with steam Vivian couldn't see what Victoria was doing. She could only hear running water.

Vivian wanted desperately to say something, but no sound came from her mouth.

She saw how the water was flowing over the edge of the tub. The water was red, and in it Victoria lay lifeless with her eyes wide open and her wrists slashed. Vivian stared at Victoria's body with tears running down her cheeks. Everything seemed so real.

When she woke, it took a while until Vivian realized where she was and that everything she'd just witnessed was just a dream. Now Vivian understood why Victoria kept appearing in the mirror. She had tried to warn her, and Vivian deeply regretted that she had ignored her.

Five hours remained until the plane would land in New York. Vivian asked a flight attendant for a cup of coffee. In her mind, she returned to the dream. She knew Victoria had committed suicide, but she didn't know how. Did she really slash her wrists? Vivian had never dared to ask George.

Her heart was filled with deep sadness to see what had happened to Victoria in her dream. In a way, Vivian could understand why Victoria had done it, because the same thought had crossed her mind. She remembered how she had lay on the floor after Ethan kicked her hard in the stomach.

She wanted to die there and then. Anger boiled up inside her. How could Ethan live with himself after all the things he had done?

Vivian knew that there were two victims, but God knows how many women had committed suicide after being abused by him and his friends.

Vivian was grateful to have escaped Ethan's dangerous grip. How on earth could she have fallen for him. Was she that desperate? She needed to pick up the pieces of her life and try to forget all about him and all the horrific things that had happened in Dubai.

Vivian had never felt happier than she did the moment she set foot in her apartment. A deep sense of tranquility washed over her. She felt safe and secure. After a quick shower she unpacked everything, then sat down on the couch.

She grabbed her handbag and noticed the black velvet bag containing Victoria's hair ornament. She removed the ornament and gazed at it. It was then she realized that it perfectly matched her bracelet. Both were made from platinum, and both sparkled with sixteen diamonds.

Suddenly Vivian saw a flash from her dream that she hadn't seen the first time. She saw Ethan slip the ornament into Victoria's hair. Why did Ethan want it back anyway, and what would happen if he realized Vivian had stolen it back?

She removed the bracelet and put it in the velvet bag along with Victoria's ornament.

With her phone in hand, she got up from the couch and walked over to the window. It was silent outside. Soft rain fell, completing the night's sadness.

She glanced at her phone, which had been inactive since she'd left Dubai. Vivian didn't dare turn it on because she was sure there'd be a message from Ethan. After careful consideration, she decided to turn it on. She'd guessed right. There were three text and two voice messages from him.

Angel, you've only been gone for half a day, and I miss you already. As soon as I think about you, my dick gets so hard it's torturing. Can't wait for you to return. I will make sure you are always by my side so you can satisfy me day and night. I'll call you again later. I love you. Ethan xxx

Vivian opened the second message.

Viv, I miss you so much. I want you to be by my side. I know for sure you will feel at home here. We will have a wonderful life together. Love, Ethan xo

Then the third.

Vivian, I just got home. Something is missing from my bedside drawer. When you get home call me immediately!!!

She knew he was furious after discovering she had stolen the ornament back. She didn't know what to do. She decided to listen to his voicemail.

Vivian, I know you took the hair ornament. Call me now.

His voice sounded cold as stone, but in the second voicemail he was infuriated.

You filthy piece of shit. You stole something that doesn't belong to you. This is going to have serious consequences, I can tell you that. I swear, damn you, you are going to seriously regret this. You may think you're smart, but you just wait for my revenge, you dirty whore. No one, I repeat no one makes a fool out of me.

Vivian quickly turned off her phone. She'd heard enough of Ethan's fury. Her heart was pounding, and adrenaline flowed through her body. He had called her a whore, and the sad thing was that he was right. She had acted like a whore – but not by choice. He had forced her to do so. Vivian felt dirty and disgusting. For the second time that night, she decided to take a shower. She scrubbed and rinsed her whole body, but the feelings of disgust and shame remained.
Unable to sleep, Vivian wondered whether it had been a mistake to steal back the ornament.

Various thoughts haunted her. Should she still fear Ethan? What could he do to her? A glance at her clock told her it was pointless sleeping because in an hour her alarm would go off.

Vivian arrived at the office at seven-thirty. No one else had arrived yet. She opened her office door and was surprised to see a vase of white roses waiting on her desk. With a smile, she walked to her desk and sat down. Were they from Ferris? Vivian immediately dismissed this thought. She no longer wanted to fill her head with men – not even Ferris. Not after what she'd just suffered.

While she waited for her computer to start up, she went to the coffee counter and found Trisha next to the machine. 'Trisha, I'm surprised to see you here this early!'

'I have an appointment with Lily, for the annual Frenay & Iams party. Today we're going to assess whether everything is ready for this Friday.'

Because of her trip to Dubai, she had completely forgotten about Friday's party. 'Ah, right. The staff party. Can you tell me the theme?'

Trisha laughed. 'Sorry, Viv. I have to make sure no one knows. It's going to be a surprise for everyone.'

'Come on. I'm not going to tell anyone.'

'Okay, I'll give you a hint... Monte Carlo and Las Vegas.'

'Ah, casino.'

'Yes, you guessed it.'

The invitation with the dress code will be circulated today. The dress code is Glamor.

'Cool, I can't wait,' Vivian chirped, thought she didn't want to attend at all.

Trisha looked around to make sure they were alone. 'Hey, Viv, how does it feel to be that close to Ferris all day long?'

Her question took Vivian completely by surprise.

'What can I say. It's nice to work with him. He's very professional.'

'Nice working with him? Come on, Viv, be honest with me. Every woman here is jealous of you, do you know that?'

'Jealous? Why?'

'Come on, Viv, don't act stupid. And you haven't answered my question.'

Vivian felt her face flush. She didn''want to talk about Ferris at all and certainly not with Trisha.

'Trisha, as I said, Ferris is a fine colleague to work with. I'm sorry, but I have a pile of work waiting for me. See you on Friday, Trisha.' Without giving Trisha a chance to answer, Vivian returned to her office. Vivian looked out the window onto the street. Since her return from Dubai, it hadn't stopped raining. The sky was gray, and she felt like it would rain all day.

Vivian looked at Ferris's tidy desk and remembered back to the last time she saw him. How he caught her holding the rose petal to her chest, and the strange look on his face.

She also remembered how he had disappeared for the rest of that day. The sound of the door opening interrupted her thoughts. Ferris entered, and looked straight at her.

'Good morning. Did you have fun this weekend?' A smile spread across his lips.

'Yes, it couldn't have been better,' Vivian lied as she walked to her desk. 'What did I miss when I was away?'

Ferris looked at her earnestly. 'Nothing special.' Ferris glanced at the vase of white roses and said, 'The cleaner threw out the rose petal from Shanghai. I didn't know if you wanted to save it, so that's why there are new ones.'

'Thank you.' Vivian forced a smile.

'You're welcome. Is everything okay, Vivian?' He looked at her, worried.

'Yes, I'm fine, thank you.'

The day passed quickly. Vivian was pleased because her work was a calming distraction, and prevented her from dwelling on her horrible weekend.

At the end of her workday, her car wove through the busy traffic on the way to George and Edward's. During the day Vivian had called Edward to ask if she could visit. Edward agreed, but told her George might already be asleep by the time she arrived. In truth she wasn't too disappointed, because she actually just wanted to ask Edward about Victoria.

Their apartment door was ajar when the lift's doors opened. A delicious aroma filled the corridor.

In the kitchen, Edward was busy cooking.

'Hi, Edward.' Vivian walked towards him and kissed his sunken cheek.

'Hi, dear. Sit down first. We can eat in a few more minutes.' Vivian sat down and realized her stomach was rumbling. She hadn't eaten lunch that day.

'What are you cooking?'

'Oh, nothing special. Just a leg of roast lamb with broccoli and baked potatoes.'

'Sounds absolutely delicious to me.' A few minutes later, they ate together quietly. Vivian broke the silence. 'How's George?'

'He's been prescribed new medicines to reduce the pain, and he's responding well.'

'That's good to hear.'

Edward looked at Vivian earnestly. 'Say what's on your mind. I can see something's troubling you.'

Vivian felt like crying. 'Oh, Edward, I don't know where to start.' Edward held her hand lovingly.

'From the beginning. That's always best.'

Vivian took a deep breath before starting. 'When George forced me to go on vacation, I met a man.'

'Oh, dear, that's wonderful! Why didn't you tell us before? George would love to hear this story.'

Vivian took another deep breath. 'I didn't tell you because I wasn't sure about my feelings for him, because of how I feel about Ferris…' Vivian told Edward the whole story, from what her friends had warned her about Ethan, to how he approached her in Aruba. With tears streaming down her cheeks, Vivian told Edward about the sexual abuse and humiliation committed by Ethan and his friends.

Edward listened intently. 'God, honey. How shocking. You should never let him back into your life. You need to ignore him and try and forget all about him.'

'Edward, there is one more detail I need to share with you.'

'You can tell me anything, dear.'

Vivian shifted in her seat and sipped her steaming coffee. 'I know I'm out of line and that it's none of my business, but how did Victoria commit suicide?'

Edward was startled by her question. 'Why are you asking?'

'Victoria has appeared to me several times, both while I'm awake and in my dreams. In my dream, she showed me something, and that's why I ask. I want to know if it was just a dream or if she really tried to communicate with me.'

Edward rubbed his chin, and with a deeply grave expression he said softly, 'She slashed her wrists.'

Vivian's face turned pale, her breath became erratic and she felt dizzy. 'Vivian, are you okay?' Edward asked.

'She cut her wrists in a bathtub, didn't she?'

It took a while for Edward to answer, 'Yes, Vivian, how did you know?' Tears rolled down Edward's cheeks.

'In my dream Victoria showed me how she'd lay there with her eyes open and the water still running.'

Edward nodded.

'The only thing she didn't show me is who found her.'
Suddenly Edward rose up, and his chair clattered on the tiles. 'I found her Vivian. It happened here. Sometimes I wake up in the middle of the night, thinking I can still hear the water running.'
He knelt on the kitchen floor and started sobbing. Vivian sat down next to him and cried with him.

'Edward, was Vicky seeing anyone before she ended her life?'
Edward thought hard then replied, 'Yes, she was, but I believe they had already broken up.'

'Do you remember his name?'
Again Edward thought hard but shook his head.

'Was it Ethan Stein?'

'Ethan... yes, that sounds familiar, but I don't know his last name. How do you know all this, Vivian?'
Vivian told him everything she knew about the rumors she'd heard about the two young women who'd committed suicide, and that Ethan might have had something to do with it. She also told Edward about the hair ornament that George had given her, and that after she'd stolen it back, Ethan was furious.

'Vivian, if that is true, then you might be in danger. What if he caught you? I can't imagine what could've happened.'

'At that time I didn't think. I just wanted it back because it was a gift from George. Edward, did Vicky leave a suicide note?'

'No, nothing.'

Later that night in bed, Vivian hoped Victoria would visit her in a dream and explain why she had killed herself. The next morning, she was disappointed because Victoria hadn't appeared.

The week went by quickly, and soon the day of the Frenay & Iams party had arrived. Glancing at her watch, Vivian realized she needed to hurry because Ferris would pick her up at seven. She wore a long cream Lanvin gown with matching shoes and bag. The color of the dress accentuated her tanned skin. She was content with her ensemble, especially as the gown's long sleeves were necessary as her bruises were yet to completely fade.

It was six-thirty – she still had half an hour. With her shoes in hand, she walked into the kitchen when the doorbell rang. She opened the door to a breathtakingly handsome man in a tuxedo. He gazed in awe at Vivian and said, 'You look amazing, Vivian.'

Her cheeks turned bright red. 'You too, Ferris.'

CHAPTER 20

Ferris held out his hand and helped Vivian get out of his Range Rover. The touch of his hand gave her shivers all over, but she suppressed her reaction immediately – she still felt traumatized after Dubai.

Trisha and Lily stood near the entrance, undressing Ferris with their gaze. Vivian even got a dirty look from Lily. Ferris didn't even glance at them as he was completely occupied with accompanying Vivian to the bar.

Vivian looked around and was quite charmed by the glamorous decorations and glitzy casino décor. Ferris passed her a glass of white wine.

'Thank you. Do you think Sean and Clive will be coming?'

'No, I don't think so. They prefer to be behind the scenes.'

Vivian realized her female colleagues were glaring at her jealously. Some even deliberately approached Ferris and tried to make small talk.

Vivian couldn't blame them. Ferris was utterly unaware of what was happening around him as he casually talked with Alex from the administration section. Even though the event was festive, Vivian felt a little sad because it seemed no one realized that George was not there for the first time. He always came to the staff parties. Had they all forgotten him already? Because they were oblivious to the fact she was standing behind them,

Vivian overheard a conversation among a few of her colleagues.

'Pff... did you see how they made an entrance together?'

'Let me guess who you're referring to... Ferris and Vivian?' The women cackled together. 'Yes, did you see how she held his hand? Do you think she wants him as a boyfriend?' Vivian took a step closer so she could hear more clearly.

'I don't think he's into women. He never looks at me. He's obviously gay.' They cackled again.

'Yeah, I think you're right. It's such a shame that some gay men are so incredibly good looking.'

'Well, I've heard from a reliable source that he's definitely not gay. He was with a woman for a very long time.'

'Are you sure?'

'Yes. However, even if he does like women, what's he doing with that spoiled brat? Have you noticed she's been reticent lately? I think she misses the privileges George used to give her.'

'I heard that George is very sick, so it won't be long before there's nobody around here to save her.' The women laughed again. Vivian was filled with anger and sadness, even though she knew they were simply jealous of her. Vivian then began to think of ways to make them even more jealous. With a teasing smile, Vivian walked over to Ferris while staring at the women watching her. Did she dare to do it? Their eyes met and Vivian knew there was no turning back now.

'Ferris, please put your arm around me. I'll explain to you later,' she whispered.

Without hesitation, he enfolded Vivian in his toned arm, and brought his face close to Vivian's ear. 'Tell me,' he whispered teasingly.

'I heard people talking about us.'

Vivian saw that all eyes were on them, and Ferris noticed too. Suddenly, he grabbed her hand and pulled her onto the dancefloor. Everybody kept watching them.

Once again Ferris whispered in her ear, 'I thought you were above all that the gossiping.'

'You know I usually am, but just not at this moment.' They danced throughout the song, and when it ended Ferris kissed the back of Vivian's hand sweetly. They walked together back to the bar. Vivian felt everyone's eyes stabbing into her back.

'Let's give them something they really can talk about.' Vivian looked at him questioningly, and before she replied, Ferris kissed her on the cheek and put his arm back around her shoulder. Vivian stood close to him. Her whole body began to glow, and Ferris's hand gently stroked her shoulder. All the women in the room glared at her, stricken with jealousy. Vivian shivered underneath Ferris's touch because it reminded her of her time with Ethan. Ferris noticed and stopped caressing her, and Vivian immediately regretted giving him the wrong signal. The night was still young, but Vivian felt tired. She looked at Ferris.

He seemed to be enjoying himself while conversing with Alex. She approached Ferris and put her hand on his arm carefully.

'Ferris, I'm going to get a cab home so you can stay here.'

'No way. I picked you up so I'll take you home too.'

'No need. I don't want to ruin your night.'

'You're not, Vivian. Let's go.' He put his arm around Vivian for the third time that night, and they left the room. They both knew very well that there'd already be a lot of gossip about them floating around, but neither of them seemed to care. Ferris helped her into the car, closed the door, got behind the wheel, and turned on the engine. Both of them were deep in thought, and they drove to Vivian's apartment in silence. When they'd arrived Vivian asked, 'Do you want a nightcap?'

'If you have some Barbaresco left, I won't refuse.'

Ferris unbuttoned his jacket, removed it and draped it neatly over the back of a chair. This pleased Vivian as it seemed he wasn't in a hurry to go home. He rolled up his sleeves and undid the top two buttons of his shirt. While he poured the Barbaresco, she noticed how he did everything gracefully.

'I feel guilty because you missed out on the rest of the party.' Ferris smiled at her as he relaxed on the couch. 'Don't worry. I wasn't too fond of the party either. Now tell me about the gossip you heard.'

Vivian told him exactly shed heard.

'I can assure you, I'm not gay. So, don't let them get to you, because believe me, there isn't a straight man on this earth who wouldn' be proud to have a woman as beautiful as you by his side.'

Vivian had no idea how to respond to this compliment, so she searched for a safe topic. 'I'm just sad that nobody seems to have missed George tonight.'

'You're right. Have you visited him since you returned from Dubai?'

'Yes, but he was asleep, so I only spoke with Edward. The whole situation is really taking its toll on him too. He's getting thinner day by day.'

'I understand,' Ferris said softly, as he placed his empty glass on the table. For a moment, they stared at each other in silence, and Vivian thought she could see desire in his eyes. Her heart pounded, and she pressed her thighs to stop the tingling between her legs.

'Would you like another glass?' Vivian stood up and took their two empty glasses back to the kitchen.

'No, thank you. I'd better get home.'

'Are you sure? It's still early.'

'I'm sure.'

Deeply disappointed, Vivian walked Ferris to the door. He kissed her cheeks tenderly, and left. Vivian stared out the window at Ferris's Range Rover as it disappeared into the dark. She told herself that it was for the best that he'd gone home after her traumatic experience. Her feelings of dread and discomfort returned when she realized she hadn't heard anything from Ethan after his three text messages and two aggressive voicemails. Vivian knew he wouldn't give up so easily. She even considered changing her phone number, but that would only mean more dishonesty to her friends. Vivian hated the fact she'd been lying so much lately.

Although her best friends were an essential part of her life, Vivian had avoided contacting them because she was sick and tired of her dishonesty.

That night Vivian had a nightmare. She was raped by Yasar and Farouk in exactly the same way they raped Victoria. Vivian woke up crying and soaking in a pool of sweat. For the rest of the weekend, she locked herself in her apartment with her phone switched off. She didn't want to hear or see anyone. Vivian desperately needed to figure out how to get her life back on track again. She hated Ethan for what he had done to her, and she wondered if she could ever return to the Vivian she was before she met him. She knew that the best way for her to cope was to bury herself in work.

In their office the following Monday morning, Ferris would glance up at Vivian occasionally, but he didn't say anything. He stood up and left the office and returned with a cappuccino and a cafe latte for Vivian.

'Thanks, Ferris, I really needed that.'

'You're welcome.' He sat back behind his desk. The clock on her computer showed ten minutes to two. With her coffee in hand, she gazed out the window.

The weather was gloomy, the rain relentless.

As she went to take a sip of coffee, she dropped the cup, and her face drained of color. She stared without seeing anything and was unable to make a sound.

Ferris was shocked and within a second has knelt beside her. 'Vivian?'

She could hear the panic in his voice but still wasn't able to speak.

Ferris pulled her out of her chair and wrapped his arms around her. Vivian was shaking and felt her surroundings spin. Ferris held her tight. Once again, he called her name, 'Vivian, what's wrong? Say something. Should I call a doctor?'

She shook her head. 'No, no. No need. Everything is fine.'

Ferris slowly helped her to sit back on her chair and knelt beside her. He gave Vivian time to calm down. 'What happened?'

She looked confused and struggled to find the words to describe what she'd just experienced. 'It felt... I felt George passing right through me. I could feel him and smell his scent.'

Vivian stared at Ferris, who was still on his knees holding her hand. He was just about to say something before the phone on Vivian's desk rang. She quickly picked it up and held it close to her ear.

'With Victo...' Her voice faded as she dropped the phone. Tears streamed down her cheeks. Ferris grabbed the phone from her lap, but the connection was already cut off.

Ferris knew precisely what news Vivian had just received. He pulled her into his arms and rocked her gently. Vivian hugged him tightly, as though she was afraid of falling. She cried and sobbed in Ferris's arms.

'Oh Ferris, he's gone. He's left us.' Ferris's arms gave Vivian a deep sense of safety, despite what she'd just heard. She felt his muscles pressing gently against her. His woody scent pierced her nostrils, making her feel tranquil.

'Come on. I'll take you home.' Ferris let go of his arms and wiped Vivian's tears with his thumbs.

In the car, Vivian covered her face with hands and sobbed quietly.

'Vivian?'

With a face still hidden behind her hands, she answered, 'Yes?'

'Look at me, Vivian.'

She looked at Ferris with tears still flooding her cheeks.

'Should I take you somewhere else, because you shouldn't be alone in this situation.'

She couldn't go anywhere. She didn't want to see her friends, and her mother was the last person she wanted to see. Vivian shook her head. Ferris nodded and started to drive. The car entered a parking area, and Vivian looked at him, confused. Drowning in her sadness, Vivian hadn't noticed that he hadn't driven her home. As usual, he helped Vivian out of his car. They walked toward an elevator. He tapped his keycard on a panel, and the doors opened.

They entered the lift and headed for the top floor.
Vivian was still leaning on Ferris when the elevator door
opened onto a vast, elegant apartment.

'Welcome, make yourself at home,' Ferris said gently. Vivian
suddenly realized he'd taken her to his home. Ferris pointed to
a large couch in front of a fireplace. 'Why don't you take a
seat. I'll make us some coffee and call the office.'
Vivian nodded and nestled into the couch. She could smell his
masculine scent on the cushions. Ferris returned with coffee
and sat beside Vivian. She held the glass tightly to warm her
hands.

'Are you cold?'

'A little.'

Ferris placed a few blocks of wood into the fireplace, stoked it
with an antique steel rod, and in minutes the wood crackled,
the fire blazing.

'Better?'

'Yes, thank you.'

'How are you feeling now?'

Vivian thought for a while before answering. 'Numb, sad and
empty.' Tears started to flow down her cheeks again.

'I understand. That's why I brought you here because I don't
want you to be alone. Hopefully, you don't mind.'

'No, I don't mind. Thank you for understanding, because I
really don't want to be alone right now.'

Ferris took off his jacket, and Vivian noticed how his tight shirt clung to his muscular, toned chest. Embarrassed, Vivian looked away.

'Do you want to look around?'

It was a welcoming distraction for her to get her mind off her sadness for a minute. Ferris's penthouse was classically furnished with a few modern touches here and there. It had fantastic views over Central Park.

Each room was tastefully and practically decorated. There were two large guest rooms, each with an en suite bathroom and walk-in closet. The kitchen was very lavish with top-of-the-line utensils and equipment.

A beautiful wooden staircase brought them to the upper-level. It was an open space with big windows and a complete gym. Now she understood where his muscular body came from.

Ferris stopped at the door. 'This is my bedroom,' he said softly. He pushed the door, and Vivian was surprised to see the Renaissance painting of the half-naked woman surrounded by angels, which she wanted to buy at William Doyle's auction house. With raised eyebrows, Vivian glanced at Ferris.

'So you were the one who bought it!' A teasing smile appeared on Ferris's lips.

'What do you mean? I don't understand.'

Now a smile appeared on Vivian's lips. 'That painting.' Vivian pointed towards the painting above his bed.

'I didn't know you were interested in it too,' he said, genuinely surprised.

'I was, but it suits your home better than it would mine, I guess.'

'Thank you.'

They returned to the living room where the fire still crackled.

'Do you mind if I take off my shoes?'

'Not at all. Like I said, make yourself at home.'

Vivian took off her shoes and sat on the carpet in front of the fireplace. 'I really wanted to have a fireplace too,' she said while staring into the dancing flames.

Ferris sat down in a chair beside the fireplace. 'It's very calming, and I often use it when it's cold.'

Vivian looked around the living room. 'You once asked me to work on your apartment, but it's all very classy yet cozy, and I wouldn't change a thing. Why do you want to redesign it anyway?'

'If you say so, then I won't change it. I trust you. You're the expert.' For the first time that day, Vivian laughed.

'I'm glad to see you can still manage a laugh. Do you know what I usually drink in front of the fireplace?'

Vivian looked at him curiously. 'Let me guess, cognac?'

'Wrong. Hot chocolate with whipped cream.'

'Really?'

'Do you want me to make some?'

'Yes, please!'

They spent the rest of the afternoon chatting in front of the fireplace, while a thunderstorm outside made it even cozier.

After dinner, they sat on the couch and watched television. Vivian fought to keep her eyes open. That day had taken a real toll on her. Completely exhausted, she drifted off to sleep on the couch. In her sleep, she cried.

'What happened, Vivian?' Ferris's voice sounded sleepy but full of concern. It took a while for her to realize she had fallen asleep on the couch next to Ferris.

'Sorry. I didn't mean to wake you up. It's just I still can't believe that George is gone, Ferris.'

'You know, Vivian. Apart from your sadness, this is for the better. George is free of pain now.'

'I know... but there are just so many things I still want to ask him, and so many things I want to tell him. The worst thing is, I never told him how much he meant to me and how much I loved him.'

'I can understand that you'd regret that, but you have to believe me when I saw that George knew. That feeling was mutual. I worked with him for a long time, and every time he talked about you, a smile always grew on his face, and his eyes shone. Don't forget that when he died, he immediately came to you. It proves how much he cared for you.'

Vivian thought of Ferris's words and wished to God that it was true.

'Thank you, Ferris.'

'What for?'

'Thank you for today. Thank you for not leaving me alone.'

He kissed Vivian's forehead tenderly. 'You're welcome. I know you'd do the same for me.'

If only he knew that she would do anything for him. 'Of course I would.'

Vivian could feel the tension building in her body. She wanted him so badly, and suddenly realized that he could heal her and make her forget all about Ethan. His sexy voice brought her back to reality.

'Let's try to get some sleep. Tomorrow I must get back to the office. I arranged for you to have some time off so you can help Edward if you want.'

Vivian was overwhelmed by how thoughtful he was, and now she knew for sure that she would die for him. She nestled into the couch in front of him.

'Goodnight, Ferris.'

'Sleep tight, Vivian.'

CHAPTER 21

The next morning, they drove to the office together. Ferris parked his car next to Vivian's.

'Are you sure I don't have to go in and talk to Sean and Clive?'

'Don't worry. I took care of that yesterday. They're aware of the situation, so you take all the time you need.'

'Thank you, Ferris.'

'Vivian, if you want, I can prepare a guest room for you at my place, so you don't have to be alone.'

Ferris's offer sounded so tempting. 'That's so nice of you, but I can't.' For a moment she thought she saw an expression of disappointment in his eyes, but she wasn't sure. 'I really have to accept that George is gone.'

'I understand. But the offer still stands if you need it, you're more than welcome. What will you do when you get home?'

Vivian thought for a moment. 'Take a shower and then go to Edward. I'm sure he needs support more than anyone right now.'

'If there's anything I can help with, please don't hesitate to call me, okay?'

'Will do. Thanks again, Ferris.'

Ferris opened the car door and helped Vivian out. When they were hugging goodbye, Lily passed by and glared at Vivian with hatred in her eyes.

Ferris noticed her glare and quickly kissed Vivian'[s lips. Lilly quickened her pace, a look of complete shock on her face.

'Sorry, Viv. Please forgive me. I just couldn't resist doing that so now they really have something to gossip about.'

Vivian, caught by surprise, lightly touched her lips.

'No... Yes... I understand,' she stammered.

Under the shower, Vivian's mind drifted away. She still couldn't believe George was gone, and that she had spent the night at Ferris's place.

Vivian's thoughts returned to Ferris's gorgeous home. How could he afford to own such a luxurious penthouse in an elite location like that?

She touched her lips again, where not long before he had kissed her. She remembered the look on Lilly's face and knew for sure that by now the whole office would know about it.

As fast as she could, Vivian got dressed and rushed over to Edward, after calling to tell him she was on her way. Ralph opened the door for her, but this time, there was no smile. He simply nodded compassionately.

'My deepest condolences, Miss Foster.'

'Thank you, Ralph. You too.'

The door was already open, and as she walked in Vivian heard voices coming from the living room. Edward was talking to someone from the funeral home. She decided to wait in the kitchen, but Edward called out to her. 'Vivian, please come and join us.'

Edward looked pale, and there were dark shadows beneath his red, swollen eyes. He must have been crying relentlessly.

'I can't decide between these two grief cards. Which one do you think is best?'

Vivian introduced herself to the funeral home clerk, who was dressed in an oversized black suit that made him look older than he was. She stood beside Edward, who was holding the cards with trembling hands. Vivian took the cards from him and hugged Edward tightly, while whispering into his ear, 'Edward, I am so, so sorry for your loss.'

'Me too, baby. I'm so grateful though that he left peacefully, with a smile on his face.'

The clerk cleared his throat to get their attention.

Vivian took a good look at each of the grief cards and pointed to one. 'I think this one is best,' she said gently.

Edward nodded, and the funeral home director noted their choice.

'If you don't have any further questions, then I'll be on my way. Today the cards will be printed and sent out.'

Edward sat in a chair while Vivian walked the clerk out. With two cups of coffee, she returned to the living room where Edward was still ensconced in his chair.

'Edward, are you okay?'

He looked at her with a teary face. 'Yes, I'm doing okay, sweetie. I'm really glad you're here.' He stroked Vivian's cheek gently.

He told her that the day before, George had made jokes after lunch and that his eyes were bright. Afterward, Edward had helped George to take a shower. After taking his medication, George had told him how much he loved and appreciated Edward, and how lucky he felt to have shared his life with him. The last words he said were, 'I love you with all my heart.' He squeezed Edward's hand, closed his eyes, and a soft smile appeared on his lips. Then he crossed over. Vivian cried as listened to Edward's story.

'He looked so peaceful. I thank God that I was with him and that he saved his last words for me.'

'I'm so happy to hear that, Edward. What time did he leave?' Vivian wiped away her tears.

'Around a quarter to two.'

'Before you called me, Edward, I experienced something inexplicable.'

'What was it?' Vivian told him in detail what happened. Edward hugged her and said, 'I experienced the same thing. But I thought it was just my imagination. I believe it was his way of saying goodbye to the people he loved the most.' Vivian looked at him in surprise. She was grateful they had shared the same experience.

'When is the funeral?'

'Friday at two o'clock.'

'Is there anything else that needs to be taken care of before Friday?'

'No, George had arranged everything meticulously. From the music, to the flowers, to the coffin – only the grief cards needed to be decided on.'

'Yes... That sounds just like George, arranging everything in minute detail.'

A small smile spread across Edward's lips.

'Have I told you how grateful I am that you're here?'

'Yes, you did. There's nowhere I would rather be right now than here with you. Is there still a chance to see him for the last time, to say goodbye?'

'From Tomorrow until Thursday night, friends and acquaintances can say their goodbyes. You can see him now if you like.'

'Now?' Vivian stared at Edward with wide eyes.

'Yes. George was very explicit with his instructions. He hated the idea of a funeral hall, and the mortuary. He chose to be in his own home, in his own warm and comfortable surroundings.'

'Isn't that hard on you, Edward?'

'No, I like having him here. In that way, I can stay with him just a little bit longer.'

They walked to the library where the coffin stood in the middle of the room. 'I''l give you some time alone with him.' Edward left the room. Slowly she walked to the coffin and saw George lying peacefully in a debonair gray suit and soft purple tie. Wrinkles adorned his eyes.

Crying silent tears, she stroked
George's face. He was freezing, and Vivian wanted to cover
him with a blanket and light a fire in the fireplace to warm him
up, but she knew it didn't make sense.

'George, you've gone too soon. There are so many things that
have been left unsaid. I wish I could turn back time so I could
tell you how much I love you, and how much I cherish our
friendship. I want to thank you for welcoming me into your
life, which has enriched greatly enriched mine. Edward told me
that you left in peace. I'm thankful for that. Now you don't
have to fight your disease anymore, you are free. You can
reunite with Victoria, and hopefully, you will watch over
Edward and me. George, I know you loved Edward, but please
don't worry about him. I'll keep visiting and supporting him.'
Vivian stood for a moment beside his lifeless body before she
left the library. Edward sat waiting for her in the living room.

'How was he?'

'As if he was only sleeping. Like he could wake up any time
soon.'

'Yeah...' Lost in thought, they sat next to each other on the
couch.

The sound of Vivian's phone broke the silence. She pulled it
out and saw Ferris's name on the screen.

'Hi, Ferris.' With the cellphone to her ear, she looked at
Edward. 'Wait a minute, let me ask him. Ferris has offered to
bring us some takeout.'

304

'Yes, please, that would be lovely. I just don't have it in me to cook right now.'

Vivian delivered Edward's answer to Ferris, and they talked a little more. She then felt her cheeks flushing red as Edward started to look at her curiously. Vivian ended the call and sat back down next to Edward.

'What?' She asked, with her cheeks still glowing.

'How are you getting along with Ferris these days?

She told Edward about the party, the kiss, and about the night she spent at Ferris's place. She noticed that her chatting was taking both their minds of their sadness, so she kept on talking until Ralph announced that Ferris was on his way up.

Vivian waited at the door. When the elevator door opened, Vivian's heart skipped a beat. Ferris looked incredibly rugged and handsome, wearing jeans and a tight t-shirt. She thought about how often he'd been coming to her rescue lately.

'How are you doing, Vivian? You look tired,' he kissed her quickly on the cheek in greeting.

'I'm holding up ok. Thank you for taking the trouble to bring us some takeout.'

'No trouble at all. It's the least I can do.'

In the kitchen, Ferris expressed his condolences to Edward, while Vivian prepared the table with the Italian takeout and poured some red wine. Cannelloni, gnocchi and fettucine her favorite comfort food.

Vivian sat between Edward and Ferris.

The atmosphere during dinner was warm and relaxed, as they each shared some of their favorite memories of George.

They moved from the kitchen to the living room where the fireplace was burning, and continued sharing happy memories. The two men enjoyed a glass of cognac while Vivian sipped green tea. Their conversation slowed. Edward was trying hard to stay awake.

'Edward, why don't you try to get some sleep?'

'No, dear. I want to keep vigil over George tonight.'

'Let me do it, Edward. You need to get some rest. Otherwise, you'll be exhausted at the funeral. That won't do you any good.'

'Vivian is right, Edward. Try to get some sleep. You need to save all your strength for the next few days. Vivian and I can watch over George together.' Edward looked doubtful but eventually gave in. 'Okay, I'll try to sleep. Thank you both for the offer. But first let me get some blankets for you because it's freezing out there.' Edward disappeared and returned with warm fleece blankets. Ferris took the blankets and poured another glass of cognac.

'Here, Edward. Drink this. It'll help you sleep.'

Edward took the glass from Ferris's hand and kissed Vivian's cheek. 'Thank you, dear. I'm so glad you're here. I already mentioned that, right?'

'Yes, Edward, you did, several times. I'm glad to be here with you.'

The library was freezing when Ferris and Vivian went inside. Ferris stopped next to the coffin and looked at George. 'Rest in peace, George. You will be missed, my friend.'

'Ferris, you don't need to stay here, I can do it myself. You have to go back to the office in the morning, so you need to rest too.'

'Don't worry about me. I have special privileges at the office.'

'You do? What kind of privileges?'

'Trust me, Vivian. When the time is right, I will let you know.'

'Let me guess, that time isn't now?'

'No. It isn't.'

She had the urge to tease him, but wisely she refrained. It amused her that this would be the second time in a row that she would spend the night with him. Vivian covered her body with a blanket and sat by the window. Ferris followed her and sat on the couch.

'The view from here is almost as beautiful as the view from your place.' Vivian gazed down at the Hudson and watched a boat gliding across the water, which was illuminated by the moon. 'You haven't seen anything yet. The view is even more spectacular on New Year's Eve.'

'I'll take your word for it.' Vivian pulled the blanket tighter around her body.

'Cold?'

'Freezing.'

'Come join me over here. It's always colder by the window.'

With a blanket draped around her shoulders, Vivian padded over to the couch and sat beside Ferris. He embraced her and rubbed her arms to warm her up. Vivian leaned into him, and the cold disappeared.

The sun had risen when Edward entered the library. Ferris and Vivian had watched over George all night. Edward walked towards George's coffin and kissed him lovingly on the forehead, just like he did when he was still alive.

'Come on, dears, breakfast is ready.' Edward poured them all coffee and sat at the kitchen table.

'Were you able to sleep last night, Edward?'

'I did manage to, yes. Thanks for recommending that second glass of cognac. You were both right. I needed to rest because today and tomorrow I expect many will come to say their last goodbyes to George.'

'Let me go home to take a quick shower and change clothes. Then I'll be back to help welcome and guide the guests, so you won't have to do anything. You can withdraw whenever you want.'

Edward appeared as though a huge burden had lifted from his shoulders. 'Do you mean that Vivian? I would be truly grateful.'

'Of course, Edward.'

'She must be an angel sent by God, Ferris,' Edward said while glancing at him.

'She sure is. I'll call a friend to arrange catering here,

so you don't have to worry about food and beverages for the guests.'

'Thank you. What would I do without you two?' Edward sighed with relief.

When she entered her front door, Vivian was overcome with a strange, uncomfortable feeling. She had never felt anything like it before in her own home. After spending two nights with Ferris, of course she only wanted more. It crossed her mind to accept his offer to stay at his place for a while, but she quickly quashed the thought. The shower slowly faded the fatigue from her body.

She carefully selected her outfit, deciding on a black pant suit with her yellow blouse. She also packed a small overnight back with some extra clothing, just in case she needed it. After closing her door, the uncomfortable feeling that had haunted her immediately disappeared.

Vivian arrived moments before the first guests arrived. She offered them coffee or tea and guided them to the library. The catering Ferris had ordered had arrived earlier, and elaborate platters of pastries, cakes and sandwiches were arranged throughout the kitchen, with a large pot of pumpkin and nutmeg soup on the stove for the evening. Friends of George came and went throughout the day, with Edward spending most of the time next to George's coffin.

The following day was the same, with more platters and soup arriving in the morning.

Vivian had no idea that George and Edward knew so many people. It was late at night when the last guests left. Vivian rested in a chair while Ferris helped to clean up the catering. The antique clock chimed, indicating it was midnight. The day of George's funeral had arrived.

Morning came, and a violent storm brought heavy rainfall. Vivian poured coffee for herself, then sat beside Edward. She wrapped her hand around his tightly. 'How you're holding up, Edward?'

'I'm fine, dear.' He got up from his seat, walked to the closet, and retrieved a neatly wrapped gift.

'Here.' He handed it to Vivian. 'Before I forget. I had planned on giving this to you after the funeral, but I want you to have it now. Because after the funeral I'll spend some time at my mother's, mainly so I can get some proper rest.'

Vivian opened the gift, and tears immediately rolled down her cheeks. It was the recipe book Edward had written for George, which contained all his favorite recipes.

'This is the first copy. It was supposed to be for George, but unfortunately it came back from the printers after he passed away.'

Vivian stood up and cried in Edward's arms.

'Are you sure you want me to have it?'

'Yes, Vivian. After all, I know how much you appreciate my cooking.'

'Thank you, Edward. I will treasure it forever.'

The funeral was very crowded despite the heavy rain. Sean and Clive were present, as well as some of her other colleagues. For Vivian, it all passed like a dream, and before she realized it, people were leaving the cemetery. The only ones remaining were Edward and his mother, Ferris, Sean, Clive and herself. Edward said goodbye to Ferris and Vivian and thanked them for all their help and support over the previous few days. After hugging Vivian tightly and shaking hands with Ferris, he walked away with his mother by his side. Sean and Clive shook Vivian's hand before they left.

'Come on, let me take you home.' Ferris put his arm around her and helped Vivian into his car.

Vivian suddenly realized how cold the air was outside. She couldn't even feel her legs anymore.

Ferris pulled over in front of her apartment. 'Are you okay, Vivian? I don't want you to be alone. It just doesn't feel right.'

'I'm fine. I want to take a hot shower and go straight to bed.'

'Well, if there's anything at all, please don't hesitate to call me, even in the middle of the night.'

'I will. I promise. Thank you, Ferris, you've been such a great help to me and to Edward.'

She climbed the stairs to her apartment, as there was no lift in her building. Vivian was reluctant to be alone. Since George's death, she had hardly been home, and had spent the whole time surrounded by people. She opened the door feeling empty, numb, and deeply sad.

Suddenly she was shocked to see that the lights were already on. She was certain she hadn't left them on when she'd departed. Vivian padded barefoot into the living room.

'Well, well, well. Look who we have here.'

Her breathing stopped and her face turned pale as fear and panic engulfed her. Ethan stood by the window with his arms crossed in front of his chest, waiting for her.

CHAPTER 22

The room was spinning around her, and her body started to sway. She grabbed the couch to prevent herself from falling. Dozens of questions raced through her mind and her mouth dried up. How did he get in? How did he know where she lived? She'd never told him that. What was he going to do to her?

Ethan walked towards her, his dark eyes fixed on her in a malicious scowl. Vivian stepped backward until her back pressed against the wall. There was no escaping him as Ethan completely blocked her way.

He lunged toward her and grabbed her neck, chocking her. Vivian was paralyzed by fear.

'Did you think you could get rid of me that easily? Did you think you could escape me?' Ethan's grip on her neck tightened. She was having serious difficulty breathing. She struggled with all her might until he punched her left cheek, then grabbed her hair and threw her onto the couch.

'I came here to get back what is mine.' Tears flowed down her cheeks, and she coughed severely after the strangulation.

'Where is it?' he screamed.

Terrified, Vivian was unable to say a word. For the second time, he punched her, this time on her left temple. She could taste blood in her mouth.

'Stop crying, bitch! Answer my question!'

'I don't know what you're talking about.' Vivian rubbed her throbbing cheek. She knew she was bleeding.

'You don't know what I'm talking about?' Before she could answer, he grabbed her hair and dragged her into the bedroom, then threw her on the bed.

'I am going to ask you one last time before I really lose my patience. Where are you hiding my hairpin and bracelet?' With trembling fingers that were covered in blood, she pointed to the bedside table. He pulled open the drawer roughly, took out the small black velvet bag, and stuffed it into his pocket.

'So this is your bedroom,' he said while glancing around.

'How many men have you invited in here to fuck you? What about the guy who drove you home? Did he fuck you in his car, or did you give him a blowjob?'

The way Ethan disparaged Ferris made her furious. She narrowed her eyes and challenged Ethan. 'He is more manly than you will ever be. You can't even stand in his shadow…' Vivian couldn't finish her sentence because his fist landed hard on her left eye. For a moment she couldn't see, she could only feel the intense flash of pain. What she had said made him even more violent.

He tore Vivian's clothes off and pinned her on the bed. Vivian tried her best to fight him off, but she simply wasn't strong enough. After forcing her legs open he locked her arms down, then rammed his cock into her again and again, raping her brutally. He continued to slap her face and her breasts.

Vivian had given up completely. She was only able to lie back like a helpless cloth doll beneath him. Her salty tears stung the wounds on her face.

Vivian could tell he had almost reached his climax as he continued to slap her over and over. After he came with a violent growl, he pulled his cock out, put on his pants, and laughed at her mockingly. He turned and walked away. Vivian quietly prayed he would leave.

Ethan turned around and came back. Because of the swelling on her face, she could barely see what he was doing.

'Oh yeah... I almost forgot. I have an interesting movie for you.' He threw something on the bed and Vivian trembled with fear. He threw his head back and laughed. 'That's right, you stupid whore, fear me. For as long as you live, fear me.' He spat on Vivian's face before he left the bedroom, but then quickly returned. 'Now you can join the others, Victoria and Melissa. Believe me. I will make sure no other man will ever want to fuck you again.'

Before she lost consciousness, Vivian heard him laughing as he walked out and slammed the front door.

In the middle of the night, Vivian woke up covered in sweat. She'd had a nightmare. She tried to calm herself down by convincing herself it was just a bad dream. When she went to wipe her forehead and her body flashed with pain, the cold hard truth hit her. It wasn't just a bad dream. She struggled to get out of bed.

The clock on her bedside table showed four in the morning. She had been unconscious for more than ten hours. For a moment, she sat on the edge of the bed because she wasn't sure her legs could carry her to the bathroom. She tried to stand up and walk. The pain was extreme, and there wasn't an inch of her body that didn't hurt.

As she turned on the light and saw her reflection in the bathroom mirror, she screamed. Her whole face was swollen and covered with dried blood. Tears flowed when she saw the wounds on her eyes and lips. Ethan had abused, assaulted and raped her in the one place she should have been safe and secure her own home.

Vivian lowered herself to the bathroom floor and cried until there were no more tears left. After a while, she started to think rationally. She couldn't just sit here. She needed to do something. In her mind, she listed who she should call. She couldn't call her friends because she'd alienated herself from them lately, and she couldn't tell them the truth about Ethan. It was impossible to call Ferris, because what should she say to him? George was no longer around, and Edward was out of town, staying with his mother in San Francisco. She didn't dare to call her mother, because again, what would she say? The only thing left to do was call the police. After all, Ethan had forced his way into her home and abused, assaulted and raped her. With all the strength she could manage,

she pulled on her bathrobe and stumbled to the living room.

With trembling fingers, she dialed 911.

About ten minutes later, there was a hard knock on the door. With a pounding heart, she shuffled toward it.

'He... hello?'

'Police.'

She felt incredibly relieved to hear that word, and opened the door. With blurred vision due to her swollen eyes, she noticed how the two middle-aged officers looked at her in pity. They quickly realized Vivian couldn't support her own body any longer and guided her to the living room. One of the officers asked Vivian if she could explain what had happened. While Vivian told him, the other officer recorded everything in a notebook.

'So, if I understand correctly, this person entered your house without permission?'

'Yes, that's right.' The officer walked to the front door because it was the only way anyone could get into the apartment.

'There are no signs of forced entry.'

'He must have made a spare key when I visited him in Dubai.' With great pity, the two officers looked at Vivian closely. 'Is there anything missing in your house ma'am?'

Vivian couldn't answer properly as she hadn't checked her home yet. 'Not to my knowledge, no. Only the hairpin, and the bracelet.'

'Okay. I think that's enough information for the moment.

The next step is to take you to the hospital for a medical examination, and to collect physical evidence such as hair and semen.'

Even though Vivian was enormously reluctant to do it, she knew it had to be done.

One of the officers glanced at her bathrobe. 'Would you like to change clothes before we leave?'

'Yes, please. Just give me a minute.'

With great difficulty, she got dressed while they waited for her. Fortunately, it was the middle of the night, so no neighbors saw her leave in the police vehicle. She was shocked by how busy it was in the emergency room. The other patients glanced at Vivian and then quickly averted their gaze when they saw her battered face. She was extremely grateful to the officers because they ensured she didn't need to wait. A female doctor whom Vivian believed to be around her age guided her into a room and asked the police officers to wait outside.

'I'm so sorry this has happened to you Miss Foster. I'm going to clean the wounds on your face first.' Vivian felt searing pain as the doctor gently wiped her wounds with disinfectant. Even though she tried as hard as she could to hold back her tears, a few still fell down her swollen cheeks. 'I'm sorry...' Vivian apologized.

'There's no need to apologize. Just let it all out. It does help, you know.' With thorough care, the doctor cleaned Vivian's face and examined her lips and eyes.

'Thankfully, you don't require stitches as these cuts aren't that deep, so it's unlikely they'll scar.'

'Lucky me,' Vivian said sarcastically, even though she knew she'd carry invisible scars for the rest of her life.

'If you're ready, I'll proceed with the internal examination. Are you okay with that?' Vivian nodded her agreement. The doctor examined her and collected a sample of Ethan's sperm.

'Did you have unprotected sex before this happened to you?'

'Well, yes, with the man who did this to me,' Vivian said softly.

'We will of course test for venereal disease.' Vivian suddenly remembered that she'd also been violated by Ethan's two friends in Dubai, and that she'd witnessed Ethan having sex with another woman.

'Yes, thank you.'

The doctor proceeded to take another swab. 'That's everything. Thank you for being so calm.'

After Vivian finished dressing, the doctor allowed the police officers to enter the room.

'Ma'am, do you want to be taken to a relative's house? We think it's best if you're not alone.'

'No, there's no need. I'd rather go back to my own home.' Both officers looked at her doubtfully. 'You are aware that the perpetrator still has the key to your house?'

'Yes, I know, but I can padlock the front door for now. First thing tomorrow I will have the locks changed.'

'As you wish, ma'am.'

'Doctor, when will I receive the test results?'

'I will ask a colleague from the lab if she can prioritize your results. I'll contact you at four o'clock tomorrow.'

'Okay, thank you doctor.' The two police officers escorted Vivian to her front door, and checked the property to ensure there was nothing suspicious.

'Are you sure you'll be all right here alone, ma'am?'

'Yes, I'll be fine. Can you please tell me what the next step will be?'

'We'll return to headquarters to file the arrest warrant. We don't expect things to move quickly as we're unaware of the perpetrator's whereabouts.' Vivian looked disappointed.

'Can you please give me the front door key? So I can check whether the door really can't be opened from the outside now that you've padlocked it.' The officer checked it and couldn't enter.

'Now, please make sure the door is locked at all times, and if anything suspicious occurs, please call us.
We'll contact you if there are any updates. Get well soon, ma'am.'

'Thank you.' Vivian walked them out and returned to the living room. She looked around and saw where she had struggled when Ethan first grabbed her throat.
Vivian picked her phone up and saw that she had a missed call from Ferris and a voicemail message.

'Vivian, I tried calling you several times to ask how you are. Please call me back. I'm worried about you.'

She heard the sincere concern in Ferris's tone. Before hanging up he sighed heavily and said,

'Please, Vivian, call me.'

For a moment, Vivian thought she should call him. She needed support from someone, but she dismissed her thoughts quickly. She couldn't tell Ferris what had happened. Everything she experienced was just too embarrassing and vile. So she decided to ignore him, thinking it was for the better.

While taking a shower, she couldn't cleanse herself of the feeling of being tainted and dirty. After the terrible incident with Ethan, she hadn't had time to wash herself properly. Deep sadness and raging anger flared after she saw her reflection in the bathroom mirror.

Her face was still swollen and she had large bruises around her eyes and mouth. After a closer look, she also saw bruises around her neck, and on her breasts, hips, thighs, arms, and wrists.

Vivian didn't know how long she stood there looking at her injuries and feeling sorry for herself. But she knew she couldn't continue like that forever she needed to pick up the pieces and go on as best she could.

After tenderly pulling on sweatpants and a sweater, Vivian contacted the locksmith. Surprisingly, he arrived within forty-five minutes, swiftly changed the lock, and handed her a new set of keys.

Vivian crawled onto the couch and pulled a blanket around herself. The sun that was peeking through the window illuminated her battered face as she fell asleep.

Her phone rang, waking her up. She looked around anxiously and realized it was only two-thirty, so she knew it couldn't be the hospital calling. Vivian waited until her phone stopped ringing.

To keep herself busy she cleaned her entire living room, before doing the same in her bedroom. She wanted to cleanse every surface Ethan had touched.

She pulled off the sheets, and underneath one off the pillows she saw a DVD. Ethan's words echoed in her head, 'An exciting DVD for you. It really is worthwhile watching.'

She grabbed the DVD and threw it in the trash, then made her bed with fresh sheets. She couldn't ignore her fear and curiosity however, and retrieved the DVD from the trash and inserted it in her player.

Vivian sat on the couch, her eyes fixed on the TV. She felt the blood pumping in her veins as Yasar and Farouk appeared on the screen.

The footage was taken on Yasar's super yacht. The men were talking and laughing in Arabic.

It was clear that Ethan was behind the camera because she could hear his voice clearly, but couldn't see him. She watched as the men left the deck and walked into a bedroom. Vivian recognized the bedroom; it was the one where the orgy had taken place.

With her eyes and mouth wide open, Vivian couldn't believe what she saw. She was lying naked on the bed. She appeared to be conscious because her eyes were wide open, staring vaguely into the camera.

Farouk stroked her nipples, which immediately peaked. He knelt beside the bed and suckled on Vivian's nipples greedily while staring straight at the camera. Yasar removed his clothes and lay next to Vivian. He touched her other nipple and squeezed her breasts, while inserting his fingers into her. Vivian heard Ethan say something but she couldn't understand it, and then Yasar replied while changing his position. He shoved his cock into Vivian's mouth and pulled it out repeatedly.

In the next scene Vivian was having sex with Yasar and Farouk, and she appeared to enjoy what the two men did to her. With Yasar straddling her face, Vivian looked aroused as he repeatedly plunged his cock into her mouth, while Farouk pumped his thighs between her legs. She heard Ethan growl behind the camera, 'Show us how much you love it.' Vivian writhed and panted as Farouk thrusted quickly on top of her. Vivian had zero memory of this happening.

Her mind went into overdrive as she tried to recount her time in Dubai.

Slowly she put the puzzle pieces together... Ethan must have drugged her. She remembered how she'd caught the three men satisfying their lust with the two women, and that Ethan had forced her to join them. When she refused, he brutally abused her on the chair while forcing her to watch in the mirror.

After that, he'd given Vivian a cocktail, and she immediately fell asleep. She suddenly realized the same thing had happened at Yasar's party.

The images on the screen increasingly made her sick. Even though the woman on the screen was her, she didn't recognize herself at all.

Vivian watched how Farouk kept pumping into her from the front, while Yasar pulled his cock from her mouth then quickly lay down behind her and rammed his cock into her ass. With tears streaming down her cheeks, she witnessed how she seemed to enjoy the double penetration.

She groaned and panted while clawing at Farouk's back with an expression of pure pleasure. The scene changed and this time she was kneeling in front of the two men, taking it in turns to swallow their throbbing cocks while she gazed lustfully at the camera. In the next scene, Ethan was now in front of the camera while someone else filmed. He squeezed her breasts hard, bit her nipples and flipped her body into various positions.

As Vivian came she screamed Ethan's name loudly. Then it cut to black.

Vivian stared at the screen, the images engraved on her memory. What in the world had they done to her? Vivian would never have done such a thing; the cocktail Ethan gave her had to have been spiked. Several times she witnessed these men using cocaine. God knows what other drugs they had on them. Vivian couldn't erase the scenes from her mind. It disgusted her to the depths of her soul the whole thing was nothing but a cheap porn video with her as the lead. She picked up the DVD case, and a note fell out of it.

Don't you dare report this to the police! If you dare, this video will be shared online so everyone can see how you like to fuck three men at the same time (what would they say at Frenay & Iams?). By the way, there's another surprise coming your way, but you'll find out what it is soon enough. At least my mission was successful: if I can't fuck you then no one will. I've made sure of that!

Vivian panicked. She had already reported Ethan. There was already a warrant out for his arrest. Vivian dialed the police station to withdraw her report. The employee asked her repeatedly if she was sure of her decision. She assured them she did not want to continue to press charges, and that she wanted them dropped.

She paced back and forth in her apartment. Vivian didn't know what to do. What would happen if Ethan leaked the video? It would destroy her life. Also, what did he mean by "another surprise"? Vivian's whole world seemed to collapse around her. For the rest of her life she would be haunted by this video. She threw herself on the couch and cried. A few minutes later she was startled by her phone ringing. Glancing at the clock, she knew it must be the hospital with her results. Vivian wiped her tears and picked up her phone.

CHAPTER 23

With trembling hands, Vivian answered the call.

'This is Vivian Foster.'

'Hello, Miss Foster. This is Doctor Jones from St. Vincent's Hospital. I'm calling with your results. Is this an ok time to talk?'

'Yes, it's fine, please, just give it to me straight.'

'Is it possible for you to come into the hospital so I can explain the results in person?'

There was no way Vivian wanted to leave her house with her battered face. 'Can't you please explain my results over the phone? I'm not too anxious to drag myself to the hospital right now.'

For a moment, there was silence.

'Miss Foster, we shouldn't really discuss this over the phone because I have some bad news for you.'

Vivian laughed sourly. 'Believe me. I don't think it could get any worse than it already is. Like I said, just give it to me straight.'

'Okay, as you wish. The outcome of your blood test is HIV positive, which means...'

'I know what it means. I wasn't born yesterday,' Vivian interrupted furiously.

Once more, there was silence.

'Miss Foster, are you still there?'

'Yes, I'm still here.'

'I suggest you make an appointment for as soon as possible so I can explain how to proceed from here.'

'Yes, I'll be sure to do that. Good afternoon, Doctor Jones.' Before she could answer, Vivian had ended the call.

The room around Vivian started spinning. She had to hold onto the table tightly so she wouldn't fall. She struggled to draw air into her lungs, and her heart was racing so fast she could hear her heartbeat thudding in her ears.

Suddenly there was total silence. No racing heartbeat. Vivian stood calmly in the middle of the living room and looked around. She looked at the crystal vase she'd bought in Milan, and at all the other artifacts she'd collected over the years during her work all over the world. Silence was replaced by outrage as she walked towards the vase. Vivian lifted it and smashed it on the floor. She then proceeded to hurl various ornaments across the room, causing as much damage as she could. When she finally stopped taking her anger and frustration out on her home, she gazed around at the broken glass and ceramics and picture frames. The words of Ethan's note echoed in her mind.

By the way, there's another surprise coming your way, but you'll find out what it is soon enough. At least my mission was successful: if I can't fuck you then no one will.
I've made sure of that!

Vivian felt like her whole life had been stolen from her. How did she get here? What kind of monster was Ethan? He had deliberately infected her with HIV. Did he do the same thing to Victoria, and the other woman he mentioned? Is that why they committed suicide? Vivian could relate because at that moment she also wanted to die.

Thankfully, her common sense quickly returned. She needed to be strong and refused to let Ethan win by ending her own life, despite how tempting it was.

While sitting on the couch, various memories whirred through her mind. All the beautiful, tender moments she had shared with Ferris had now come to an end.

Darkness had fallen, and Vivian was still sitting on the couch when someone knocked on the door. She held her breath, completely petrified.

They knocked again.

'Vivian... are you home?' She recognized the voice. It was Ferris. For a split second she wanted to open the door, so he could put his arms around her and comfort her. Instead, she sat there in silence as she heard his footsteps going down the stairs. She peered through the curtains and watched him drive away. Now he was out of her life for good. The thought broke her, tears spilling from her eyes and flowing over her swollen face. Her physical pain was nothing compared to the pain in her heart that she suffered upon realizing she could never see Ferris again.

After a while, it became clear that she desperately needed to speak to someone. She soon realized that the only person she could ask for support was her mother. Vivian called her.

'Ellis Foster.'

'Hi, Ma. It's me.'

'Hi, dear. How are you? Wasn't it George's funeral today? How did it go?'

Vivian counted to ten in silence. Of course, it was no surprise that her mother didn't know which day George was buried, because she didn't care.

'No, Mom. That was yesterday.'

'Oh, sorry, my mistake. Tell me about it.'

'I didn't call you to talk about George, Mom. I called to ask if you could come to my place.' Vivian heard her mother sigh.

'To your apartment? Now? Honey, it's Saturday night. I'm just about to meet with Nora. You remember Nora, don't you?'

Of course she remembered Nora, her mother's best friend who drank too much and loved to play with men.

'Yes, Ma. I know Nora, but believe me, it's very important for me that you come over.'

'Can't you just speak to me over the phone? Or wait 'til tomorrow?'

Vivian had almost lost her patience. She counted to ten again so she wouldn't scream.

'No, Mom. What I need to tell you shouldn't be said over the phone. You know what? Just forget I called.

Obviously your friends are more important than your own daughter.'

'Viv, don't be so dramatic! Of course you're more important to me. If it's that big of a deal, I'll come now.'

'Thank you.'

'It's fine. I'm on my way.'

Vivian turned on all the lights and made coffee. The knock on the door scared the hell out of her, and she wondered if that fearful response would ever go away. She walked slowly to the door and peered through the small viewing hole. Her mother stood at the door with her cellphone pressed to her ear. Vivian overheard her mother talking. 'Yes, yes, I won' be long. It's just a quick stop at Vivian's. I'll still be there on time.'

Vivian opened the door. Her mother's face contorted in shock when she saw Vivian's swollen face. Her cellphone slipped from her hand onto the concrete floor.

'For the love of God, what happened?' She reached out to Vivian, who immediately collapsed in her mother's embrace. For a moment they stood there hugging each other. Vivian couldn't remember the last time she'd felt her mother embrace her like this.

'My dear child, what happened? Who did this to you?'

'Oh, Mom…' Her mother let her go and stared in horror at Vivian's body. Vivian saw various expressions flash across her mother's face; sympathy, sadness, confusion and anger.

'Vivian, who did this to you? Who is responsible for this?'

A wave of sadness washed over her, and Vivian began to sob. As they walked into the living room, Vivian watched her mother scan the broken glass on the floor with wide eyes.

'Come on, dear. Let's sit down.' Her mother helped Vivian to sit at the dining table, then poured two cups of coffee before sitting next to her. Ellis tenderly took her daughter's hand in hers, and stroked it softly.

'Tell me, honey. Who did this and why?'

Vivian could hear the anger in her mother's voice. 'Ethan.'

'Who is Ethan?'

Vivian repressed her embarrassment and shame and told her mother the whole story. Her mother listened attentively. For the first time, she didn't interrupt her.

'What should I do now, Ma? My life is over. What can I do?'

'First, let's pack some clothes for you. You're coming with me to my place. You must rest and sleep well in a safe environment. You can't stay here.'

Vivian was relieved that for the first time in her life she felt she could sense her mother's concern without her saying anything painful.

'What about Nora?'

'To hell with Nora. I'll call her when we get home to say you need me now.'

'Thank you, Mom.'

Ellis winked. 'Let's pack some clothes.'

Two hours later, Vivian was lying in bed at her mother's house, tucked under a thick blanket. After her mother urged her to, she'd taken two sleeping pills, but was still wide awake. Vivian felt she needed to go to the bathroom, and her throat was dry. After she went to the toilet, she walked to the kitchen. From there she could hear her mother talking on the phone.

'No, Nora! I feel so embarrassed.'

Vivian stood still so she could eavesdrop. It seemed her mother was ashamed of her. Vivian's heart broke. Why was she telling all of this to Nora? She might as well broadcast it on national television.

Vivian wanted to open the door to yell at her to stop.

'Nora, you don't understand. I'm ashamed of myself because I was never there for her when she was growing up. I am a terrible mother, and I've only just realized it now. I never showed her enough love. I was always too busy with work.

'If only I had been a good mother to her, maybe all of this wouldn't have happened. You have to see her face, Nora. He used her as a punching bag. Every time I look at her, my heart breaks.'

Vivian had always felt that her mother didn't love her, but now she was seeing another side of her.

'I always kept my distance because she's the spitting image of her father. Nora, I've made a colossal mistake. I can only hope and pray that I can make up for the years that I've wasted with her.' Vivian wasn't sure what to do; whether she should go back to her room or approach her mother.

Her mother's conversation ended. Ellis was still sobbing while sitting on the couch hugging her knees. Carefully, Vivian opened the door.

'Mom? Are you alright?'

Ellis looked at Vivian with tears in her eyes and reached out while saying, 'Come here, honey.'

Vivian approached her and nestled into the couch next to her mother. They didn't say anything to each other, but enjoyed the rare closeness between them.

Vivian broke the silence. 'I can't sleep, despite having taken those two pills.' Her mother gently caressed Vivian's long hair.

'Mom?'

'Yes, dear?'

Vivian straightened up and looked at her mother. 'I overheard your conversation with Nora. I want you to know that I don't blame you at all for what happened. I'm an adult, and I should have known better.'

'Vivian, If I were a good mother to you, you would've confided in me, and then I would've given you advice and warned you, so all of this might never have happened.'

Vivian thought for a while before continuing. 'You told Nora that you kept your distance from me because I resemble Dad. Why? I don't understand.'

Ellis took her daughter's hands and squeezed them softly.

'Vivian, when I met your father, it was love at first sight for me. That feeling wasn't mutual.

He was in love with someone else. At some sleazy nightclub, we got drunk and ended up in bed.' Vivian relaxed into the couch as she listened to her mother's story.

'The next day, your father regretted that he had spent the night with me because of that other woman. A few weeks later, I realized that I was pregnant, and I told your father. He did what a man should do, and took his responsibility as your father, even though I knew deep down he wanted to be with someone else. I always felt like the second choice, and after you were born, even the third choice. Your father stayed with me for you, and that thought always kept me from loving you.'

'But, in my memory, Dad always loved you very much.'

'Your father had grown to love me, in a friendly sort of way, but it wasn't the kind of love that should be shared between husband and wife.'

'I never realized this.'

'You couldn't have known. Your father was a good and caring man. He was always very patient and understanding, while I occupied myself at the office and built a wall around me. The bigger you got, the more you resembled your father, and the more difficult it was for me to get close to you. You two had a close and strong relationship. Sometimes I envied you because of the close bond you shared with him.'

After sighing heavily, Ellis took a sip from her cup of coffee. Vivian was silent. This was the first time in her life her mother had talked so openly about something.

'Vivian, you are unique in every way, just like your father. You are beautiful and charming, with a friendly and gentle character. Your face is so similar to your father's, especially your eyes. Many times, when I looked into your eyes, it felt like your father was looking back at me. What I want to say is... I love you and that I'm here for you. I'm just so terribly sorry that it's taken this horrible thing to happen to you for me to finally be honest with you.'

Now it was Vivian's turn to reach for her mother and hug her.

'On Monday I have a doctor's appointment. It would mean so much to me if you could be there.'

Ellis kissed Vivian's bruised cheek softly. 'Of course I'll come with you, but for now, you have to try to sleep. It's getting late.'

The following morning, when Vivian woke up and realized where she was, a small smile spread across her lips. Her teenage room, which she had redesigned and redecorated countless time, still felt warm and familiar. In the en suite bathroom, she looked at herself in the mirror, and her face turned sour.

Even though the swellings on her face had gone down slightly, the reddish marks had turned dark purple. In the corner near the door, she noticed her panda slippers, and she managed a small smile out of the corner of her mouth.

Vivian's stomach rumbled as she walked into the kitchen. Ellis was busy making pancakes. As a child, Vivian had spent a lot of time in this kitchen with her father.

'Hmm... it smells good, Mom. I could really get used to this!'
Ellis turned around and couldn't mask her expression of severe
concern as she stared at her daughter's face.

They sat at the dining table, and Vivian couldn't decide what to
drink first, coffee or orange juice.

'Honey, don't you think it's for the best if you sold your
apartment? You will always be reminded of what happened if
you stay there. You can stay here until you find a new place to
call your own.'

Vivian considered her mother's suggestion. It would be painful
to sell her apartment but what her mother said was true. She
could no longer feel comfortable and happy there.

'Maybe you're right, but it isn't a buyer's market these days.
Who wants to buy at times like this?'

'Melanie.'

'Melanie?' repeated Vivian.

'Yes, her rental is soon to be demolished to make way for a
shopping center. She's searching for another apartment.'

'Can she afford to buy my apartment with her salary?'

'Don't worry. We can find a way around the situation.'

The thought of Melanie purchasing her apartment made Vivian
happy, because she knew how much she loved the place.

Vivian spent the morning in the kitchen with her mother,
talking about her childhood and her father.

'I have to make some phone calls. After that, you can help me
make lunch.'

Vivian didn't hear her mother return to the kitchen. 'What are you thinking about, Viv?' Ellis asked, her voice full of sympathy.

'How do I go on from here? It feels like I'm in some sort of nightmare that won't end. The worst thing is, I have to give up my job the job I love so much. There's no way I can face Ferris ever again. He can't ever find out what happened.' The thought of him brought tears to her eyes, which she quickly wiped away. 'It's all so unfair, Mom. I really had the feeling that Ferris and I were finally getting somewhere, we were growing closer and now... now it's all over, because of that bastard!' Vivian got up and began to pace up and down in the kitchen. 'Why wasn't insulting, molesting, raping and that filthy sex-tape enough for him? Why did he deliberately infect me with HIV? He has destroyed my whole life. I might as well end it right here and now!'

Ellis jumped up from her chair.

'Vivian Foster!' Her mother's shouting rang loud in her ears. 'Don't you dare to say things like that ever again! I know everything looks dark and twisted right now, and it may feel like you have nowhere to go. But you won't give up that easily. You will fight like hell, not only for yourself but also for all the other women he destroyed. You will not give him that damn satisfaction. Honey, you have to report it again.

Don't let him stop you, don't let him win. You owe this to Victoria.

He is counting on it that you will hurt yourself, just like the other women. He won't expect a fight, so if you don't fight back, there will be other victims who fall into Ethan's trap, and you won't be able to prevent it from happening. I know this won't be easy, but you're not alone. I'll fight with you all the way.'

Vivian was completely taken aback by her mother's outburst. She had never seen her like that, so fiery, driven, powerful, and intense. She hoped that she had the same strength somewhere deep down inside of her. 'But Mom... if I report it, he'll release the tape. I'm so ashamed.'

'I know, dear. However, you can't take his word for anything. For all we know, he might release it whenever he feels like, whether you report him or not. As bad as it sounds, you have to learn to live with the fact that there is a tape out there somewhere. As soon as you accept that, you can move on with your life.'

After hours of talking, Ellis made sure that Vivian resigned from Frenay & Iams. They would look for another house or apartment, and Vivian would become an equal partner at her mother's architect's firm.

The following Monday afternoon, Vivian and her mother were waiting for Dr Jones. Several times Vivian wiped her sweaty palms on her jeans. She was equally nervous and scared.

Dr Jones came in and sat in front of them.

'Good afternoon Miss Foster.

I'm pleased to see that the swellings have reduced significantly since the last time I saw you.'

'Thank you, Dr Jones. Before you continue, I want to apologize for my behavior over the phone the other day.'

'No need to. I know you had a lot to process, and I understand that this situation is difficult.' She glanced at the document in front of her and looked back at Vivian. 'Fortunately, antiretroviral therapy for treatment of HIV will enable you to live a normal life.'

Dr Jones explained the treatment to Vivian, and advised her that she'd require a medical check-up once a year. The doctor gave her a folder of her prescriptions and brochures containing information about the treatment.

'Vivian, as your doctor, I also need to emphasize the importance of informing any potential partners that you are living with HIV.'

A few minutes later they stood outside the hospital, and Vivian took a deep breath, filling her lungs with fresh air. For the rest of the week she locked herself up in her mother's house. She was still struggling to process all the events that had happened to her. One thing that made her relieved was the fact that her mother had made sure she could immediately resign from Frenay & Iams, without giving them an explanation of why.

CHAPTER 24

'Viv, isn't it time for you to start doing something? You've locked yourself up at home all week. Like it or not, you have to start a new life.'

'How can I leave the house looking like this?' Vivian pointed to her face. The swelling had almost disappeared, but the bruising was still clearly visible.

'Okay, you have a point. How about we invite your friends to have dinner here?' Her mother's proposal made her grimace. 'You can't avoid them forever, you know. When was the last time you talked to them? Did you give your new phone number to Salfina and Genieva?'

Guiltily, she shook her head.

'Vivian, they are your closest friends. You have to tell them.'

'Have you told Melanie, Mom?'

'No, the only thing I told her was that you were facing a problem and had to stay with me temporarily. She doesn't even know that she can buy your apartment.'

Vivian had to admit that she missed her friends and was eager to see them again. 'Okay, let's invite them.'

'Great. I'm heading out to the office now, and will tell Melanie so she can contact them. I'll be home early to prepare dinner.' After her mother left, Vivian's uneasiness returned. She paced back and forth.

She felt like a prisoner trapped in her own body. What she really wanted to do was to grab a cab and go back to her apartment, but her bruises prevented her from doing so.

Her mind drifted to Ferris. She hadn't seen him for a week. Vivian missed his friendly face, the calmness of his voice, his scent. What hurt the most was that they had become closer, and now she would never know if it was destined to become more than friendship. Later that afternoon, Vivian saw her mother pull into the driveway. She went outside to help carry the grocery bags. 'Melanie and Salfina will be here at six, Genieva will come a little later because of a meeting.'

'Oh, okay.'

A neighbor from across the street who was walking her dog stared with her mouth open at Vivian's face. Vivian fled inside while her mother confronted the curious neighbor.

Vivian waited impatiently for her mother to get inside.

'What did she want? What did she say? What did you say?'

'Don't worry. I told her you had an accident and that you're recovering here.'

'What was I thinking. I shouldn't have gone outside. Now you have to lie and make up stories for me.'

'Don't make such a big deal out of it. Come on, help me with the groceries so I can start making dinner.' At six, the doorbell rang. Vivian's heartbeat suddenly accelerated because now she would have to tell her friends the truth about what really happened.

'I'll get it.' Ellis walked to the front door, and Vivian heard Salfina's cheerful voice greeting her mother.

'Gosh, how long has it been since I last saw you?' You still look young and beautiful,' Salfina gushed to Ellis.

Footsteps came closer while Vivian nervously waited in the living room. Melanie and Salfina stood frozen on the spot when they saw Vivian's face.

'Vivian, what happened to you?' Salfina hurried over and hugged her best friend tightly.

'Ouch, Sal. It's still painful.' Immediately, Salfina released her embrace. Melanie stood right next to them with tears in her eyes.

'What happened, Viv?'

Vivian looked at her mother with a pleading look to help her deal with this situation. Ellis understood she had to intervene.

'Should we wait for Genieva first? Otherwise, we'll have to tell everything twice.'

'Tell me about your pregnancy, are you still feeling nauseous?' Vivian tried to change the subject.

'You girls sit down while I get you something to drink.' Ellis walked into the kitchen.

'What happened, Viv?' Salfina whispered.

'Later, please. Tell me about you, Sal. I need a distraction.' Ellis returned with wine and juice for Salfina. Salfina spoke about all the ups and downs of her pregnancy.

She thought the only positive thing about it was that she no longer had to wear padded bras because she'd already gone up three cup sizes. Even though she spoke cheerfully with a smile on her face, her worried eyes remained fixed on Vivian.

Half an hour later, Genieva arrived and had the same reaction as Melanie and Salfina when she saw Vivian's face. Now that the three friends had gathered, Vivian stood up, and all eyes were on her.

'I know you're all waiting for me to explain what happened.' Silence filled the room as Vivian paused and prepared to continue the story. 'I know you're expecting an explanation and I will give it to you, but please, let's have dinner first so I can enjoy this happiness a little longer.'

During dinner, they talked and laughed as usual. As always, Salfina was the loudest, and Vivian realized just how much she had missed her friends.

After dinner, they returned to the living room, and Vivian could feel the tension rising again. She took a deep breath as she knew she could no longer postpone it. 'What I'm about to tell you isn't easy for me. Right now, I'm still feeling very fragile. So what I want to ask you is to please listen to my story without interrupting me.'

The three women nodded in agreement. Vivian coughed to clear her throat before she continued.

'Do you remember the night at The Club when Sal received a strange text message from Ethan? So, here it is…' Vivian told her story from the beginning to the end.

She left nothing out. Her friends were in shock after hearing the full story, and couldn't say a word. Melanie was the first to shed tears and Salfina and Genieva were not far behind her. Vivian could read the emotions on their faces. They were precisely the same as her mother's when she heard it for the first time. It took a while until finally someone broke the silence. Salfina got up and started to pace. Several times she turned to Vivian with her mouth opened ready to say something, but she abandoned those thoughts. Finally, she spoke.

'How the hell could you let this happen? Didn't we warn you about him? Did you not listen to a single word I told you about him?' Melanie jumped up from the couch to defend Vivian.

'Woah woah woah, Sal, this is no time to blame Vivian.'

'Mel is right, Sal. Vivian doesn't need this. She needs our love and support, so keep the lecture to yourself, will ya?'
Salfina looked at Mel and Genieva angrily but quickly realized they were right. Melanie walked towards Vivian with her arms outstretched and hugged her.

'Oh, Viv, I'm so sorry... If only I could do something to make you feel better, but I don't know how!'

'You don't need to do or say anything. Your presence is enough for me.' Salfina embraced Vivian and Melanie.

'Please forgive me, Viv, for my outburst.'

'No need to apologize, Sal. If the tables were turned, I probably would've reacted the same way.'

Genieva joined her friends and gave Vivian a tight hug. 'Do you know what we need? A weekend getaway together! What do you think?' Genieva looked at her friends excitedly.

'I think that's a great idea,' Ellis said to Genieva.

'I like it too, but can it wait until my bruises have completely gone? I don't want to go anywhere looking like this.'

'Deal!' The girls shouted in unison.

The three of them prepared to go home, but Ellis asked Melanie to stay for a while to discuss something. Mel sat on the couch while Vivian walked her friends out.

Ellis sat down next to Melanie and poured her another glass of wine. 'Tell me, Mel, how is your search for another apartment going?'

'Difficult, actually. I've looked at several already. The ones I like are way out of my price range, and the ones I can afford are in unsafe neighborhoods.'

'What about my apartment?'

Melanie looked at Vivian with wide eyes and laughed, 'Are you kidding me? Your apartment is like a palace to me, but I can't afford it.'

'What if I make you a good deal and my mother increases your salary?' Melanie glanced at Vivian and then Ellis.

She couldn't believe what she'd just heard. 'Are you two for real? Even though it would cost me a fortune to furnish the place.'

'No need, because you can keep all the furniture.

I'll only take my clothes. I need to make a fresh new start and try to forget the past.'

'In that case, I'm thrilled to accept your offer, but what are you going to do in the meantime?'

Ellis joined the conversation. 'Vivian will work with us, Mel. I asked her to become my equal partner in the firm, and she's accepted. And yes, Vivian will stay here until she finds a new home.' Vivian took her house key and handed it to Melanie.

'Mel, I hope you'll feel at home staying there, just like I did before. The paperwork is just a formality, so if you want, you can move in right away. The place is yours.'

Melanie's face, exuberant at first, swiftly turned gloomy.

'What is it, Mel? Is it going too fast for you? Do you want to think about it first? Or do you feel pressured?'

'No, no, Viv, it's nothing like that. It's just that I feel guilty because dark clouds are overshadowing your life. It doesn't feel right for me to feel happy, you know.'

Vivian reached out Melanie's hand and held it. 'You shouldn't think that way. What happened to me is no reason for you to be unhappy. Whatever it is, life goes on, and so will my life. I just need to figure out how to get back on track but believe me, I will come out of it stronger, and before we know it, we can all laugh and have fun again like we used to.'

Tears pooled in Melanie's eyes. 'I honestly admire you so much, Viv. I'm pleased and grateful to be your friend.'

Vivian kissed Mel's cheeks with affection.

The following weeks passed by quickly. Vivian had started working, and Ellis was amazed by Vivian's performance and praised her talent.

The relationship with her mother was getting closer, and Vivian was enjoying it. Even though she loved staying at her mother's place, she was eager to live on her own again. After browsing the market for a short time, Vivian bought an apartment in the same building as Edward.

Every day, after work, Vivian spent her evenings redecorating her new home. There was a lot that had to be done to satisfy her flare for design.

The connections she had built up with the auction houses while working for Frenay and Iams were very useful in her search for furniture and artworks.

Vivian was pleased that her new home had a fireplace. She consulted different auction sites to look for the right one.

Vivian was often so occupied that she forgot all about the fact she was living with HIV.

The only thing that reminded her was the medicine she took daily.

During the day while working around the clock, Vivian felt energetic and optimistic, but every night in bed, she cried herself to sleep. Not because of her illness, but because she thought of Ferris.

When Melanie moved into Vivian's apartment, she found a letter in Vivian's mailbox. It was from Ferris.

Vivian, I don't know where to start. Many times I tried to call you, but the number is disconnected. Several times I knocked on your door, but there was no answer. So the only thing that's left is to write to you.

What happened? It seems like you completely disappeared after George's funeral. I didn't hear anything from you. Did I do something wrong? If so, please tell me what it is, so I can apologize. It was a huge shock for me to hear you had quit your job. Even Sean and Clive were completely surprised because the reason for your departure wasn't clear at all.

I must admit that I'm very sorry about your decision, because not only did I lose a great colleague, but also a good friend. Of course, I can only speak for myself, but I really do consider you a good friend.

What worries me is that the Vivian I know isn't the type of person to avoid or run away from problems.

So that tells me that something serious must have happened, but what? What happened, Vivian?

Why won't you want to talk to me? At least let me know that you are all right?

Anyway, through this letter, I want to tell you that you are an amazing woman and you can always count on me as your friend. If there comes a time when you want to talk about it, please don't hesitate to call me, even it's in the middle of the night. I will always be here for you.

Regards, Ferris

Every night before she went to sleep, Vivian reread his letter. No matter how good her days were and how energetic she felt, she knew she couldn't never erase him from her mind. After crying herself to sleep, she dreamed of Victoria, George, Ethan, and Ferris. The dreams always ended the same, with Ethan abusing and raping her.

The day that Vivian could move into her apartment was approaching. She took three days off work to supervise the installation of the furniture. Vivian was very grateful that Melanie often came by to help out.

The following Friday was the getaway weekend Genieva had planned. They would visit Niagara Falls, and after returning from the trip, she would move into her new home.

She was very curious about how Edward would react when he found out about everything that she'd been through, and that she'd become his neighbor.

He was still in San Fransisco at his mother's house, recovering after George's passing, but had promised to cook for Vivian when he returned home.

Vivian asked Ralph not to say a word to Edward about her moving there.

Vivian began to rediscover the rhythm of her life and was ready to start over, even though her sadness about losing Ferris was still deeply rooted and impossible to erase.

His letter was engraved on her memory she had memorized every sentence.

On the Friday afternoon, they'd arrived at their destination.
Genieva jumped like an excited child when she saw the chalet.
'Ohh... isn't it gorgeous! Look!' She pointed to the wooden
jacuzzi in the backyard under a large grape vine.
'Cool, we can relax in there while sipping cocktails.
Except for you, Sal,' Melanie said enthusiastically.
'Fine, I'll drink orange juice out of a wine glass, who knows,
the taste might change.' The four girls laughed out loud. Vivian
was looking forward to having a good time with her beloved
friends.
The interior of the cabin was cozy and luxurious. The furniture
was arranged around the fireplace with a bear carpet in front of
it.
'Okay, let me recap the agenda,' said Genieva. 'After dinner,
we will soak in the jacuzzi with wine or cocktails or orange
juice, and later on we'll have hot cocoa with whipped cream in
front of the fireplace. Everyone agreed?'
'Uhh, did anyone bring cocoa and cream or anything else for
that matter?' Melanie asked while looking at her friends.
'I saw a supermarket on the drive up here. I suggest we make
a list of all the things we need,' Vivian said.
Everyone started shouting about the items they wanted, and
Vivian laughed at her noisy pals. It had been a very long time
since she'd laughed like this. Vivian realized just how much
she needed her friends in her life.The fire in the fireplace
crackled, and the four of them sat around the fire wearing thick

351

fluffy bathrobes. Melanie and Genieva sat on the floor while Salfina and Vivian sat in the lounge chairs beside the fireplace.

'I would like to take this opportunity to thank you for your support and affection. Also, I'm glad and thankful you didn't judge me for my actions.'

Melanie wanted to say something, but Vivian stopped her by gently raising her hand.

'I'm fortunate to have friends like you. I know that there are people out there who look down on people like me. I also know people who have lost friends because of their illness, but luckily, I still have you by my side. Therefore, I want to say thank you…'

Salfina raised her hot cocoa and said, 'Cheers, to friendship.' The spent the rest of the evening in front of the fireplace, laughing and talking. 'Hey, Viv, have you heard anything from Ethan since all of this happened?'

'No I haven't, and I would like to keep it that way. That's why I changed my number.'

'Gosh, Nieva, you really want to talk about that bastard now?' Salfina rolled her eyes in exasperation, but Genieva ignored her and continued. 'He's cunning enough to get your new number, Viv!'

'If he does, I'll just have to change it again,' Vivian answered firmly.

'Aren't you afraid of what he might do if he finds out about the police report?'

'The worst he can do is release that tape. If I can overcome the knowledge of HIV, then I surely can overcome some stupid sex tape. Now, the report is still pending, and I can submit it again at any time. I wanted to ask Edward's advice first. I hope he can connect me with Vicky's mother, who knows she can provide additional information.'

'Okay, enough about Ethan. Let's think about what we'll do tomorrow. We're here to have a good time, not to talk about that lowlife.' Melanie tried to change the subject, and Vivian was relieved.

'Duh... of course tomorrow we will go and see the waterfall. Isn't that our main destination?' Genieva's bemused expression triggered all three of them to laugh again.

The next day they went to see the spectacular waterfall. Its power and natural beauty was exhilarating. Unfortunately, cold air ruined the atmosphere, and Vivian overheard Sal and Nieva talking.

'We should go. We can't just think about ourselves anymore. We have to think about her condition.'

Back at the cabin, Vivian excused herself and went to her room. It hurt her that her best friends pitied her. The last thing she wanted was to be treated like a sick person. On her bed, she freed her tears until she fell asleep, and the dark and twisted dream awaited her.

CHAPTER 25

The low temperature outside indicated that winter was coming, but Vivian didn't mind because she loved spending time in her new home.

After work, she headed straight home to her apartment. Her new favorite thing to do in the evenings was curling up in front of the fireplace with a good book. Even though she was surrounded by people at work, she still lived a very private life. Since the weekend at Niagara Falls, Vivian had again put some distance between herself and Salfina and Genieva. She still was upset by their comments about her condition. She only remained in contact with Melanie.

Ellis often tried to persuade her to have dinner with her, but Vivian always excused herself. She was too afraid to run into Ferris, even though the odds were small in such a big city. Vivian was looking looked forward to Edward's return the following weekend. He'd called and invited her for dinner on Sunday.

During their phone conversations, Vivian hadn't told Edward anything about what had happened to her. She'd also kept the fact that she was now living in the same building a secret.

Vivian poured herself a glass of Asti and sat in the chair in front of her roaring fireplace, her mind drifting away.

Was she strong enough to continue with her report to the police?

Maybe Ethan would make her life a even a bigger hell than it already was. Would it be worth it? Could she handle it? Vivian remembered the powerful speech her mother had delivered about needing to fight Ethan, but did she have the same fighting spirit as her mom?

Without realizing it, a small smile appeared on her face when she thought of the woman who'd given birth to her. Recently her mother had played an essential role in her life something Vivian had never imagined possible before.

She was working and collaborating well with her mother. Several times Ellis mentioned that it wouldn't be long before she would hand the company entirely over to Vivian, so she could finally start enjoying other things in life, like traveling. Vivian also insisted that Melanie expand her tertiary qualifications so she could participate more in the company. Melanie often invited her to stop by to eat at her place, but Vivian always refused. She just wasn't ready to return to her former apartment yet.

Yes, her life had changed tremendously since Ethan had entered it. She used to love the hustle and bustle of the city, but now she seemed more like a hermit who stayed at home all the time. A massive thunderstorm rolled across the steel grey sky. Vivian glanced out her window and realized it had been raining for days now. Vivian hoped that the rain would stop tomorrow so she could visit George's grave.

She hadn't visited his grave since the day of his funeral.

Vivian bought two bouquets of flowers at Tiffany's flower stall in front of the cemetery, one for her father and one for George. Vivian guessed Tiffany, who was tall and pretty, was about the same age as her. Throughout the week, Tiffany was kept busy with flower deliveries, and during the weekends she opened her little shop for the visitors to the cemetery.

Tiffany told Vivian about a deal she offered for a fixed monthly amount, one could receive a fresh bouquet each week.

Vivian subscribed to the deal, so she would always have peonies and orchids at home.

Vivian walked with the two bouquets into the cemetery. She looked to the sky and crossed her fingers it wouldn't rain. After she visited her father's grave she walked quickly over to George's, but the moment she placed the flowers on it rain started pouring down. She ran to her car and drove home, soaking wet. When she'd finally made it back, a hot shower washed away the cold from her body. She chose a very casual outfit then cleaned her apartment a little before she visited Edward. Vivian called Ralph so that he could tell Edward she was coming up. As usual, the front door stood open. Vivian had to hold back laughter because Ralph played his role so well. Vivian walked in and went straight to the kitchen.

'Mmm... Edward. It smells so good, as usual!'

Edward turned around and hugged her. 'Hello dear. Goodness it's been a long time.' Edward looked at her from top to bottom.

'Slippers?'

Vivian could no longer hold back her laughter. 'That's right, neighbor.'

'Neighbor? Huh, I don't understand,' Edward said in surprise. 'I moved into this building!'

'Get out of here, are you for real?'

'Yes, a few weeks ago, and now it's finally all set up. But enough about me. How about you, Edward. Did you find the peace you needed at your mother's?'

'Yes, I did. My mother is a real sweetheart. She spoiled me rotten. I wasn't allowed to do anything. The first few days I spent sleeping and crying, but then I found the strength to start writing a new cookbook.'

'Oh, Edward. That is wonderful to hear. I'm so glad that you're back and looking healthy again. You really were a mess when you left.'

'Yes, I know, but fortunately my mother took good care of me. It seems like I inherited her flare for cooking. She knows how to create incredible dishes from simple ingredients. We agreed to write a cookbook together when I finish the book I'm working on now.'

'Very good! What about the last book you printed?'

'The publisher and I agreed to wait until Christmas to promote it.'

'Good strategy.'

'Come on dear, let's eat. I can't wait to see your place.'

After they enjoyed a crisp and comforting chicken and leek pie, Vivian and Edward walked the short distance to Vivian's apartment. Edward wandered around in awe. He brushed the white sandstone wall and said, 'I absolutely love what you've done with the place. It's so interesting and tastefully decorated. George always told me how good you are at your job, but now I can see for myself.'

Vivian passed him a glass of wine and felt proud.

'I know it's none of my business, but how could you afford to buy an apartment in this building? I still remember how George and I struggled to buy ours, and since then its value has almost doubled.'

'I no longer work for Frenay & Iams.'

Edward raised his eyebrows and looked at Vivian with wide eyes. 'Gosh, Viv. What did I miss since I left?'

Vivian's heart beat faster, and her breathing became irregular every time she had to recount all the terrible events she'd experienced.

'Edward, I need to tell you something that's quite upsetting. It might be better if you sit down.'

'What happened, dear? You can tell me everything. You know that, right?'

'Yes, I know.' Vivian took a deep breath and poured her heart out to Edward, who stared at her with a horrified expression without ever interrupting her. When Vivian finished the story, Edward got up from the couch and pulled her into his arms.

'Oh my God. I'm so sorry for you.' Because of Edward's warm embrace Vivian burst into tears.

'It's good to cry, dear. Let it all out,' Edward said softly as he rocked her gently in his arms.

'You know, Edward, I'm so embarrassed by all of this. I don't like to go out in public anymore. After work, I immediately rush home and lock the door. I don't even see my friends anymore.'

'I understand what you mean and what you're going through. My brother also had HIV.'

'Sorry, I didn't know that.'

'No problem. Vivian, you can't let this virus determine your life. I know this is not something you can be proud of, but you don't need to be ashamed of this. That man infected you intentionally, he didn't inform you that he had the virus, so please, Viv, don't be ashamed.'

It was a huge relief to talk to Edward, and she felt lighter after finally being able to share everything with him.

'Regarding the police report, you need to do what you want, not what others tell you to do. There is no need to feel guilty for Vicky or the other woman because it won't bring them back. You need to regain control of your life, and you know lock yourself up isn't going to help.

'Do the things you did before all of this happened. Life will be easier once you accept the fact that you have the virus. I know plenty of people living with HIV, and they still enjoy their life every day.'

Vivian wiped her nose with a tissue and gave Edward a tight hug. 'Thank you, Edward.'

'You're welcome, dear. Promise me you'll do your best to live your life as you did before.'

'I'll do my best.'

'Well then, if you'll excuse me, I'm going home to do some writing because the best inspiration comes to me at night.' He kissed Vivian's forehead. 'Goodnight, neighbor.'

'Goofnight, Edward. Thanks again.'

Two weeks had passed since her dinner with Edward and the promise she made to him, but nothing much had changed. She still didn't feel comfortable going out in public. The only thing that had changed was eating with Edward. Every day after work, she came home and slipped into something comfortable, and on Tuesdays and Thursdays, she spent the evening with him. That was the rhythm of her life.

Vivian sat at Edward's kitchen table and saw how expertly he plated and put the finishing touches on his creation that evening a Moroccan lamb tagine with dates and apricots.

'Smells fantastic, Edward. I don't think I've ever had Moroccan cuisine before. My stomach is rumbling. Today work was piling up, so I missed lunch.'

Edward laughed and winked at her. 'Today I received a report from Ralph.'

'Ralph? Since when does Ralph report to you?'

'Since I asked him to. Didn't you promise me to start living your life again? According to Ralph, it looks like you haven't gotten far yet. He told me you've never received a visit from your friends, and that you only leave the building to go to work.'

Vivian looked at Edward in disbelieve. 'I'm just not ready, Edward.'

'Nonsense. Listen to me. What you experienced was terrifying and traumatic, but what you're doing now is not good. At this rate, you'll only continue to isolate yourself.'

'Not true. I have you, my mother and my friends,' Vivian defended herself.

'Then tell me, why don't you invite your friends to come over, or go out with them like a normal person at your age?'

Vivian got up from her chair and began to pace back and forth in the kitchen. 'Because... because I'm not normal, Edward. I'm sick.'

'Well, see for yourself, then. That's exactly what I mean.'

'What?'

'You're hiding behind this virus. You're letting this disease control your life. Give yourself a chance, Vivian. I'm sure you'll see that life is precious and that it needs to be lived.'

'That's easy for you to say. You don't get strange looks from people.'

Edward laughed, clearly amused.

'Why are you laughing? What's so funny about that?'

'Oh, Vivian. You are truly unique. People look at you because you are gorgeous and beautiful. You're noticed not because of the disease you have. Is "HIV" written on your forehead? It's all in your head. I know what you need, Vivian. If you want to eat together with me on Thursday, you'll need to dress a little sharper. We're dining out.'

She panicked. 'Please Edward, don't.'

'Do you trust me?'

'Of course, you know I do. What kind of question is that?'

'Good. Then stop questioning me and trust me on this one.'

For two days, Vivian was distraught. Where was Edward going to take her? What was his plan?

Edward opened the door of a small bistro and let Vivian go in ahead. The waiter couldn't take his eyes off Vivian as he led them to the table. They sat facing each other.

Vivian looked around and felt very insecure.

'Cozy restaurant. I've never been here before, have you?'

'I often came here with George, it was one of our regulars. According to him, they serve the best roasted ribs in town.'

'Oh, now you've got my attention.' Vivian had actually wanted to order something else, but she didn't want to disappoint Edward.

Edward looked pleased as Vivian enjoyed her food.

'Edward, you're right! These are the best roasted ribs I've ever had.'

'Tony Roma is indeed the king of roasted ribs.'

'They're delicious. We have to come here again.'

Edward glanced at his watch. I'm glad you like it. If we want to order dessert, we need to hurry because I don't want to be late for our next stop.'

'Next stop?' Vivian swallowed. She was hoping they'd go home after dinner, even though she was enjoying her evening with Edward. She just wasn't sure if she was ready to go anywhere else so soon.

'Where are we going?'

'You'll see. I only want to ask you to listen with an open mind. You don't have to say anything, just listen.'

'Are we going to some kind of show?'

'No, it's definitely not a show.'

Edward took her to a complex where various foundations and associations were located. When they entered, Edward asked her to wait while he walked to the information desk. Vivian saw Edward engaged in a conversation with a woman who seemed very friendly as she pointed to one of the corridors.

'We're a little early, but we can go inside,' Edward said while leading Vivian to one of the doors.

The room was medium-sized, and in front there were speakers, a podium and a long row of chairs. On the left was a long table where a few people were enjoying coffee, tea and snacks. They sat in the back row and saw the room slowly fill with people.

Vivian realized that most of them knew each other and that they swiftly fell into warm and friendly conversations.

Several times Vivian tried to extract information from Edward, but without success. The only thing he said was, 'Open-minded.'

The buzz from the crowd disappeared when a man stood on the small podium. All eyes were on him as he unfolded a piece of paper in his hand while looking at the audience.

'I want to welcome you all, especially those who are joining us for the first time. I'll give a brief explanation of what we're doing here. Every Thursday we gather here to meet people who have something in common with each of us...'

Vivian tuned out and stopped listening to what the man on the podium was saying as she racked her brain. Had Edward taken her to some kind of support group, like an AA meeting? She glanced at Edward.

'Open-minded,' he whispered.

A young woman appeared on to the podium. 'Hello, my name is Samantha Walker. Four weeks ago, I was diagnosed with HIV, and, maybe as some of you here can imagine, my world fell apart.'

Vivian sat on the edge of her chair while listening carefully to what the young woman saying. Immediately Vivian felt sympathy for her and was touched by her story.

Three other newcomers shared their stories. Vivian recognized her life in each of them.

They were not only sharing the obstacles they faced, but also suggestions to overcome them.

After everyone had finished sharing their story, the group drank coffee and tea at the long table. Edward turned to Vivian and took both her hands and held them tightly.

'If I'd told you I was going to take you here, you would've fought me. I strongly believe it can be helpful to talk with people who can understand what you're experiencing. During the session, I was afraid you'd walk out in the middle of it, and I'm so proud you didn't.'

Vivian looked at Edward lovingly. She understood that he only wanted the best for her. 'To be honest with you, I was ready to leave until the first young woman shared her story, which I immediately sympathized with. I can understand and imagine what she's going through.'

'That's why I brought you here. You can exchange ideas with other people like that woman, who is brave enough to appear in public and share her story.'

Vivian thought for a moment and had to admit that she was impressed by this program.

'Let's grab a cup of coffee before we go,' Edward suggested. Everyone at the table was engaged in enthusiastic conversation with frequent laughter. Vivian sensed just how relaxed and familiar they all were.

Samantha, the young woman who had spoken first, stood alone at the table.

Vivian walked up to her. 'What an amazing speech you gave.'
Samantha looked at Vivian with a friendly face. 'To be honest,
I was scared to death about giving that speech. It's my first
time here, you know.'

'Actually, this is also my first time here.'
Samantha laughed and held out her hand to Vivian.

'Samantha Walker.'
Vivian laughed to while shaking Samantha's hand. 'Vivian
Foster.' She immediately clicked with Samantha. In a short
time they'd talked about many things. They exchanged
numbers and promised to return to the group the following
week.
Edward waited for Vivian in the corridor outside. When Vivian
walked over to him, a wide smile appeared on his face.

'Sorry for the wait Edward.'

'No problem.' He hugged Vivian and kissed her on the cheek.

'Thank you, Edward. If it weren't for you, I never would've
come here.'

'Don't mention it. My brother used to come here regularly. It
was hugely beneficial for him. I can only hope and pray that it
will do the same for you. What do you think about it?'

'I already believe it can make a difference. I even promised
Samantha I'd see her here next week.'

'Wonderful, then my mission was successful.'

CHAPTER 26

For the first time since her life had been turned upside down, Vivian was starting to feel more confident about herself and her life. She was excelling in her new job, and found new assignments and challenges extremely appealing.

Following Edward's advice, she invited her friends over for dinner, but only Melanie accepted her offer because Salfina couldn't make it and Genieva had to fly to Vancouver for a meeting.

Ralph announced that Melanie was coming up. Just as Edward did for her, Vivian left her front door open for Melanie.

Melanie was carrying a big bouquet of flowers when she entered Vivian's apartment, and looked a little disappointed when she saw the flowers around the room.

'If I'd known, I would've brought you something else.'

Vivian laughed at Melanie's disappointed face. 'No problem, Mel! I'm always happy to receive flowers. Thank you.'

'Did you arrange all of these by yourself? They're exquisite.'

'No, I'm a regular customer at a florist. Every week she delivers a fresh bouquet of my favorites.'

'Wow, that's convenient. That's something I'd like to arrange for my place.'

'I'll give you the address later. I hope you're hungry. I made pesto and a big green salad, and there's garlic bread too.'

'Sounds great. I'm ravenous, Viv.'

They walked towards the kitchen where a large dining table surrounded by twelve high-back chairs stood. Vivian always dreamed about having a large kitchen, and now she did.

'Have a seat. What can I get you to drink? I think white wine will suit our dinner best.'

'That sounds wonderful. The pesto smells delicious, Viv.'

'Thanks, I made it from Edward's cookbook.'

'I'd like to meet Edward sometime. You always speak so highly of him.'

A smile appeared on Vivian's face when she heard his name.

'He also lives in this building, right?'

'Yes, he does.'

'So?'

'So, what?' Vivian laughed.

'Call the man so I can meet him. Then he can judge your pesto and see if you did his recipe justice,' Melanie said with a cheeky smile. 'Okay, I'll call him.'

Five minutes later, Edward joined the two women in the kitchen. Vivian made the introductions, then the three of them quickly became entangled in a conversation about food. Edward praised Vivian's pesto, and after a while excused himself because he wanted to get back to his writing.

'Goodness, Viv, what a charming man he is.'

'Yeah, I know. George's passing has really brought us together. He's taught me to look at things differently, and I must say that it's helped me greatly.

I feel so much better these days because of his support and advice.'

'I noticed that. I wanted to ask you about it yesterday.'

'About what?'

'Well, you look more relaxed, and you smile more often. You're almost the same old Vivian again.' Vivian thought for a while before she answered, 'The old Vivian is gone and won't come back, but believe me, the new Viv will be better than the old one. I'm working hard on that.'

'What's changed, Viv? What made you look at things from another perspective?'

'Three weeks ago, Edward took me to a meeting for people who are HIV positive. Every Thursday I go there with a friend I made at the first meeting I attended, Samantha. That opened my eyes. I see how people continue to live and enjoy their lives, and then it hit me. If they can do it, then so can I.'

'Thank God for Edward.'

'Yes, that's right. I hope his luck will come around too one of these days.'

'Do you think he'll find a new partner?'

'I hope so. I don't think George wanted him to stay alone.' Melanie took off her shoes and rested her feet on a chair.

'Did Edward tell you anything else about Victoria? Did he put you in contact with her mother?'

'I've talked a lot with Edward about it, and he thought I should only file the report when I'm ready to,

369

and not out of guilt for Vicky or that other woman.'

'He's right, you know.'

Vivian also took off her shoes and shifted a little closer to the fireplace. 'What's so great about Edward is, he can see my situation more clearly than I can. He pointed out to me that it could take years to carry out a lawsuit against Ethan, which would mean I'd be reminded of it all the time. I'm not sure if I can do it, because I just want to forget about it and move on with my life. Do you know what I mean?'

'I understand. You must do what's best for you. Whatever your decision is, I will always support you.'

'Thank you, you are a good friend.'

Melanie moved from her chair to the floor and sat next to Vivian by the fireplace. She brushed her shoulder against Vivian's and glanced at her with a small smile.

'Can you keep a secret?'

Vivian giggled at her behavior. 'Sure I can.'

'But you have to promise me that you'll pretend you don't know, when this person says it to you directly.'

'I promise.'

'It's about Genieva.'

'What's wrong with her? Is she pregnant too?'

Melanie laughed. 'Impossible! You know how she thinks about men.'

'Yes, exactly.'

'No, the news is, her boss gave her an offer she probably

won't refuse. You know how she's always in Vancouver, right?'

'Yeah.'

Melanie sipped her coffee before continuing her story. 'The thing is, her boss wants to open a branch in Vancouver, and he asked Nieve to become the CEO. What do you think? Cool, right?'

Vivian thought for a moment about what she'd just heard. She rarely saw Genieva these days, but if her friend had to move to Vancouver, the chances of them hanging out would be even smaller. The only good girlfriend she'd have left would be Melanie, because Salfina would soon be entirely preoccupied with her baby. Suddenly Vivian felt jealous that Genieva had shared this information with Melanie and not with her. Vivian's heart hurt because she'd known Genieva since kindergarten.

'How do you know all of this?'

'We bumped into each other at Sarabeth the other day. While having breakfast, she was a little lost in thought, and that's when she told me. She's considering the offer seriously, but if I were her, I'd take it in a flash.'

'Goodness, and she asked you not to tell us?'

'Yes, as she wanted to tell you and Sal in person. But I don't think it'll be long before she goes because she's already negotiating her salary.'

'Genieva is a born negotiator. At kindergarten she already knew how to trade her cheese sandwiches for candy with the kids in first grade.' Vivian smiled at the memory.

'It amazes me how the three of you knew at such an early age what your talents were. Don't you miss Frenay & Iams?'

Vivian took a deep breath. 'Yes, very much, especially Ferris. I just can't forget about him, Mel. Have I shown you the letter he wrote me?'

With a sad expression, Melanie shook her head. Vivian went to retrieve the letter and then let Melanie read it. Vivian watched how tense her friend became as she read it.

A smile appeared on Vivian's lips when Melanie read the letter a second time.

Melanie gave the letter back to Vivian and said, 'I hope you don't mind me saying this, but I'm very curious to know what he looks like. I have a feeling that he must be gorgeous.'

'Yes, he is, he's an extraordinary man. Not only in terms of his appearance, but also in terms of how he communicates. I thought he'd finally opened up to me, and that he'd broken down the defensive wall he'd built around him. Thanks to Ethan, now I'll never know for sure.'

'Oh... Viv, I'm so sorry for you.'

'I know.'

'Listen, I know that men aren't your priority right now, but I'm sure your knight in shining armor will come along eventually. Maybe he won't be as handsome as Ferris, but he'll be someone who can give his whole heart to you, and love you for who you are.'

'Thanks, Mel, you truly are a good friend.'

Melanie looked at the clock. 'I'd better go home now. I've got to finish my college assignment. It's hard you know, working and studying at the same time.'

'I know, but believe me, your efforts will be rewarded. You want to know how?'

'Yes, tell me.'

'Ellis is currently making the arranges to hand the company entirely over to me.'

Melanie's eyes widened. 'Are you kidding me?' Vivian laughed at her. 'No, I'm not kidding. When everything is settled, I will move you from the reception desk, because I know you have so much more to offer than that.'

'Oh Viv, are you serious?'

'I'm serious, but you need to complete your studies first, and you have to keep it a secret. No one at work may know, okay? I don't want the rest of the staff to speculate.'

'I promise I won't tell, and I'll work damn hard to finish my degree. Your secret is safe with me,' Melanie put her hand on her chest with her face beaming.

After Melanie left Vivian's apartment, she called Samantha. The foundation was looking for two volunteers to manage the coffee and tea service during the meetings. Vivian had been thinking about this all week, and it turned out that Samantha was also considering it. They decided to register together for the position. With a pile of documents on her desk, Vivian kept looking at the clock.

She was looking forward to the meeting tonight. Besides the friendship she'd built with Samantha, she'd also become friends with three more group members, Sven, Philip and Kaitlin. They always sat together since the second meeting that Vivian and Samantha had attended.

After dinner, Vivian skipped coffee with Edward and decided to arrive early to enroll as a volunteer.

Samantha was already waiting when Vivian arrived.

'Are you early or am I late?' asked Vivian with a laugh as she saw Samantha's relieved expression.

'To be honest, I'm early because I've been looking forward to this since last Thursday! It just love meeting up with you, Phillip, Sven and Kaitlin.'

Vivian laughed loudly. 'I must confess that I feel exactly the same!'

Arm in arm they walked towards the hall to register. Sara, who was responsible for preparing the coffee and tea, was pleased with the help they offered. They'd start their new role the following week.

'Well then, now that's taken care of, shall we wait here or in the main hall for the others?' asked Vivian.

'Let's wait here.' Sara poured coffee, and as they were chatting about the lousy weather, Kaitlin ran into the room excitedly.

'Wow, what's got you all worked up?' asked Samantha.

'Because tonight is the night!' Kaitlin sang with a big smile.

Vivian and Samantha looked at each other and raised their eyebrows.

'Let me tell you why I'm so excited. Every second month the most gorgeous man in all of New York City comes and speaks here. I've forgotten his name, but anyway, that's what I'm so thrilled about, because he's coming tonight.'

'What's so special about him that makes you jump up and down like this?'

'Hello. Didn't you hear me say he's the hottest man in town? Just wait till you see him, then you'll know I'm right.'

Samantha asked Kaitlin about his physical characteristics while Vivian thought about Ferris. She couldn't imagine a better looking man than him.

Vivian missed him so much that sometimes she had the urge to call him, but she always abandoned the thought. She still read his letter every night, and each word was engraved deeply on her memory. Although she was feeling better about her life, some things hadn't changed the horrible nightmares still haunted her.

Vivian was startled by Kaitlin poking her arm.

'Viv, are you daydreaming?'

Vivian returned to the real world. 'I was just thinking of someone I used to know.'

Philip and Sven arrived soon after, and as always Sven chatted non-stop. Phillip bowed politely, and while looking at Kaitlin said, 'Good evening, my lady.'

Sven punched Phillip's shoulder.

'Save it, knight. Look at her. Her face is glowing. You know what that means, don't ya?'

'Gentlemen, let me help you to wake up,' said Samantha. 'Tonight Kaitlin is on cloud nine, thanks to tonight's speaker.' Now it was Philip's turn to punch Sven's arm. 'Now you're a lost cause. Your plan will have to wait another week.'

Vivian looked surprised when she found out there was a special connection between Sven and Kaitlin. She was overwhelmed with curiosity. 'Oh, what plan do you have in store for Kaitlin?' Vivian asked, and Kaitlin turned her head at the mention of her name.

'It's not just a plan for Kaitlin, but for all of us. I thought it would be nice if we eat together every Thursday before coming here. We can eat out, or we can take turns cooking.'

'What a great idea, but we just registered as volunteers to manage the drinks service,' Samantha couldn't hide her enthusiasm.

'How early do you need to be here?' Sven asked with a frown.

'An hour before it starts.'

After a short discussion, they found a solution that was satisfying for all.

Vivian was already looking forward to welcoming all of them into her kitchen. She suggested starting at her place next week.

'Next week is Thanksgiving, so aren't you all gathering with your families? Since I was diagnosed with HIV I've been estranged from mine, so I don't have plans yet,' Philip said forlornly.

None of the others had plans to spend the holiday with their families either. In that moment Vivian realized she should be grateful for her mother. Ellis never ostracized her, and neither did her friends. Vivian's heart ached when she found out that the four people in front of her didn't have the support of their friends and families since learning they had HIV.

Vivian decided she was going to prepare an extravagant meal for her new friends. Maybe she could convince Mel to come over too, as she secretly wanted to see if there'd be chemistry between her and Sven. Vivian gave them all her address and asked if they could come right after work.

The meeting had a large turnout that week. There weren't enough chairs for everyone, so some of them had to stand at the back. Luckily as they'd arrived early, Vivian and her friends were able to sit together. Vivian looked at her watch and poked Samantha's shoulder.

'I'm going to the bathroom. I'll be right back.'

Samantha nodded while saying, 'Hurry up. It's about to start.'

When Vivian returned, she saw the door of the hall was closed, meaning the meeting had begun. Very carefully, she pulled the handle down and pushed the door open. Because of the loud creak, all eyes turned to her, including those of the speaker. Vivian's face suddenly turned bright red. She looked around the room and her eyes stopped on the man standing on the podium.

Her heartrate jumped through the roof, her ears began to buzz loudly, and her knees grew weak. Vivian dropped her bag to the floor, turned around, and ran as fast as she could. She kept running, and several times heard her name being called, but she didn't stop. Vivian bolted out of the building towards the street. She couldn't see anything through the tears. A cab driver had to slam on his breaks to avoid her as she dashed across a street. She could still hear the voice calling her name and the sound of footsteps chasing after her. Vivian kept running until she tripped over and fell hard on the ground. Within a second, she felt strong arms lifting her up. Her heart seemed to stop beating altogether when she saw who was in front of her.

CHAPTER 27

Confused and overwhelmed, Vivian still tried to escape the hands that gripped her. She could no longer think clearly because the thing she feared most had just become reality. How could this have happened?

'Let me go!' Vivian shouted in tears. The grip of his arms became tighter. There was no escaping. Some pedestrians looked at them suspiciously, but they didn't stop.

'Please let me go!' This time she begged.

The familiar voice whispered softly in her ear, 'I won't let go until you calm down.'

It was difficult for Vivian to think straight, but for a moment she tried her best to calm down. Her body began to relax slightly, but the grip of his arms remained tight.

'I'm fine. You can let go now,' Vivian was surprised how calm her voice sounded.

'Are you sure? Because I don't want you to get hurt. Just seconds ago, you were almost hit by a car right in front of me.'

'Really, Ferris. I've calmed down.' Vivian heard him sigh heavily.

'I'll let go only if you promise you won't start running again.' His voice was stricken with concern.

'I promise.'

Ferris slowly let go of Vivian's body. His face was tense and alert, as though he was on guard to chase her again.

'Let's find a place for a coffee. It's too cold to wander outside without a jacket.'

Vivian didn't realize how cold it was after running as fast as she could. Ferris hailed a taxi and before she realized it she was sitting in the back of it beside him.

The cab stopped in front of Ferris's apartment.

'I don't think it's such a good idea to have coffee here.'

Ferris paid the fare. 'I think the exact opposite. We have a lot to talk about, and we shouldn't be distracted by anyone.'

During all the years she'd known him, this was the first time his voice had sounded firm. She didn't argue.

Because Ferris's keycard was back at the foundation, the doorman let them in with a spare. The elevator brought them to his penthouse. Ferris held the door wide open and motioned for Vivian to enter. 'Please,' he said with the same firm tone. Hesitantly, Vivian stepped inside. When she'd regained her composure, she realized how cold it was that night. Ferris walked straight to the fireplace, placed several large wooden blocks into it, and lit it.

'Please take a seat. It won't be long before the place warms up.' Ferris pointed to the couch in front of the fireplace where they had fallen asleep the last time they were there together. Without saying anything, Vivian took a seat, and immediately smelled his familiar scent on the cushions.

'What can I get you to drink? Coffee, tea, hot cocoa with whipped cream?'

'Anything is fine, just as long as it doesn't trouble you.'

Ferris went into the kitchen. For a moment, Vivian considered escaping out the front door. She was certain Ferris would ask her why she was attending that meeting. She could lie to him, but he would also question the reason why she'd run away. No, no more lies, she thought. She had to tell him the truth so it would be over and done with. She also wanted to know what he was doing at that meeting.

Before she could think any further, Ferris returned with two cups of hot cocoa with cream on top.

'Still cold?'

'Yes, a little.'

He took a fleece blanket from the couch and placed it gently over Vivian's legs.

'Thank you.'

He sat on the floor, facing her. 'I'm not sure how and where to start. The first question that comes to mind is, why didn't you ever answer my letter?'

Ferris's sharp gaze made Vivian look away. She couldn't deny how much she missed his gaze, his voice, his presence.

'Vivian?'

'Yes, sorry. Of course I read your letter.'

'Then why didn't you reply? Do you have any idea how worried I've been about you? What in the world happened after George's funeral?'

Just like him, she also had no idea where to start.

Despite the fact she was deeply embarrassed about the terrible things she'd experienced in Dubai, she finally decided to tell him everything. She figured by this stage she had nothing to lose.

Before she began, she sipped her hot chocolate, cleared her throat, then wet her lips with the tip of her tongue. Vivian's face flushed when she realized Ferris was watching her tongue move. 'Are you sure you want to keep sitting on the floor? My story will be very long.'

'I'm good here.'

'Okay. Do you remember when George forced me to go on vacation?'

'Yes, I remember that.'

'I didn't want to go on vacation at all because everything I wanted and needed was right here in this city.'

Ferris shifted a chair so he could lean on it with his left arm. His shirt tightened across his broad shoulders and chest. Vivian looked longingly at his chest and face. She saw a small smile appear on his lips, and she could feel her cheeks flush even deeper.

'During that holiday I met a man.' Ferris's smile suddenly disappeared.

'I wasn't looking for a relationship and certainly not for some kind of summer love, but it just happened. I honestly didn't expect this to happen because my heart belonged to someone else already, but unfortunately, he didn't feel the same way about me. Maybe that's why I became interested in this guy, because I just wanted to forget the love of my life. But it turned out to be the biggest mistake I've ever made.' Vivian paused and looked at Ferris, who was looking straight at her.

'For a while, I thought I was in love with this man. He was very caring, loving, understanding. However, that was only one side of his character. When I found out about his true nature, I decided I needed to play along with his game in order to save my own life. There were times when I was absolutely terrified, and wasn't sure whether I'd survive.' Vivian laughed wryly at the memories, and then continued.

'I finally managed to trick him and was able to escape safely from Dubai. After my departure, he realized I wasn't as stupid as he thought, and threatened me in various ways.'

Ferris stood up from the floor and sat down beside her. His gravely concerned stare gave Vivian the courage to continue.

'Shortly after it happened, George passed away. Even though I was filled with sorrow, I was also relieved that this man was no longer contacting me or threatening me.

That was until the day you took me home after the funeral. He was waiting for me inside my apartment. I knew then that something terrible was about to happen to me.' Vivian gulped several times and tears welled in her eyes.

'He brutally abused me and raped me…'

Ferris got up and began pacing back and forth. His face was pale, with fury written all over it.

'Damn it. I should have accompanied you upstairs. I shouldn't have left you alone that day. How could I have been so stupid?' he yelled loudly. His outburst made Vivian wince. He saw her reaction, and knelt beside her. 'I'm sorry, It wasn't my intention to scare you, forgive me. Please don't think of me like that. I'm nothing like him.'

'I know you aren't. That man intentionally hurt and abused me, and destroyed my life.'

'I need another drink.' Ferris grabbed a bottle of cognac and two glasses. 'Would you like some?' His face was a storm of emotions; anger, sadness, guilt, but most of all, affection.

'Yes, please.'

Ferris was furious. Vivian had never seen him like this. With trembling hands, he poured cognac into the glasses and handed one to Vivian.

She took a small sip, and immediately the amber liquid warmed her throat. 'That's not everything. There's more.' Before Ferris could respond, Vivian had resumed her story. 'After I returned from the hospital, I found a DVD that he'd thrown at me before leaving the apartment.'

'What kind of DVD?' It was the first time Ferris had interrupted.

'Several times, without my knowledge, he slipped drugs into my drinks, so in the drug-addled daze I let two of his friends have sex with me, and he recorded it.'

Tears flowed down her cheeks as she witnessed how the face of the man of her dreams turned even paler, and his hands clenched and unclenched with rage. Once again, he got up and paced the room. Eventually, he stopped in front of the large window overlooking Central Park. Tears were still running down her face when she called his name. 'Ferris?'

It took a while before Ferris turned around and looked at her.

'He intentionally infected me with HIV.' After she said this, Vivian sank onto the floor and cried without restraint. Ferris immediately sat down beside her and embraced her.

'Shhh... it's okay. You're safe now. Everything is going to be fine.'

'How can you say that, Ferris? It's not fine. I have to live with this for the rest of my life!'

Ferris said nothing. He just gently caressed Vivian's hair and helped her to get up and return to the couch. They sat side by side and Ferris pulled the blanket over Vivian's lap as she continued to sob. He embraced her again and pulled Vivian against his sturdy chest. Vivian let her head fall onto his shoulders, she was completely exhausted. Just when she wanted to close her eyes, she sat straight up and shouted, 'My bag! I dropped it with everything in it, my cellphone, house keys, wallet, credit cards, everything!'

Ferris pulled her back into his arms. 'Don't worry. I called the foundation. Your bag and my car key are at the reception desk. What's your agenda for tomorrow?'

'I'm going to work.'

'Maybe you can call your boss and ask for the day off. There's still a lot we need to talk about.'

Vivian nodded in agreement.

At midnight, Vivian woke up. The fire was still burning, and she felt Ferris's arm around her shoulder. His face looked even more handsome by the flickering light of the fire. As if aware of her eyes on him, Ferris woke up and opened his eyes. He held her gaze.

Vivian was embarrassed because she'd been caught staring at him. 'Sorry, did I wake you up?'

Ferris caressed Vivian's hair gently, and with his thumb slowly stroked Vivian's lips. He leaned forward while staring at her closely and pressed his lips to hers. At first, Vivian thought he would only kiss her briefly, but Ferris's lips encouraged hers to open. Their breathing sped up as Ferris continued caressing her hair. He sighed deeply. Vivian gently grabbed Ferris's hair and he groaned softly, to show her he liked it. Their kiss was growing more intense, more passionate. It was like Vivian was being kissed for the very first time.

To feel his lips with hers and to be in his arms is what Vivian had longed for for so long. She still couldn't believe that the man who was kissing her was the one she loved with all her heart. Vivian pressed her body against his. For a split second she forgot about the virus. She wanted more.

Suddenly Vivian was surprised by Ferris pushing her away with his eyes wide open.

'I'm so sorry, I shouldn't have done that,' Ferris said, deeply ashamed.

Vivian got up from the couch, walked to the big window, and looked outside. She fought her tears because she understood why Ferris had refused her. She couldn't blame him. What man would want a woman with HIV and a leading role in a nasty sex tape? She felt she'd made the wrong decision letting Ferris kiss her because now it would be even more difficult to forget him.

'Say something, Vivian...'

Vivian was lecturing herself. Strengthen yourself, Vivian. Hold your head up. Say what you should say and get out of here. You can do the crying later. Slowly, Vivian turned and looked into Ferris's eyes.

'You're right, you shouldn't have done that. I don't need your pity. I got carried away. I'm sorry. I'd better leave now.'

'Please don't go, Vivian. We still need to talk. Stay tonight, and tomorrow we can continue after we've both had some rest.'

'I can sleep and rest at home. We can meet somewhere tomorrow and talk things over.'

Ferris smiled and shook his head. 'Vivian, you can't outsmart me on this one, because I'm sure if I let you go now, you'll do all kinds of things to avoid me again. So it's better if you just stayed here. I won't let you walk out of my life again.'

Vivian was distraught. Ferris had read her mind. She was still standing beside the window.

387

'I've told my story. Everything there is to know, there's nothing more I can add.'

'Yes, you have told me everything, and I've listened to you. I just need some time to process all of this. However, it's only fair that you take the time to listen to my story too.'

'Okay, I'm listening,' said Vivian firmly.

'No, it's really late. Let's sleep first. Tomorrow there is plenty of time to talk even the whole weekend if necessary.'

Vivian decided to give in. Ferris had a point it was only fair she listened to his story too. 'Okay, but I want to take a shower first.'

Ferris reached out to her, and she timidly took his hand before he led her up to his bedroom. He opened the bathroom door and said, 'Those are the fresh towels and you're welcome to use my bathrobe when you're done.' He pointed at a stack of white towels in the corner, then the bathrobe hanging behind the door.

'Thank you.' For a moment they stared at each other before Ferris left and closed the bathroom door behind him.

Vivian looked around. With its polished white marble floors and walls and large marble sink, the bathroom was very luxurious and neat. At the sink Vivian noticed his electric toothbrush and shaver, and smiled when she saw his aftershave was the same brand as her perfume, Angel by Thierry Mugler. Before removing her clothes, Vivian rechecked whether the bathroom door was locked properly.

When she kicked off her shoes, Vivian was surprised because she expected the floor to be cold, but it felt warm. The rain shower with a powerful jet was a new sensation for her. Reluctantly Vivian turned off the tap. She wrapped herself in a thick towel then took another to dry her hair. With the tip of her finger she brushed her teeth.

Wearing Ferris's bathrobe, and with wet hair and red cheeks from the hot shower, she opened the door and found him waiting in the bedroom. Embarrassed, Vivian stopped in the doorway. 'You have a great shower. I had to drag myself out of there.'

'The jet wasn't too strong? I forgot to tell you that you can turn it down if you want .'

'No, it was perfect.'

Ferris looked at her sharply. Embarrassed, Vivian looked down to her hands which were fidgeting with the sash of the bathrobe.

'You sleep in here. I'll take the couch.'

'No need. I can sleep on the couch. I don't want you to give up your bed for me.'

'Don't worry. I'll be fine on the couch. Do you mind if I take a shower here?'

'No, not at all. After all, it's your bathroom.'

Ferris passed her and closed the bathroom door while Vivian climbed into his bed and pulled the blanket up to her chin. Ferris's bed was extremely comfortable, and she could smell his aftershave on the pillows. From the bathroom, she heard the splashing of the shower. Vivian wondered if he had ever bathed with his ex-girlfriend in there.

After about five minutes, Vivian heard the running water stop. She closed her eyes and pretended to sleep when the bathroom door opened.

Ferris stood beside the bed, caressed her cheeks and damp hair, then kissed her lightly on the forehead. He turned the lights off, then left the room. Vivian opened her eyes after she heard the door close. For a few minutes she stared at the ceiling before finally falling asleep.

CHAPTER 28

Vivian woke up and stretched out. Even though she hadn't slept for very long, she felt quite well-rested. For a few minutes she hesitated about going downstairs because she didn't know if Ferris was still asleep.

Finally, she padded down the stairs into the living room. The fireplace had warmed the room, but Ferris wasn't there, so she wandered into the kitchen. Ferris stood by the countertop.

'Good morning,' she said, as bravely as she could.

Ferris turned around and looked at her carefully. 'Good morning, sleep well?'

'Yes, I did. How did you sleep on the couch?'

'It was comfortable, but I didn't sleep much.'

Vivian didn't know what to say and sat down at the table.

'Would you like to eat breakfast here or in the dining room?'

'Here is just fine, thank you.' Ferris passed her a plate and cutlery.

'The croissants will be ready in a few minutes. Would you like coffee, tea, milk, or maybe orange juice?'

The way he was trying to please her touched Vivian. 'Coffee is just fine, thank you.'

'Café latte?'

Vivian raised her eyebrows, unable to hold back a smile.

'Can you make it?'

'No, I can't, but this machine can.

It can make various kinds of coffee.'

Vivian peered at the large, sophisticated machine.

'Here you are, ma'am. Café latte with two sugars, as per your regular order.'

Again Vivian was touched; Ferris still remembered how she liked her coffee. She took a sip and closed her eyes to taste it properly, while he waited expectantly for her reaction.

'Mmm... this is great. Where did you buy it? I need to get myself a machine like that.'

Relieved, Ferris exhaled sharply. 'It's so nice to receive praise from you.' His voice was low and hoarse, which immediately triggered Vivian's desire. Ferris's eyes wandered over the bathrobe Vivian was wearing, which made her heartbeat and breathing faster. A ding from the oven indicated the croissants were ready, shattering the moment between them.

'Hungry?' Vivian only nodded. Ferris set the table with croissants, bread, butter, jam, milk, and orange juice. 'I also have cereal if you want.'

'Are you kidding? This looks wonderful, and is more than enough.' Vivian was delighted with the fresh warm croissants with jam. After her second, she leaned back in her chair feeling quite content, then slowly sipped her coffee.

'So, Ferris, now it's your turn to tell me your story.'

Ferris was somewhat taken aback by Vivian's direct statement. He leaned back in his seat and crossed his arms in front of his chest.

'What's the hurry, Vivian? We still have the whole day. Have you called your boss yet?'

'No need to, I have special privileges at work.'

Vivian felt satisfied as she used his words against him, and Ferris laughed as he knew exactly what she was doing.

'Then why are you in such a hurry? Are you feeling uncomfortable here?'

Vivian got up from her chair, took their plates from the table, and placed them in the dishwasher.

'No, no. It's nothing like that.'

'So what then? Is it difficult for you to be honest and open with me?'

'That's exactly what I want to ask you, Ferris.' Vivian's fierce reply surprised him.

'I understand what you mean. I know you're wondering why I was at the meeting last night.'

'To be honest, yes I am.'

'The foundation is mine. I founded it with Jack, whom I met at the hospital on the day we were both diagnosed as HIV positive.'

When she heard this, Vivian was still leaning against the sink. With wide eyes she slowly returned to the table. She was completely shocked.

'About ten years ago, I met a woman, and we had a relationship. Even though we had fun together, I knew deep down that she wasn't the one for me.

393

She saw our relationship differently, and wanted it all a house with a white picket fence, children, a dog, the whole nine yards. In order not to disappoint her, I decided to live with her in a small apartment.

'After two years, the fighting started. She desperately wanted to get married, but I didn't. One morning we were fighting again, and I went to the office in the middle of it. All day I felt uneasy, because it was wrong of me to just leave in the middle of an argument, so I decided to go home early that day. I wanted to sort things out because it just isn't my nature to fight.

'At that time she was in between jobs, so I knew she'd be home. Of course, she didn't expect me to be home early. When I entered our apartment, I heard noises from our bedroom. I opened the door and saw her having sex with another man. They didn't even realize that I'd seen them, because I turned around and left and went to my mother's house.

'In the evening, I called to tell her what I had witnessed, and that our relationship was over. I know it wasn't classy to tell her that over the phone, but I just didn't want to fight anymore.

'It was my mother who insisted I go and get tested, and the day I got the results, I felt like my life had ended.'

Vivian sat staring at Ferris with wide eyes, and was speechless. All she could do was remain quiet while watching Ferris as he made her another café latte and a cappuccino for himself. Finally she asked, 'Did you contact her again after that?'

'Yes, after I got the positive result. I called her because I knew she was the only person who could've passed on the virus to me.'

'How did she respond?'

'Of course she didn't believe it. She kept screaming and yelling at me that I must have got it from someone else, and that I was unfaithful to her.' Ferris laughed cynically before continuing, 'The thing is, it was impossible that I had got it from someone else, because she was the first girlfriend I ever had, and she turned out to be the last one.'

Even though it had all happened many years ago, Vivian could see it was still difficult for him to talk about it. Everything became clear to Vivian. Now she understood what George meant when he told her that Ferris had experienced terrible things in the past. Now she realized why he was never seen with a woman.

'So, you've been alone for all these years?'

'Yes, I've lived a celibate life.'

Vivian thought for a moment. 'But why?'

'Because I knew I couldn't live with myself if I accidentally infected another woman.'

For a few moments, they stared at each other in silence. The air between them was filled with tension. Vivian rushed to find a topic to break the silence. 'And now here we both are... two successful people living with HIV.'

Ferris got up from his chair and sat next to Vivian.

'I understand that it is still difficult to believe, but trust me, you can still live your life as you did before.' Ferris's voice was gentle and sincere, and her eyes brimmed with tears.

'There's nothing wrong with crying, Vivian. You need to let go of your emotions in order to find relief.'

Vivian could not hold them back, so she let her tears fall.

With his thumbs, Ferris wiped her tears and kissed her cheeks. Before she realized it, his lips were on her mouth. Just like the previous night, his kiss was tender yet passionate. Their tongues melted together and Vivian's heartbeat raced. She wanted to throw her arms around his neck when she suddenly remembered what had happened the night before, when he pushed her away in the middle of a kiss. Now Vivian pushed him away.

Ferris looked at her in surprise 'No, Ferris,' Vivian said firmly.

'What?'

'You can't keep doing that. Kiss me and make me feel like I'm special to you, and then the next moment push me away. I won't allow it anymore.'

Ferris stood up and began pacing back and forth while frantically combing his hair with his hands. 'I'm so sorry, it was never my intention to do that.'

'Do what? Kiss me or push me away?'

'Both.'

'Well, then why did you do it?' Again tears welled up in her eyes.

Ferris walked towards her and stood in front of her. 'I have wanted to kiss you for such a long time.'

Vivian looked at him with raised eyebrows. 'I don't understand. Why do you want to kiss me? Is it because you pity me?'

Ferris laughed. 'Believe me. I don't pity you at all.'

'So why then?'

'Ah... damn it, Vivian... how do I say this?'

'Say what? Who's having trouble opening up and telling the truth now?'

'Do you want to know the truth, Vivian?'

'Yes, of course I do. Isn't that why you kept me here overnight?'

Ferris looked at her longingly before he began. 'Since the first day you started working at Frenay & Iams, I've been interested in you. Even though you were young, I knew you were the one for me. If I didn't have the virus, then everything would've been different. Before you came into my life, I had built a wall around me so that no one could ever hurt me again. Then you came along, and I built that wall even higher to protect myself from you and what I thought would only be more sadness. Everything was fine until George got sick and I was asked to work closely with you.'

Vivian opened her mouth to say something, but Ferris raised his hand to stop her.

'Please let me finish. It's hard enough for me to tell you this.

The high wall that I'd built no longer seemed to work.

It's hard to keep my distance from you, and to remind myself every day of the virus that I'm living with. I don't want to harm you. Yesterday you told me that you're now also living with HIV. I felt euphoric when you told me, because I felt that now there was nothing standing in my way anymore.

I hated myself for that feeling, but it didn't stop me from kissing you.

When I finally dared to do so, your words about giving your heart to another man haunted me. Vivian, you are extremely special to me, and I don't want to be your second choice.

I didn't get much sleep last night because I kept thinking about what kind of man I am to be thankful that you have HIV now too. The kiss I gave you minutes ago came out of pure selfishness, because I wanted to feel your lips for one last time.'

Vivian stared at Ferris through tear-soaked eyes as he finally concluded, 'I want to sincerely apologize to you for the fact I felt euphoric. I'm so sorry.'

With both hands, Vivian touched his face and kissed him softly. Ferris pulled away, tears rolling down his face. 'No, Vivian, don't. Just like you, I don't want your pity, and I definitely do not want to be your second choice.'

Vivian couldn't help but laugh out loud. Ferris looked at her confused, not understanding at all how his words could make her laugh.

'Oh... Ferris.' With great difficulty, she forced herself to calm down.

'What's so funny?' he demanded.

Vivian stopped laughing. 'Ferris, you are the man who stole my heart. Have you never noticed it?'

Ferris looked at her in surprise. 'Is this some kind of sick joke?'

'No, I'm not kidding.'

Ferris looked at Vivian for a moment, then a wide smile spread across his face. He lifted her and spun her around in his arms. Vivian hugged Ferris tightly. Carefully Ferris returned her feet to the floor.

'This is the best day of my life. I never knew you had the same feelings for me.' Again Ferris kissed her but more passionately this time. Vivian felt completely drunk with happiness and joy.

She laughed and cried at the same time.

It was now late in the afternoon. They lay side by side in front of the fireplace. Ferris was still wearing his pajama pants and a shirt while Vivian was still wrapped in his bathrobe.

They'd spent several hours caressing and holding each other, crying and laughing together. Ferris jumped up and held his hand out to Vivian. 'Come on, let's get dressed. I want you to meet my father. He is the only person who knows about my feelings for you.'

Even though Vivian was moved by Ferris's invitation, she still wanted to be alone with him for a little bit longer.

'Okay, but I have to go back home first to take a shower and change clothes.'

'I'll call my father, take a quick shower, and then we'll go to your place.'

Vivian heard the elation in Ferris's voice as he told his father that he wanted to visit so he could share some good news.

His excitement and enthusiasm amused Vivian so much she couldn't contain her laughter.

While Ferris took a shower, Vivian got dressed in the bedroom. She didn't know how many times she pinched herself to make sure she wasn't dreaming.

She couldn't imagine what her mother, Edward and her friends would say when they heard her news.

When Ferris came out of the bathroom, Vivian couldn't keep her eyes off him. He walked around bare-chested wearing only a towel on his hips. Water droplets clung to his muscular arms and chest.

Ferris stood in front of her, and Vivian kissed the droplets. Her hands stroked his chest, then slid down his torso until they stopped at his towel.

Before Vivian's hands went any further, Ferris took hold of them swiftly, his eyes burning with lust.

'Vivian, believe me when I say there's nothing I want more than this. God, if only you knew how often I fantasized and dreamed about this. But I want our first time to be special, so I really think we should wait.'

They collected her bag and his keys at the foundation, then drove to Vivian's place. For a moment, Ferris was confused as they drove into the parking garage of Edward's apartment building.

'Do you want to visit Edward first?'

Vivian couldn't help laughing but she didn't say anything. They stood in the elevator hand in hand. When the door opened, Ferris still looked confused. Vivian opened the door to her apartment. 'Welcome to my home.'

'I didn't know you moved here!'

Vivian entered first and took off her shoes. 'I had to because I couldn't stay at my old place after all that happened there.'

'I understand.'

'Make yourself at home. I'll take a quick shower.'

Later that evening, Ferris pulled over into a long driveway and stopped in front of a magnificent mansion. With sparkling eyes, Ferris looked at Vivian. 'We have arrived.'

He helped Vivian out of his car. 'Dad? Hm, I think he's in his greenhouse.' His exuberant glow made him even more handsome. The greenhouse was filled with orchids of many different colors.

'Ferris, these orchids are beautiful,' Vivian whispered.

'Yes, they're my father's most valuable treasure.'

'You're wrong son. You are my most valuable treasure.'

The voice sounded familiar. Vivian spun around and came face to face with Sean Frenay.

Vivian looked at him in disbelief, and Ferris, after laughing at her reaction, kissed the tip of her nose.

'Dad, I have something to tell you.'

Together they told Sean the whole story. Vivian could read the emotions on Sean's face they were identical to Ellis expressions when she had heard the story.

Sean got up and hugged his son. 'I'm very happy for both of you. It's only a shame that this all had to happen to bring you two together.' He turned to Vivian, grabbed her hand, and kissed the back of it.

'I'm very sorry for you, Vivian, that you had to go through all this. I know it's not easy to accept, but it did unite you two. I'm convinced you two will be happy.'

'Thank you, Sean.'

During dinner, Sean explained to Vivian why Ferris used his mother's last name. It turned out that Ferris had decided to start working at the bottom of the company.

Apart from Clive and George, no one at Frenay & Iams knew that Ferris was Sean's son. When Sean and Clive retire, the company was to be taken over by Ferris because Clive had no children. It was then Vivian's turn to tell them that she would also take over her mother's company. It didn't take them long to develop the idea of merging the two companies.

After they'd finished eating, Ferris gave Vivian a tour of the house.

The three-storey house was huge and had countless bedrooms.

There was an indoor pool and a larger lap pool outdoors. The stables contained several racehorses, and there was a tennis court and home gym too.

'What a beautiful home! Does your father live here all alone?'

'I used to visit him on weekends when I was young, but yes, now he lives alone.'

Ferris and Vivian were sitting side by side on a large leather lounge suite in front of a roaring fireplace when Sean entered the living room. A smile appeared on his face when he saw his only son looking so radiantly happy.

'You have a beautiful home, Sean,' Vivian said sincerely.

'Thank you. Vivian. One day it will all be yours,' said Sean with a wink.

CHAPTER 29

It was already late when they returned to Ferris's penthouse. It was difficult for them to be physically separated they maintained contact the entire time.

'I want you to stay here with me, Vivian. I don't want to waste any more valuable time. I want to be with you all the time. I want to see your face as I open my eyes in the morning.' Vivian understood what Ferris meant too much valuable time had been lost already.

'I want exactly what you want.' Ferris kissed her eyelids affectionately, the tip of her nose, her cheeks, and finally her lips.

'You don't know how happy you've just made me.'

'Making you happy every day is my priority.'

They walked up to his bedroom. 'Do you want to take a shower first?'

'I want to take a shower with you, Ferris.' Vivian noticed how difficult it was for him to adjust to the situation after being alone for so many years.

'You go ahead. I'll be right in after you.'

For quite some time, Vivian stood alone in the shower, wondering what was keeping Ferris so long. Suddenly the bathroom door opened, and Vivian stared in amazement. Her eyes glided over Ferris's perfectly chiseled body before stopping at his huge erect cock.

Ferris walked toward the shower with blushing cheeks.
Anxious and embarrassed, he stood beside Vivian.

'This is all very new to me.'

Vivian stepped closer to him and he took a step back.

'Wait, let me look at you first.' Ferris gazed at her with desire.
Her long wet hair covered her breasts.

With both hands, Vivian pushed her hair to her back so he
could see them. After staring in awe, Ferris took a step forward
and pulled her into his arms. Vivian felt his erection pulsating
against her.

They kissed passionately until they were out of breath. Ferris's
hands began to explore Vivian's entire body, but when they
were almost between her legs, he hesitated.

Confidently, Vivian took his hand and guided it into her.
He sighed heavily when he felt how wet she was. It was then
Vivian's turn to explore his body. She stroked Ferris's chest and
bent to kiss his nipples and nibble them gently. Ferris's groans
made her more excited to continue to his lower body.

His breath caught in his throat when her mouth opened around
his cock. 'Ohh, Vivian. Wait a minute.' He guided her to stand
up.

'Please be patient with me. I haven't done this for a very long
time. I still have to get used to it.'

Vivian nodded, wrapped her arms around his neck, and pressed
her breasts against his chest.

After bathing, they dried each other's bodies carefully.

When she opened the bathroom door, Vivian discovered that Ferris had filled his bedroom with candles, and everything flickered with a warm and sensual glow. Light classical music drifted softly in the background. Vivian was sure she'd heard it before, but she couldn't remember where.

Ferris held Vivian's hand as she lay down on his bed, and then he slowly lay down next to her. After kissing her all over her body, Ferris stopped at the apex of her thighs.

She spread her legs to make it easier for him to touch her. Ferris licked her cautiously, his soft groans arousing her even more. His rhythm was very slow. Vivian moaned and writhed slowly, following his rhythm. Slowly he increased his pace and slid his middle finger into her. Her body began to tremble, unable to subdue the orgasm.

'Oh, Ferris,' she sighed heavily.

Ferris gazed at Vivian with sparkling eyes. While gripping the base of his cock, he pushed into Vivian slowly, edging deeper and deeper into her warm depths. Vivian could feel how deep he was.

Ferris moved slowly at first, but then steadily increased speed. His muscular, athletic body was tense, and he groaned with each thrust. Vivian gazed at his face, which was completely focused on hers. Just before he climaxed, he called out her name.

Exhausted and deliriously happy, they lay side by side. Ferris turned his head so he could look at Vivian.

'Sorry, I wanted you to be able to enjoy it longer, but I couldn't hold it anymore. I'm sorry.'

'You don't need to apologize. We have a lifetime to enjoy each other.'

Vivian lay her head on Ferris's chest, and became lost in the rhythm of his calm and steady breathing. She thought he'd fallen asleep, and just as she closed her eyes, he said,

'I love you, beautiful.'

Vivian's eyes opened. Now she knew where she'd heard the classical music it was in the erotic dream she'd had on the plane to Las Vegas. Ferris had tied her up, blindfolded her and made love to her passionately. She smiled at the memory, because in that dream he'd also called her beautiful.

'I love you too, Ferris.'

After breakfast, Vivian took her phone and charger from her bag. She hadn't looked at it since she ran into Ferris at the foundation. It took a while before the first messages arrived, and when they did the alerts beeped many times.

'They obviously missed you,' Ferris said with a dashing smile.

'They're all from my mom, Edward, and my friends. Oh, here's one from Samantha. I met her at the foundation.'

'Shouldn't you call your mother first, to let her know everything is fine? Maybe she's worried about you.'

'Yes, you're right. But I have a better idea.

We can visit her together so you can meet her.'

'I can't wait to meet your mom. We can visit your friends afterward if you like?'

Vivian pursed her lips, and a mischievous smile appeared on them.

'No, I want to surprise them, but before we go to my mother's place, I want to stop by Edward's first.'

That Saturday passed by quickly, because Vivian was on cloud nine. Edward and her mother were both thrilled that she was now with Ferris, and they both cried tears of joy.

Ferris immediately felt comfortable with Ellis. She was very warm and friendly towards him, and quickly joked that he was her ideal son-in-law.

Vivian and Ferris spent the rest of the weekend together at his penthouse. They made love several times, and Ferris gradually began to relax and grow more confident.

The way he made love to her so gently and passionately reassured Vivian that it was true love. It was completely different to the dark and twisted animalistic experiences she'd had with Ethan.

If they weren't in his bed, they sat by the fireplace talking for hours. With an aching heart, Vivian listened to Ferris explain that he no longer celebrated Christmas or other holidays since his diagnosis.

She couldn't imagine how lonely he must have been for all those years, especially during the holidays.

Of course, he was welcome to spend Christmas and Thanksgiving with his parents, but he always chose to be alone. Vivian described in detail her terrible experiences in Dubai, and confessed that she felt the sex tape was overshadowing her life. She told Ferris that he could watch it if he wanted to, so he could know exactly what she'd been through.

Ferris refused, admitting that if he did, he wouldn't be able to predict his actions. He tried to convince Vivian to let go of the burden, and that if the tape surfaced, they would cross that bridge together.

Something else that had also become a burden was what would become of the orphanage in Aruba. Vivian was certain it was all an act, and that Ethan had orchestrated the entire episode just to impress her. Ferris promised her that he'd look into it, and see what he could do. She was certain he'd keep his promise.

Monday morning arrived, and together they got ready for work. Vivian hated the idea of being away from Ferris all day long. She wished they could lock themselves away and spend more quality time together in their exclusive company.

Later that day, when Vivian was immersed in her work, she was startled by a new message alert from her phone. Samantha's name appeared on the screen. Damn, Vivian thought. She'd completely forgotten to reply to her the day before. Vivian quickly tapped out a reply to say that everything was fine and that she was looking forward to seeing her again

the following Thursday. A soft knock on her office door made
Vivian lift her head. Melanie was standing in the doorway.

'Come on, Viv. You have to tell me.'

Vivian glanced at her and smiled while raising her eyebrows.

'Tell you what?'

'Come on, Viv, you can't hide it from me.' Melanie did have a
great ability to read people's body language correctly.

'Believe me. There's nothing to tell.'

'I know for sure you're hiding something from me. Come on,
Viv, out with it! I'm good at keeping secrets.'

Vivian chuckled. 'Yeah, right. Just like that secret from
Genieva, or had you forgotten about that?'

Melanie blushed, and Vivian felt sorry for her.

'Listen. I really can't tell you anything right now as I still have
a lot to do today, but if you, Genieva and Salfina come over for
dinner on Saturday, I'll tell you everything there is to know.'

'See! I knew something had happened!' Melanie said
trumphantly.

'Can't you just give me a few clues? Saturday seems so far
away! Please don't make me wait that long!'

'Patience is a virtue, Mel,' Vivian said with the wink.

Melanie looked at her friend in disbelief, but Vivian stuck to
her plan to tell them all on Saturday, even though she wanted to
shout it from the rooftops.

'All right then, I'll contact Nieva and Sal, and together we'll
speculate intensively about what happened.'

410

Melanie left Vivian's office with a melodramatic scowl. When she'd just got her concentration back, Vivian was distracted again by a message alert from her phone. Her face beamed when she saw it was from Ferris.

Hey Beautiful, it's only noon, but I can't concentrate at work. My mind is floating to you. I miss you and can't wait to get home. I'll stop at an Italian restaurant, so we don't need to cook tonight. It feels good knowing that when I get home, you'll be there waiting for me.
I love you, Ferris xxx

Vivian typed a reply immediately.

Hey, handsome. I feel the same way. I'm having trouble concentrating on my work too. When I close my eyes, I can see and hear you so clearly. I can't wait to go home to your place. I want to caress you and feel your arms around me. By your side, I feel safe, loved, and cherished. Alone, I feel incomplete.
Love you too, Vivian xxx

Vivian pressed the send button, and a reply soon appeared.

It's our home now.
Ferris xxx

Smiling radiantly, Vivian put down her phone. She planned to go home early so she could surprise Ferris. The intercom on her desk buzzed.

'What's up Mel?'

'Saturday is set. We'll gather at your place around seven.'

'Perfect. Mel, I'm finishing up here and going home early.'

'Oh, okay...'

Vivian grinned. She could hear the suspicion in Melanie's voice. There was just one more thing Vivian needed to do before returning to Ferris's penthouse.

She quickly realized it would be the first time in her life she would spend just five minutes in a department store. She glanced at her watch she still had enough time before Ferris came home.

About an hour later, Vivian entered Ferris's penthouse with the spare keycard he'd given her. Even though he'd said this was their home, she still felt a little strange.

In the bathroom, she cut the tags from the pale yellow lingerie she'd bought at the department store. After a quick shower, she dried her hair and left it down. Vivian put on her new lingerie and a matching negligee. In the living room, she lit the fireplace and filled the living room with scented candles.

As a finishing touch, she opened a bottle of X, to go with their Italian take out.

Vivian was sitting by the fireplace when Ferris walked in.

'Welcome home, handsome.'

Ferris's eyes seemed to devour her. He dropped his briefcase on the floor, then yanked off his tie, all the while with his eyes fixed on Vivian.

'I really could get used to coming home like this.' His voice was low and hoarse. He sat down in front of Vivian, then caressed and kissed her left shoulder . 'You are so indescribably beautiful. You take my breath away, Vivian.' She threw her arms around his neck and kissed him passionately. They made love in front of the fireplace. Ferris's confidence and self-control increased even more.

They didn't sleep all night, as they didn't stop exploring and enjoying each other's bodies. Even though they hadn't slept, they still felt fine the next morning. They agreed to meet at Edward's house after work because Vivian wanted to keep her promise to have dinner with him every Tuesday.

After a very long and productive day, Vivian finished all her tasks, then took a cab to Edward's. With a beaming smile she walked into his apartment. Ferris was already there.

Her heart skipped a beat when she saw her two favorite men chatting at the kitchen table. The minute Ferris saw Vivian walk in, he stood up and kissed her passionately. Edward smiled at their happiness.

'I hope you're hungry. I mean hungry for food, not the other type of hungry.'

They both laughed at Edward's taunts.

'I'll set the table,' said Vivian.

Edward had spent the afternoon creating one of his many specialties, a rich and creamy beef bourguignon. Vivian and Ferris expressed their pleasure and delight throughout the dinner, with Edward smiling more each time.

During dinner Ferris told Edward and Vivian that earlier that day he'd discussed with Sean and Clive the process for him to take over the company, and how they would inform all employees.

'And what about you, Vivian? Are you thinking about returning to your former workplace now that you've snagged your dream colleague?'

Vivian playfully pushed Edward on the shoulder. 'Actually, it's even better than that. My mother is also passing on her company to me, so we've decided we're going to merge our two companies.'

'Well, this really is when two become one!' Edward said with a cheeky smile. 'Hmm, Frenay & Foster is a good name, or are you going to use your mother's last name?' he asked Ferris.

'No, I will use my father's last name. I've already set about the process of changing it legally. If all goes according to plan, everything will be settled before Christmas.'

'And you, dear. How about your apartment? I assume you won't need two houses?'

'As much as I love my home and living so close to you Edward, you're right, we don't need two houses, so yes, I'll sell it. Hopefully the price doesn't fall when it hits the market.

Otherwise I'll rent it out for a while.' While she spoke, Vivian noticed Edward trying to hold back a smile as he witnessed how much Ferris adored her.

After dinner, Edward walked them to the elevator.

'I am so, so happy for you both, even though it saddens me to think about the challenges you had to face to finally be able to unite with each other.'

His words touched Vivian, and she gave him a big, warm hug.

'You know, Edward. I wish I knew from the very beginning that Ferris is living with HIV. It would've saved us so much time.'

'I'm not sure I understand what you mean by that, dear.' Edward looked confused.

'What I'm saying is that had I known from when we first met and I fell for him, it wouldn't have stood in my way, I would love him regardless.'

'Are you serious?' asked Ferris

'Yes, it wouldn't have mattered to me.'

Ferris stared at her, his eyes glazing over with astonishment.

'Edward, can you believe that I am the luckiest man in the world?'

'I believe you, my friend. George always said that Vivian was a very special woman.'

Later that night as they lay side by side in bed, Ferris tickled Vivian's arm and said, 'Thursday is Thanksgiving, how would you like to celebrate it?'

Vivian turned to look at him.

'Actually, I'm sorry, but I already have plans. Samantha and some friends from the foundation are coming to my place to have dinner. It will be the first time they celebrate Thanksgiving for a long time. I also owe them an explanation after running off last week.'

'You don't need to apologize. I think that's very sweet and generous of you. Will you also go to the meeting afterward?' She looked at Ferris shyly. 'Yes, because I registered as a volunteer to serve the coffee and tea.'

Ferris laughed. His genuine laughter always made her heart swell.

'You always manage to surprise me, Viv. Edward is right. You really are an exceptional woman.' He kissed the tip of her nose.

'I hope you'd like to join us on Thursday. Edward and I are planning quite a feast.'

He rubbed Vivian's cheeks and lips with his finger.

'You know I'll be there.

'Ferris?'

'Yes, my darling?'

'Do you mind if I tell Samantha and the others about us?'

'Actually, better not,' he said, and before she could reply he continued with a smile, 'We'll tell them together.'

416

CHAPTER 30

Vivian took the day off work to prepare the Thanksgiving dinner with Edward. In the morning they went grocery shopping together, and Edward's connections at the specialty delis and fresh produce markets ensured they were able to get the finest ingredients.

Edward was in charge of the turkey, while Vivian prepared the roast vegetables, salads and dessert with recipes from the book of George's favorites.

Tiffany delivered three beautiful bouquets, and Vivian gave her a bonus in the spirit of the holiday. Throughout the day as they were busy in the kitchen, Vivian noticed Edward was constantly humming.

'Should I play some music?'

'Yes! I always listen to the radio when I'm cooking,' Edward said with a laugh.

'What station?'

'My favorite is Radio New York Live.'

Moments later they were both singing as loud as they could to Queen's *I Want to Break Free* while boogying around the kitchen. When the song ended, Edward said, 'My dear, that could be your new theme song, because now you are finally free.' Vivian poured drinks for them both.

'Yes, you're right! I would never have thought I would find this kind of happiness after my diagnosis.

Did you know that Ferris has never celebrated any holidays since his diagnosis?'

'You're kidding…'

'When he told me my heart broke. So I want to do my best to make this holiday season special and truly unforgettable for him. I want him to enjoy and embrace special days again, especially Christmas.'

Edward looked at Vivian with a cunning smile. 'I've just had an idea. Want to hear it?'

'Yes, of course! Please share it with me!'

After listening carefully to Edward's idea, Vivian got very excited and was convinced that with Edward's help, everything would turn out wonderfully.

'Well, dear, it looks like my job is done here for today. You just have to wait until the timer on the oven rings and ice the strawberry cake once it's cooled down to room temperature.'

'Are you sure you don't want to join us for dinner? You know there's plenty for all of us.'

'Yes, I am sure. But thank you. I really want to work on my book now.'

She hugged Edward and thanked him for all his help, then continued in the kitchen. She set the dining table and placed a wreath of orange and red flowers from Tiffany in the center. Looking at her reflection in the mirror made Vivian smile. She had to admit to herself that she looked good.

In black pants and her pale yellow wrap blouse with her hair hanging down to her waist, Vivian knew her ensemble would please Ferris. The thought of him made her blush a little. Ralph announced that Samantha was heading up.

'Vivian. Hello?' Samantha's voice sounded apprehensive.

'Hi, come in Samantha.' Vivian walked ahead of Samantha and heard how she whistled in astonishment when she saw her apartment.

'For a minute I thought I was in the wrong place. Is this all yours? Your living room is even bigger than my whole condo. Do you live here alone?'

If Samantha was impressed by this apartment, what would her reaction be like when she saw Ferris's penthouse? Vivian wondered to herself. 'Yes, it's mine, but I'll be selling it soon.'

'Selling it? Why?' They walked to the kitchen, and Samantha continued to gape in amazement. Before Vivian could answer Samantha asked suddenly, 'So, what happened last Thursday? It looked like you'd seen a ghost or something, the way you ran away like crazy out of there. Then that speaker jumped over the table to chase you. You should've seen Kaitlin's face. I must admit she was right, though. That guy was incredibly handsome.'

Vivian didn't know what to say and sighed with relief when the intercom rang. They waited for Philip, Sven, and Kaitlin in front of the lift. Before the lift's doors had fully opened, they could already hear Sven's voice talking rapidly.

Just like Samantha, the three were very impressed by Vivian's apartment.

They entered the kitchen, and Vivian opened a bottle of champagne, filled five glasses, and plopped a strawberry in each one. She then handed everyone a glass and invited them to sit down.

Philip soon said, 'Hey, Vivian. You set the table for six. Who else will be joining us?'

'You still haven't told us about what happened last week, Vivian,' Samantha said.

Kaitlin soon followed with, 'That's right. You'd better have a good explanation for that. Thanks to you, we barely got to look at that extremely handsome guy. Now I'll have to wait all over again to get a glimpse of him.'

'Next time you should try to talk to him, Kait, instead of just staring at him from afar like some sixteen-year-old teenager,' Sven taunted.

'Good evening.'

Everyone turned towards the voice. Kaitlin's face went pale and Samantha's eyes widened while Philip and Sven looked completely confused. Ferris walked straight over to Vivian, wrapped his arms around her waist, and kissed her.

'Hi, beautiful. I missed you.'

Vivian's face glowed. 'I missed you too, handsome.'

It took a few moments for everyone to recover from their surprise, and then Ferris introduced himself.

Samantha then helped Vivian bring the turkey and side dishes to the table. While they ate, Ferris and Vivian explained what had happened the previous week. Vivian kept glancing at her watch she didn't want to arrive late for her first volunteer shift. Ferris recognized her anxiety and smiled warmly at her.

'Don't worry. I've contacted Sara. Tonight, you don't need to prepare anything I've arranged full Thanksgiving catering for tonight's meeting.'

Vivian smiled at him appreciatively while her friends stared at him in wonder. Ferris then explained that he was the founder and director of the foundation.

The rest of the evening was wonderful success. Everyone enjoyed Edward's and Vivian's dishes, and Vivian was delighted that Ferris seemed to thoroughly enjoy the evening. As they were getting ready to go to bed, Ferris told Vivian that it was the best Thanksgiving he'd ever had.

At breakfast, Ferris told her he had to go to the office to meet his father and Clive, even though it was a holiday.

'Of course I'd rather be here with you, but there are quite a few legal documents that need to be reviewed and signed.'

'No problem, I have some errands to run for tomorrow's dinner with my friends.'

After Ferris kissed her and left for work, Vivian called her mother.

'Hi, Mom.'

'Hi, baby. Was the Thanksgiving dinner a success?'

'Yes, it was, but there's a different occasion I'm calling to speak to you about.' Vivian explained to her mother that Ferris hadn't celebrated Christmas for years and told her about the plans she'd made with Edward. Her mother loved the idea, and they decided to meet within the hour to go shopping.

After a few hours, they'd got everything they needed, and arranged for the delivery on the 4th of December.

After ensuring everything was ticked off their list, Vivian and her mother enjoyed cake and coffee.

'Where is Ferris now?' Ellis asked.

'He's meeting his father and Clive to discuss the legal documents required for the company takeover in January.'

Before going home, Vivian told her mother about her plan to merge the two companies. Ellis responded enthusiastically.

'Maybe we should speed it up too, baby.'

Vivian looked in surprise at her mother. 'Are you sure, Mom? I know how important your company is for you.'

'Your happiness is more valuable to me. Also, I've been talking to Nora about the possibility of traveling together, and she loved the idea. So an early retirement is now very appealing to me!'

'I want you to do it when you're sure, Mom, and not because you feel pressured.'

'Nonsense, and besides, I'm sure you and Ferris will build these companies into something far greater than I could ever have hoped for.'

Later that day, as she was busy preparing dinner for her friends, Vivian couldn't ignore how tense and nervous she was about seeing them. To confuse them even more, she'd texted them to say that dinner would be at a different address.

Wearing jeans and a T-shirt, Ferris walked into the kitchen. The curves of his broad and muscular chest were visible beneath his shirt, and his hair was wet.

'Wow, are you trying to seduce me?' Vivian asked in a low, husky voice.

'That's all I ever want to do,' Ferris's reply was even huskier.

'I'll take over from you in the kitchen so you can take a shower and get dressed. Try to relax a little. You look very tense.' He placed his hands on Vivian's hips and pulled her closer to him. Vivian felt his erection. She rubbed her body against his, which made him growl.

'How about you take a shower with me. I want to feel you inside me.'

Ferris couldn't resist Vivian's invitation and carried her to the bathroom. After they quickly undressed, Vivian pushed Ferris to the wall of the shower cubicle and knelt, taking his manhood in her mouth. Slowly and tenderly, she sucked and licked while Ferris leaned against the wall with labored breath. When his legs started trembling she knew he had almost reached his climax.

She sucked harder and faster so he would come in her mouth for the first time.

'Vivian, stop… what are you doing... I'm almost there.'
She looked up at him and watched his face tighten.

'I... can't hold it anymore... I'm coming... Oh my God I'm coming.' His cum filled her mouth and Vivian swallowed, looking up at him with a seductive smile.

He needed time to catch his breath before he could bury himself deep inside her. Each time he penetrated her the size of his cock almost shocked her, but the pain felt good.

Vivian stood up, and Ferris picked her up and pinned her against the wall. She wrapped her legs around his torso, and then he thrust into her with all his strength. Her moans of pleasure made him pump even harder and deeper. Vivian's orgasm was so mind blowing that tears ran down her cheeks. Ferris was shocked and caressed Vivian's face while wiping away her tears. 'Did I hurt you?' his face was panic-stricken.

'No, you didn't hurt me. These are happy tears. I've never come so hard before.'

Ferris's worried expression slowly faded.

'It looked so incredibly sexy when you had me in your mouth, and the pleasure you gave me was so good. My God, you have awakened a beast that has been resting in me.'

'Hmm... I don't mind if that beast stops by more often and gives me an orgasm like the one just now.'

'Don't worry. I know for sure that you'll always be able to wake him up. But hey, we should hurry. Your friends will arrive any minute now.'

They had just finished getting dressed when the doorman informed them that their guests were on their way up. Ferris sat in a chair next to the fireplace while Vivian greeted her friends at the lift. Her face shone with happiness when she saw them. Salfina hugged her first. 'Gosh, Viv. You're looking good! Let me see you.' She pushed her back a little from her embrace.

'Thank you, Sal. You look great too. You've started to show,' Vivian said while looking at Salfina's belly.

'I told you, something big has changed for her,' Melanie said. Genieva was the most relaxed of the three. 'You really are looking different, Viv.'

Vivian was still beaming with a big smile on her face. Melanie looked very curious.

'Why are we having dinner here and not at your place? This looks like a very luxurious apartment complex, and even the doorman looks cool.'

Vivian could only laugh happily.

'Please, come in. I want to introduce you to someone.' Her friends followed her inside, and Vivian heard Sal say something to Mel.

'I'll bet you a hundred dollars that she has a boyfriend.' When they entered, the large living room with the floor to ceiling window overlooking Central Park took away their breath away. 'It must cost a fortune to live here. Only the rich and famous could afford to buy something at this location,' Genieva gushed in awe.

While her friends took in the view of the park, Vivian walked over to Ferris, wrapped her arm around his waist, while he lay his arm around her shoulders.

'I'm delighted you love the view as much as we do,' Ferris said in a friendly manner.

The girls turned around together and looked at Ferris from top to bottom. Vivian used to hate it when women looked at Ferris this way, but now she could only feel proud.

'Girls, I'd like to introduce you to Ferris Aus... uhh... Ferris Frenay. Ferris, these are my best friends, Salfina, Genieva, and Melanie.'

Ferris shook each of their hands warmly. 'Ladies, it's a pleasure to meet you.'

Genieva was the first to ask. 'You mean this is THE Ferris!?'

'Yes, he is. The one and only.'

Genieva walked with open arms towards Vivian and hugged her and kissed her cheeks. 'Ohh, Viv. I'm so happy for you, now please tell me how this happened!'

Ferris again placed his arm around Vivian's shoulders and kissed her temple. 'Why don't we eat first. We'll tell you the full story of how we got together later. According to Vivian, some of you can think and function a little more clearly with a full stomach,' Ferris said while smiling at Salfina. They all laughed.

While rubbing her belly, Sal walked towards Vivian and Ferris.

'I like him already, Viv.

However, for your information, I can think clearly in all circumstances these days,' she said with a mischievous grin. Everybody laughed again, and were soon in raucous conversation. Vivian enjoyed watching her friends as Ferris explained everything. He was flooded with questions because of course they needed to know every details.

Underneath the table, Ferris held Vivian's hand and constantly stroked it affectionately. Genieva also had news about her move to Vancouver for the very lucrative job offer. They all talked late into the night.

Vivian couldn't stop smiling, because the day she'd been greatly anticipating had finally arrived. It was December 4th, when all the items she'd bought with her mother would be delivered.

Ferris studied her carefully he knew she was up to something.

'Okay, spell it out.'

'Spell what out?'

'Come on, Vivian. I can tell you're up to something,' Ferris grinned.

'I'm not up to anything. I'm just really happy today,' she tried to say as convincingly as she could.

'Damn, I have to go. I can't be late. I've got an appointment with my father, Clive and some lawyers.' He stood up and kissed her goodbye. 'I'll call you after the meeting. Then you can tell me why you're acting so mysterious today.'

Vivian laughed and watched him leave the kitchen. 'I love you,' she called after him. Moments later, she heard the front door close.

At half-past nine, her orders arrived. It wasn't long until the entire living room was full of boxes and packages of various shapes and sizes. She started unpacking everything and quickly realized she would need help in order to finish on time. She called her mother and asked if she was available, but she had a series of meetings to attend. Instead she sent Melanie to help.

An hour later Melanie arrived, and she couldn't believe her eyes as she glanced around the room at the towers of boxes and packages.

'Gosh, Viv. Did you leave anything at the department store for other people, or did you buy the entire store?'

Vivian suddenly felt uneasy. 'Do think it's too much, did I go overboard?

'No, Viv. I understand why you're doing this. When I was growing up we were happy with almost nothing because there was no money. So if the tables were turned and I was you, I'd do the same thing.'

Vivian hugged her friend and thanked her for her comforting words. The two of them started unpacking the boxes and unwrapping the packages, working non-stop to get everything done on time. Ferris called four times, curious about what Vivian was up to.

She didn't even hint at her surprise.

She only reminded him to meet her on time at the Rockefeller Center for the launch of Edward's new recipe book.

Finally, Vivian and Melanie finished everything, and were satisfied with the result. Vivian thanked her any times, telling her she couldn't have done it without her.

On the back seat of a cab, Vivian glanced anxiously at her watch. The traffic was terrible, so she got out of the cab to walk there instead. As she approached the Center, she saw Ferris's tall and dashing figure standing with his hands in his woolen coat pockets. The air was freezing, and snowflakes floated down. Ferris's face lit up with a big smile when he saw Vivian walking toward him. He greeted her with a kiss then said, 'It's freezing. I hope Edwards's book launch is somewhere very warm.'

'Uhh, how do I say this. There is no book launch.'

'Is it canceled?'

Vivian burst out laughing.

'Actually, there was no book launch to begin with. I just used that as an excuse to get you here.'

'So, I was right this morning! You were hiding something from me!' Ferris laughed, lifted her up, and spun her around. Vivian laughed along with him and wrapped her arms tightly around his neck. Ferris placed her gently back on her feet and kissed her passionately in the middle of the busy street.

'Hurry up. It'll start soon.' Vivian pulled his hand and weaved her way through the crowd.

All around them people were counting down... six, five, four, three, two, one. Then came deafening applause, whistles, and cheers, as the lights on the giant Christmas tree were switched on.

Vivian gazed at Ferris. She could tell it was an emotional moment for him.

'Thank you, beautiful, for bringing me here. Now I realize what I've been missing all these years. Tomorrow we should buy a tree for our home.'

'Yes, let's do that.' They stood for a while in their warm embrace, admiring the towering tree and its splendid lights and decorations.

'Let's go home. It's cold.'

In the elevator, Vivian stood close to Ferris to warm herself up.

'Still cold?'

'Freezing,' she replied.

'I'll light the fireplace as soon as we walk in the door.'

Vivian smiled but didn't say anything. Ferris opened the door and stood completely still. He couldn't believe his eyes.

The entire penthouse was decorated in red, green, gold and white tinsel, ornaments and statues. In the middle of the living room stood a Christmas tree that reached the ceiling. The golden fairy lights strung around its branches twinkled, and above the fireplace hung two Christmas stockings with their names embroidered on them. Ferris walked in amazement through the living room, touching everything gently as he passed, before clutching the new Christmas quilt that was draped over the couch. 'Vivian, this is amazing. All the years I've lived here, it was just a house to me, but now it really feels like a home. Did you create this Christmas wonderland all by yourself?'

'I shopped for everything with my mother a few days ago, and Melanie came today to help me decorate.'

'Wonderful, and what are all these?' With wide eyes, he pointed to the piles of presents stacked neatly beneath the tree. Vivian enjoyed how much he admired her work.

'Some gifts are for you, but there are also some for your father, my mother and our friends.'

'You are such a kind-hearted, thoughtful, generous person, Vivian. I feel so lucky to have you in my life. In such a short time, you have brought me so much love and happiness. I can't imagine living without you anymore.'

Vivian was deeply touched, and her eyes began to fill with tears.

'I only want to see you smile,' she continued. 'If you're happy, then I'm happy too.'

Vivian knelt beside the tree and studied the pile of gifts. She then took a small box and gave it to Ferris.

'But it's not Christmas yet... and I haven't got you anything yet.'

'Never mind, it's only a little something.'

Ferris carefully unwrapped the gift, his eyes sparkling.

He gazed at Vivian while holding a rich brown leather glove with his initials neatly embroidered on the cuff.

'Oh, they're perfect. Earlier today I was thinking I should get a new pair. Thank you, beautiful.' Ferris kissed her gently.

On Christmas day, Vivian and Ferris welcomed their family and friends, except Salfina, who was celebrating Christmas with Jake and her in-laws.

When Melanie met Sven, she was smitten immediately, while Kaitlin and Philip seemed very close. Throughout the night Edward talked with Genieva, as they both shared a strong passion for cooking.

Vivian had insisted to Ferris that she wanted to prepare Christmas dinner, but Ferris wanted Vivian to be free to completely enjoy the evening, so he arranged for everything to be catered.

After all their guests had left and they were lying in bed in each other's arms, Ferris thanked Vivian for an unforgettable Christmas. They then made love for hours.

They spent the next day at home, deep in conversations about the past and future. Vivian asked whether Ferris had forgiven his ex-girlfriend, and whether he'd seen her since their relationship fell apart.

He told her that he had forgiven her but hadn't seen her again, because not long after he ended things, she committed suicide. As they gradually pieced things together, they realized that

Ferris's ex Melissa was also a victim of Ethan's, just like Victoria and herself. All the mysteries had finally been solved. Ferris also found out that Ethan hadn't kept his promise to the orphanage in Aruba, and told Vivian that he would fulfill the promises himself. Even though everything had fallen into place, Vivian still had serious doubts about whether she should file the report against Ethan. Ferris advised her to consider all the facts first, especially because such a lawsuit would probably take years and would reopen old wounds for Melissa and Victoria's families. However, he insisted that whatever her decision, he would support her.

Vivian decided to drop all the charges against Ethan because she didn't want to waste her time and energy on him anymore. She felt it would simply be better to spend her time living happily with Ferris, taking care of the company, and the foundation.

'What do you want to do for New Year's Eve?' Ferris asked while nibbling her ear.

Ferris had once told her about the fireworks that could be seen from his penthouse.

'I only want to spend it with you, here, just the two of us,' Vivian said softly, as she offered her neck so he could kiss it. The year was almost over. They stood side by side in front of the window with a glass of champagne in hand. From television, they could hear the countdown.

At midnight, the spectacular fireworks display began.

'Happy New Year!' they said to each other in unison, before a long, slow kiss. After a minute they were interrupted by the intercom. With raised eyebrows, Vivian looked towards Ferris, who smiled mischievously.

'Wait here, don't move.' Ferris strode to the front door and returned with a basket. 'I actually wanted to give you this for Christmas, but at that time she was too young to leave her mother.'

From inside the basket, Vivian heard soft mewling. With both hands she lifted a kitten gently from the basket, and immediately recognized it as a British Longhair, the same breed of cat she'd had when she was a girl. Vivian held the tiny kitten up to her face. Just like with Ferris, it was love at first sight.

'Oh, Ferris. She is adorable. Thank you.'

Ferris stood beside her. 'Do you like her collar?'

Vivian looked closely at the collar, and her mouth fell open. There was a diamond ring dangling from it.

Ferris took the ring and got down on one knee. He took Vivian's left hand and slipped the ring on her ring finger. It fit perfectly.

'I know we've only just started our relationship, but I couldn't imagine life without you. Because of you, I feel complete, like a real man again. Vivian, you are the reason I can smile and enjoy life to the fullest. You have given me a reason to live.

Thanks to you, my life feels meaningful again. You bring me so much joy, happiness, and love. Without you, my life would be meaningless. What I'm trying to say is... Vivian, will you marry me?'

Tears of happiness flowed down her cheeks. Vivian dropped down to kneel in front of Ferris and peered at the exquisite ring on her finger. When she looked up at Ferris, he was completely still as he awaited her answer, his eyes fixed on hers.

With both hands, she grabbed his cheeks and kissed his soft lips, before replying, 'Yes, yes, I would be honored to be your wife. I love you, Ferris, with all my heart, body, and soul.'

The End

Printed in Poland
by Amazon Fulfillment
Poland Sp. z o.o., Wrocław

54257208R00258